Mrs.
ENGELS

Gavin McCrea

Catapult ❀ New York

Published by Catapult
catapult.co

Copyright © 2015 by Gavin McCrea
All rights reserved
First published in Australia and the UK by Scribe Publications

ISBN: 978-1-936787-29-6

Catapult titles are distributed to the trade by
Publishers Group West, a division of the Perseus Book Group
Phone: 800-788-3123

Library of Congress Control Number: 2015933696

Designed by Strick&Williams

Printed in Canada

9 8 7 6 5 4 3

To Iñaki

Contents

Phase
the Now

1870

September

I. Fair Warning

No one understands men better than the women they don't marry, and my own opinion—beknown only to God—is that the difference between one man and another doesn't amount to much. It's no matter what line he's in or which ideas he follows, whether he is sweet-tempered or ready-witted, a dab at one business or the next, for there isn't so much in any of that, and you won't find a man that hasn't something against him. What matters over and above the contents of his character—what makes the difference between sad and happy straits for she who must put her life into his keeping—is the mint that jingles in his pockets. In the final reckoning, the good and the bad come to an even naught and the only thing left to recommend him is his money.

Young lasses yet afflicted with strong feeling and seeking a likely subject for a tender passion will say that money has no place in their thoughts. They make exceptions of themselves and pass

on good matches, for they believe that you must feel a thing, and that this thing can be pure only if it's a poor figure it's felt for. To such lasses I says: Take warning. This is a changing world, we don't know today what'll happen tomorrow, and the man you go with will decide where you're put, whether it's on the top or on the bottom or where. The fine feelings love will bring won't match the volume of problems a pauper will create. Odds are, the handsome fella you go spooney on will turn out to be a bad bargain, white-livered and empty of morals; the gospel-grinder is sure to have his own blameworthy past and will drag you to the dogs; the flash charmer will come to act the tightwad, insisting you live on naught a year; the clever wit will loiter away his hours believing others must provide his income, and the happiness you anticipated will never turn into happiness enjoyed; there'll always be something wanting.

Better—the only honest way—is to put away your hopes of private feeling and search out the company of a man with means, a man who knows the value of brass and is easy enough with it. Make your worth felt to him, woo his protection as he woos your affections, in the good way of business, and the reward will be comfort and ease, and there's naught low or small in that. Is it of any consequence that he isn't a looker, or a rare mind, or a fancy poet, as long as he's his own man and is improving you?

This must be calculated on.

Love is a bygone idea; centuries worn. There's things we can go without, and love is among them, bread and a warm hearth are not. Is it any wonder there's heaps of ladies, real ladies, biding to marry the first decent man who offers them five hundred a year? Aye, young flowers, don't be being left behind on the used-up shelf. If you must yearn for things, let those things be feelings, and let your yearning be done in a first-class carriage like this one

rather than in one of those reeking compartments down back, where you'll be on your feet all day and exposed to winds and forever stunned by the difficulty of your life. Establish yourself in a decent situation and put away what you can, that, please God, one day you may need no man's help. Take it and be content, then you'll journey well.

II. On the Threshold

And there's no doubting this carriage is high class. The wood
and the brass and the velvet and the trimmings: I see it in bright
perspective, and though we've been sat here since early morning,
my mind has been so far away, up in the clouds gathering wool,
it's like I'm noticing it now for the first time: a sudden letting in
of daylight. I reach out to stroke the plush of the drapes. Tickle
the fringe of the lace doilies. Rub the polished rail. I twist my boot
into the thick meat of the carpet. I crane my neck to look at the
other passengers, so hushed and nice-minded and well got up.
None of this is imagination. It is real. It has passed into my hands
and I can put a price on it all.

  Across the table, on the sofa he shares with his books and
papers, Frederick cuts his usual figure: face and fingernails
scrubbed to a shine, hair parted in a manly fashion, an upright
pose, feet planted and knees wide, snake pushed down one leg of

his breeches; a right gorger. He fidgets round and tries to throw off my gander.

"All fine with you, Lizzie?" he says.

"Oh, grand," I says, though I'm slow to take my eyes away. I can't see the crime in it, a lady taking a moment to admire.

"Lizzie, *bitte*," he says, rustling his newspaper, and slapping it out, and lifting it up to hide himself, "I'm trying to read."

I click my tongue off the roof of my mouth—for him, naught in the world has worth unless it's written down—and turn to look out the window. Outside, the country is speeding by, wind and steam, yet not fast enough for my liking. The farther we get away, and the farther again, the better.

I forbade anyone from coming to the station to see us off, for I didn't want any scenes, but of course Lydia, the rag-arse, disobeyed me.

"Don't let it change you," she said, gripping my hand and casting anxious glances up at the train as if it were a beast about to swallow me. "Find a friend as'll listen to you and don't be on your own. It's no fine thing to be alone."

We embraced and she cried. I squeezed her arm and fixed the hair under her bonnet and told her she was a good friend, the best.

"Find your people, Lizzie," she said then through her tears. "I'm told St. Giles is where they be. St. Giles, do you hear?"

I sat backways in the carriage so I could leave the place looking at it. To go from a familiar thing, however rough-cut, is a matter for nerves, and I suppose that's why so many people don't move. Manchester: leastwise they know the run of it.

At Euston, Frederick stands on the platform, waist-deep in smoke and soot, and takes it all in: heaves it up his nose and sucks it through his teeth and swallows it down as if all these years in

Manchester have weakened his bellows and London is the only cure. Around him, around us, a mampus of folk, mixed as to their kind. Men and men and men and men, and here more men hung off by ladies dressed to death and ladies in near dishabbilly and ladies in everything between. By the pillar, an officer in boots. Over there under the hoarding, a line of shoe-blacks. A pair of news vendors. An Italian grinding tunes from a barrel organ. And passing by now—charging through with sticks and big airs—a tribe of moneymen in toppers and showy chains, chased at heel by beggar boys so begrimed it's impossible to tell if they're Christians or coons or what.

I stop one of the railway porters and ask him to tell me what time it says on the station wall.

"Ma'am?" he says, unsure whether I'm playing a rig, for the clock is large and plain for all except the stone-blind to read. "That there says a quarter past two o'clock."

I nod him my thanks. He bides for the penny. I wave him away; a tone won't win any favors from me.

"On time," I call to Frederick. And then again to be heard over the music and the patter and the tramp of boots on the pavement: *"I says we're right on time."*

Frederick takes his watch from his fob and holds it up to the clock, makes sure the one isn't fibbing to the other. "So it seems," he says.

I push through to stand in front of him, my arms folded against him. "Now don't go being slippery, Frederick, and remember what you said. You said if there were no delays we'd be able to go and see the house today. If we got here before three, you said, we wouldn't have to put it off till tomorrow."

He drops his watch back in and wrestles his hands into his gloves. "We'll see."

We wait in the waiting room for our bags to be loaded onto the cab, then we wait in the weather for them to be removed to a second cab, on account of the lame nag that's preventing the first from moving off. These added minutes spent in the strangeness of this strange place—a smell of drains just like Manchester, only with a special whack to it—has given me a sick headache and has me wanting, more than ever, to get to the new house. To close the doors and be safe behind my own walls. I become impatient. I huff and stamp my foot. And by the time we climb up and are on our way, my tongue is aflame with speeches, even though I've promised not to bring them out again.

"Frederick," I says. The bump and jolt of the wheels makes my voice tremble. "*Frederick?*"

He sighs. "What is it?"

"My love, forgive me if my insistence bores you, but still I don't understand why we must stop with the Marxes. If our house is ready, why don't we go there direct and move ourselves in? Then we could see Jenny and Karl at our leisure, when we're right and settled."

He lets loose another sigh. Crosses his leg over and lands a sharp elbow on the windowsill. "Really, Lizzie, I cannot discuss this with you again."

"I just don't see the need, that's all. Causing trouble for Jenny, when our house is there, biding to be walked into."

"For blazing sake, Lizzie, you know well it was Jenny's idea to have us for these few days. She desires us there so we can make the final arrangements together. Besides, it's too late to change the plans. We've been kindly invited, we've accepted the kind invitation, and that, if you'll be so kind, is the end of it."

And though it feels to me like the depths of unkindness,

I know this must indeed be the end. When a man's mind is set, there's rot-all you can say to change its direction.

I turn to watch out the window. Soon the giant station hotels give way to workshops and warehouses; now to rows of brick and stone; now to terraces and park. Like Manchester, the whole of human history is here, only more of it. I make to point something out to Frederick—the door of a house on a better kind of street—but he's not looking. He's quiet in his seat. Like a statue he sits stock-still, his gaze on his lap, his mouth pulled down.

"A penny for your thoughts," I says.

"What's that?" he says, blinking at me like a dazed child.

"You looked a hundred miles away. Were you thinking anything?"

"*Nein, nein.*" He brings a fist to his mouth and clears his throat. "I wasn't thinking anything. Nothing at all."

He says this, and of course I ought to credit it, but his face and manner go for so much; I can tell he's lying. He's thinking about *her,* and it makes me sad and envious to know it. Spoken or unspoken, she hangs there between us; an atmosphere.

I arrange the cuffs on my wrists till I'm able to look at him again. When I do, I can tell he has noticed a hurt in me, though I'm sure he doesn't know what's caused it. He brightens, his mood freshens, and he speaks in the tone of a man who wants to make up for he doesn't know what.

"I have always thought it interesting," he says, bringing his face close to the glass and squinting through it, "I've always thought it interesting that the English divide their buildings perpendicularly into houses, whereas we Germans divide them horizontally into apartments."

I shrug to tell him I've never thought to think about it.

"In England," he goes on, "every man is master of his hall and

stairs and chambers, whereas back home we are obliged to use the hall and stairs in common. I believe it is just as Karl says: the possession of an entire house is desired in this country because it draws a circle round the family and hearth. *This is mine. This is where I keep my joys and my sorrows, and you shan't touch it.* Which is a natural feeling, I suppose. I daresay universal. But it is stronger here, much stronger, than it is in the Fatherland."

I make a face—"Is that so?"—and pull the window down to let the breeze in.

Don't I deserve to have some days that aren't about her?

The cab stops outside a detached house of fair style: three up and one down, a good-sized area, a flower garden and a porch. That they live bigger than their means—that they live at the rate of knots and don't use their allowance wise—isn't a surprise to me. Even so, I feel called on to speak.

"It won't be long now before they have us cleaned out."

I take the cabby's hand and kick my skirts out so I can land my foot without stepping on my hem. I've bare touched down before the door of the house flies open and two dogs come surging out with Tussy close on their tails: "*There* you are!"

The larger of the dogs runs to Frederick and puts its paws up on his good waistcoat. Frederick bends and allows himself to be licked on the cheek and the ear. For a man so neat he has a queer love for what roots and roves. The other dog, the ratty-looking one, comes to make circles around me. I stand frozen while it sniffs at my privy parts.

"Don't be frightened." Frederick laughs. "He's harmless."

I give him a look that says I'll scream and make an episode if it's the only way.

Snorting, he takes the animal by the collar and shoos it off. "Come on, Whiskey, come away from that mean woman."

Tussy kisses Frederick on the lips and tells him he's late getting to London, twenty years late. He laughs and says something in the German, and she tosses her head and speaks back to him in the same, and between them now they release a mighty flow of language, one so foreign that, if you were to judge from their faces and features only, you wouldn't know what they were feeling.

When their business is done, Tussy comes and wraps herself round me, making me feel the child, for she's taller than me now and has a bust bigger. "At last you're here, Aunt Lizzie, at last."

"Tussy, my sweet darling, let me see you." I hold her out and look her up and down. She has her hair in braids and a jewel at the neck and a dress that shows a new slightness of waist. Only a year since her last visit to Manchester—what a prime and drunken affair that was!—and yet, from the look of her, it'd be easy to believe thrice that time has hurtled away. Fifteen and out of her age, never to be a child again; it'd break your heart.

"You've grown all out of knowledge," I says.

"Have I?" she says, and does a twirl, and curtsies. She sticks out her tongue and winks as she rises from the dip.

I swat her on the arm with my glove. "You're getting more and more like your father."

"You mean, more like a Jewess?"

I laugh. She hasn't lost her mouth. "Mind your father doesn't hear you saying such things."

Frederick instructs the cabby to take our belongings inside, suitcases first, boxes and gifts last. Tussy takes my arm and walks me up the path to the porch.

"I have missed you so, Aunt Lizzie."

"And I've missed you, child."

"And now, finally, we get to be neighbors."

"Aye, it's been a long time coming."

"You know, it's only twenty-two minutes away. Your new house, from here. I've been there often and have counted the distance. Door to door, twenty-two minutes on foot."

"Is that all? A mere hop and a skip."

"We shall do all sorts together, shan't we, Aunt Lizzie?"

"There'll be time for it all. We'll not lack for things to do, nor time to do them in."

The rest of them are stood in the hall passage: the family display. Mother, father, and eldest daughter, biding to bask in the honor they know we must feel to be connected with them. Frederick walks in and is greeted by more of the German, and more again, till the air is full of it. I leave them to have their minute. Lingering on the matting, I marvel at the tree they have in a tub on the porch.

"A tree," I says, "in a tub." I tug on Tussy's sleeve. "I wouldn't let that grow any farther or it'll burst out."

Giving vent to a howl of laughter, Tussy pulls me up the step and presents me as the ringmaster presents his lioness: hip cocked back, arms stretched out, fingers twinkling, a giant grin. Young Janey comes forward first and she's a winsome sight to see. It's a beauty that might need a little bringing about, true, but it's a beauty all the same, and I wouldn't take it from her. Next comes Karl, his whiskers like bramble on my face, his lips like dried-out sausage.

"*Willkommen,* Lizzie," he says.

And final now, Jenny herself. The changes in her face speak to how long it's been. Five or six years, by my count, though she looks to have been drawn out by a decade and more. Well settled she is now, into the autumn of her time.

"Welcome to our home, Lizzie," she says with a bit too much energy. "Welcome to London."

I offer a grateful smile and now blush at the falseness of it. We're not used to playing this visiting game with each other. For some reason or another, I always decided to stay at home when Frederick took his trips to the capital; likewise Jenny never joined Karl or Tussy on their visits to Manchester, and no one ever seemed to wonder at it, no excuses were given for us, our tabsences were taken to be the normal and wanted way, which I suppose they were.

"And Laura?" I says, in case I forget to mention her later and am judged thoughtless for it. "Are there tidings from Laura?"

"Safe," Jenny says. "They have moved from Paris to Bordeaux. They will be safe there."

I open to inquire further, but she grips my arm to say there'll be plenty of time for that, I'm not to worry, now is a moment for reunion and celebration.

Behind us, Karl and Frederick start a scuffle over who ought pay off the cabby, as if it made a piddle of difference on earth which pocket it came from: isn't it all water from the same fountain? Jenny can't help but to get involved, and I'm glad of the free moment to take off my bonnet and have a proper look. The hall, I see, is papered gay. There's a table with pottery animals and a bust. A mirror and a line of pictures, and in every wall a door. The carpet is rich and unworn and goes up to the first landing and into the beyonds. The banisters are painted three coats of white.

Once the cabby has been dealt with, Jenny sends the men into the parlor and out of the way. She smiles a moment through the silence, and now she says, "Nim?" only the once and bare over her breath, almost a sigh.

Miraculous-like the maid comes up from the kitchen. She's wearing a simple dress and a white cap and apron. I've heard so much about her, how good she's supposed to be to look at, I'm

relieved to see she's plainer in true life. Fine bones, to be sure, but the work tells upon her.

"Nim, the cases, please," says Jenny. She whispers it, as if the giving of orders hurts her and must be made soft. "Into the guest-rooms. Thank you."

Nim nods at her mistress and, as she passes, gives me another as a greeting. I step aside to give her way, but not so far that I can't measure her up.

Her nose doesn't reach my shoulder!

The sight of her knocks me out of myself, for when a figure has been made famous to you—when she's been talked about till her name sounds louder in your ears than Jehovah's—you expect her to tower over and be massive, and yet here she is now, a tiny thing. As I watch her go up the stairs, I'm left in no doubt as to the solid-ness of her frame, and her limberness—she manages to haul two burdens at a time and not be tripped by the dogs whirling about her—but there's no getting clear of the fact that, God bless her, she's but a pip. If you didn't keep an eye on her, you'd lose her.

"Oh, and, Nim," says Jenny when the maid is already gone round the bend of the stairs, "when you're done with that, we'll have some refreshments in the parlor." Jenny now turns to me and makes a gesture to indicate that it's a relief to be rid of ugly tasks. She takes the bonnet out of my hand and leaves it down on the table. "Come," she says, and puts me on her arm and walks me off for the tour.

I count a parlor, a morning room, a conservatory, a cellar, five bedrooms, three cats, and two birds.

Says Jenny: "It is indeed a princely dwelling compared with the holes we have lived in before. In fact, to my mind it is far too large and expensive a house. I am forever telling Karl we ought to move, that we live too grandly for our circumstances. I for my part

wouldn't care a damn about living in Whitechapel. But he will not hear of it. He thinks the house is the one means by which the Girls can make connections and relationships that can assure them a future." She unfurls a finger and makes circles in the air with it. "*Surrounded* as we are by doctors and lawyers." The shape of her mouth is supposed to tell me that such people are a necessary unpleasantness to her, like the stink of the slop pail. Pondering a moment, she lets the face fall away. "But I daresay Karl is right. A purely proletarian setup would be unsuitable now, however fine it would be if we were alone, just the two of us, or if the Girls were boys."

We've stopped outside Karl's study. By the way she puzzles at the half-open door, I can tell she's queasy about whether to venture in or to pass over it. Shamming ignorance of her unease, I unhitch myself and go through.

"It might look like a mess," she says, following after me, "but it has its own peculiar method."

I make my way to a clearing on the rug, a small circle of carpet bordered by piles of books and papers.

"It may not be immediately evident, but this room is actually the brightest and airiest in the house." She picks her way through and draws the curtain back. "The Heath right there. The air the best in London. One has only to leave the windows open a moment and that cigar smell is killed."

I'm close enough to the chimneypiece to have a proper gander at the things littered on it: the matches, the tobacco boxes, the paperweights, the portraits of Jenny and the Girls.

"Look, here's yours," she says, pointing at the picture of Frederick.

On the way back out, I take the liberty to push in a file that looks ready to topple from the bookcase.

"He calls them his slaves," says Jenny, meaning the books.

Back downstairs a tray has been made ready in the parlor. Nim stands beside it, biding our wishes. Frederick and Karl have already been served liberal shorts of gin.

"Lizzie, what shall it be, tea or coffee?" says Jenny.

"Whatever you're having yourself," I says.

"What do you say to coffee?"

"Nay, I won't have coffee, but thank you."

"Tea, then."

"Not much up for tea either, you're very kind."

Karl slaps his thigh and gives out a good-humored roar. "Can't you see it's a drink the woman wants!"

The color runs up Jenny's neck. She lets out a little laugh, glances at the clock and now down at her hem. "A drink, Lizzie?"

"Aye, I'll have a nip, if it's going." To put me into the spirits.

Nim comes to me with a half-measure. She refuses me her eyes when she hands me the glass; keeps them low on the floor.

"Thanks, Nim," I says, loud and clear so I'm heard. "You're awful good."

Her mouth twitches. Someone coughs. She scuttles back to the tray and sets about readying the Girls' tea. Sat in the chair closest to her is Frederick. I watch for his behavior, but in actual fact, he bare notices her. More than that, he ignores her. I'd even say rude, if I didn't know Frederick to be so particular about his graces.

From his royal spot on the settee, Karl proposes us. "To Frederick and Lizzie," he says. "After the darkness of Manchester, may you find happiness and rest here in London."

Tussy rummages in a drawer and comes out with two wrapped gifts. Frederick is served first: a red neckerchief. He ties it on and marches up and down and gives a blast of the "Marseillaise," and

everyone laughs and claps. Mine is a jewelry box, and inside, lying on a bed of velvet, a silver thimble and a pin with a bit of thread already fed into it. I hold up the needle between my fingers, and they all brim over.

Says Karl between his guffaws: "The revolutionary finally settles down to her fancywork!"

I make as if to pour my drink into the thimble. "It'll come in handy for measuring my poteen." And that—easy as falling off a chair—brings the house down.

When the laughter drains, the room settles into a tired silence. The tick of the clock. The sucking at glasses.

"Uncle Frederick," says Janey after a time, "have you finished your history of Ireland?"

This gets Tussy excited. "Oh yes, Uncle Angel, when do we get to read it?"

"Oh, oh," says Frederick, trifling with a corner of his jacket and frowning. "Thank you for your interest, my dear children, but I'm afraid I've been distracted of late. It's all about France now."

"Hmm," gurgles Karl, "indeed. And speaking of that damned place, we need to take a clear position on the situation. Our initial support of Prussia is proving quite an embarrassment—"

"Karl, please," Jenny interrupts. "Can't you leave this outside talk until you are actually outside?"

Karl puts his hands up in surrender.

Tussy giggles.

Jenny catches my eye and gestures at the tray. "Lizzie, there is some tart here," she says. "But if you are hungry for something more filling, I could have Nim fix you up some cold cuts."

I shake my head, perhaps a little too fierce. "Please don't go to any trouble. We ate on the train."

Frederick, always liable for a man-faint if he doesn't have his

in-betweens, looks about to contradict me, but he sees the arrangement of my face and checks himself. "I fear Lizzie is getting restless. She is anxious to see the house. I promised to bring her to see it today." He looks at Karl, as if begging leave.

Karl waves a woman's wave. "Go on, Frederick. Show Lizzie your new home. We'll have time to catch up later."

While I'm putting my coat and bonnet back on, Jenny tells me what she's done to the house. She calls my attention to certain arrangements and wonders if I'd like them altered.

"When I see them, I'll tell you, Jenny," I says. "You'll be the first to know."

The air outside runs into me, a respite. I wouldn't mind walking the twenty-two minutes. "Will we foot it?" I says, thinking Frederick is beside me, but when I turn, I see he's clean gone. "Frederick?"

Of a sudden, I feel him behind me, and then I see only black.

"This way it will be an even bigger surprise!" he says, bringing forth more laughter and clapping from the family gathered on the threshold, and though I notice I'm allowing it to happen, I do say to myself, I says, "Can't I just see the blessed thing? Must it be one of their games?"

He's gone and put his new neckerchief over my face as a blindfold.

III. A Resting Place

A donkey's age, it takes him, to get the wretched thing off. Two, four, six taps of my boot and still he's behind me, fighting with the knot.

"What's keeping you?" I says.

"Patience, Lizzie," he says, and I know it'd be no use telling him again, at this late stage, that his time in Manchester has turned him into a northern stumpole.

I feel him wiggle his finger underneath the neckerchief; now I hear him bite into it and grind it between his ivories. The cotton presses tight against my nose, which tells me it's not really new, this rag. It's one of the old ones from the Club, still smelling of cigars and bear's grease.

With a last wet groan, he gets it free. A curved terrace of houses—dream palaces—unrolls itself in front of me.

"Primrose Hill," he says, and turns me round to face the hill of

grass that rises out of the ground where the terrace ends on the opposite side of the road.

"Are those sheep?" I says.

"And this one"—he turns me again, this time to meet a giant face of plaster and brick—"is ours."

I have to creak my neck back to see to the top of it. The brightness of the day gleams up its windows. Three floors. Iron railings. An area. A basement.

"Well?" he says.

My heart feels faint, which can happen when you make the acquaintance of a real future to replace the what-might-be.

"Have you nothing to say? Hot and cold water all the way up!"

Dazed by light feeling, I clutch at my throat and dither about stepping over the doorsill. "Bless and save us, Frederick, I don't know. It's awful grand."

As I make my way around—the green room already filled with flower and plant, the laundry room fit for an army, the cloakroom with hooks for a hundred, the cellar bigger than the one I myself was reared in—I can't help holding on to the walls and the tables to keep myself on end. I keep expecting a steadying hand from Frederick, but it doesn't come. Something isn't right with him. A flash temper has come over him. When I point something out, he makes sure to bid his interest the other way. When I open a door on the left, he opens one on the right. When I go to look at a wardrobe, he goes to look at a lamp.

"She's done a fine job," I says. "A fine job."

But he doesn't answer. It must be that he doesn't like what she's done.

And, to be honest, I can see why.

In her book, there's naught worse than a new house that looks

new. She said so just now before we left. "So long as the thirst for novelty exists independently of all aesthetic considerations," she went, "the aim of Manchester and Sheffield and Birmingham will be to produce objects which shall always appear new. And, Lizzie, is there anything more depressing than that luster of newness?"

And I went to myself, "Aye, the smell of decay," and took her attitude for a London attitude, set square against sense. But what do I know? She's the baroness and knows better about the styles. (How she ended up with a cruster like Karl is anyone's wager. He must have thought that, because her family tree has as many rebels as it does nobles, she'd have the right opinions about everything, already there in her blood. And she must have thought, well, *she* must have thought he was intellectual and clever, the kind of man that'll win glory on earth, which only goes to show how little true wisdom there is in young hearts.)

In decorating the house, what she's tried to do, she said, is dull the pristine down and make the place appear longer stood. I said I hope this doesn't mean there'll be dirt and dust round the place, for I don't allow it. She said it isn't a question of cleanliness but of heritage, for olden things can be clean without being shiny. I said what would I be wanting with heritage? All I need is a couple of chairs that stand upright. She said it isn't hard to give the idea of it, even in recent and modest houses, by buying the necessaries at auctions, such as movables of no modern date and art that's been handled and weathered—*and chipped,* I see now—and by scattering it all about so that two new things don't rub against each other and make a glare.

"Ending the tyranny of novelty," is what she called it.

"Spending other people's brass," is what I call it, but only to myself. And it's unkind even to think it, for I wouldn't have been able to do it—the ridding, the arranging, the fixing up—without her.

She's thought of everything. She's had the right fringe put on the draping, and the right frills put on the fringe. The few bits we sent down ourselves, she's had cushioned over. She's had the stores stocked. She's had calling cards made; there they are stacked on the hall table. Everything: first to last, start to end.

"We went a finger over budget," she said. "But I believe quality speaks for itself."

And the rooms do indeed speak. They speak dark and solemn. For in buying the movables—and by all accounts she bid like a mad-body after most of it—she thought not about what was handsome but about what was suitable to Frederick's position. And seeing them now, these hulks of bookcases and cabinets and desks and tables, I find myself wondering has she mistaken him, all along, for a priest.

"Are you thinking what I'm thinking, Frederick?" I says, as a way of cheering him.

But there's no humor to be had from him. He's gone like a brick. Closed like a door. He shrugs and disappears upstairs. I follow him up and find him on the first landing, glowering down at his feet.

"Lizzie, I wish you to favor me by showing me which room you would like to have as your boudoir. I'd rather have these matters decided for me."

"All right," I says, hardening myself now. "If that's how you want it."

Jenny has put a cabinet and a toilette table in the large room on the first floor, so she probable expects me to claim that one, on account of its size and distance from the road. As it happens, I decide to leave that one to Frederick—it's closer to his study, after all—and I choose instead the smaller one on the top floor. Here I'll have to share a landing with the maids, and it means an extra flight of steps up and down, and I know people will think I picked it out of a

fear of taking too much. But the truth is, I much prefer it. They've thought to put a fireplace all the way up here. And there's a nice washstand and a hip bath, and the flowers on the wall are so brilliant and colorful they look fresh picked. And the bed: the bed has golden posts and an eiderdown quilt, and the way it's sitting in the light, it's like God shining down over it. I sit on it and know immediate that it's mine. "That's it with the moving," it makes me think. "We'll not budge from here. This is the place that'll see me out. This is the bed that on my last day I won't get up from."

"This is the one I want," I says.

"Fine," he says, and goes to look out the little window that gives over garden and the roofs of the other houses.

There's a terrible quiet. His back is a wall blocking out the lovely bit of sun, and the shiver in his limbs makes me think he's going to put his fist out through the glass. For what reason, it's beyond me to say.

"Is everything all right with you, Frederick?"

Slow, he turns round. He doesn't look at me and heeds only the wringing of his hands. "I am sorry, Lizzie"—he shakes his head in a sorrowful way—"I am sorry that you judge the house only *awful grand*. You were expecting something more. But this will have to do for now."

Alarmed, I open to object. I rise to a stand and reach out an arm, but he raises to halt me.

"It is already a risk to take a house this size. A bigger one would be a push too far. Besides, I have already given my word on it. It has been signed to us for three and a half years."

"Frederick, I—"

"Jenny and Karl are waiting for our impressions. They, and especially Jenny, have put a great deal of time and effort into finding us this house and making it fit to occupy. So what you are going to

do, Lizzie, what I'm telling you to do, is to pretend that you think it more, much more, than awful grand."

A rising laugh makes me push my face into my sleeve. As foreigners go, he's unusual fast at picking things up. His problem— the big noke—is letting go when a thing is long done and over. There's times he'll get his whole fist round a delicate article and won't drop it till he's wrung all the sense out of it, and he holds it still, even if he knows it's crushed or broke, or anyhows beyond repair.

"Lizzie, are you laughing?"

Laughter that's sealed only builds and I think I might burst. I plonk back down on the bed and lift my shirts up to hide my face.

"*Ya,* you are laughing! What is so funny? Stop it! I said, stop it!"

"Oh, Frederick," I says, and it all spills out of me, a peal. "Come here and let me kiss you."

He lumbers over, confounded, and sits beside me.

"Frederick," I says, "the house is much more than *grand*. It's an effin' castle!"

He frowns and studies my face for any hidden rigs.

"I'm serious! I just adore it!"

He grins and lets out a sigh and takes tight of me and kisses me. And for a moment now, it almost doesn't matter that it's her he really wants to be holding, that it's her he'd prefer as his princess, for she isn't here and won't be coming back, and I'm the closest thing to her he can ever hope to get.

"You know something?" he says then, tears in his eyes but laughing too. "The Queen was right."

"The Queen? About what?"

"About the Irish."

"And what, pray tell, did the old hooer say about us?"

"That you're an abominable people, none in the world better at causing distress."

IV. Cross to Bear

Imprisoned, they have us, in their hospitality. Already here two days longer than planned. It's my own fault for not being firmer with Frederick. I ought kick up more of a row.

At first I was worried about getting in the way. I didn't want to walk in on top of anyone or trespass on their time. But, as it happens, I keep finding myself alone and lost and off the beaten course, in rooms that go into rooms, up and down and every which direction. My heart goes out to Jenny, having to govern such a monster, and I've come to admire her practice of going away to rest in case she might be tired later in the day, for I've learnt that a mere glance into the parlor is liable to dizzy you, for the depth. It certain can't be *work* that drains her. Since our arrival I haven't caught her doing anything but *make* work with her queer times. She has a joke: "Better a dry crust and manners at eight than fowl and vulgarity at five," but in actual fact, she wouldn't be content with crusts at any

hour, and the maid is left bearing the brunt. Boiling up and bringing in and fettling about, the little creature attends to all of their little wants, and she does it on her own, too, with no others to aid her (for it seems that with servants, if not with any other portion of life, Jenny knows how to make a saving).

Ah, the poor wee puppet! The petty pocket! The pigwidgeon! Nim—I can't deny it!—has succeeded in fascinating my attention. Despite my strict resolve to be cool in her company—"Don't notice her," I says to myself whenever she comes in—I always find myself flushed and susceptible. Whether it be the quiet show she makes of her modesty or the delicate manner with which she wields her influence, or her sad-sad-secret (now so-so-public) that cuts a perilous edge around her china figure; whatever it is, she absorbs me, and I'm fain to get her alone. I must find a moment, I think. I must separate her and present myself proper to her. I must hold out a hand. I must get an idea. *What is the nature of your powers? What do you do that makes the women bend to your will and the men so heated to mount you?*

My chance comes now. The a.m. of another empty day. Jenny off for her nap. The Men locked into the study upstairs. The Girls gone to play shuttlecock in the garden for want of something else going on. I'm supposed to be watching them and learning what's what, only I know my break when it comes and make an excuse of my bladder.

I find her sat on a stool in front of an open cupboard in the storeroom, drooped and snoring over a book that lies on her lap. Her dress is tucked up and the laces of her boots are loosened. She's taking her two minutes, and I'm sorry to have come in on her.

"Can I help you, Mrs. Burns?" she says before I can steal away. Her face is bleary, but her voice is bright, not a hint of sleep in it.

"Oh, Nim, I—"

Apologize, is what I want to do, for barging in and robbing her leisure. But more than that, I want to apologize for Frederick. There's no excuse for the shabby treatment he's been giving her. It's as if he believes that by overlooking her, by paying no regard to her, by passing orders for her through the rest of us, he'll convince us once and for all that she means naught to him, that not even his words are worthy of her (when, in fact, there's not a single word he speaks that doesn't fly right at her, that doesn't explode about her like fireworks, that, in the noise and the bright light, doesn't call to our minds that day some twenty years ago when her charms got such a hard handle on him that he decided the only means of release was to lift up her skirts and put his seed inside of her, not a single thought given to the harvest such behaving so unfortunate bears). Aye, that's what I want to do, apologize for all of Frederick's *behaving*. But instead I fumble with my tongue and shrink within myself and end up saying, "So how do you find it here? Do you go much to the parks?"

With red-shot eyes she pins me, and I hold her stare, and we stay like this for a time; two maids across a storeroom floor.

At last she closes her book and stands. "It's nearly time for the picnic, Mrs. Burns." She checks the floor around her and rummages in her pockets, looking to see if she's dropped anything. "We're to gather in the parlor," she says. And when she unbends and sees me still standing here: "Perhaps you'd be more comfortable waiting up there?"

Spread out on the couches, fidgeting and yawning and trying to ignore Karl's pacing, we bide for Jenny. After forever has passed, she swishes in and kisses the air about us, a hand busying itself with a button of her coat.

"If we want to make the best of the afternoon we should set

off immediately. It could be raining in an hour, and then we would have missed the fine spell, or?"

Behind her, Karl widens his eyes and purses his lips as if to say, "Don't look at me, I've had a lifetime of it."

Once outside the gate, Frederick and Karl stride ahead, arm in crook, their heads tilted close so as not to drop anything important between them. The Girls hold hands and swing their arms like children; they each lead a dog by a strap. Jenny lets them gain a bit of distance before drawing me in and sallying forwards. Nim follows with the basket.

"Nothing extravagant," says Jenny. "Just some roast veal, some bread and cheese, some ale."

I turn and smile a weak smile at Nim, the tiny doll straining under the poundage.

The Men wait for us at the Heath's edge. Karl asks whether it's a good idea to go to the usual spot, given the strong breeze. "Would some place more sheltered be better?"

Jenny suggests under one of the big oaks, and we agree. Ohing and ahing like she's just solved the National Debt, we agree. And I, for one, must be careful of my mood.

We set off again. The dogs are released onto the grass. Tussy skips after them. A sullen-looking Janey searches for flowers to press. The trees are tossed. The wind is loud in the leaves. The kites in the air fly slanted and set their owners straining. Down in my bad lung there's a pain. Naught to fret over, but there. Too much fast air after these long days spent between the dust of the mattress and the smoke of the fireside.

"Karl is so happy to have Frederick nearby again," says Jenny now. "It does me good to see him happy, he's been so nervous of late."

"I'm glad, Jenny. That's nice to hear."

"Of course, he hasn't been alone. My own hair is gone gray thinking about Laura in France. Her second baby lost, and now pregnant again. Caught up in this damned war. It has us all hysterical."

"You oughtn't worry, Jenny. Laura'll be fine. Doesn't she have Paul to look after her?"

"Paul?" she says, whipping a handkerchief from her sleeve and making a whisk of it at me. "Paul is *French*. And a *politics* man."

"*Mohme!*" Tussy is calling from about twenty yards. "*Mohme! Mohme!*"

"What is it?" Jenny says without slowing her gait.

Tussy runs to catch up with us. She comes round us and, walking backwards, her hem dancing around her boots and liable to trip her up, holds out a feather. "Look what I found. Which bird is it from, do you think?"

Sighing, Jenny takes it and runs it through her fingers. "A common magpie," she says, and hands it back.

Tussy looks at it a moment, disdainful, and drops it. Wanders back onto the grass.

"And it's not only Laura," Jenny says when we're out of earshot again. "I also worry for these two. Look at Janey there and tell me she isn't radiant? And Tussy, perhaps she even more so. But I'm anxious. I'm anxious that, for this same reason, they are all the more out of place and out of time. And with the life we give them, how will they ever meet a good ordinary man?"

"How will any of us?" I says.

She squeezes my arm and grants me a smile. "Oh, Lizzie, you *are* funny. But perhaps I am not expressing myself well. I speak of a subject it is hard for people who do not have children themselves to understand. A mother will look at her children, and if she sees that one of them has already been denied the chance of a happy

kind of life, she will naturally worry that the others will go the same way. I know I sound like a philistine when I say it, Lizzie, but if they could but find husbands, a German or even an Englishman if he had a solid position, and get themselves comfortably settled; if they could do that, I wouldn't mind my own losses so much. The last thing I want is that they have the kind of life I have had. Often I think I would like to turn away from politics altogether, or at least be able to look upon it as a hobby to take up and leave down as I please. But for us, Lizzie, it is a matter of life and death, because for our husbands it is so, and I fear it has to be the same for our children. This is our cross to bear."

I say naught. Thoughts and memories come vivid, of old desires and chances lost, and though there's regret in them, and mourning, it's not unpleasant to have their company. We walk on.

"But we must be optimistic, mustn't we, Lizzie? Rather than dwell, we must look forward to better things. And I do think we are entering a new phase, a happier time for all of us. Your move to London marks a change. I believe great things will happen now that Frederick is here. Karl has been so looking forward to it."

"Frederick also. He's overjoyed to be out of that job. Only a month wanting till he's fifty, and he's like a young drake again."

"Ha!" She hugs my shoulder. "And it is about time. Frederick's talents were wasted in that dusthole. It is true there was pleasure to be gained from taking money out of the enemy's pocket, draining it from the inside, so to speak, but enough is enough; the real work has to begin, and Frederick is essential to it. He really is a genius. Are you following his articles on the war?"

"Not myself, nay."

"Oh, but you must, they explain—" She sucks in her breath. "Oh, I do apologize Lizzie, I wasn't thinking. I'll read them to you

one of these days. Or better, I'll have Nim do it. She wouldn't mind. She likes to keep abreast."

Up ahead, Frederick has stopped at a coster's cart to buy ginger beer for the Girls. I wish he wouldn't. I've seen it done in Manchester, the ginger boiled in the same copper that serves for washing, and it's not healthful. Jenny halts us in order to keep our distance from the others. She bends down and picks some flowers from the verge.

"What are these?" I says when she puts a posy in my buttonhole.

"Snow-in-the-summer," she says. "It's rare to see them still blooming this late."

"They're lovely," I says.

She gives a vague smile and, seeing that the others have moved off, starts us up once more. "I realize I have been talking only of myself."

"That's all right, Jenny."

"Well, I do not want to talk anymore. It is only boring you and upsetting me. And distracting us from the other matter."

The other matter is, of course, the house. She reminds me that the maid, Camilla Barton, is due to arrive in a fortnight's time, and gives me advice on how to keep her, which is harder than I might think, for things aren't like they used to be, in sixty-eight and the crisis years, when the good families were letting go of their help and the registries were brimming with girls to be had for the asking and for a price much closer to their worth. Nay, things have changed and a girl will walk if she finds a better situation, and it's often not even the mistress's fault, for it's difficult to define in exact terms what's owed a girl and what she herself owes, and not everyone can learn the art of leaving the servants alone.

"I recommend a second girl," she says. "Frederick instructed me to find only the one, and I followed those instructions, but my

true feeling is that you will need two. Everything works better with two. The girls are happier because they have company and get to sit down in the evening, and you are happier because the work can be divided out and gets done. You do not want to be a slave with your apron never off. London is your retirement. If I could afford it, I would get another."

"Can't Nim manage? Has she ever threatened to leave?"

"Nim? Oh, she's different. We've had her for so long she's like family."

In the distance, Karl beckons us to a tree where he thinks we ought lay the picnic. Jenny flutters her handkerchief in answer.

"Speaking of family, Lizzie, I would like to say something to you."

"What's on your mind, Jenny?"

"I'd like to clean the air."

"Does it need cleaning?"

"About your sister."

The other matter. The *real* matter.

"Jenny, you don't have to. It's not important."

"*Nein, nein,* it's on my mind, Lizzie, and I'd like to say it out." She turns into the wind so the loose strands of her hair fly back over her bonnet. "Mary was your sister, Lizzie, and you loved her as any sister would and should, and I don't think little of you for it."

"And I'm glad for *that,* Jenny."

"You already know relations between her and me weren't easy, and I'm not going to insult you by pretending otherwise now."

"Well, we can't get on with everyone."

"But there are reasons, Lizzie, good reasons, I did not, as you say, *get on* with your sister, and I want to share some of those with you. I want to tell my side. Not to vindicate myself, you understand, or absolve myself of any wrongdoing, but to let things out in the open, so we can be friends, you and I, honestly and truly."

I shake my head and keep my gaze on the path ahead. "What's past is past, Jenny. What's to be gained from walking back over it? Mary is gone, and what spite there was between you has gone to the grave with her. There's no point digging it out and giving it life again."

She tugs on my arm in an effort to turn my eyes towards her. I don't give in to it. "You are a good person, Lizzie, and I appreciate most deeply your trying to save me the pain. But I must talk on it. Otherwise it shall always be there, haunting me. The only way to put a thing behind one is to put a name on it and to know it, or?"

She goes quiet, leaving just the wind in our ears, and it seems for a moment like her mind has countered itself and decided against naming or knowing anything, but the moment passes and she turns to me now, intent on my face.

"As you well know, Lizzie, anxieties and vexations are the lots of all political wives, but I can say with certainty that few are familiar with the misery and anger I have experienced over the years. With Karl I have lived a Gypsy life, forced from place to place, this country to that. I can barely remember a week when I did not have to struggle in some mean way to keep the family healthy and alive in the hovels our poverty pressed us to live in. I often went to pieces and saw Karl weep. Many times I felt I could no longer keep my strength. I became an expert at composing begging letters. I lost my looks." She wipes a hand across her cheek as if to remove the pits that the smallpox has left there. "And through all of this, the only means, the *only means* I had of preventing a total collapse was the show of respectability I was able to maintain. It may sound silly to you now, Lizzie, but I was young and I had certain ideas, and my public face was all that kept them alive. And when Frederick took up with Mary, it threatened to take away even that." She takes my hand from where it was warm in my skirt pockets, and she holds it. "Did Mary speak to you of me?"

"Speak, nay. She fumed. Called you all sorts. And she had some right, Jenny. It was no business of yours what she and Frederick did."

"Yes, I know, Lizzie. And if it were only that they were not married, then it would not have been a problem. Please, I am not a fanatic. But the fact was, they were using each other. Mary was using Frederick to get ahead. And Frederick was using Mary to make a splash. Nothing was real. They were playing each other like a game, and that was all. She took his money and gifts, and lived like a fine lady of society on the back of him. And he showed her about like a prize. He said it himself, she was his *finger-up* to his family and the whole blasted bourgeoisie, and it was clear they both enjoyed it a bit too much, she and he. It was vulgar and intolerable, and it was doing no good for the Movement. People, our comrades, were asking questions. I remember hearing them wondering out loud to each other why such an intelligent man was involving himself with one of his workers. They could accept he was a capitalist and a millocrat. That was the family burden he had to carry. But did he also have to behave like one? He was taking advantage of his position. He was no better than the other rich sons of Manchester who used the young girls of the proletariat for their pleasure. Frederick, they said, was an exploiter. They thought he was exploiting the—"

She stops here. She sees my face and is clever enough to know she ought. She gives me back my hand and I put it away again. "Can you forgive me, Lizzie? Do you think we can be friends?"

I'm far from charmed. It's not in me to offer any softening words. But nor do I push her to the apology she's paining to reach. At bottom she's a good woman. Her affliction is only that she believes, still, that she has a right to be free from all that's disagreeable. "Of course," I says, and touch her on the shoulder.

She moves around to allow an embrace, but before anything can happen—before I'm seen stood in this park in this woman's arms—I come away to help Nim with the final bit of carrying.

"Do you need a hand with that, Nim?"

"I can manage, thank you, Mrs. Burns."

October

V. Let Us Hear

I lie under, his whiskers like a broom of twigs and stinking of
liquor, till I've come to terms with the dark and my situation in it.
"Angels of grace, defend us," I says, "what bloody time is it?"

Our first p.m. in the new house and Frederick went out to the
Club to celebrate. "Karl is insisting," he said. "There are some people he wants me to meet. I'll be back before ten." At midnight and
no sign of him, I went to bed. Alone among the unfamiliar walls,
I slept in a state close to waking. Now—some unholy hour—the
weight of man collapses onto me. When God wants to punish you,
he answers your prayers.

"My Lizzichen," he moans, grappling for a grope through sheet
and dress, "forgive me, but I'm in need."

"You rotten scoundrel," I says, using my elbows against him.
"Get you to your own chambers."

"Come now, *mein Liebling,* show some mercy."

"I'll show you more than mercy, Frederick Engels, now ske-daddle. Away with you. Can't I put my head down a minute?"

He kneels over me and, mocking-like, clasps his hands together as if to beg. "Have pity on a rogue," he says. "Am I not good to you?" he says. "Is a moment of comfort too much to ask?" he says, and other such phrases that he thinks will wheedle him in.

"Mary Mother, give me patience." I yank up the linen to stole myself. Knowing neither my own forces nor the degree of his im-pairment, this sends him rolling—*thump!*—onto the carpet. I sit up and hold my breath. Rain is falling outside and there's a barking of animals off and yonder. Bellows of laughter rise up from under the bed. I fall back and sigh.

Boys kept like monks by their mothers go one of two ways: they turn womanly or they turn wild. Frederick's rearing among the Calvins—kept behind curtains drawn tight and doors too thick for the world's vices to get in—has done naught for him but disease his head with what it's been deprived of, and now look at him: single-minded and seeing no ends that aren't low. He keeps pictures. He makes foreign requests. It's not always the Council he runs off to.

After some scratching about and some fumbling, there's a striking at lucifers and the lamp flares up. I cover my eyes from the sudden light. "Still in fit shape, I think you'll agree," he says. I see, when I've come to terms with it, that he has his clothes off and is showing himself. He clasps his hands behind his neck, which makes the skin run up over his bones and the hair jump out from under his arms. He holds this pose as long as the lush in his veins allows it. Now he wobbles and, giggling like a little girl, staggers over to lean on the wall. The lamp shines hard against him.

Growing up, no one sits down and tells you what the man's bit is going to look like. Knowledge is got from the snatches you

catch. The hole in your father's combinations. The neighbor man washing at the pump. The surge in the gent's breeches on the bus. The Jew Beloff pissing in the bucket. Frederick's is like none of those. In its vigors, it points up and a bit to the side. Its cover goes all the way over the bell and bunches at the end like a pastry twist. Before he does anything, he spits on his hand and peels this back. Then you know he's right and ready.

Personal, I have my limits with it. There's things I'll not be brought to do. I'll maw it: no harm in that if he doesn't shove too. And I'll let him turn me over: let go of your vanities and there's pleasure to be got there. But the hooer's trick, that's crossing the pale. What's the draw of an act so cruddy? And what's the purpose, anyhows, when the normal carriage road has been clear of courses these past twenty years? "Keep dreaming, General," is what I says whenever he starts to rub up that way. "Not for love nor lush."

Tonight, though, he wants the usual, and I don't quarrel with that. I bring my hands down his back and put them on his arse, his little arse that hasn't dropped with the years but has stayed upwise and firm. Where it meets the leg is like the underneath of swollen mammies, and when he pushes, its sides dip in to make dishes smooth enough for your morning milk. It turns heads, the round of it under his breeches. I've seen it with my own eyes. When it's late in the parlor and hot with bodies, and when he himself is sticky from all the hosting, he sometimes takes off his coat and turns to throw it somewhere; that's when they nab their peek.

He puts his arms under my knees and bends my pins over them. I know he'd like them hooked over his shoulders—my ankles clutching his neck, my toes taking hold of his hair so sleek, his whiskers tickling skin that usual only feels the itch of a stocking—but I'm no longer the young thing I once was, and

neither is he, though he likes to think his physical senses are as hale today as when he first fetched a lass.

His eyes are open. He doesn't ever close them doing it. He likes to pin you, pierce you through. I swear with those eyes he'd stare into naught and find something. Even when he's lushed they stay clear and bright, and seem to let you into his head, though this can only be a fancy, for afterwards there remains the mystery of what he thinks when he gets on top of you, whether it's dark or light or what.

I begin to feel it, the quiver down in my cunny, but I've to conjure it up if I don't want it to fade, the last lick of oil in a lamp. I help it with my hand like he himself has taught me—a French recipe—and I let out a gasp. Reading this a sign, he comes down bricks on me.

If he says anything now, dear Jesus, I'll credit it.

There's never been anyone like him.

It's rare I sleep the whole night when he stays. I go off easy enough, but am woken early by his kicking. For some reason, I can't bear to roll over and see him there grunting and happy. There's others, I'm sure, who lie and watch for the sun to rise up out of him. He'll not get that from me. I stay with my back turned.

In actual fact I ought be up already, doing the round. The maid doesn't get here till Sunday and I've to look after everything myself. The pulling back of the blinds and curtains. The opening of the shutters. The drawing up of the kitchen fire and the polishing of the range. The checking of the boiler. The putting on of the kettle. The cleaning of the boots and the knives. Then the other fires. And the hearth rug. And the grate. Then the rubbing of the furniture. Then the washing of the mantelpiece and ledges. Then the dusting of the ornaments. Then the scattering of the tea leaves

and the sweeping of them up. So many things, and for every one a thought. So many thoughts at a time, for so many things, it's hard to know the ones you ought be hearkening to. By thinking you're forever running behindhand you make things the master of you.

The worst, though, will be the answering of the door. I can already see it in their faces: "Why *her*?" The butcher boy, the shop girl, the milkmaid, the grocer, the letter carrier: "Can't see what makes her stand out." Every day of every week, somebody, some way: "If she can do it, any old beggar can."

I'll try to turn blind from it. I'll pass them my coins and tell them my orders and make as if I've not remarked a thing. But afterwards, I know, I'll be left with something inside, a prickling feeling like a hair in my collar or a pea in my bodice; a reminder of the fact that, when it comes to my hike to the higher caste, there's no getting away from the chance of it. Would I know what I know, would I have done what I've done, would I be here today, swelling it up, if I'd gone down different alleys, taken up with other souls?

Fortune first spins her wheel in my favor in the summer of forty-two. It's the summer the wages are cut and the mills are turned out. The summer the coalpits are shut and the boiler plugs are pulled and the workers gather and the riots flare and the soldiers march. And while all this is happening I'm at home, locked into the basement with Mary. Though I don't know it yet, though it will take me time to understand, my being here, inside away from it all—my sitting it out—will be the chancest thing I ever do.

I *want* to join in. There's rebellion enough in my heart to spark a hundred rallies. But Mary has other plans for me.

"If you go out that door," she says, "you'll not be getting back in."

"Well, maybe I won't want to get back in."

"You want to be a corner girl, is that it? You want to be a loafer and a beggar till you die? Go out there now and that's what you'll be, and that's what you'll stay. If anyone from the mill sees you with that crowd, or even a girl who looks like you, you'll have no hope of a situation when the mill opens again, no hope in hell. And I'll not support you. I'm over with looking after you and being your mother."

She touches something with that, the proud bone in me. With Mam passed over, and now Daddy at the workhouse, I've come to depend on Mary for what I can't beget on my own, and though I'm grateful for her good offices and will live to thank her for them, they come at a dear cost.

"You want me to be a knobstick, is that it? You're telling me to break the strike?"

"I'm telling you to pull your weight. When a girl gets to fifteen, she ought know how to walk for herself and not tug on other people's sleeves."

"The neighbors will make it hard for us. They'll shut us out."

"Let the neighbors act for themselves. They can throw stones at us, for all I'll cry, as long as we can feed ourselves."

"Who wants to work in the mill anyhows. It's the mill is keeping us down. It's the mill that's killing us."

"Fine sentiments, sister lady, but I hate to tell you, it's the clemming that's killing you right now, and unless you find yourself a swell and marry up quick, it's the mill or a pauper's grave for you."

And true enough, it's the hunger that eventual brings me round. Weeks, the mills stay closed, the Ermen & Engels the same as the rest, and without Mary's wage, we're brought to winking distance of the workhouse ourselves. I feel I'd like to cry, only I don't have the forces, and I know then I'm in the last ditch and sinking,

for I'd like to and I can't. And in that moment I know that when the gates of the Ermen & Engels are thrown back, I'll be there in the horde, elbowing and stepping on heads to get to the front.

An animal, that's what chance makes of me.

On my first day, the girls are already talking about the owner's son. "Soon he'll be coming," they says to each other, for there isn't much else to amuse them in the yard. "Soon he'll be coming from Germany to learn the strings, and one day he'll be the boss man himself." And they're excited about this idea. They can't wait to slap an eye on him, for they've heard he's quite the looker.

They haven't a good head between them. Most of them are yet young like myself, some of them well under the age, and every morning that he doesn't appear makes the next morning a thing for them to look forward to. Me, I dread the next morning as a plague, for it only promises more of the same: a job that lays you low and saps you. And I can't picture how the owner's son, however dapper, could change it.

I'm unhappy, but more than that, I'm raging. In the place bare a month and I'm already having urges. To scream and shout. To climb on top of the yard wall, and from there to get onto the roof so there'd be no one in Manchester who didn't hear me. But in actual fact, I do what I'm told. I stay quiet, just as Mary has warned me, and don't let tell of my affairs. I keep my opinions and my illnesses hidden. I put a rag over my mouth to keep from coughing. And I work hard, harder than I've ever worked at anything before, by putting my cholers into it.

"The strikes came at a good time," we're told at assembly one morning. "The strikes came at a good time for *you*." The mill has bought new machines, the latest crop of mules that need but a fraction of the hands to work. They were planning to let go of the people they no longer needed, given the advances. But—luck and

behold—the job was done for them, the troublemakers weeded out natural. Leaving us, the new, leaner, better Ermen & Engels family to march with the banner.

Mary is thankful to be given one of the new mules. I think better of reminding her of the people her mule is replacing, people she knew and declared to care for; or of the meanness of her new wage, lower than what they were giving her before. I think better of it because she knows these things well and is choosing not to give them their proper weight, for if she did, they'd crush her.

I'm to follow her on the floor, pick up the new ways, and then take over a mule of my own. "Be fast," she says to me. "Be fast and you'll be seen, and you'll move up," for it's a fine spinner she wants us to be, a spinner of the Diamond Thread, which she believes to be a situation that can't be robbed by the machines or by the children. "If we don't learn the fine spinning," she says, "we'll go the same way as the men. Out on our backs and not a situation in Manchester to be had."

Though it makes me bitter to do it, I give in and learn, and what I do well I try to do better and faster, for that's the way to beat the weariness and to sleep at night. I come early and leave late. I join in the talk in the yard. I spend my Sundays with the girls in the halls and the fairs. And when the time comes, in spite of myself, I have to own that he's handsome.

He holds himself slim and erect, and has a good forehead, and—still so young—all the color is yet in his hair. At assembly he talks quick and short, ashamed, it seems, about the foreign in his patter. He's going to make a tour, he says, and he promises to get to know each and every one of us, which makes everybody giddy. Except Mary. It makes her regular cross. "When he comes," she says, "keep at it and put on you don't even see him. The last thing he wants is a mill full of girls losing the run of themselves."

Of course, it's herself, then, who goes and loses herself entire.

His laughter comes into the room before he does, and it's catching. "Lethal as the consumption," Mary will say later.

"My lucky day!" he belts from the doorway, stretching out his arms to get the full lung into it. He looks around. Even from a distance I can see his eyes take in the world and see to the bottom of things, and though he keeps his face, I know he's disappointed by us. Fine lookers between us, there aren't many. There's only Adele in the carding room, but she's got very thin and looks to be down with something serious. And Maggie two rows up, I suppose, if that's your dish of tea.

As he moves around, he waves his hand in front of his face to keep off the dust, and I'd like to tell him it's a useless exercise, all that waving, for it only wafts the flyings in, but of course I keep my trap shut. He's nowhere near me yet anyhows, and I don't know if he'll even get close, for time's ticking on and work hasn't been taken up proper, and he's stopping at every girl and asking them questions—about themselves and where they're from and their work and how they're finding it—and he doesn't seem to be putting on, he appears sincere enough and waits for their answers, though the bulk of them can only stretch to a blush and a curtsy.

Soon Mr. Ermen loses patience and hurries him on—something about having to finish the tour before Christmas—and then all he can spare is a flash of his whites as he passes. He doesn't even stretch that far with me, but strolls by without so much as a glance. I see his cheek out of the side of my eye: skin like the back of a babby. He goes past Lydia, too, without a look, I'm glad to see. And Mary. And soon all there's left of him is his little arse, swaggering away out of our lives.

Only what happens then is, he nigh on catches his side against a wheel. Mary rushes over to steady him, for she's the closest. She

takes tight of his arm and pulls him away from the danger, and while he's still reeling in his boots, heedless to what's happening to him, she says to his face a curse in the Irish, something our mother used to say when we were being hazards to ourselves.

The room catches its breath. Speaking out of turn costs you sixpence of your wage, and that's on an ordinary day. Mr. Ermen makes for Mary and looks ready to handle her, but Frederick, now recovered, waves him away and tells him not to be so jumpy. Can't he see this woman has saved him from an injury? Then, God bless him, he asks her to repeat what she said, for he loves a joke.

"Let us hear it," he says.

She wipes her brow and looks about at all the faces, and in that moment I wish her looks were doing her better justice, for she's recent taken on a touch of jaundice and isn't as flush as God wants her.

"Come on, do share," he says, and folds his arms across like someone biding to be impressed.

Mary coughs. "It's only something Mammy used to say when we were little."

There's a shuffle of feet as we prepare for the worst.

"Go on," he says, not annoyed but eager-like, fain to be on the inside of things.

"She used to say it when she'd see us knocking over things," she says, and bites her lip and looks down.

He waits for her to look up again before addressing her. "Your accent, young lady," he says, "is most unusual," and he asks her where it's from. She says it's from Manchester, like herself, but the Irish part. Then he asks was it the Irish-Celtic her mother spoke when she scolded her.

She says, "Is that the old language you'd be referring to, sir?"

And he says he supposes it is.

And she says, "Well then, aye, it was."

Then he asks does she speak the Irish-Celtic herself, and she says she does, but only the few phrases she has. And then he asks has she ever been to Ireland, and she says, "Nay, though I hope to go before it pleases God to call for me."

There's a tense air about the room. He's spent more time with Mary than anybody else, and in a manner more intimate than most would judge her worth. But it's to get worse, for instead of calling it a day and leaving it at that; instead of being happy with saving her a fine and taking his leave, he puts a hand on her back and draws her out of her place, as if to make something special out of her, a fine example. The two of them are standing apart now, Mr. Ermen several paces back, and he begins to ask her about the firesome spirit of the Irish he's heard so much talk of, and he wonders if it's true that we're more related in character to the Latins— to the French and the Italians and the like—and if, like them, we're more interested in the body—*the body!*—than in the mind.

There isn't a sound in the room, and the heat makes it all seem like a feversome dream, and Mary, I can see, is struggling to understand whether she's being mocked, whether this foreigner is using her for his fun, and it's all a trap, and these are the last agonies of her situation. So what she does is, she hardens against the doubt and says the only Italians she knows are the organ boys that come into the pub, and they're only good for making a racket and slipping their dirties up your skirts, and she wouldn't like to be put in a basket with them.

At this, he roars. So shocked are we by its quickness and its power that at first we don't understand it's laughing he's doing, and we're relieved when we see that it is, and that it's the good kind, not the sneering kind, and then we let ourselves do it too. For we can see he's no longer behaving like one of them—listening from across a fast river—but has dropped his distance and waded

in, like a hunter that's lost his fear. His arm reaches farther around Mary's waist.

"Where would a man have to go in this town to meet a girl like you?"

I know now that a bold manner goes well with women and impresses men. I've seen it work a hundred times since. But back then I think he's gone too far, crossed over too quick. It isn't the species of thing a mill man ought say—though it is, I know, the truth of what they do without saying—and I'm not prepared for everybody laughing, and Mr. Ermen clapping his back and calling him a sly trickster, and the girls turning to measure their disbelief against each other, and Mary giving him a soft elbow and asking him, scut-like, what type of man he is at all. Nay, I'm not prepared for any of it—the fainting and the adoration that no mortal body deserves—so when I see it, it sickens me.

He takes to walking out with her, I believe, because she talks well and he enjoys hearkening to her. And he keeps walking out with her, he doesn't bore of it, I believe, because he doesn't understand her and wants desperate *to* understand her, for it promises so much.

She likes to say it's because of her ankles. They have a peculiar allure, she thinks, that he can't get full of. She takes to flashing them at him in the yard. He'll be up in the office looking down, and she'll be walking with us and putting on not to notice anything but the ground in front, but then, easy as you please, not a whiff of warning, she'll lift up and step one out from under the hem. They aren't bad as ankles go—of the two of us she has the better—and I'm sure they don't put a damper on proceedings, I'm sure he likes them regular enough, but what really keeps him interested, I'm also sure, is her blather.

He's like a young scholar trying to pull truth out of a foreign gospel. If he learns to understand her, and to speak like her, he'll know what it's like to be her, and by there to be poor. Of course, what he's chasing is a shadow down a passage, for you can't learn that species of thing. To have your vittles today and to know it doesn't depend on you whether you'll have them tomorrow, that's something you've either lived or you haven't.

"What do you talk to him about?" I says to her, for I want her to be ashamed, going around at night with the owner's son.

"Oh, everything," she says.

"Everything?"

"My life. His life."

"You're telling him our affairs."

"Arrah, don't be at me, Lizzie. He's not like the others. He wants to learn about how things are for us. To help us."

"Help? Well, we know what *that* means."

"It's different."

"Why is it different? Why would he want to help you? Hasn't he enough to be getting on with? A mill to run."

"He doesn't like what he sees here, Lizzie. In Manchester and thereabouts. He wants to understand it so he can change it."

"He has ideas, all right, and for that he's no different than any other man. You'll be ruined."

Listening to me, you'd think I'd become the eldest and she the youngest. The truth is, I'm scared for her. She's gone deaf to her own advice. Isn't it herself who says that the higher-ups only marry their own, and if they want your time it's only to lie down with you, and then only for the thrill: it's *you* who pays the final price? Hasn't she gone back on her own words? It's a part of Mary I'm not patient with, this habit of not heeding herself, but I don't punish her with it either, for she punishes herself enough on the days he doesn't call.

No doubt he goes with other women—he's been seen wandering alone down the District—and the thought of it makes her suffer, deep and miserable. He stays away for weeks on end. She sees him in the mill and pours all her hurt into her eyes, but he resists her willing and stays upstairs where he is. Then when it suits him, he appears again, raps his ashplant on the door, and goes to the end of the passage to wait. So strong is her wanting, she throws a shawl around her pain, and runs out.

"What do you do when you go out with him?"

"I show him around."

"Around where? What's there to be shown?"

"He wants to see where we live."

"We? We who?"

"We the Irish. We the workers."

"Jesus."

"The Holy Name, Lizzie."

"Well, he's not coming in here, he's not welcome."

"He'll want to come inside eventual. And I'll not stop him. And you'll not stop him neither."

She enjoys her new position, anybody can see that. It's easy to picture her leading him down the passages and into the courts, choosing the meanest of the doors to knock on, pointing out all the things that are filthy and wrong, speaking to the bodies for him and getting them to show him their children, and their hips and their sores. Oh aye, all that would come to her like breathing. But what it takes a sister to see—and what I can't keep my eyes off once I've seen it—is what she's doing her best to hide: her love illness.

For it's ill she is. Ill and pure struck-blind. The moments when he needs her and wants her—"Precious moments," she calls them—these moments are when she's fullest and happy, and she wishes them to go on and on into forever, for she doesn't want to

go back to being empty of him. She wants him to be unable to do without her. And he leads her to believe this is so. Just by looking at her a certain way he leads her down that lane—she herself tells me it's all in his eyes—and she forgets her own person there, gets lost in the maze of his possibilities.

She falls, just as he does, for a promise.

Then comes the night he comes inside and stays for tea. He brings pies and ale, too much for the three of us, so he orders the neighbors out from behind the curtain and divides it all up. I'm sure I'm not the only one thinking, Who in God's name does he think he is?

He gets the good chair, and the best cup and plate, and a knife and a fork, and everybody watches how he uses them, on a pie. No one dares talk, so he has to do the talking himself, though he leans on Mary for help, there being so much in what he says that's hard to get. He tells us many things, gossip most of it, about the foremen in the mill and their romances, and the practical jokes he likes to play on Mr. Ermen. And a whole other heap, too, about growing up in Germany among the Calvins, and hating it because the Calvins credit that all time is God's time and wasting a minute is a sin, and life isn't meant for enjoying but for working only.

As for working, he hates his situation at the mill. He hates the position it puts him in, up there on a pillar, for he's happier down here with us lot. But he judges it good for himself also. "Because Germans of my particular caste know too little of the real world. It's an education of sorts, and will do me good."

What he's learnt so far—and he swears to learn more before he leaves for Germany again in a year's time—is that the workers are more human in daily life, less grasping, than the philistines who employ them, and that the philistines are interested only in

money and how much it can buy them. The least grasping of all, he thinks, are the Irish. And, as far as he can see, they work just as good as the English.

Says he: "It's true that to become something skilled like a mechanic, the Irishman would have to take on English customs, and become more English, which would be a formidable task, for he's grown up without civilization, and is close to the Negro in this regard. But for simpler work which asks for more strength than skill, the Irishman is just as good."

All this sort of science, he talks, and more besides, but what's stayed with me—what my mind lingers on oftenest—is what he says about the way we talk. At this stage, we've all imbibed a fair amount, and most of the neighbors are already sleeping: Seamus is on the ground away from his straw, the children are in their different spots, only the wife, Nan, is still with us. It's late, and I'm trying to signal to Mary to put an end to it. We all have work to get us up in the morning. But she'll not break in on him, not in his stride, and what he's saying is interesting to her, or so it seems from the way she has her chin in her hands and is staring at him, tranced.

What he's talking about is the old language. He says he has heard it spoken in the thickest of the slums, as if this is something to wonder at. From there, he gets to talking about the English as it sounds in the Irish gob.

"I can read and understand twenty-five languages," he says. "But I admit to being tested by the English spoken by you and your people."

Then he gets us to say a few things, and he laughs and repeats what we say, and then we laugh.

"*Grand* this and *grand* that," he says. "Everything is always so splendid for you! Through it all, you manage to stay so cheery and optimistic!"

At this, Nan near on falls off her stool for the laughing. "I'll tell you something for naught, girls," she says. "These foreigners are shocking queer!"

Then we all roll around, and Frederick does too, though he's only allowing himself to be taken along, for he doesn't really know what we're laughing at.

Mary takes it on herself to let him in. "For the Irish," she says, "*grand* doesn't mean more than *middling*."

Nan sees Frederick's muddled arrangement. "We'll need something strong to get us through this," she says, and goes to get the bottle she keeps safe for the priest.

Meantime, Mary goes over and sits down on his lap—right there in plain sight—and scratches his whiskers and plucks his cheek. "Listen now, Foreign Man. If a thing is *grand,* it's holding together. If a situation is *grand,* it's tolerable good. If a body is *grand,* she's alive and likely to do. No more and no less than that."

Nan can barely get the spirit into the glasses for all her snorting and shaking. I'm just mortified and want the pageant to end so I can face the mill tomorrow with some of my honor intact. Frederick, for his part, takes to pondering what he's been told, and when he's over with that, he looks about our little room.

"And a house?" he says, being the type who wants to know the in-and-out of things precise. "If a house is *grand?*"

Mary stops smiling then, and puts down playing with his necktie, and turns to us, and takes us in—stunned-like—as if remembering us from a distant past. And then she says, "If a house is *grand,* my love, it comes with a rent that will leave you enough to go on."

Now, awake, Frederick gets up and dodders about for his clothes. He's having another cock-stand. I watch him muffle it into his breeches. In his room he keeps a tin, lozenges meant for sustaining your piss and vinegar, though I can't see the use of them myself, it being a fine and thirsty animal God's made of him.

"Are you well, Lizzie?"

"Well enough."

He puts on his shirt, leaves it tucked out to hang over the stubborn article. "I've missed the morning. Why didn't you wake me? I'll have to skip my walk and work late to make up. Can you bring my meals up?" He picks up his shoes and puts his coat over his arm. "Lizzie, did you hear me?"

I nod. I heard you.

I put onto my side, haul the covers up. "Frederick?"

"*Ya?*"

"Jenny thinks it's a good idea to get another maid."

"There's one coming on Sunday."

"Another one, I mean, over and above her."

"Oh? Jenny thinks so? And what do you think?"

"I think it'd be a good way to get Pumps out of Manchester."

"Pumps?"

"My niece. Half-niece. Thomas's eldest."

"Oh, him."

"Aye, him. He has her in a bad way. When she's not locked at home looking after her nine brothers, she's on a corner selling bloaters till all hours. It's only a matter of time before she gets into trouble. She could come down and help me here. It'd be a chance for her."

"Let me think about it." He goes for the door.

"Oh, and, Frederick?"

"What now?"

"Can you open the curtain before you go?"

He looks at me like I've just asked to be fanned.

VI. Capital

Not shy of the curtsies. Round-boned. Clean-cuffed. Plainness of a good human sort. Frederick sits her in the morning room and reads us through her character.

"It says here that you can read and write. That will be helpful. And you can milk a cow. Interesting. *And* make butter. A country girl?"

"Devon, sir."

"Oh, and look, how about that! You can do the scales on the piano."

Aye, with her feet. Blindfolded.

"Listen here now, Miss Barton," I says. "Do you know anything?"

"I beg your pardon, ma'am?"

"About keeping a house?"

"Well, as it says there—"

"I don't care a whit for what it says on that bit of paper. I want you to use your voice and tell me out. Can you cook?"

"I can."

"Good. Because it's for the kitchen I want you. My niece will be joining us in a few days, and she'll look after the hearths and the upstairs. You're to tend to the cooking."

"Aye, ma'am."

"I don't know what you're used to from your last place, but here there'll be fish on Fridays."

"Course, ma'am."

"You're to keep the counters and pots clean, I won't stand for mice. And most important, you're to look after the kitchen store. Groceries for the day, the week, and the month are to be put in the book. You must keep a check on what's lacking and you must do the writing yourself, do you hear? I won't do it for you. I'll count what comes in and you'll cross it off the list. Not a penny is to be spent that does not have my approval. Breakages must be mentioned within the day or they'll be made good from your wages."

She nods a biddable nod.

"Now come with me and I'll introduce you to the kitchen range."

I lead her downstairs. "Don't be shy now. Get familiar."

She makes her way around, opening into cupboards and checking for what she'll need. *Naught much to her* is what I think. *Improvable* is what I think. She'll do, she'll do. But she has another think coming if she thinks I'm going to spend my days calling hoity up the stairs.

Nim. Skim. Spin. Spiv.

"Spiv," I says. "We're going to call you Spiv."

"What's Spiv?"

"It's your name from now on."

"What does it mean?"

"Naught, only I like the ring of it."

Once I've taken her on the full round, I go up with his middle-p.m. cheese and beer. I come in on him pacing. He freezes and turns from where he's stood, feet outspread in the center of the carpet. "Lizzie, I must ask you to knock."

"Oh, I would, Frederick, I would, only I'm holding this"—I nod down at my burden—"and I would have kicked, only I saw the door half-open."

"Excuse me, Lizzie, I'm a brute. Come in, come in."

I put the tray down on the sideboard and take up the old one.

"Thank you, my love," he says, not moving from where he is. Then, as if a brilliant idea has just occurred to him: "Why didn't you let the maid do it?"

"Sure if I gave it all to her, I'd never see you."

He laughs. "And how is she settling in?"

"Early yet," I says. "We'll see."

"*Ya.* Indeed. Good." He claps his hands, rubs them together, now strides over to his desk, lifts the moneybox out the drawer. "Actually, I'm glad you came. I wanted to talk to you. Karl and Jenny are giving a party in our honor."

"Oh, aye?"

"Tomorrow. To celebrate our arrival and to introduce us to some of the London-based comrades." He rummages in the box and comes out with four sovereigns. "I want you to take this and buy yourself something nice to wear. We're dandying up, making a bit of a fuss."

I give him a stern look.

"Come, Lizzie," he says. "It's all right to spend a little to look good."

"Where would I go?"

"Well, to the dressmaker's. Have something pinned that will leave their jaws hanging."

"What dressmaker's would have anything ready for tomorrow?"

"Go to Barrow's"—he speaks like a man who knows—"they will be able to help you, I guarantee it."

I crinkle my brow on purpose. "Barrow's?"

"It's not far, in Camden. You won't find anything here in Primrose Hill. Get a cab. Give them my name and pay them off a few extra shillings, you'll see. A new place recently opened opposite them and they're begging for the business. They'd have it sewn while you waited, if that was what you wanted."

He comes and puts the coins on the tray by his dirty plates. Seeing them there, twinkling among the pork rind, I feel a fresh lightness in my heart. "You might be right, Frederick. I wanted to get abroad of the house anyways, and a run round the shops might be just the ticket."

"That's the spirit, Lizzie."

"I'll go right away."

"Ha!" he laughs. "No time to lose."

"And I might have something out."

"Of course," he says, and searches his pocket for an extra guinea. "Good idea."

I leave as I am, only a light shawl and a reticule as excitements, and I leave the house as it is too, shambled with unfinished tasks, the new girl with the dinner yet to prepare, and I can't say I'm bothered about it.

I cross the road to the lamppost at the bottom of the Hill and flag a cab from there. On the journey, I watch out the window and put the roads to memory so I can walk back and save the fare.

The bell in Barrow's brings two girls beetling out from the back room. They're got up in identical silk dresses with short sleeves and lace caps, but to look at, they couldn't be further apart: one tidy and pinched, the other large and dusky-skinned and curled about the face.

"I need a dress," I says.

"Um, certainly," says Pinch, leading me over to a counter so polished you can see yourself in the black. "Is it for a special occasion, or do you require something useful?"

"I suppose you could call it special."

"Oh. Well, in that case might I recommend our antique *moiré,* which we have on special offer at the moment, nearly half price?" She throws a length of rippled silk over the counter; gold so gold it glows. "We have this in a range of shades. Unfortunately, one cannot see its full effect here. It's most becoming at candlelight."

"Half price you say?"

"Half price, madam."

"So how much would a dress of this cost, at half price?"

"Four pounds, eighteen shillings, and sixpence."

I splutter. "You must be barking. I won't be spending more than a pound."

She purses. Beside her, Curly laughs an appeasing laugh and whips the gold silk away, replaces it with another, this one a high-shining blue. "Am I right to say that madam is of the more sensible sort? Less interested in the novelties of fashion than in value for her spend?"

"Well, you wouldn't be wrong anyhows."

"In that case, we have this plain *glacé* silk in over thirty shades of color, commencing at only two pounds, fifteen shillings, and sixpence for the extra full dress."

I give an impatient cluck. "Maybe I didn't make myself clear—"

She shakes her curls. "Madam, you made yourself perfectly clear." She rolls away the blue silk and puts out a green muslin. I touch it. Stiff as a board. "This is French organdy, one of last year's designs, which we are giving away at the very reduced price of one pound, six shillings, and sixpence for the extra full dress."

I put my hand under my chin and tap my lip with a finger, as if considering. "Do me one without the frills and I'll give you a pound for it."

"Without the frills, madam?"

"None of those ridiculous trimmings you have in the window there. All that unnecessary bib and tucker."

"We have other models we can—"

"I want it plain, plain as can be."

"You don't want to see—?"

"Do you understand the word *plain,* young lass?"

"Of course."

"Well, that's what I want. And I want it for a pound."

"I shall have to speak to—"

"Speak to whomsoever you like. Mrs. Engels is the name. One-two-two Regent's Park Road. I'll be here."

Curly curtsies and goes into the back room. Pinch forces a smile into her cramped little face and goes to busy herself with the show dummies. I turn my gander to the carpet to keep from catching myself in the looking glasses that leer from every side.

"All right, Mrs. Engels," says Curly when she comes back, "that should be fine. If you would like to come this way, we shall get you measured up."

"That won't be needed, I can tell you straight off what I am."

"I do not doubt it, Mrs. Engels, but at Barrow's we like to measure all our customers to ensure the best style and fit."

"Listen, chicken, do you have a book to write in?"

"Of course."

"Well, put this down."

Flushing, she picks up her feather. Dips it.

"Bust thirty-four, hips thirty-six, length-to-foot just as you see me." I step back to give her a full view. She frowns at me and scribbles down. "I'll be back at five tomorrow to pick it up."

"Tomorrow?"

"That's right."

"Madam, I'm sorry, but we usually need at least three working days. We could have it ready by close of business Monday."

I pick a sovereign out of my reticule and put it down on the page of the book.

She waves her hands over it as if to magic it away. "No, madam, please, you can pay when you come to collect it."

"Take it now and be done with it. And I'll be seeing you tomorrow."

I find a cookshop a little up the road and order a chop and a pint of Bass's ale, and now a slice of plum pudding and a cup of ready-made coffee with cream and sugar. I take the table in the window, for I like to look out.

Passing by, streams of people with bags and boxes: gone out for a ribbon and coming home with the stock of an entire silk mercer's. These places, they do it on the cheap and make their capital out of pressure and high prices. It takes cleverness and steel for a woman to get her fair portion.

Exhausted, I look into my cup and try not to feel like the only one fighting.

VII. The Party

When it comes to the dangers of a bit of food, the Germans can be as afraid as the English, so I eat before we leave. Spiv heats me up a kidney pudding, and I have a glass of milk with it to line the gut, and after that some cold saveloy and penny loaf.

As it happens, I needn't have ruined my stomach, for there's vittles enough to feed a battalion: tables of meat and fowl and fish and cheese, salvers of delicates and dumplings carried by livery servants in silk hose, all sorts of strong-tasting aliments smelling up in our noses. Who's died? I think as I marvel the fare.

Tussy appears beside me. "I've been looking all over, Aunt Lizzie."

Embarrassed to be the only one grazing, I drop my pastry roll onto the damask. "Tussy, my sweet darling."

"Come on, I want to present you."

She takes a glass of red from a tray, puts it in my hand, and

pulls me with her into the crush. "I don't think I have ever been in a room with so many interesting people at once," she says.

The men have changed the usual shab-and-drab for frilled shirts. The women are in clothes above the ordinary but not showy. I feel in tune, glad to have put my foot down at the dressmaker's. Tussy introduces me to everybody, even to those I've met and know.

"This is Mr. Engels's wife, Mrs. Burns. An Irishwoman and a true proletarian."

The strangers bow. The familiars wink and smile along. There's more women than I expected to see. One sitting beside Karl on the couch. A pair by the window, looking foreign and bored. And by the chimneypiece, in a circle around Jenny and Janey, several gathered. Frederick—no surprise—has dug out the one with the lowest neckline.

"I'm not going to remember all these new names," I whisper to Tussy, mortifying of the fuss.

"Don't worry," she says. "What's important is that they remember *yours.*"

From where he's sat, Karl makes a big act of twisting his monocle in to show he has it tied on a new ribbon. Janey's wearing the Celtic cross I sent her. Jenny has made more of an effort than anyone else to draw attention onto herself: a feather in the hair, yards of a color not found in the wild.

"Oh, ladies, please," she's saying to her audience, the lush sending her voice up a pitch. "Before the illness, I had no gray hair and my teeth and figure were good. People used to class me among well-preserved women! But that's all a thing of the past."

Loud protests.

"Come now, ladies, I am not looking for your reassurance. I speak from a place of solemn awareness. I can see the reality.

When I look in the glass now I seem to myself a kind of cross between a rhinoceros and a hippopotamus whose place is in Regent's Park Zoo rather than among members of the Caucasian race!"

Reddening for her, I busy myself with the only bow on my bodice.

"Now, Lizzie," she says when the required objections die down, "I'd like you to meet some extraordinary women. Mrs. Marie Goegg, chairman of the International Women's Association. Mrs. Anna Jaclard, writer and Communist. Mrs. Yelisaveta Tomanowski, thorn in the side of every Bakuninist, real or suspected. And Mrs. Elisabeth Dmitrieff, Karl's own private reporter in Paris. Elisabeth is just here for a few days before going back into the *mêlée*. And what exactly are you going back to do, Elisabeth?"

"Well, I certainly won't be sewing sandbag sacks, that is for sure!"

They cackle and clap and swat the air with their gloves and fans. I drink and look around. Nim is by the door ordering one of the hired men down to the kitchen. Her hair is looped and she's put earrings in, but apart from that, she's the selfsame: sensible petticoat, two pleats in her dress. It's said she's had many suitors and could have made a good match more than once, even with the shame of Frederick's bastard hanging over her, but here she has stayed, devoted and constant, both when the wages have come and when they haven't. She sees me looking and comes over.

"Your glass is empty, Mrs. Burns," she says, taking it from me and replacing it with a full one from a passing salver.

"Thanks, Helen," I says, for that's her real name; I know it to be so.

"Lizzie!"—Jenny is calling—"I was just about to give the ladies a tour of the upstairs. Do join us."

"Well, thanks, Jenny, that sounds nice, only—"

Laughing, Tussy takes my arm. "Don't be such a bore, *Mohme.* Lizzie is going to stay here with me. The band is going to start soon, and the men aren't nearly drunk enough to dance, so I'm relying on Lizzie to be my partner."

Tussy leads me to the bay window where the band has set up. "Music, please!" she cries, and they start up. She spins me from one side of the empty floor to the other till, three songs later, I start hacking and I've to sit down.

After a time—no sooner do I finish one drink than another is pressured on me—the women come back from upstairs. "Finally!" says a voice, and the men approach with outstretched hands. I refuse the two who ask me up.

"Maybe the next one," I says. "I need the rest."

But the truer truth is, I've become interested in what's happening by the second fireplace; to get up now would be to miss it. It appears the woman Dmitrieff is telling something of her life. Sat on an easy chair like it's a throne, enough space between her legs to fit a violin-cello, she has the place rapt. Frederick, Karl, and some others have made a ring round her and are fighting with each other to laugh loudest at her utterings. I strain my ear to catch a scrap.

"So I said, *I only married you to get a passport,* and he said, *Well, I only married you for your—*"

She widens her eyes in mock horror and peers down at her bust, as if noticing for the first time how smooth and well-looking it is.

Now *there's* a body to contend with.

Refusing another round of dancing, I rise and make for the empty chair beside her. But Jenny, who must have been watching too, is faster. She slips through the band of men and takes Dmitrieff's hand.

"If none of these men are brave enough to ask you up, then

you shall have to make do with me."

Dmitrieff laughs. "Oh, Mrs. Marx, I thought you would never ask!"

The two skip to the floor, and the men look after them, murmuring and scratching and wondering why all women aren't like them.

Stranded now on a bit of empty carpet, I hasten to the nearest free seat. I watch the array over the lip of my glass: Jenny and Dmitrieff, Karl and Goegg, Frederick and Janey, Tussy and Dalby, Tomanowski and Lessner, Jaclard and Eccarius, Dr. Allen and his wife, the Lormiers, and maybe ten others, swaying and reeling. The number dawns on me: thirty or more altogether. A good way to clear off those who are due a visit, but the expense must be—well, it must be effin' mighty.

Of course, it's easy to spend when you haven't done a tap to have it. Three hundred and fifty pounds a year, in three installments, straight from Frederick's accounts, that's what they get. I'm sure they think it's a secret; I'm sure they think I'm oblivious because I'm unable to make out what Frederick writes in the books. But in our house, having keen ears is just as good as having snooping eyes of your own, for half of the time he's forgetting to speak in the German; half of the time he's shouting through the walls instead of keeping his talk to a whisper; and the other half of the time he's at the street door barking orders to messengers and letter carriers; it was never going to be long before I caught wind. Three hundred and fifty pounds is the digit, and that's before the gifts and the sneaky envelopes; that's before he sweeps in to level the bills and promises-to-pay that they leave to pile up on their desks and dressers and drawers (and not, where they ought be, on their memory and their morals).

Careless charity is what the world would call it, if it knew.

Helping those who beg and not those who really need the help. And who needs the help more—can someone please tell me?—than Nim's son? Lord knows what condition of roof that boy is living under, and yet I don't see a single tormented penny leaving the house in his direction. Would Frederick even know where to send it? One day justice will have to be done the poor lad; one day he'll have to be cut his sliver.

"You know, there's a story told about them," I says, turning to the man sat beside me.

"About whom, madam?" he says, his breath wafting through his moustache.

"The Marxes."

"Ah, yes. Such a remarkable family. Stories are bound to be told about them."

By the fireplace, Karl has taken up the fire blower and is making smutty jokes with it. Watching him brings a smile—like a secret understanding—to the man's face.

"You one of the Party?" I says.

His smile drops. "The Party?"

"You know, the International."

"Madam, the International is not a *party.* It is an association. A free association of workingmen."

I make a face to say I stand humble and corrected. He accepts it with a nod. Brings his glass under the hair of his lip to suck from it.

"Well, sir, the story I'm thinking about—"

"Is almost certainly just that, a story. Tittle-tattle from the bread queue."

"You haven't heard it yet."

"I don't need to hear it to know that it's false."

"If it's false I tell it, it's false I got it."

"Precisely."

I take a sup and ponder this a moment. "Only I don't believe this one is false. And if you only listened a minute, I'm sure you'd find you agree."

He shakes his head and groans.

"The way it goes is, her mother, I mean Jenny's mother, gave them some money for their honeymoon, and they took it with them in a chest."

"Please, madam, must we do this?"

"And what they did was, they left the chest open on the table in the different hotel rooms they stayed in, so that any old body who visited them could take as much as he pleased from it. As you can imagine, *empty* the chest soon was!"

The man stares at me. He joins his brows together and frowns. "That's it?" he says. "That's your story?"

I push a finger into the soft bit of his arm and whisper into the black of his ear: "But don't you see, this is the root of it! One generous thing done a lifetime ago and they think the world is in debt to them since. There's no fairness in it. In the first place, I don't think you can call giving your parents' good money away *generous*. If you can call it anything, it's—"

The blood now comes beating to his face. An angry flush overspreads his features. He shifts his chair so he can face away from me. I take my hand back and sigh. These foreigners have no notion of the banter. The Irish, there's not much I can say in their favor, but at least they allow for a woman's words when she's lushed; they know it's only the drop talking.

The music stops and the remaining dancers bow and clap, and now make their way back to the chairs and sofas. A woman rushes in from the hall, as if summoned by the new quiet.

"Where've you been?" rasps her redheaded friend, just two

paces from me. "All this time, I've not seen you."

"I was in the kitchen playing cards with the hired men. What a lark! I won this." She opens her palm to show a threepenny bit.

Jenny walks into the center of the room and calls for a final applause for the musicians, then orders us up the stairs to the parlor for the performance.

"The moment we've been waiting for!" someone shouts.

Frederick comes to take me up. "Are you safe?" he says when my foot squeaks on the carpet of the stairs and I have a little wobble.

"Go to blazes, Frederick," I says.

In the parlor we get seats, but the men have to stay on their feet. Jenny comes to stand in front of a counterpane held up as a curtain by two menservants. She gives a little speech about the effort she and Karl have made towards the Girls' education, and how unfortunate it is they couldn't do so much for them in music as they'd have hoped. "In any case," she says, "their real strength is drama and elocution. And tonight my youngest daughter, Eleanor, whom many of you know as Tussy, shall be playing Hamlet. This is apt, for her father used to always say she was more like a boy than a girl."

A chuckle goes round.

"Good old Tussy!" someone calls out.

"My eldest daughter, Janey, shall be playing Gertrude, and although she knows not yet the joys and pain of motherhood for herself, I think you shall find she does the role full justice."

Cheers and claps.

"The Girls would like to dedicate their performance to their sister Laura and her husband Paul, who are now safe in Bordeaux, thank heavens, and expecting a child."

Applause.

Jenny bows and the servants let drop the curtain. One of the

men has given Tussy a military jacket. Jenny has put Janey in one of her ball gowns.

"Now, Mother," says Tussy, "what's the matter?"

"Hamlet," says Janey, "thou hast thy father much offended."

"Mother, you have *my* father much offended."

This stirs up such laughter in the crowd that Janey is forced to hesitate before speaking her next line. "Come, come," she says once there's quiet, and the two set off into their theatricals, speeching off and casting their limbs about. I don't know if it's the lush or the heat of the room, but I'm finding it hard to stay with the meaning of it. My head pounds. I feel all face. I look around to see if anyone has noticed the wrong with me. Nim, I see, is stood by the door. That's where I must go.

"Excuse me, excuse me," I says as I make my way down the line.

"Are you all right, Mrs. Burns," Nim says when I reach her. She gestures into the room to remind me of what I'll miss if I leave. I turn back to see Tussy striking a blow at a figure wrapped in the drapes, and now Karl spinning out from behind them and falling onto the floor.

Dizzying, I rush down the stairs and out the street door. I take the air and am thankful for it; it keeps what's down from coming up. A moment and Nim is outside with me.

"Here," she says, wrapping a shawl around me.

"You don't have to worry, Helen. I'm grand."

"Shall I fetch you a glass of water?"

"Nay, nay. Just stay a minute."

"Well, all right. But not too long. I must get back." She puts the door on the latch. Rubs her arms. "It's getting cold now," she says. "It will be fully winter before we know it."

"Aye, that it will."

Some minutes pass. The noise from upstairs comes through

the windows and out into the night. All down the road, the houses are dark.

"I shall have to leave you now," Nim says.

"Nay, wait—"

Knowing no way to proper introduce it, I go ahead and bring out the money: the savings from the dressmaker's and a few other morsels I've managed to gather up.

"Here," I says, "I want you to have this."

She takes a step away.

"Take it. It's from Mr. Engels. He wants you to have it."

"Mr. Engels? For what?"

For what. For what. She must believe my head emptier than the Savior's tomb.

"Helen, please. I'm not just another of these silly women. I know how many beans makes five."

"I'm sure I don't know what you mean."

"Mr. Engels and me, we have so much. More than we can cope with."

"I'm not going short. I'm looked after."

"I don't doubt it. This is just an extra bit. You have full claim to it."

She shakes her head and pushes open the door. "I have no claims to anything."

"Your son does. Think of your—"

But she's already gone. Leaving me to hold the whole weight of my purse.

Back upstairs, I find the performance over. Port and sweets are being tendered round. Tussy pushes through to reach me.

"You missed the whole thing, Aunt Lizzie!"

"Not at all, I saw you up there. You were a star. I've never seen

such—"

But she'll not be cozened, nor condoled, and she doesn't spare me any of her pouting, and I don't have the force to bring her round, so it comes a relief when, from across the room, the woman Dmitrieff calls her away with the lure of her smoke. I watch her go, the man's jacket spilling over her shoulders, and it occurs to me now which one *Hamlet* is: it's the one where she marries her husband's brother and, by there, sends it all down-falling to shite.

November

VIII. Inverted World

Pale as royals, the pair of them. Wouldn't know a day's work if it shone on them blazing. Put their backs into naught, far as I can see, except giving me gob.

Only this morning Spiv says to me, she says, "Don't mind me, ma'am," when I find her dangling her feet while she ought be cleaning the slops. "Don't mind me, I'm only resting up on account of my courses." Then, when I catch her putting the woolens through the mangle: "But, Mrs. Burns, this is how I did them in the last place, this is how the missuses are doing them."

You come to London, get a nice home about you and—blight your innocence!—you think you're over with the toils and the trouble.

The other one can hear me chiding from two flights up, and comes down in her night rail. "Don't stand there, Pumps," I says to her. And then, "For the love of Christ, Pumps, don't stand there

gawping," for she'll not hearken to something spoken only the once. "Make yourself useful and go do the grate, it's a blind disgrace and needs blackening."

She bobs a curtsy and goes, and I'm left relieved by how easy she's toed, for on your regular day she's the worse of the two, all her energies spent trying to get one over me and prove I'm not up to the dodge. With the passing of the moments, though, my relief turns to suspicion—the lass so yielding is a forecast for bad goings-on —so when I've done with Spiv and sent her into the kitchen to think about lunch, I go to the parlor to give it the once-over.

Just as I pictured: the grate still undone, the drapes covered with paw marks, and Pumps herself in front of the mirror rubbing black onto her face. Which is to say, it's worse than I pictured, and we're back to the usual.

"Pumps, what's this?" I says.

"What's what?" she says.

"This here, on the drapes."

"That? Was there when I got here."

"Why didn't you get the benzene to it, then?"

"Thought you wanted it that way."

"And on your face? Did you think I wanted you with whiskers as well?"

"Oh, this? I just thought you could use another man about the place."

This, for the London missus, is life. Not the fancy ball you might have imagined, but this. Which only goes to show you can't foreknow the shape of things to come. For if you'd told me this day twelvemonth how it was going to be—that my hours would be spent poking in nooks and sniffing in corners, running the finger and dancing at heels; that every day would be a scrub, and every week a starch, and every year a white; that tomorrow's coals

would turn to yesterday's ashes, and time would burn my wick both ends—if this day twelvemonth you'd told me the God-glaring truth of it, I'd not have credited you. I'd have thought you unkept in your mind.

Get away with you, I'd have thought. It can't be shabbier than Manchester, can it?

Yet nowadays I oftentimes think we oughtn't have flown the old kettle at all. I oftentimes think the mill wasn't so killing as this. Topsy thinking is what this is, but topsy is how it goes up here; topsy and wrongways.

Advice: if you come, leave your senses back where they were common.

IX. Island Dwellers

I like to do the step myself. Which is a lucky thing. For Spiv refuses to be seen out front. And Pumps is too afraid of a bit of exertion to take her shoes and stockings off and get down into the scrub. It's a task I ought stay away from, on account of the knees, but I've learnt it gives me more pain to watch them do it than to do it myself. They're likely to be content with less than the right white. And there's no precise measure for the clay, the blue, the size, and the whitening; you have to judge the mixture by its look.

I go hard at it—my sleeves rolled, my face lathered—and I don't let off till, out the side of my eye, I light on a crowd of four women coming up the road from the Hill side. They, in return, catch sight of me when they're a few doors away. By my own deeper wisdom, I know they're headed in my direction. I put my attending back on my cleaning, but I'm aware of myself now and don't feel inside the task.

They come to stand in a line over me. I twist my neck to look up at them.

"Might we see the lady of the house?" says the one in the high-boned collar.

I stand. Brush the hair off my brow. Flatten my pinny. "Come on, Lizzie," I says to myself, "don't be put so easy to the blush."

When it dawns on one, it passes through the others like electricity. "Oh!"—they clutch their chests in the spot where the air has been knocked out—"How novel!"

Sat on my sofa, gummed together in a talcumed clump, the committee members of the Primrose Hill Residents' Association tell me what they saw: a woman and a girl viewing the house, and then the same two overseeing the arrival of the furniture and making all the arrangements. They describe both figures in a detail that'd chill the devil: the size and shape of their noses and mouths, the height of their brows, the color and curl of their hair, the cut of their clothes; it's as if they've painted picture portraits of Jenny and Tussy and hung them in their heads. They expected to be received by them. They look disappointed to have got me.

"Relations of yours?" the woman named Stone asks, pulling out the end of her dress and floating it out over her boots.

"Nay," I says. "Just intimates."

"I've seen her before," Leech says. "The woman, I mean. Does she live nearby?"

"Aye, not far. Near the Heath, up that way."

"Foreign?"

"A baroness."

"Oh, I see."

"And her name?" says Westpot, jigging her leg in a manner that says she's unprepared to sit here, in these uncomfortable visiting

clothes, and bide for the required particulars to come out of their own accord.

"Von Westphalen," I says, giving Jenny's maiden name to avoid mention of Karl.

"Von Westphalen. Let's see. German?"

"Aye."

Westpot ponders a moment. "Doesn't ring any bells. Does she go much into society?"

"I'm not sure, you'd have to ask her."

"And yourself?"

"Me? Oh well, I'm not the outsy-aboutsy sort."

I ring for tea and sandwiches and cake. Pumps bites the side of her finger and glares at the women through squinted eyes.

"Go on, girl," I says. "Don't be dallying."

While we're waiting, I bring the talk round to the house—that's what they're here for, isn't it?—and mention the hidden costs of living in a new area: the uncivil distances, the bad roads, construction everywhere, hoarding blocking the paths. It's a speech I've heard Jenny give on several occasions and it's always been well received. Here, now, I'm met with a row of faces longer than a day with no bread.

Pumps brings in the tray and I give out the tea.

"And you are Mrs. Burns," says Mrs. Westpot. "Isn't that what you said?"

"That or thereabouts," I says.

Leech looks about for signs of children. Halls sighs into the emptiness.

Sensing an edge to our nerves, Stone says I'm not to be embarrassed, there'll always be duties the householder will reserve for herself. She, for instance, makes the beds of her own choice, for the servants aren't to be depended upon to put down the same

number of blankets every night. Leech looks shocked that Stone would let go of her home secrets to a stranger; she tries to turn our minds away from the blunder by lashing herself into an enthusiasm about my draping. I ought keep the windows open as much as possible, she says, so the smoke doesn't linger on them. This prods Halls to air her loath for women who insist on smoking, especial out in the public.

"It can only be taken as a kind of challenge."

Leech tut-tuts and says she heard there were women smoking at the funeral of Mr. Miller, a man who used to live down by the Canal. Fifty people for breakfast, there were, a table covered in cakes and biscuits and oranges and nuts, and all species of wine and exotics, and though Leech herself didn't attend—she wouldn't dream of it, for it wasn't her place—she was told there were women there, attending; women with flowers in their bonnets and fags in their mouths, and it had the atmosphere of a wedding more than anything else.

"It's hard to imagine a grieving widow having to serve delights to such a rabble, but that's exactly what Mrs. Miller had to do, as it was ordered in the will. Then, after all of that, he didn't leave her enough to get by on her own."

There's a pause to allow the shaking of heads. I pass the plate of sandwiches around. "Thank you, but no," they each say in turn, for they don't want to ruin their appetites; they're on the route to other engagements.

Saucers under their chins, as if to catch every precious thing that might fall out, they take it upon themselves to explain the area to me. It's best, they say, to think of Primrose Hill as an island, with the railway forming the northern boundary and the Canal the southern one. The better sort of residents live this side of St. George's Road. This is because here, one escapes the murky results of the railway

activities, thanks to a benevolent wind that blows the smoke and dust eastways over the Chalk Farm Road and Camden. On the opposite side of St. George's Road, running towards Gloucester Avenue, the residents are working types, three families or more to each of the houses. It is, they say, like a little northern town, dominated by the railway and with a strong bond between the bodies living here. The houses are impossible to keep clean, of course, due to the flakes of soot that float about and settle everywhere. But the people are happy and tend to their own. Nevertheless, it's best not to walk there at night, for the roads can be rough, with families of boys patroling about. And the railway bridge is to be avoided at all costs, and at all times, for it provides dry arches for the congregation and accommodation of street Arabs and gutter children.

Their speech causes me a twinge, to be sure, but if I'm honest, I don't despise them in my heart. Perhaps this is because I don't feel beneath them. I'm no great lady and I don't know the fashion of the months, but I'm aware of my new position, in the middle class of life, and I don't think I'm faring so shabby.

Once satisfied that I'm a woman with the right information, they allow their talk to move to other subjects. It comes to rest on the banks. They're thankful the crisis years have passed.

"Dreadful, was it not, ladies?" says Stone.

"Dreadful, dreadful," the heads nod.

"When I heard that Overend and Gurney had gone under, well, I got such a shock I called my husband in and I said to him, *Gregory, take all our money out of the banks immediately, our savings would be safer under a board here at home.*"

Halls laughs. "Did he do as you commanded?"

"Are you mad? He just snickered and told me to not to worry my head over affairs which aren't mine. They can be such rotters, can't they?"

A chuckle passes round.

"Speaking of rotters," says Leech, "have you heard about Mr. Wagner?"

At this, they all sigh together and say it's a shocking and terrible thing. Such a disappointment, they say, when a genius fails his public with immoral private doings.

It's clear they've talked about this Wagner character before. He might even be someone they regular use to take the corners off a meeting, to make it feel rounder and sister-like. I take him to be another neighbor and am glad I don't ask further about him—that instead I sigh along in my ignorant stead—for it soon becomes clear to me that it's a musician he is, not a neighbor, and by the sounds of it, a bit of a hound too. Once I know the facts, I'm resolved to tell them some true and shocking stories about musicians, stories that will go all the way to their cores: about the Manchester halls and what the singers and fiddlers got up to there, the fiddling they did in the dressing rooms, and not only with the loose women from the boxes but with the higher-ups too, who would bribe their way down the corridors and hide themselves between the costumes. But my chance doesn't come, their fast manner of talking to themselves makes it hard to break in, and when the subject passes on, it irks me that there's things I could have said on my own side, about musicians.

"You're not from London, are you, Mrs. Burns?" Westpot says, impatient to be getting on.

"Nay, from down Manchester way. But my kin, they're from across the water."

"France?" says Leech, making Stone and Halls giggle.

"The other way."

"Ah, of course." She looks at the other three. They twitch their faces back at her.

"So you and your family," Westpot says, "you are, um, shoppy people, then?" She talks to her nails, as if abashed by having to bleed this personal vein.

"We were in the cotton, if that's what you mean. But we've stopped with that. Now we're in something else entire."

"Well, that's a relief," says Stone.

"A relief, indeed," says Halls.

"Shoppy people are bad enough," says Leech, "but the Manchester ones are supposed to be a whole grade down, if that's possible."

"Always behind the counter, even when they're not," says Stone.

I can't gainsay what they're saying about Manchester and the rest, but I don't like how they're saying it, so I says, "If the Manchester men have a bad name, it's their own doing and they deserve it, but they're not all the same, there's good eggs between them."

"Good eggs?" says Westpot. "Like Mr. Burns, you mean?"

"Mr. who?"

"Why, Mr. Burns, woman! Your husband!"

When you're called a missus, oftentimes you forget yourself, and it's a good idea to have a story to tell, to cover over. But I have no such story ready. "There's no Mr. Burns," I says.

"Oh, my dear woman."

"Oh, Lord."

"No Mr. Burns?"

"Where is he?"

I clear my throat. Scratch an itch that takes hold of the scalp under my bun. "He's in his grave," I says, undressing the lie by thinking of my father.

Stone allows herself a gasp. Leech takes a napkin from the tray

and offers it to me. Halls gives me a Protestant "Bless you" and looks down, virtuous-like, at her clasped hands.

I nod my thanks and reach once more for the sandwiches, happy to be off the hook as light as that. But Westpot has drawn back her lips and is thirsty for the truth. For that's how they bite you: smiling.

"But I've seen a man," she says, "I've seen a man coming in and out."

"You have?"

"Yes, Mrs. Burns, a man."

"Oh, aye. Now that I think of it, there's a man who lives here."

"But he's not Mr. Burns?"

"Nay, he's not Mr. Burns."

"Oh?"

"Oh!"

"Oh."

"Who is he, then?"

"He's Mr. Engels."

"Mr. *Angles*?"

"Engels. Mr. Engels."

"Is he here now, this Mr. Engels?"

"Nay, he's away from the house on business."

"And who is he? A lodger?"

"Nay, not a bit of a lodger."

Westpot simpers, understanding. "You're not married, are you, Mrs. Burns?"

"He's my husband, I just haven't taken his name."

"You can't take a man's name unless you're wedded to him." She turns to the others. "She's not married."

"I'm his helpmeet is what, Mrs. Westpot."

"You're his—?"

"She said *helpmeet*."

"Shh, ladies, let's try not to be rude."

They suck themselves in. Leech's stays creak. Halls, so fascinated by the proceedings, forgets herself and takes up a slice of cake. Her eyes darting around for the next move, she feeds the whole thing in.

"Mrs. Burns," says Westpot, "if you don't mind me asking—" She hesitates.

I meet her gander full force. I've naught to hide from no one. "Aye, Mrs. Westpot?"

"What I was going to ask was, what business is Mr.—?"

"Ah!" Halls lets out a splutter, and now a gullet-bursting cough, and now the contents of her gob drops out—*pat!*—onto her lap. "Pepper!" she yelps. "There's pepper on the cake!"

Pumps—I could hear her ear scratch against the door the whole time and now I know why—shimmies in, calm as a cucumber. "You all right, ma'am?" she says. "Can I help you there?" She walks around, positions herself behind Halls, and serves out four slugs to her back.

Stunned, I watch the scene, the perfect horror of it. And I'm still sat here, unable to move, while the women file out, crinolines crumpled, bunches bounced; and still now while Pumps fettles up the tea things.

"Those were some bitches," she murmurs to herself as she makes a pile of the plates. "They got what was coming."

Her behavior is a credit to those who brought her up. For she was raised in thoughtlessness. Reared to be someone who'd have none of the advantages. Just one more of the poor tattery children of Little Ireland. Like all of us, she would've seen much brutality within the circle. A crooked look would've caught her a larruping at

the hands of her slack-spined father and rag-and-scram brothers. Her face and the bent of her back bear the marks of this ill usage. I can't blame her for feeling angry and wanting to defy the laws of the wide world. I've been her. I *am* her.

My punishment, so, is not the belt or the starvation. Nor is it the water pump or the locked door. Rather, it's the needle.

"Come and help me with the stitching," I says to her. "Come, please, and salvage my efforts."

And she comes. And she looks at my work: a bundle of botched and broken thread like a wild shrub. And she bursts out. And I can't help but join her. We hang off each other now and laugh till we're sick.

X. A Free Education

I'm not clever with the needle. I can't keep my mind full on it. When it comes time for it—this hour after lunch is the usual, though I'm told some ladies can't stop and have to have it torn from them at bedtime as a babby from the breast—but, aye, when the lunch is cleared and way is made for the buttons and patches, I'm hindered from settling into it by a draft that, no matter what the weather outside, comes under the door and cuts into me like a knife.

Over my shoulder, it does blow, and into my ear. Then, whirling in my head, it swings my weathercock round and points it backwards and northwards, and sets me to believing that because I've done my time spinning cotton, I ought be handy at this fancy-work too. "Lord bless us and save us, Lizzie Burns," the wind roars. "All those years at the mill and you can't do a simple cross-stitch?"

I know it's only the devil trying to make me pucker a seam or prick my finger; it's only himself trying for my soul before the Lord calls for it. So I try to pay no heed. Though it gives me an ache to have to listen to him, speeching off like one of the mill men—"What we do today, London does tomorrow!"—or whistling the sound of the mule, dandier to him than a lark, I make as if I'm taken up with the feeding of thread and the making of loops, for I don't need to answer for myself.

That's just how it went in Manchester. The way it was, we were the ones who went out to earn the fire and candle, and it was the men who sat home and did the darning. That was the custom of the place, on account of our wages being the lower. I can't be faulted for that.

Mr. McDermot, down Parliament Passage, he even does it for the mint, like he's a seamstress. You pass your clothes in to him in the morning—he has a basket set out under the window, so all you have to do is drop them through and shout in your name—and he sews them up grand while you're at work and has them ready for collecting the same p.m. Mrs. McDermot is a spinner like the rest of us, but at one of the shabbier mills that doesn't let you out till nine or ten, so when you pass by and gander in, you see her man there, pinny-tied and stool-sat, sewing panels and fixing hems and putting strings in caps, looking all alone only for the bits of clothes and children spread about him. You only ever see him getting up to stir the supper.

They wouldn't believe you in London if you told them.

Nor would they understand—though it's a simple thing to grasp—that when you're out working all day, you don't learn how to knit or to mend, or to have any of the home virtues other mis-

suses might have. Indeed, if today I've any skills to boast of at all, it's only thanks to the Jew, Mr. Beloff, from up Ancoats Street way.

I run in with Beloff during my second year at the Ermen & Engels. Having served out his year at the mill, Frederick has gone back to Germany, leaving Mary with a head full of dangerous notions. She thinks he's coming back. She believes that, one day soon, when he's done with his business on the Continent, he'll ride back into Manchester and carry her off to the good life, the foreign life. It's a bad moment. When she's not demented with high feeling, she's sitting in the dark and letting the blue demons waste her. And on those frightening occasions when she's neither up nor down but normal, she's entertaining men, one after the other, in an effort to forget. I often fear she is near to downbreak. But I don't know how to reach her. My words she screams over. My attempts at embrace she throws off and resents. "You don't understand," she says, "and you never will."

It's not long before I feel worn away by it all, and I begin to spend my evenings from home, and my Sundays too, in the dramshops and the pubs. Soon enough I'm getting thick with a boy called Sully from Spinning Field, who takes to walking me over to where the Medlock meets the Irwell, and to kissing me, and to putting his hands inside my dress, and to telling me that Manchester is in England, and England is in London, and as soon as he's saved a bit of money, he'll quit the whole damn place and boat it back to Ireland, make a big family there. Sully has no regular situation. He spends his days collecting bits of smoked cigars from the gutter, which he then dries out and sells back to the tobacconists for a price. And when there's no cigar butts to be had, he looks over the streets for sticks and handkerchiefs and shawls that have been dropped in the night. Or he digs out the cracks between the paving stones with rusty nails to find a penny. Or he collects dried-out

dog-dirt for the tanning yards, and bones for the glue makers. And he never sticks to anything. Spends most of his time wandering about, looking for a bit of amusement. And when I've finished my day at the mill and have no desire to go home to Mary and her wailing, I join him, for I like his way of living outside.

Push to shove, we fall in with the mudlarks, and we fare grand with them. We sit by the Medlock, Sully and his gang and me, waiting for the tide's retiring, throwing stones and shouting oaths at the old women who make a headstart by wading straight into the water and fishing down to their elbows, not minding what they stand on, for their feet have long gone to leather. We wrap scraps around our own to keep them safe, but we're young and still have imaginations about what we can't see, so we decide it better to bide for the mud. What we find in it, we sell. Bits of coal, we knock off to the neighbors at a penny a pot. A pound of bones gets you a farthing at the rag shop. Dry rope is worth more than wet. But copper nails are the real treasure: fourpence, you get, a pound. You get naught for the bloodworms, their having no use or value, but we collect them anyhows, fill our pockets with them and then take them out in fistfuls to show the fine ladies on Deansgate.

The worms are all the wildlife there is in Manchester, apart from the pigs in the courts. But oddtimes—it's true—a wind comes down the Medlock and brings a seagull with it. You don't remark on it hanging there till one of the others points it out to you. Then you're not able to stop remarking on it, the way it stays up without moving a limb, and you go all envious, like a fool.

Mary's livid about my larking. "When you sink so low," she says, "it isn't easy to pick yourself up again. What if the mill people find out what you're doing? What if one of the foremen sees you running about like Miss Jim Crow, all torn and covered in muck? What would Frederick think? You're going to ruin everything!"

And eventual things do go Mary's way. I get a nail in the foot and, in the same unlucky week, a bit of glass in the other, which leaves me lame. I can't get up from crawling and have to go about the place like a dog. I'm still suffering for it in the knees.

"Serves you right," Mary says. "That'll learn you."

All the same, she makes sure to put a word in for me at the mill, and she gets a promise—it's no secret how—that I'll get my job back once I'm healed.

I spend most of the days pent up in our room. But if the weather's nice, I sit on the step outside and watch the course of the passing day. Sully from Spinning Field doesn't find his way to me—he must be a dullard or just a laggard, for I told him precise how to get here—but as chance has it, the Jew Beloff passes by regular to visit the boghole, his own court having none. And one day, when he gives me a farthing for no more than a salute, I get to speaking with him.

"See you about the place, sir," I says, for he's hard to miss, as tall as he is, all long and black, and with very little whisker on him; not a bit like Karl. "I see you about, but I'm not familiar with your people. Is it Irish you are?"

He enjoys that, he does. He stops and gives me his gums and leans on the wall beside me and tells me his kin isn't a bit of Irish but comes from the other direction, far out East.

"Out Ardwich way?" I says.

"Farther," he says.

The way he explains it, the Jews live in England like a people apart: private rites and holidays, and a separate parish to give out relief. Most of them work as clothesmen, like himself and his own father before him, buying and selling. Hats, he says, are valuable and always will be, as long as there's heads to put them on. He

opens out his bag and shows me his wares, and I'm surprised how quality they are, fit for a different caste altogether.

From now on, every time he comes by, he stops to talk, and when I'm not on my step but inside, he takes it on himself to knock on the door and ask for me, much to the fright of Mary, who sees no good reason for a Jew to be calling and wants him sent away. I do no such thing, of course, for I'm fain to go out to him, and we get to knowing each other well.

When we're together I even forget he's a Jew, for it isn't like when you see a darky musician in the halls or a stray Chinaman off the Liverpool boats and your heart falls to thumping and you don't want to get close. With Beloff you can pass the day beside him and not think about it, for he's skin-colored and doesn't appear that queer when you check him over proper, and you can laugh with him just the same as with one of us. Like the time he tells me he gave me that first farthing because he thought I was a cripple and a cripple is as good as a corpse in his book, no good to the living except as a weight to carry around, and there's something about that—the picture of the living carrying around the dead—that makes us buckle.

From my blather, he gets intimate with our affairs. Mary warns me about talking to strangers and letting on how hard things are for us, and dragging us through the muck that way.

"The less people who know our worries the better," she says. "No name is a good name."

But the way I see it, Beloff knows anyhows that we're down a wage on account of my wounds, and he can hear the bang and clatter of Mary inside, and can see for himself how hard it is to be cooped up with it all day, obeying rules made by an ill woman. He isn't blind to the thin stick of my arm either. It won't do me harm to play it up a portion is what I think.

And sure enough, one day he says to me, he says, "As soon as your feet are better and you can get around again, you should come and work for me."

And in that moment I come to the knowledge that a man can indeed help you rise in the world. All you have to do is pick him out right and play him well.

A matter of weeks and I'm going to Beloff's house every Friday p.m. after the mill, and again on Saturday till nightfall, for that's when the Jews keep their Sabbath and won't touch anything, so he gives me my vittles and a couple of bob to do it for him. Snuffing the candles is what I do, and poking the fire and scrubbing his collars and doing the dishing-up, and he says if I ever get good at it, I'll one day be able to do the sewing too: the sewing of all the clothes that come to him broken. What he gives me in return isn't enough to get a room of my own, but at least it gives me time away from Mary, with the added thrill of a regular lot to eat: supper on Friday and fried fish on Saturday, and dinner then, and tea, and supper after that, and that suits me.

A one-room, back-to-back in a court same as our own, is all he has, but he has the luck to live alone, his wife being passed over and his children gone to try their chances in London and such fields. This means it's only ever the two of us: me going about my business and him at the table or on his mattress, rolling cigarettes and calling out his orders. "Do it with two hands is better." "It's not going to come out, Lizzie, if you don't bend down into it." "You'll take your eye out like that. The needle needs to come at you and over your shoulder, not away from you like you're doing."

I don't see it yet, but what I'll eventual realize is that he's training me for home service, for that's the only way out of the mills.

"You're ignorant on the fundaments," he says. "It's best not to show you know anything, they'll not stand for a know-all, but for

the sake of your mind and the mind of your people, you should know the fundaments, everyone should know the fundaments," and then he starts pumping me on subjects I feel young yet for grasping.

I don't trust him at first, for there's one thing I do know for myself: there's always someone trying to improve you, especial if you're Irish. But over time I come to understand that Beloff is different from the higher-ups who pity you to the amount of a lecture. Over and above being a Jew, he's a separate species of man and fond of learning, and wants to pass it on, for he thinks that important in itself. He thinks learning alone can smarten you. He even thinks it's better than mint or land.

One day he notices my suspicions and he says to me, "What motivates me isn't charity, Lizzie. Ask anyone who knows me, I don't have a compassionate bone in my body. Nor am I looking to have power over you by making you a fool to myself. Believe what I say only when it agrees with the dictates of your own common sense. When it doesn't, I want you to speak up, for perhaps there is intelligence you can give me in return," and that gives me pause to consider, and the fears I have of him turning me into a queer body like himself fade, and I begin to hearken proper.

He gives me many lessons. About the earth and the sun, and which goes around which. And about how to speak, like you don't says "worser" but "worse," and unless you say it a hundred times a day till it comes out natural you'll be put down as an unread and no notice will ever be taken of you. And about England and how it's a place where the people spend too much time inside, thinking, and this gives them notions about themselves and sets them to believing they're masters and can rule over other people who live in other places. And about the difference between the English and the Irish, how one are Protestants and have to choose between

High and Broad and Low, and the other are Catholics, plain and simple, and slaves to the English, and will keep on being slaves until the Catholics from other places, Spain and that neighborhood, come to free them.

A lot of what he says is thick-spread like this and hard to swallow, and I oftentimes feel like telling him that a Jew has no right to be talking about things that don't concern him, and he'd better shut his trap in case anybody hears and slaps it shut for him. The only thing that stops me is a feeling I have, strong and deep down, that liars don't talk like him.

My last ever lesson with Beloff I remember like I had it yesterday.

"Stick clear of the religions, Lizzie. There'll come a time in your world employment when they'll want to save your soul by making you read passages and live by rules written down. There'll be little you can do to avoid it, you being the pauper and them being of the conviction that you're such because you lack faith. You won't have a say except to listen, but you shouldn't let it in. Mouth the words they ask you to speak, but don't put your believing in them, do you understand me? Learn the words, but don't credit their meanings."

It's the sad hour of a Saturday evening. When I finish putting this last bit of polish on the candlesticks, I'll have to cook his tea, then it'll be time to go back. I rub as slow as I can to stretch out the minutes.

"But I already have a religion," I says. "I even go to Mass for it."

He's over by the fire, wrapped in the bed things. "What matters your religion if it's the wrong one? They'll want to change it, and you should be ready for them."

"Sounds like you've quarrels with the Protestants, Mr. Beloff."

"Yes, and with your kind too. And my own kind most of all,

make no mistake about it. Each as bad as the next, thinking they know the secret to living and dying, and fighting each other over it all the while."

"But you obey the rules. You don't work on a Saturday."

"Ignoramus girl. You mistake something born of blind conviction and something done out of mere habit."

"You don't believe at all?"

"It's not a question of believing. It's about suspecting the ideas they're putting into your head. Always look at who is telling you something as much as what he's telling you."

"What are you saying, Mr. Beloff? I oughtn't hearken to someone if I don't like the look of him?"

"No, you should listen *more*. That's how you'll learn to be the good judge."

I put the sticks I've shone back where he likes them—one on the windowsill, two on the table, the rest on the dresser by the pictures of his family—and put the water on for the potatoes, but low. If he keeps on like this, it'll go past the hour for my leavetaking and that'll be grand by me, every minute away from Mary being a minute from the scourges saved. I peel with the blunt knife. Instead of bringing the fork and plate to the table together on the salver, I make trips back and forth.

"You can stay, young Lizzie, if it'll take the stones out of your shoes."

"Mr. Beloff?"

He takes the bite off his pipe, spits into the fire. "If it's such a vexation for you to go back, you can remain."

"Where'd I sleep?"

He whirls round, looking horrored. "I said nothing about sleeping!"

"Oh."

He makes a gesture to say his heart is pierced by my look. "All right, all right, I suppose we could find something for you to lie on."

I smile and put the bacon in to fry and, over the sizzle, try to comprehend my feelings.

I'm put on a mat in front of the fire with a rolled-up rug under my head and a coat thrown over.

"How's that?" he says.

"Warm enough," I says.

All night I keep my eyes closed, but am kept alert by the expectation of a snore or a fart or any sign to show Beloff's gone off into his slumbers so that I can go off myself without fretting about keeping him up with my own noises. But naught comes, bare even a breath. When I open my eye a slit and look through the dark, I can make him out on his back on the mattress, stiff and ironed out like a corpse.

It's the first time in my life I don't say my prayers.

As soon as there's light, I get up and make a new fire. I take out the ash and the night soils. Seeing the volume that comes out of the bucket, I realize I must have slept after all, for I didn't hear Beloff getting up. I spend in the lane myself so as to leave the bucket empty. While I'm haunched over, I watch the flapping of the oilskin in the window of the house opposite, which satisfies me and gives me no short measure of peace, it being early and there being no bodies yet risen to distract me.

Back inside, I'm surprised to find Beloff up and waiting for his breakfast.

"Am I getting something for the extra day?" I says.

He grumbles something about asking no questions till he's had his coffee.

"Where do you go to the Mass?" he says, once served. "I want you to take me."

"To Mass?"

"That's right."

"Do the Jews not have their own churches?"

"They do, but I want to go to yours. That's the humor I've woken up to."

On the road there, he must realize I'm not bringing him to my regular place, for I lead us out of the way, far from the passages and over past the lots. But he doesn't let on or allow his good mood to change. He whistles through his lips and skips through the puddles, jumps over the lushed-out bodies sleeping on the road. When a scrawn of a cat comes out of a sprung door, he lifts it up and presents it to me for petting.

I'm having trouble finding the church I'm thinking about, for I've never stepped inside it but only wandered by. The third or fourth time we circle past the same court, Beloff stops and leans on the pigpen that takes up most of it. From a window a bit of something is thrown and the animals snort and climb over each other to get it.

"You know, Lizzie, most of the Jews who don't eat pork don't know why it shouldn't be eaten, only it's wrong to eat it. Do you see the lunacy of that?"

"The only lunacy I see, Mr. Beloff, is yours for the bacon."

He laughs. "I'm no bigot, Lizzie. I don't care where I get my meat, so long as I can get it. I often go and buy it without looking at what it is or how they've killed it, whether it has a seal or not. And why?"

I shrug.

"Idiot girl. Because I don't think it's wrong. The Chinaman eats cats and doesn't think *that* wrong. He'd be shocked and appalled if you told him it was. Does that make him bad and evil?"

When eventual I find the church, I'm appalled to see that, despite it being first Mass, it's squeezed to bursting. Have we come

on a feast day without my knowing? I go to stand at the back with the men who, hungover and coughing, have been pulled out of the beds by their women. Beloff is having none of that. He bends his arm out, puts my hand on the inside of his elbow, and marches me up to the top as if giving me away. I don't think my heart has ever beaten so fast or my face taken in so much blood.

He genuflects. He kneels. He stands. He bows. The old beggar even clasps his hands and speaks out the prayers, word for effin' word, and all I can think is, Will this ever be over? Then, just as I begin to see a light shine at the end, he joins the file of bodies going up, and my worst fears come to be.

"You oughtn't of taken the host," I find the boldness to say on the walk back home.

"Why on earth not?" he says, putting on to be surprised by my displeasure.

"You're not a bit of a Catholic and you oughtn't of."

"Oh, but, Lizzie"—he's enjoying this, the hooer's donkey—"I was hungry."

"You were making a mockery."

"And do you see me burning up for it? Has the lightning come to strike me?"

"You're going to hell."

"Which hell is that?"

"Whichever one'll have you."

He shakes his head and chortles. "Oh, child of the Irish benighted—"

"Lizzie's my name. Lizzie Burns."

"Well, Lizzie, it's time you grew up and climbed out of your swamp."

Mary is waiting outside his door. She has a shawl dragged over

her head and pulled across her nose against the cold. I'm almost glad to see her.

"How long have you been out here?" I says.

"Long enough," she says, muffled through the cloth. "Where were you? I was worried sick."

"It's Sunday, young Mary," Beloff breaks in. "Where else would we be but at the Mass?"

Mary's hand comes out from under her coverings to bestow on me an almighty whack. The pain of it rings as far as my toes. Before this violence, I was resolved to leave Beloff, to skivvy no more for him, for he's a man with no respect to show for anything, but now I find myself conflicted.

"And you, sir," Mary says, pointing a finger at him, "you ought be ashamed of yourself."

Beloff doesn't look the slightest bit fussed. "Sister child, why don't you come in and we'll boil up some tea, get the cold out of those limbs?"

"Tea? Here's your tea, you dirty Jewish."

She frees her mouth of its veil and spits on the ground by his feet. Turns on her heel and storms away.

When I leave I know I'll never be coming back, so I stay a while drinking tea and looking into the fire, and another while frying up the midday dinner.

Says he: "Don't look so hard at it or it'll turn."

When it begins to darken, he tells me he has a card party to go to and it's time I faced what I had coming. I hate him then and wish him dead. How dare he send me away when it's his own hide that ought be tanned? All the same, I know that when Mary comes at me, it will be pleading his honor I'll be doing.

XI. With Radical Chains

"Here! Spiv! Pumps!"

Five in the p.m. of another day and I'm feeling compunctions about being over-hard. Five in the p.m. and, again, I decide it's time for a fresh start. Five in the p.m. and I call them to the morning room.

Pumps arrives, her hand in her mouth as usual, finger rubbing tooth. "Are we expecting?" she says, making sheep's eyes at the tea things I've put out, the cake I've cut.

"Nay," I says, "I thought we'd have a sneaky tuck-in, the three of us." I smile—muster all I can—and spread butter onto the slices and put them onto the plates. "With all the running round we do, it's rare we take the time to sit down and have a chat like us girls ought do together."

Spiv appears in the doorway. Folds her arms across. "I made that cake for Sunday."

"You did?" I take the prize slice with the cherry for myself.

"Well, no harm, can't you make another?" She opens to give out, but I'm faster: "And aren't there always the shops? The world wouldn't stop without you."

I pour. Spiv perches, ready to jump up and gainsay any involvement if it all turns out to be a rig. The more effort she spends keeping the saucer from falling off her knee, the more fidgeted she gets and the more tea that spills over. Pumps, on the other side, slouches like it was onto cushions she was born. A parish pip warming her hands, she makes, the way she's holding her cup underneath.

"Now, girls," I says, "I've been thinking. It's nigh time we looked at your half day."

Pumps takes her bit of cake up and bites into it. "The half day's fine as it is," she says, wet crumbs flying. "Why fix something that isn't broke?"

"For goodness sake, child," I says, "if from time to time you hearkened before you spoke, you might actual learn something. You've neither of you to worry. I don't want to take any of your time away. It's *more* time I want to give you. An extra hour seems fair to me for all the work you've been doing, helping us settle in and the rest. Believe it or not, it's already two months since we came to live under this roof, and that makes—how long?— a whole quarter of a year, and it's not always been roses, I know. There have been high emotions and some bad scenes. I own I've not been the easiest, this being a new arrangement for me. But now I want to wash the plate clean. I want us to be friends."

Glad of myself, I push my cake in and wash it down, press my thumb onto my plate to collect what's fallen. We all of us ought remember that, though it's no small task to be large and humble, the pleasures got from it make it worth the trouble.

Spiv clatters her cup down and narrows across at me. "Pumps is right, the half day ought stay put as it is."

"But—" My tea goes down the wrong way. "But Spiv, *cough cough,* don't you understand, *cough,* I'm trying to *give* you something? A reward for your services?"

She curls at me. "The name's Camilla, ma'am."

Lord have mercy, not this old bone.

"Your name's what I call it, Spiv"—how swift a rising ire can gulf the finer feelings—"and it'd do you no harm to remember there's girls who get only an afternoon a month, if they're given pause at all."

As if to remind me of the times, she throws her eyes up. "Adding an hour'd be no help, ma'am. With the lunch, I can't get out before two, and if I come back after seven, there'd be everything still to do for the morning. It'd make Thursdays unpossible."

Camilla Barton, Camilla Barton, it's higher than your hole you're fartin'.

"All I want," I says, putting the rage into the stirring of a fresh cup, "all I want is for us to be a bit closer. I'm not asking us to be bosom familiars or any such thing. I understand you must live according to your age and have your own secrets. I don't expect you to have older heads than you do, nor give out all their contents. But wouldn't it be right to share ourselves out a touch, to take our spare time together now and then, to do things more like a family? I'm sure Frederick would like to see it that way. You know how he hates ill feeling in the house."

"Listen, Aunt Liz—" Pumps puts on that voice she's learnt from listening to the Men in the parlor, that *reasonable* voice they like to use. If I wasn't busy with my handkerchief getting a splash of milk off my sleeve, I'd flatten my hand and silence it that way. "Aunt Liz, it's very nice of you to offer, and we love Frederick right well and want him happy in every feature, but I'm telling you, you wouldn't like what we do. We run about and get up to young tricks,

it wouldn't fit you right. You're a bit past it, if you don't mind me saying."

This brings a new rush of gall to my embittered mood. Lucky she'd be, at my age, to have hair half as black, not a gray strand on show, and no lady do-naught in London has it so shiny and thick. "Mind yourself, Mary Ellen Burns," I says. "If you're let out at all, it's because I license it. And if you're *here* instead of freezing your derriere on a Manchester street corner, it's also because I license it," and she knows it good and she knows it well, which is why the colors come up her face and she withers back into her cap.

By now our little Burns dramas must be as familiar to Spiv as any she can recall from her own childhood, but I don't think it's in her natural nature to be generous in her comparisons, or to own that her bad feelings towards us might actual be the flutterings of envy, on account of being so far from her own kind and having so little opportunity to quarrel with them. So she sits through it silent and judgeful, and when it's over and Pumps has begged her pardons, she stands up with a sigh and starts to clear.

"Mrs. Burns, if I may," she says, licking a blot of icing that gets on her finger while scraping.

"What is it, Spiv?"

"Mrs. Burns—" She doesn't look at me but between her fingers, in those warm spaces where the mites sometimes gather, for any icing she might have missed. "Mrs. Burns, can't you go out with Mrs. Marx and her intimates? Isn't she forever inviting you? And wouldn't you enjoy that much the better?"

"Put those plates down, Spiv."

She gives me a wary look.

"I said put them down. I'll do them."

Once free of her burden, she bobs a curtsy.

"Now get out of my sight. You too, Pumps."

Heads bowed, they hare for the door.

"You both ought be married by now," I call after them. "You ought be married and not here bothering me."

I'm left feeling too much to move. A cruddy humor has come and teased away my goodwill, the hopes I had of refreshing the heavy airs in this wretched house. Of course, the proper thing now would be to turn my affliction to good, to rise and come over it with busyness and tasks. *Trial and emotion strengthen the constitution and ought be cheerful borne* is how the saying goes. But to *look* at the half-eaten cake and the pool of tea in Spiv's saucer— just to look at them—tires me right out, weighs me to the carpet.

Jenny says that the Revolution will better our fare. That it will pay us for our home tasks and make us self-supporters. And I'm ready to put my doubts in a drawer and believe it isn't a swindle; I'm ready to follow the wind. But what she's not saying—what I've to keep to my own sorry self—is that at the pace the Revolution's going, with the comrades divided on themselves and squabbling over trifles, we'll not live to enjoy it.

I stay in my chair like this till I hear Frederick's step coming down the stairs. Of a sudden I'm charged with a desire to squeal on them. I must let it out, I think. I must reveal to him how they really are before it burns me away. A fire lights in my chest and roars in my ears. "We could do without them," I'll say. "We could live alone, just you and me, and get by regular well."

I hear his feet hitting the tiles in the hall. I stand and take up a stack of plates and hold them in front so that, if he comes in on me, I'll be seen to be doing something. He shuffles about outside the door. Picking things up and knocking things over. Giving out German curses.

"*Scheisse*," he's saying, "*Scheisse, schei—*"

A moment and he bursts in, the skirts of his coat flying. "Ah, here you are," he says. "Have you seen a letter lying around?" He spies over the tables and sideboards, turns over the clock on the chimneypiece, peers under the mats and the doilies. I can't work out if it's me who's looking slow or him who's moving train-speed. "I put it on the hall table to take to Karl, but someone seems to have moved it."

By his tone I know he's holding down a temper. I decide now to be the wrong minute to come at him with the house doings. "I've not seen any letter, my love," I says, putting down the plates to help in the search. "What did it look like?"

He turns to look hard at me, the conch shell in one hand and the ballerina figurine in the other. "It looked like a letter, Lizzie."

Folding open the doors to the parlor, he has to fix his elbow to his side to keep the papers under his arm from falling. I go to help him. "Here, give me those."

"*Nein*—" He puts them down on the writing desk. "Leave them there, do not touch them." He pulls the doors open the rest of the way and goes through, begins tearing at every blessed thing: the plants, the vases, the albums, the pressing books, the sewing box.

I sigh and follow him in. Lift the newspaper off the seat of the armchair. "Is this it?"

"Which? *Ya*, thank the devil." He whips it up. "I wish people would keep their hands off things." He puts it under his arm, where he had the other papers before. "Right, Lizzichen, I'm off"— hand brushing light on my arm, whiskers tickling my cheek—"I'm with Karl for dinner tonight."

"But I've ordered fowl. Spiv is going to roast it."

"Have it yourselves. Or I can send Jenny down to help you."

"Nay, nay. I'm sure the girls will be happy with an extra helping."

"Superb."

"Don't forget these." I give him the papers from the writing desk.

"Ah, *ya,* thank you. *Bis bald.*"

I wait till he's halfways out the door. "Oh, but, Frederick—?"

He twists and looks at me over his collar.

I point to his shoes, all scuffed and muddied. "You're not going out with those looking like that, are you?"

He looks down and curls his toes up. "I don't have a clean pair left. These will have to do."

Being so peculiar about his appearance—his lines he likes straight and his colors in tune—I thought he'd be pleased to have his eye drawn to the lapse, but I see now I've only nettled him further. A flush comes to his cheeks, and his response is mottled by it, and it makes me feel down-low and contrite, for I remember now that I promised to polish them yesterday, and it's only on account of his high manners he's not mentioning it. There's people, I know, that write down their tasks in a ledger, and the hours for doing them, but I count on my own brains, and I'm not a machine, time and times there's things that slip through.

"Come on, then," I says. "Take them off and I'll do them this minute. I won't have Jenny saying I send you out on your business looking like a rural."

"I have a cab waiting. They are fine as they are."

"Sit down there now. Flick of a lamb's tail and they'll be done."

I draw him over to the chair by the occasional table and put him into it. He moans. Throws his papers down. Takes out his watch and studies it. But he stays sat all the same.

I'm about to ring the bell for Pumps to bring the polishing box when the earwigger herself comes running in with it. "Here we go, Uncle Angel," she says, and kneels in front of him. "Give me your foot here and we'll get those spick and span for you."

The bell-cord still tight in my grip, I glower down at her. "I'll do that, Pumps, thank you. I'm sure you're busy at other things."

"Not at all," she says. "I can't think of any task that would better merit my attending." She smiles up at Frederick and takes his foot onto her pinny. He meets her mooning face and—begad the weakness of men!—his arrangement softens.

"Pumps," I says, coming to stand over her, "this is something I've promised Mr. Engels to do and I'd like to do it."

"For godsake, Lizzie," he says, chucking an arm at me, "let the girl do it."

I'm still holding the newspaper I took from the armchair. I slap it now against my skirts and take the chair on the other side of the table. All right, let her do it, but she'll need watching over.

While Pumps works, he fans himself with a magazine, sending the smell of spices across. "What would I do without you, Pumps?" he says. "You're a good girl, you're learning well."

She looks up at him, and they beam at each other, and it's enough to make the juices rise from your stomach.

He lets her work for as long as he has the patience. "I'm going to be late," he says when it's final exhausted. "Are we nearly there?"

"Nigh on, Uncle Angel," says Pumps. A few more lashes of the brush and she lifts his foot down to the carpet. "There we are. Good as new."

"Thank you, *mein Liebling*," he says. "Good enough to eat from." He leans over and kisses her on the cheek.

She reddens and bows down, hides her face under the fringe of her bonnet. "You're some fine charmer, Uncle Angel," she says, putting the tubs and the brushes back in the box.

He tips his head and grins. Gets up and stretches. Puts his papers under his arm. "Don't wait up!"

He's gone—*slam!*—and I'm left with the task of bursting the

little grubber's head, though I find now I don't have the energy for it. She mutters something about clemming for a smoke, and I let her go.

I gather up my ends and make the window in time to see Frederick climb into his cab. But there's only a flash of him to catch, and it strikes a chill in me, the fact that I see less of him now I'm living with him than in Manchester when he had us separate; the fact that we were better off the old way, better friends to each other. And there's other facts, too, that come dashing towards me like the rain against the glass, but I turn from them and come away, for I'd hate for him to look back and see me here, watching at his coattails.

December

XII. The Holy Family

Like flies on gristle, the mad bodies of London swarm the Zoo. A thicker brew of hatters in this corner of the Park than in the whole rest of the city. In the parrot house, weird old women trill and chirp and throw buttons to the birds. In the aquarium, gents softened by idlement leer into the murk and, by the looks of it, dream of sprouting fins of their own. The reptile house, the giraffe house, the camel house, the pelican house: little asylums, all, for those nuts with the shillings to spare for the turnstiles; wealth enough to be separate and peculiar, the busy world not daring to put on them or hinder their temper. It makes me queasy to be here, in and among them, and I worry that Tussy's love of the place is a sign she's headed the same way.

"I beg you, Auntie Lizzie," she said. "Come with me to see the moving crib."

"The what now?"

"The moving crib. Every year before Christmas they build a stable and fill it with exotic animals. And instead of statues, they have real people playing the holy family."

Am I the only one who sees it?

I agreed to come, against my own wishes, for I was afraid that alone she'd be approached, or in her innocence would do the approaching herself and, by there, get herself into situations. I'm so fond of the poor child, I'd hate to hear of her tricked or fouled. "All right, all right, the Zoo it is," I said, and no sooner was it out of my mouth than I began to look forward to the hours spent away from the house, and to the hand-holding and the secret whispers. "We'll bring a picnic, make a day of it," I said.

But, of course, by the time today arrives around, bright and free of rain, she's assembled herself an entire army of keepers, in the middle of which I vanish, bare noticed.

Frederick leads us down the paths with the confidence of a man who has come to see this Christmas spectacle before. With his women, it's probable; the ones he fears will go to the bad if they're not given proper distraction. He's dressed light for the freezing weather, in a frock coat built for September. Beside it, Karl's broadcloth suit, buttoned up to the whiskers, appears a solemn demand for respect: from the season, from the people, from the animals the same.

Scattered around are the comrades Tussy has convinced to come. One of them, a young strap I don't have a name for, looks to have tied invisible twine from his sleeve to Janey's, so firm does he stay by her, so little does he let her drift from his air. To watch it makes my heart sink, for I've seen it before, the clever and quiet eldest girl dashing into the arms of a rake, not for love or money but

to avoid remaining at home as help to failing parents. My wager is she'll be engaged before we even realize.

Two others, old enough to know better, are making circles around Tussy like stalking dogs. She puts a sweat on them by darting from cage to cage, pointing at the fur and feathers, lecturing on the ins and outs of the mating business, and now, for breaks, insisting they repeat the English names of the beasts till they can say them proper and with no foreign slurring.

Pumps is climbing a railing to get a better view of something. I watch her and worry that I've made a mistake by allowing her to come while keeping Spiv at home. She's getting used to the little privileges that come with having Burns in her blood and it's hard to know whether that's right or wrong.

Jenny is far off with the women Jaclard and Goegg. I'm being tanned by her, I can tell. Every time I come near her, she turns her head towards the bars and puts on to be interested in the life going on behind them. And her face: a window once wide open, now closed fast. Her behavior is no mystery to me, of course. She acting like she is because I refuse her invitations. Because I don't call to see her. Because I've not turned out the way she'd planned.

Walking alone, I follow the company into the tunnel. Our noses closed against the reek, our eyes lowered against the loiterers in the shadows, we soon come out by the deer paddock.

"This way," Frederick calls out, and marches us towards a stable where a small crowd has gathered. A collection of forlorn-looking boys in sandals and robes and false beards are stood, shivering, around a cot lined with straw. The Virgin Mary has blue paint around her eyes and red on her cheeks and a shadow where her fluff has been sheared. The Babby Jesus is a doll in winding sheets. The Wise Men have gold slippers and blackened faces. Scratching around the sad scene is a collection of impossible

animals. Trunks, tusks, horns, hooves: it's all there, a ridiculous array. Saddest and loneliest of all is an animal half-zebra and half-donkey standing on three legs in the corner of the stall. Tussy lures it over with some grass she's pulled up from someplace.

"I consider that nothing living is alien to me," she says when, final, it takes her offering.

It chews. Flaps its lips. Trundles back to its place. Lifts its tail and pisses a gush.

"What *is* that thing?" I says.

"It's called a quagga," she says, reading from the plaque.

Fact: the hippopotamus is the only thing worth the fare.

Frederick suggests taking tea in the rooms by the bowling green, and we agree.

"Everyone, follow me!"

Jenny takes Tussy by the hand, steers her onto Frederick's arm, leaving her admirers to tussle over Karl's attentions. Karl humors them the length of the llama pen (it's Tussy, again, who tells us what they are), before breaking away and coming across to me.

"Do you mind, Lizzie? Can I beg the favor of a word?"

"Of course, Karl. What can I do for you?"

He applies just enough tug on my arm to draw me to the back of the pack. I watch Tussy move farther and farther away and, trapped like a bird, curse myself for having left the nest at all.

"As you can probably see," he says, "my wife is not in the best of shape."

I look at Jenny giggling onto Frederick's shoulder. "I've seen her worse."

Karl can't hide his surprise. "I must object, Lizzie. Please do take into consideration that she likes to put on a good face. I can assure you the woman is—"

Suffering. I get it. The lot of the thoroughbred.

"My wife loves company," he says. "Even when the season is over and the days are shorter, she likes to receive guests and to get out as much as possible. True, she is beginning to understand that she must cosset herself a little more and not try to make every single event. But, on the other side, when she spends too much time at home she becomes, well, she becomes weary and crabbed, and her temper fires quick at the trigger. Like one of these animals here." He looks around and rubs the back of his hand in a fretful way. "Please do call on her, Lizzie. She would benefit greatly from your company. We all would."

"I'll do the best I can, Karl. I've a house to run."

He turns and, with desperate eyes, searches me through.

"I'm sorry, Karl. What I mean to say is, it would be a pleasure. You don't have to worry. I'll make sure Jenny is well looked after for the winter."

He sighs and smiles and lands one on my cheek. "Thank you, Lizzie. I just wanted to mention it."

"Of course, Karl. Any time."

The bogwork done, he brightens. "And now we have Christmas to look forward to, don't we? We're delighted you will be joining us. We are inviting all the comrades who have no families to go to. Making it special for them. I guarantee a ruckus. I know Jenny will love to have you there. And Nim will appreciate the extra help from Pumps and Camilla."

He grins and pecks me again, his beard dipping down into my collar and tickling my neck, and like a ninny I let out a titter, but inside there's a fury bubbling, fired by the feeling that, once again, I've been tricked.

"What's this about Christmas at the Marxes?" I says to Frederick when I get him alone later.

"Didn't I tell you?"

"Nay, you didn't. As usual I've to find out from the wrong people."

"Are you angry?"

"What do *you* think?"

"I thought you'd like the idea. Less work for you."

"Oh, by the willful ass of Mary and Joseph."

"You don't want to do it?"

"Of course I don't want to do it! Our first Christmas in London? Spent with Jenny and the whole wide world? Why can't we have it alone, as a family, quiet-like?"

"All right, if that's what you want, that's what we'll do."

"Nay, it's too late now. You've already committed us."

"We can change our plans. I'm sure Jenny would understand."

"Nay, we can't do that."

"Why not?"

"Blessed be, Frederick, for a man who claims to know the destiny of mankind, you understand diddly-dick about the laws of womenfolk."

Where the greatest crime is to have your own mind.

XIII. An Irish Lie

I know I ought to go up to her. There's things she'll want me to do. A list. To buy and to do. But I can't rouse myself to it. Tomorrow the spirit might be in me, but not today. Today my duty is to my own. My own place. My own house. And Lord knows it's long overdue a laundry wash.

"Frederick, I'm going to need your help."

He's bent over his desk, scribbling. "Uh-huh," he says without looking up.

Sighing, I get down and check under his chair for slut's wool. "It's going to be a busy day, Frederick."

"I understand. If you need a hand"—he waves the free one in the air over his head—"all you have to do is ask."

"Well, that's what I'm here doing, Frederick. I'm asking."

"Ah." He turns his eyes up and looks at me through his fallen fringe.

"It's laundry day," I says, "the last before Christmas. And I've no intention of putting it off or getting the woman in. If we're to get it done before suppertime, we'll all have to pitch in our bit."

"What do you want me to do?"

"Follow me."

"Now?"

"Take that plate and those dirty glasses with you."

Down in the scullery Spiv is bent over the washing book.

"Sir," she says, "what are *you* doing here?"

"He's going to help," I says.

He winks.

She looks him up and down, a lick of scorn, before getting back to her list.

"Right, Frederick," I says, "you can start by sorting the pile out into aprons, collars, shirts, body linen—and what's else?—nightclothes, pinnies, and petticoats."

"I am not certain I—"

"Any muslins, colored cottons, or woolens, leave to me. Unusual-looking stains, put them at one side and I'll have a look."

"But, Lizzie, I have not yet eaten lunch."

"You'll be having a big dinner."

"I do not think I will make it that far alive."

I take the old cheese from his plate (he's still holding it, of course, for he has no idea where to put it down) and push it into a bit of yesterday's bread. "There, that'll keep you going."

The aggrieved look he pulls doesn't prevent him from stuffing it in.

"Spiv, where's Pumps?"

She nods towards the storeroom.

I shake my head, not grasping.

"Hiding," she says.

"Oh, by the burning hole of Moses." I pull on the storeroom door but it doesn't come. "Pumps, let go of the handle." I try again, but it stands with. "Pumps!" I bang on it with a fist. "Get you the blazes out of there!"

The silence of a cringing animal.

"Mr. Engels is here, do you want him to see you acting the brat?"

A yelp, the sound of things falling from the shelves. The door gives, swings open.

"Git!" I says.

She stays cowering in the gloom.

"I said, git!"

Keeping herself as far from me as the area allows, she creeps into the light. A scarf is tied round her face to cover her nose and mouth.

"What in the name of—" I tear it down: a line of blisters across the top of her lip.

"She's been at the arsenic again," says Spiv.

"Shut up!" Pumps screams.

Spiv mimics her—*Shut up!*—before turning to Frederick. "She spreads it on her lip to burn her runner off."

Middle-chew, Frederick lets his mouth fall open, crumbs and wet bits falling. He puts a hand to his own whiskers, hides them away, as if they too were in danger. You forget they can be a shock, the home doings, when you're not used to them.

Pumps runs crying from the room. I follow her out. "Spiv, I'll deal with you later."

She shrugs, dips her pen in the pot, scribbles something down.

"Frederick, when you're done separating, take the sheets out from soaking and rinse them. Spiv'll show you how. We'll be right down."

He swallows and gawps like a man out of his depth, a man sunk too deep.

I find Pumps upstairs, slumped and sobbing.

"The consequences of vanity," I says.

She buries her weeping puss deeper into the crook of her elbow.

"Shall I call Dr. Allen?"

She shakes her head.

"We'll dress it, then, and you'll be right. I hope you've learnt your lesson this time."

She lifts her head and wipes her face.

"Come now, Pumps. It's not the end of the world."

Laying on liberal with the sniff and blubber, she lets herself be led to my room. There I put a tincture on the wound that leaves a purple stain all about her mouth and cheeks. It looks a fright, from three paces like a regular mutton chop, so I allow her to put the scarf back on, but only as far as the nose and not over it; I'll not have her going around looking like a sneak-thief. I tell her where I've hid the cake and send her down to it.

"Get it into you quick and don't dawdle, there's work to be done."

Left alone, I stop a minute at my dressing table. Take my favorite brush from the tin. Run it through once. Pull a handful round. Start at the ends. There's relief in this stolen moment, and I'm certain there'd be pleasure too if the tart I baked yesterday hadn't just now crowded in on my mind. I wince remembering how Spiv and Pumps looked at it coming out of the oven, hard as stone from too much rolling.

I put the brush down. It's not the big but the petty things that keep us from sitting. It's against the little mistakes that we bear on, on, on. Through the mornings of upped nerves and wasted breaths, the breakfasts warmed with a sup to steady us. On into the lonely lunches and the afternoons of blaspheming in the mind

and reflecting on what can't be helped. On across the halls and landings, the seeing-afters and well-doings, the fires and folds. The book room. The cook room. The privy. The parlor. On and on and into the bedroom again, where again we pale at the filth of the windows and the chimneypiece caked and the mirror smeared, and we catch the cut of ourselves, nuddy but for our workaday dress, head bare of a cap and in want of attention, exhausted and deserving of a sit-down, if only we could learn proper how to air the dough.

Back downstairs, Spiv has the possing stick and is beating the linen. I send her out to make a start on the supper—I suppose we can't have Frederick starving—and I give the job over to the man himself. He takes the stick without complaint. But then he starts to enjoy himself too much, whacking at things and creating a mess, and making lewd gestures to put Pumps into convulsions, so I put the two of them to shave the soap and do it myself.

We take turns rubbing in the jelly and throwing the water. I wait till the soda is done before coming away to the kitchen to check on Spiv, leaving them alone to do the blue. When I come back some minutes later, I see they've come round to be on the same side of the copper, and are stood close enough to hold the holy host between their hips, three hands in a line down the stirring pole—hers, his, hers—and for an awful minute I'm reminded of himself and Mary, standing in that boat in the river, the hold of the oar shared between them, him showing her how to push off.

I elbow between them and look down into the pot. "Have you mixed it well through? If there's streaks it'll be your head, Pumps."

After a minute, I take her off to the kitchen to dab the woolens and silks. "Start with this light conduct and you'll always be taken light. Easy to put on, easy to cast off." I leave her there to sulk.

Back in the scullery, I tell Frederick to follow me to the garden with the load, for there's a strong breeze and still an hour or two of good winter sun left in the day.

"I'm sorry about my niece, Frederick," I says when the largest sheets are up and hiding us from the house.

"She is certainly a personality," he says.

"Do you find her handsome?"

"Lizzie!"

I snatch at his sleeve. "She's a young thing yet. I'll not have her meddled."

Startled, he steps back, tugs at his arm to free it. "Lizzie, I am appalled." He looks about as if waking up in a place he doesn't recognize. "Do you need me for anything else?"

"Nay, go on."

He shakes his head and marches back inside.

"Don't disappear, Frederick," I call after him. "We'll need you for the flatirons."

Is there a loneliness more lonely than mistrust?

Boating on the river was his idea. He comes back to Manchester from the Continent full of them. His first, straight off the boat, is to take up with Mary again, to take up with her as if no time has passed to make him wiser, though in fact it's been a full eight years. *Eight years* he's stayed away, writing his books and chasing the great revolutions around Europe. And for the same length she has lived here, as she has always done, a tiny cog in the Manchester machine, only now with her heart locked in a secret box that she believes only he can open. And here he returns, the prodigal son, to run his father's mill—the job that family duty more than poverty has forced him to resume—and he comes to Mary with his idea, his big idea, which is

to have her again as his woman. And what does she do, only spring open with gratitude. And from there are born further ideas. To travel to Ireland on holidays. To move in together. To one day marry . . .

But first there's the river: what will be Frederick and Mary's first daytime outing as a reunited pair. They've been seeing each other as they always did, at night and behind curtains, but now they've decided to go broad with themselves, and they insist I come along (not for my good company, mind, but to take some of the philistine gape off them). I've vowed never to play the goose for them again, not since last week, when they dragged me around every music hall in Ancoats and then ditched me in a hush-shop to go up the stairs together, so I tell them I'll come only if I can bring a friend.

"Which *friend*?" says Mary.

"Lydia," I says. "Lydia from the carding room."

Says Lydia: "Not a chance in highest hell."

But she shows mercy when I grease her with the promise of beer and a free lunch. "He'll pay for everything," I says.

"Is it right, though?" she says. "Going about with yer man?"

"It's himself who wants it, Lydia. And Mr. Ermen knows about it and can't do anything. Isn't it a free country? Don't worry, you won't lose your place, you have my oath."

She thinks on it a long time. "All right," she says, "I'll do it." But only if she can bring her sweetheart Jamie. Which puts me right back in the muck. There's no road left for me but to tell Lydia to bring someone else, a man, to even the numbers.

She brings Moss. His real name is Donal Óg, but they call him Moss because of the fair hair that grows in small clumps on his cheeks, never quite joining to become the full beard. It's a name born out of envy, of course; a name devised by men who won't ever look half as handsome as him. He's a dyer at the same place our

own father used to work. We once met at a wedding in the Grapes, and I've noticed him on other occasions since, but in truth I could whistle down the wind for all I feel for him. His fifteen shillings would never get you anyplace.

We meet at the park gates. Moss is late, but he comes with flowers.

"Picked not bought," Mary whispers.

Frederick puts himself between Jamie and Moss, takes their elbows. "They're called Pomona Gardens after the Roman goddess of fruit trees and orchards," he says, and leads them ahead towards the water.

The men made themselves neat, but put beside Frederick they seem but cadgers, their efforts to spruce and shine themselves only making them look wretched, as if they've come straight from the early house. Understanding this, and prickled by Frederick's high talk, Jamie flashes back and gives a face. Lydia and Mary trade tittles. Moss understands the rareness of the occasion—it's not every day you're put level with the powers—and acts the brown-noser, looking to where Frederick points and nodding along to whatever he's told, the effin' eejit.

I look down at my flowers. Not bought and looking beaten. But fair's fair, Mary, he'd have had to walk out to the fields to find them.

We spread the rug while Frederick goes to talk to the boatmen about renting a boat.

"Don't come with us," says Mary when we're sitting. "Let me go out alone with him. Say you're scared of drowning or something and you'd prefer to watch from here."

The men shrug. Lydia winks. I look daggers.

"I got us a good deal," says Frederick when he comes back.

"Two hours for only a little more than the price of one." He looks thrilled with himself. "It's always worth your while to bargain."

They nod. I pick at the grass.

Mary gets up and takes his hand, makes a show of dragging him away to the banks.

"Aren't you coming?" he calls back to us.

"You two go on and have a turn," says Lydia. "We'll join you in a bit."

Jamie moves to take Mary's place on the rug to be closer to Lydia. In the fuss of arses and limbs, I stretch my legs and spread out my dress, leaving only the corner for Moss. He doesn't seem to care. He takes two bottles from the basket and walks on his knees into the sun. There he rolls up his sleeves to the shoulder and his breeches to the knee, and puts himself out to bask. He's watched by the people drinking tea at the little tables under the creepers. Farther down river, there's a spot where the men swim in the next-to-nuddy and the women take off their boots and show their shins, but we're not there now; we're *here.*

"Piss-artist," goes Jamie, as if to say he himself is the kind that stays covered if there's ladies about and drinks only what he's offered or can afford.

Lydia is glad to gob the bait. "One beer goes further in a poor family than two in an oiler like him." Her smile is crooked. His is cruel. Mine is faint-livered and craven, for though I want naught from Moss and wouldn't be happy if folk put me together with him, I do hate to hear a bested man drubbed further. He's had it harder than most, I've heard, a father that ill-used him and kept him from his meals, and he's turned out a lovely looker and kind enough, considering.

"Moss," I says, putting the sandwiches on a plate, "come and have something to eat."

"In a minute," he says without turning his face from the heat.

For a time then there's silence, just the flies and the moving water, and for another time we play a game where we guess what dodge Mary is going to try next to make Frederick handle her. Rock the boat? Splash the water? Grab the oar? When we tire of this, we turn our attention back to Moss.

"You'll get burnt," I says. "Come back into the shade."

"I'm grand," he says.

"Arrah, come on, Moss," says Jamie. "We're missing you here. Come and tell us one of your stories from Ireland."

"I'll do no such thing, I'm fine where I am."

"Arrah, Moss, don't be like that," says Lydia.

"I'll be how I like."

"Leave him be," I says. "Isn't he grand where he is?"

I bring him a beer and a sandwich.

"*Go raibh mile,* lovely Lizzie," he says, and gives me his teeth. White and strong, they are, the ones that haven't been knocked out. He bites the sandwich, takes a gulp, then puts the bottle and what's left of the bread onto the grass and rolls onto his side as if to sleep. I pick up the old bottles and bring them back to the basket.

"I'll tell you what, then," says Jamie once I'm settled, "I'll tell one of Moss's stories."

"Go on," says Lydia, nudging him, "go on, tell us."

"Oh, Christ, Jamie, spare us," I says.

"Lizzie!" says Lydia. "Remember yourself! We're only here for you. Doing you a good turn."

He tells a story of Moss when he was a boy back in Tipperary. How one day at the river—a river like this one, only called the Ara—he had his clothes robbed and had to walk home stitchless except for the bit of sack he picked up to cover his vitals. It takes Jamie an age to tell it, going into all the particulars about Tipper-

ary town and who did the robbing and how, and making sure to mention that Moss already had clumps of hair growing up and over himself even though he wasn't yet ten.

I watch Moss through the telling. He doesn't show himself to be hearkening. He doesn't kick up or cut in. Doesn't move at all, except to swat a wasp or scratch his tummy. It must be he knows Jamie's jealous. It must be he knows Jamie would take on all of his troubles if it meant being a stunner the same. So he turns the deaf ear.

But when Jamie is over and Lydia has balled out her laughs, and when there's been pause enough for a bit of guilt to be felt for telling another man's tale, Moss does get up and come over.

"You didn't tell the end of it," he says, dropping his empty onto the rug and rummaging in the basket for another. "What you've told is only the beginning."

He keeps us biding while he drinks from the new one, and then while he swallows and wipes and staggers over to lean on the tree. When final he gets round to it, I can't help but think he's putting on to be tipsier than he is, for the scene it makes.

How he tells it, when he got home from the river, starkers as he was, his mother wouldn't open to him, the news of his shame having reached her before.

"Off with you and find your father," she called at him through the door. "If the sight of you doesn't bring him home, Christ only knows what will."

Knowing she'd not be talked round, he set off on a tour of the drinking houses and, by the time he'd found the one holding his father, the whole of Tipp was laughing at him. His father himself was laughing till he understood it was his own son that had come through the doors. And when he understood this, he was quick to turn the laughing to his favor, the cute hooer, by keeping on

laughing and making a song and dance of ordering his son a spirit from the bar.

"Give the boy something to warm him," he said. "Can't you see he's half-froze?"

To the delight of his intimates, he gave Moss his shirt for the walk home.

"A double act! There's a pair of you in it now!"

Some sight they were on the roads, father bare of chest and son bare of leg, the two of them three sheets to the wind. Moss—watching his father wave at the people who turned to mock, listening to how his father caught their sly sniggers and threw them back as heartful bellows—began to feel light, near happy, and well nigh forgot what he was going home to receive.

His father's high mood vanished when the door of the homestead was thrown closed. But when Moss looked at his father, he saw that it wasn't only his humor that was changed but something else too. What it was, his hair had gone white. White complete. Some time between the pub and the house, he'd lost all the color out of his locks. His father's hand was raised to start the thrashing, but seeing how Moss was looking at him, not with fear but with gaping disbelief, he broke off and went to check himself in his shaving mirror. Being as vain as he was handsome, he thought the thing was lying, and he put his fist into it. Then he pulled it out of the wall and used it on Moss.

"That's how I got these scars here," Moss says, opening his shirt and taking it down to show his neck and shoulders and back.

I turn away. On the other side of the green, at the little tables, people are peering out from under their hats. "Cover yourself up," I says.

He obeys. Puts his hands in his pockets. Spits in the grass. "I'm going for a jimmy-riddle."

We watch him go off towards the bushes. A fine figure, no question, but it's his own fault everybody knows his trials.

"Do you even think he's *from* Tipperary?" I says.

Jamie and Lydia shrug together.

While he's gone, Frederick and Mary bring the boat to the banks and beckon us to join them.

"You two go on," I says. "I'll bide here for Moss."

I'm still here waiting when the four get back.

"Where is he?" says Jamie.

"Must still be looking for a private spot," I says.

Lydia hisses and folds her arms across. "Well, we're going to the roundabout. Are you staying here?"

I look at the hole in the briar where he disappeared. "Nay, I'm coming with you."

Frederick buys tickets for everybody. Jamie and Lydia take theirs without a thanks and climb up onto the same horse.

"Woo-hoo," cries Jamie.

"Yippee," cries Lydia.

Frederick laughs and calls out to Mary. "Come, Mary, let us ride together like Lydia and James!"

"Nay, nay," she says, waving her hands and shaking her head. "Nay, please, Frederick, nay."

I look at her. *Nay, please, Frederick, nay?* Aren't these public displays what she lives for?

"Come on, Mary," says Frederick. "It is going to start in a minute. It would be fun!"

"I'm sorry, Frederick, but I can't, I can't."

I give her a stern look. "What's wrong with you? Can't you get up there with him now he's paid for you?"

"I can't, Lizzie," she says, touching her belly. "Not in my condition."

I want to fetch my picnic up. And in fact, that's what I do, only I put a hand up to stop it coming past my lips.

"Are you all right, Lizzie?"

The roundabout creaks to a start, and the three of them, the wanton couple and the lonely German, go round. The music rings a pain in my temples. I swallow down and look around for somewhere to sit.

"You're no more pregnant than I am," I says as I move away. "Wasn't I washing the run out of your sheets just two weeks ago?"

I sit on a bench by the bandstand. Mary stays by the roundabout, gives a weak-looking wave every time Frederick passes. When it stops, Jamie and Lydia come off arm-in-arm, swerving and wobbling and all-round acting like topers. Frederick rushes to Mary and pours his foreign concern over her. From where I'm sitting, I can't be sure if he knows what game she's playing. He brings her over to sit at the tables. I wait till the tea is brought before joining them.

"We ought get the rug and basket," I says. "They'll be robbed."

But no one moves.

Moss doesn't come back.

"Typical," says Jamie.

That night Frederick doesn't stay the night, for he can't be seen walking to the mill from this direction in the morning. I hear him leave around midnight. Mary comes straight into me.

"I'm tired," I says. "And we're up early."

She pays me no heed. Gets into the bed beside me. "I've told him," she says.

"Told him what?" I says, though I know well what.

"About my circumstances."

"Oh, for Christ sake. Good night, Mary."

"If I'm not pregnant now, Lizzie, I will be before long. It's not a real lie."

I shake my head in the dark. "And is he happy about your *circumstances?*"

"That's the thing. He's over the moon."

"Suffering Jesus."

"He's going to stick by us."

"Is he now."

"He's going to put us in a bigger place, maybe even farther into the country, for the fresh air, and as soon as I start to show, he's going to tell everybody and move in with us himself."

"Us? Who's this us?"

"You, me, and the babby. And him."

I laugh. "Have you lost your senses?"

"What do you mean?"

"You think I'm going to stick round here and take on the burden of your mistakes? Sit up for your dirty issue? Clean the crap out of his nappies?"

"You're twisting my meaning."

"You're the one that's twisting, Mary. Twisting the good out of everything."

"You're my family, Lizzie, and you'll soon be Frederick's too. He vowed to look after you."

"Look after *me?*"

Out of naught a vision of Moss comes: nuddy as Our Savior on the cross. "Better to marry me," he says, "than to burn in this hell."

The next day, after the bells ring, I go looking for him. He's not hard to find. I take the seat beside him.

"Two more of those," I says to the tapstress.

"What do *you* want?" he says.

"I'm sorry for yesterday, Moss."

He shakes his head. "Arrah, you don't have to be sorry, Lizzie Burns. You're a good woman. I'm not worth you."

I touch his hand. "Enough of that, Moss. You're worth more than most I know."

He looks at me then, and through his blinking eyes, I can see his urges.

"I'm getting you out of here," I says.

And he follows. You don't understand the power you have till you test it.

We can't go to his house, for he shares with other men, and I'll not bring him to ours, not with Mary there to fling the dirt, so I lead him up the passages. We start a couple of times, but we're not left alone for long.

"I know a place," Moss says. "But it costs."

"Don't worry about that," I says.

He brings me down Great Ancoats and into a neighborhood I can't name. The room is bright enough and tidy. The lass who shows us up is younger and has a plainer, cleaner face than you'd suppose.

"Thanks," I says when I hand her the coins.

"You have till the morning," she says. "Nine on the clock. If you leave before, you don't get it back."

His bit is a thick log that sobers me and gives me second thoughts.

"You ought know something, Moss," I says.

"What?" he says, lifting his head out of my mammies.

"I know my way around a man, but I've never let one inside."

His eyes go wide and his brow creases, and I can't tell if he's more surprised by my frankness or by my maidenhead.

Once it's in, there's little in the act that surprises me. I lie

under and he goes over, and I search in it for the pleasure, though it's over before I catch more than a spark.

Afterwards he stretches out beside me, puts an arm across my belly.

"If I'm up the pole," I says, "will you run off like you did in the park?"

"I'm sorry about that, only I didn't feel right. I was riled up, and when I'm like that my manners are not of the best. I hope you can forgive me."

"I suppose." I put my arm to rest over his.

We're like this till I'm almost asleep. But then he chooses to say, "I was engaged to be married, you know. In Ireland."

"I don't need to know about that, Moss."

"She was a fine girl and I loved her, but I had to leave. It was the only way."

"Please, Moss, that's all none of my business."

He sits up on his elbow. Looks down at me. "I hope you'll make me your business now."

"Let's see what happens."

What happens is not a babby but ulcers on my fingers and about my cunny.

"You filthy bastard," I says to him when he comes to see me at the lock hospital, "you big dirty filthy bastard, you've given me the Old Joe," and if I'd strength enough to mete him out a lashing I'd do it, in front of the nurses and all.

"I didn't know, Lizzie," he says, holding out another posy of his picked flowers. "Please believe me, I didn't know."

I wave the weeds away. "Well, you don't have to worry any-hows. Frederick is paying for the mercury."

"Lizzie, please forgive me."

"You'll have to take the same yourself before you get another lass into this mess."

"Oh, Lizzie—"

"I can talk to Frederick for you, if you want. About covering the costs."

He falls into the chair by the bed, white as death. Around us, the women cough and moan.

"Lizzie, let me marry you," he says after looking at me for a long while.

"Proposals, Moss? This is not the time."

"I've naught only what I stand upright in, but I love you and want to look after you."

"Are you talking out of shame, or do you mean it?"

He doesn't have to reply. I can tell by the way he takes grip of the bedsheets that he means it, violent.

It's men are at the bottom of every plague in this world. We come to the lock with this frontmost in our minds, and as we lie here stewing in our cures and wondering if we'll be next to go cripple, or walk off into fits, or turn so childish we've to be washed in bath chairs and given to drink with a spoon in a teacup, our knowledge turns to action: sometimes screams or fists but most often somber vows of chastity breathed out into the late-night miasmas. "Dear Lord," we says. "Dear Lord God Our Father, if You find the grace to spare me, I'll never go near another one again." And we're dead earnest. We believe ourselves new-made saints. And we make the same vow the next night and every night after, till we're told by some twist-whiskered pup that we're saved and can likely leave in the morning. And now we're so grateful—so effin' overglad—our holy promises are dropped and we forgive the dirty drakes everything. More than that, when we see them biding by the door

to take us home, it's Lucky me! we think. Lucky me to have such a morsel worrying after me!

Moss goes for my elbow and I let him have it, but when he uses it to slow my walk, I take it back from him and says, "I don't need a crutch, I can get around grand." And farther on, when he lays hold of my hip to help me cross a road: "Don't handle me like I've lost the use of myself. I'm well and not changed."

We stop for a pause at Ducie Bridge. Shoulder-to-shoulder, we lean over the parapet where the bricks have fallen away. The weather being dry, the river is shrunk to a string of pools. Caught in the weirs, the slime sits out to dry and rot. The stink is enough to make you dizzy, but we close our noses to it and stay.

"Look," I says, pointing to the sky above the tanneries.

"What?" he says, searching in vain. "What is it?"

"Arrah, you're too slow. It's gone behind. It was a seagull."

We come away. My knees are sore after the weeks of lying slack, and by the time we reach Salford, I'm in a mighty sweat. We buy ass's milk and brandy balls from a coster outside Weaste station, and eat and drink sitting on an overturned cart.

"Moss, you need to know something."

He stops chewing and looks at me in a tone of "Ah, Lizzie, what's this? Do I really need to know anything?"

"If you don't like what I say," I says, "you can walk. I'm giving you license to turn on your heel and go. I won't hold it against you."

He looks at me, afraid.

I throw what's left of my sweet to the mice and rub my fingers on my skirt. "I can no longer have children. That part of me has been taken."

He drops his face down to his boots. "So we'll do without and we'll live better for it."

His answer comes too fast and I don't trust it. "Look at me, Moss."

He lifts up, his eyes ashiver from too much talk.

"Don't you want a family? A homestead of your own? Without the hope of little ones, would there be any sense to us?"

"I'd go on happy with just the two of us."

"You says that now."

"I says that now and I mean it. The most I can give in this life is my word."

And what more, for brutal truth, could I ask?

Sat on the cart, we stay, and watch the bodies come out of the station. The swells and sailors coming from Liverpool. The Manchester men climbing into their gigs.

"Did you make friends at least?" he says.

"In the lock?" I says.

He nods.

I smile and poke him in the side. "All I'll miss from that place is the laudanum."

We get up and walk the rest of the way. At the end of my road we kiss.

"Leave me here, Moss."

"I want to go in with you."

"Nay, I'll do this alone."

"I'll bide here."

"Go home and I'll call on you tomorrow."

"Don't change your mind, Lizzie. Don't let them talk you against me."

"Don't be fretting and git."

He doesn't move till I peel him off and push.

"Go on, skedaddle."

I don't have the key, so I have to knock.

"Here she is, back," says Mary, opening. She kisses me on the side of the head above the ear.

Frederick is here. "Look at you," he says, taking me from her and planting on my cheeks. "More ravishing than ever."

She's cooked a fish, I can smell it.

"I hope you've not gone to any trouble. I'm not terrible hungry. It's more tired is what I am."

"You're out of breath," Mary says. "Have you been walking?"

"Just a little."

"Why didn't you get a cab back? The money I gave you yesterday, didn't you use it to get a cab?"

"It's not the walking. I'm just tired out after all the time on my back."

"Well, come on, you'll sit and have something."

"Just a drink, Mary, please. That's all I want."

From the armchair I listen to them eat. The whiskey softens the noise of them, their scrape and swallow. It softens Mary's ire, too, when final she decides to release it.

"Oh, but she's some willful one," she says, the same as if I'm not sitting here two paces away, "insisting on going into the lock like a pauper when she'd have been cared for best here at home."

"Leave it be, Mary," says Frederick.

I don't look over. I keep fixed on the window and the day that's darkening on the other side.

"Well, she's cured," she says. "I suppose that's the main thing."

When they're finished, they bring their glasses over to the sofa.

"Aren't you going to give her the gift?" says Mary to Frederick after he's sat.

"Ah, *ya*," he says, getting up again and going off to the bedroom.

When he's good and gone, she leans in. "Aren't you the lucky one."

"Aren't I the *what*?"

"Getting away with only your womb lost?"

"Only?"

"Well," she says, "it could've been your hair. Or your teeth."

He comes back and hands me a basket of soaps.

"That's awful kind of you, Frederick."

"With these you can take lots of hot baths and rebuild your forces."

I smell them. Lavender. And rose. "They're lovely."

"Lots of baths and fresh air and rest, that is what I prescribe. And I forbid you to go back to the mill."

"I'm not intending to go back, Frederick, not till next week at least."

"Not next week, not ever. Mary has left for good and so should you."

I look over at her. She sips from her glass, then holds it out to the side, dangles it between two fingers as if threatening to drop it on the carpet, as if such a spill wouldn't be *her* mess to fettle. "What're you looking at me like that for, Lizzie? It was only a question of time. It's not right for me to be there anymore."

"Not right?"

"The rumors were putting Frederick into too many awkward corners. The Ermens were asking questions, only dying for the excuse to smoke him out of the business. And the Club, he couldn't even pass it without jokes and whisperings coming out at him. And the Communists up in London, well *they* are—"

"They're not rumors if they're true."

Frederick coughs. He has to sew his mouth to keep the lush from showering. Mary doesn't flicker a lid. Slugs the end out of her

glass and puts it down. "Lizzie, you wouldn't believe how jealous those bitches got, what a misery they were making of it for me."

It's *bitches* they are now. Once upon a time, they were careful and kind. Once on a time, they were the salt of her earth.

"At first I laughed along, put on like I thought it was funny, but then the slighting speak began, and the games in the yard crafted only to make me suffer, and I realized I'd crack before they'd ever stop, that's how cruel they'd turned. It's best I got out before"—she rubs her belly like a trencher woman brewing a belch—"before, you know."

I know, I know. It's enough to see her changed out of her bodice and into her loose shimmy. Fraught. In foal. Brought to bed. On the straw.

Sighing, I hold my glass out. "Where did you put that bottle?"

Frederick jumps up and goes for it. Tilts me more in. Puts it on the floor beside my chair.

"So what's all this got to do with me?" I says when I have it downed. "Why ought *I* leave *my* situation on account of *your* troubles?"

Mary darts Frederick a fearful look. He clears his throat. Crosses his legs. Looks about to speech off, but I hold up to halt him. I don't need to hear it. I can suspect for myself. The rumors have my name in them. They say it's the two of us he keeps for his pleasure. One Burns one night, the other Burns the next, the two Burnses together on feast days and strikes. They say it's *him* who put me in the lock.

"Are you discharging me, Frederick?"

"*Nein, nein,* of course not."

"Am I to lose my earnings to keep *you* safe in your circumstances?"

"Christ, Lizzie," says Mary, "we thought you'd be happy to leave the place."

"Happy? What'd I do instead? Can you tell me that? What'd I do?"

"That's what we want to talk to you about."

"I couldn't go out to service. No respectable house would have me after so long in the mills." And I'll not sit here all day stitching and learning the melodies, going soft on a foreign man's mint.

"Lizzie, would you listen a minute? It's been arranged. We've it all drawn out."

And now she lays it out visible, the picture of us. In the middle is herself, of course, glowing under her own halo. And around her, sitting and standing and draped over, are her stout, German-faced children. And around them, circling with velvet arms and a grinful of perfect teeth, is Frederick. And behind him, the faint color of wallpapering, is myself, the starve-acred relative without a sprig of her own to tend except her breakdowns abloom. And around us all, built solid and flush and clean, is a house on Burlington Street: two floors, two gardens, three bedrooms, an inside bathroom, and an attic for lodgers to cover the extra expense of me.

"Nay." I nigh on snap an ankle in my rush to get upstanding in my boots. "Nay, nay, nay." I'm wag-wag-wagging my finger in their faces. "Nay, nay, nay, nay, you can rub me right out. I'm not going any place with you two, not to Burlington nor any other street. I'm staying in my job and earning my wages as usual. And I'm going to live with Moss O'Malley."

Now Mary bats. "You're going to *what*?"

"You heard me. It's all been settled."

"Settled? When?"

"Today. Over the past weeks. He's been coming to see me. I paid off the nurses to let him in."

"Mary Mother of Jesus. With *our* money, too." She gets up, takes the glasses out of our hands, and brings them to the kitchen.

"I wasn't over with that," I says on her way out. We hear her putting the kettle on for the dishing up. A pause while she gathers herself.

"What're you playing at, Lizzie?" she says when she comes back.

"I could ask the same of you, Mary."

"Ladies, please!" says Frederick from way below on the couch. "Sit down and let us talk this out like civilized human beings."

"He's no good for you," she says.

"He wants me no harm."

"Harmless, aye, that's the right word for him. Wet and harmless. A big man gone damp."

"You're one to talk, a prime tippler yourself."

"And his intimates? All the same. Jamie, Kit, Dan, Mick, Joseph, the whole crowd of them. Naught doing but passing their time in swilling ale and smoking like the beasts that perish."

"He's a good man."

"Arrah, he's a tosspot. They all are. Talking for the good of Ireland when they're the worst of its examples."

Furious, I point down at her shame. "Well, he'd never do something like this by me."

"And how could he, even if he wanted to, with your insides taken?"

I clasp my mouth and teeter back. That's the end of it. No gain to be got in keeping on. She has her mind and she can keep it.

Turning from her, I pitch a pleading eye to Frederick. "All we need is a few pounds to set ourselves up. Then I'd be out of your hair for good." I already owe him—God knows I owe him, and not a little—but if I've gained any sense of the man, he's above

keeping personal accounts. "It would be a loan, Frederick. We'd pay you back a bit at a time."

Behind me, Mary foams over. Frederick silences her with a finger. Comes to the edge of his seat. Signals towards the armchair. "*Bitte,* Lizzie, sit down. You too, Mary."

We obey. The furniture creaks. He studies me a minute. Then he says, "Is this truly what you desire, Lizzie, or do you feel pressured, by him or by us? If it is the former, I would be glad to help. But if it is the latter, then we should talk and try to come up with a different solution."

His question puts a knot in my innards. Am I starting out of my own mind, or am I being forced against the grain? If I'm honest, I know the answer. My accidental life was bound to put me swimming upstream eventual. But I can't say it aloud.

Mary sees me shally. "What Frederick's asking you is, are you going with him to get away from us, you ungrateful ax, or do you love him plain and true?"

Love?

Love?

The way I've heard Mary speak of it over the years makes me doubt I've feelings in my body at all. But I've seen enough of this world to know that most of us have to accept men we don't feel for, and I'm not sure it's for the worst in the end. A marriage of emotions can't be lasting. It wouldn't be healthful if it was. You only have to look at Mary, gone thin and nervous, to know it doesn't do a woman good, and she'll waste away entire if she doesn't soon understand it.

"I have to be practical," I says.

"How is making house with Moss O'Malley *practical*? God, it's like you've not heard a word I've ever said to you, about anything."

"I'm prepared to give him the benefit of a doubt." It's a stranger he is, but a man too, and most men lean to the good.

"You're a fool, Lizzie, to cast your life on such a die."

"I'm not with him for what he'll win me. I'm with him for his character. His morals."

And just like that, it's said. The whole "morals" bit. Said and heard, and certain to come back and scorch me.

We find a room in Hulme, Moss and me, a fair walk from our situations but where the Irish are few and nobody bothers with our private affairs. The place costs more than we can afford, but we'll manage, for Frederick has put me in charge of the Diamond Thread and added three and sixpence to my wage, and with his loan I've paid an advance on the first three months. For that's what I'm giving it: three months.

"Three months?" says Moss.

"Aye. After that, I'll decide."

"You mean you haven't yet decided?"

"Nay."

"Oughtn't we do it straight off? Isn't that the normal way?"

"Three months. A trial run. A chance to prove yourself."

"Prove myself?"

"You can start with your drinking. I'll not be ballyragged by a soaker for the rest of my days."

"Is that what you think of me?"

"It's what I've heard of you. It's what they're saying. You're lucky I'm not one to put faith in the voices. I'm giving you three months to make liars out of them."

"And what about our living together? What'll we tell them about that?"

"Why must we tell them anything?"

"Passing as man and wife, isn't that a sin? Doesn't God look down on it?"

"He might, but He also knows my reasons and will forgive me for them."

"They'll be expecting a wedding. Everybody'll be."

"Well, they'll have to bide."

"Bide? Begorrah, woman, don't you have any Church in you at all?"

When not at the mill I keep close to home and watch him, and what I see is a man raised on naught to be naught, thankful for any crumb he has and not particular as long as he gets the needful. I tend to the meals, but I give out the stitching and steer wide of the baking, and I make sure not to take him anything to the bed, for then he'd expect it every day. He does what he's required about the place, fixing it up and making it a bit of a home, and he makes an effort to be cheerful, striving against the sorrows of the past that sometimes sore beset him. Though we're not yet joined in God's eyes, in my own he's within his rights, and I give myself over to the fetch whenever he wants it, to keep him manly and also to relieve him. And though he's inclined to be quiet, I press him to speak and to tell his stories, and the odd time we bring the chairs out to sit, the neighbors stand in their doorways and hearken, for I understand that in his soul he holds a deep well of feelings, and that, without a means to draw down, it could boil into a storm and burst out of its own willing. On Saturday nights he goes out with the lads, which keeps him in bed most of Sunday morning, and he often comes home from work with the whiff, but he never gets in too late or without his legs full under him, and what he spends doesn't make us poorer, so I make it my business not to complain. And for some weeks we live like doves together, never having disputes.

Some time in the second month, Frederick summons me to the office.

"How are you getting on?" he says, closing the blinds against the clerks at their desks outside, then changing his mind and opening them again.

"At the Diamond Thread? Pretty tidy, Mr. Engels," I says. "The girls are good workers."

"Good, good." He comes away from the windows to fiddle with some papers on his desk. Takes a file out, puts it back. When he looks at me again it's with a sly twinkle. When he speaks it's in a whisper. "What I mean is, how are *you plural* getting on? We have not seen you since you left."

"Oh, we're getting on grand."

"You have not come to visit."

"We'll come when we're proper settled."

"Mary misses you. We both do."

"Nice of you to say."

I brush some flyings off my sleeve. I don't intend to give it easy, whatever it is he wants.

"We would like to see where you live."

"I'll do you a dinner when the place looks halfway decent."

He comes round the desk and takes a box from the cabinet. "Do you need any—?"

"Nay, not a bit of it. And we'll start paying you back as soon as the wedding is over and paid for."

"Ah!"—he shakes the coins in the box—"there is to be a wedding!"

On the other side of the glass, the men look up from their business. I pinch myself through my pocket. "No date yet, but I suppose it will have to happen sooner or later."

"Well, this calls for a celebration."

"Nay, Frederick, please."

He puts the box down and goes to pour two drinks from a bottle on the sideboard. I try to hide behind a hand. "I oughtn't, Frederick. They're watching."

"Do not pay attention to them. I shall tell them you have had a faint."

"I want my head clear going back to work."

"Oh, pish-posh," he says, handing one to me and touching his own against it.

"Cheers."

"Cheers."

My throat is dry from the mill air. The lush burns it farther and I cough. One of clerks lowers his papers to peer at me. I take another sup and catch his eye over the rim. He turns away.

"It is good to hear you are so happy, Lizzie," Frederick says now, sitting down and leaning back in his big chair. "You deserve it, more than anyone I can think of."

"Well now, Mr. Engels, *happy* is a stretch." My time under Frederick's protection made the hobble of life foreign to me, and I've been alarmed by the difficulty of returning to it. But it's also true that I've been enjoying the simple-and-straightness of it. It's what it is, and it's a struggle, and it doesn't put on to be anything else.

"Well, you certainly look happy, Lizzie."

"I do?"

"I only wish Mary were the same."

So we're *there* already.

He sits there looking at me, biding for a word—advice and such—but I don't give it. I put the glass on the desk and my hands on my lap. I cross my feet in front of me and look straight back at him. He doesn't need me to say what he already knows. She'll

never be happy. She'll always be like a child, ever wanting what she doesn't have.

"Please come and visit," he says when the silence gets too heavy for him to carry.

"I will. Maybe when the babby's here."

He flinches at the mention. Grimaces like he's been jabbed. And that's how I get to know the babby's gone. Come out before its time. I put on not to understand.

"Mr. Engels, I'll get behindhand if I sit here any longer."

"*Ya,* of course. Be on your way."

"Thanks anyhows for the drink."

I leave him pale and scrambling to look busy.

"What was that about?" says Lydia when I get back to the workroom.

"What do you think?"

"Is she all right?"

"She's made her bed, now she may lie in it."

When I get home that evening I find Moss sitting outside, making speeches to some of the local children.

"Don't be giving them nightmares," I says, going in.

When the supper is on, I decide to go out and join them, but something stops me on this side of the door. I put my ear against it, but it's only the usual racket I hear: the Liberator O'Connell and the landlords and the Great Hunger, things any Irishman with a head would know, though to hear him you'd think he was a prophet of the news.

"You'll get those children into trouble," I says to him later, when we're eating.

"Not a bit," he says.

"They'll get some hiding if they go home spouting about the suffering sister island."

"Well, it'll be good for them if they do. They'll learn what their folks are really like. The history they carry."

"Just be careful," I says, and leave it there.

But it'll not be left. There's something I heard him say to the children that stays with me like a tick, burrowing down and making a wound. And a few days after, while I'm scrubbing his back in the bath, I find myself saying, "Moss, I need to ask you something. Do you mind if I ask you?"

"Jesus, not so hard, Lizzie!"

"The other day when you were talking to the neighbors' children."

"When?"

"A few days back."

"I don't recall, but what about it, anyhows?"

"I heard you say something and I didn't like it."

He looks over his shoulder at me. Big worried drops fall from his lashes. "What didn't you like?"

"It's probable naught."

"What was it?"

"You said that if you weren't born in the Catholic provinces of Connaught, Leinster, or Munster, you weren't Irish at all."

He laughs. "Is that what has you so nerved up these past days? Stomping around and clattering the pots?"

"If it's anything particular, aye, it's that."

"Christ, it's well for some, having so little to worry them."

I slap him on the arm with the brush. "What did you mean by it?"

"Ah, for feck sake, Lizzie, it's only a way of talking." He rubs his arm. Lifts some water out and pours it over the spot. "A way of talking is all it was."

"Well, I don't want any more talk like it."

"Well, you know what, Lizzie Burns—"

Of a sudden he's up standing and the water's rushing off him onto the flags and he's grabbing the towel from my shoulder. "I'm getting sick of your rules. Sick to the teeth."

"If you don't like my rules, what's keeping you here?"

"I'm beginning to ask myself the same."

He leaps out of the tub and strides across the room, leaving his wet on the only bit of carpet we have, and has to last us.

"You're dreeping every place," I says. "Can't you wait till you're dry?"

He tears at the fresh clothes I've put out on the bed. His breeches stick to the damp and he has to hop round to get into them. "A better man would have raised his hand to you long ago." He slaps his cap on and makes for the door.

"Where're you going?"

"Out."

"Off with you, then." I follow him onto the road. "Off with you back to Tipperary, if that's where you're from at all."

He reels back, comes to giant over me, though what I see is only a boy in his tantrums. "What did you just say to me, woman?"

"You heard me. How can we know for sure where you're from? We only know what you tell us, and any amount of that could be tarradiddle. There's voices saying you were born in Cheetham and your accent is only what you kept from your kin."

He slams his fist into the brick behind me. Draws his hand back slow. Puts it under his arm. Bares his teeth. Growls through them. "And what are you, Lizzie Burns, only an effin' Brit-licker?"

Four whole days he's gone. Sunday night, Monday night, Tuesday night, Wednesday night, till the Thursday when his money is spent and he shambles in looking like he's been pulled through the bush.

"Did you go to work at least?" I says.

He doesn't answer. Instead, he heaves himself by the limbs to the bed, falls down on it full-clothed. I leave him there and finish my tasks. At supper, I put out a plate for him, but he doesn't get up for it. What'll not keep till tomorrow I eat myself.

"I'll not having you running off every time you don't like the sound of something," I says when it's time to get in beside him.

He says naught, but I can tell by his breathing he's not asleep.

"Do you hear me, Moss? Do you hear me?" and I keep at him till he groans and pulls the sheets over his head, for he needs to understand the health of a thing is told by how fast it recovers, and four days is too long by any measure.

I blow out the candle and in the dark allow a hand to rest on him. It's late, after all, and he's learnt.

After so many days with only broken rest, sleep comes quick, but I'm hauled from it young by the sound of the springs grating. "I'll not be made a mocking stock anymore."

I blink up at his shadow. "What's the matter with you?"

"We're to marry. This week, we're to do it."

"I told you three months."

"And I'm telling you, Lizzie Burns, I'm finished with your tricks and your tests. We're getting married or we're calling it off."

"All right," I says, "all right," for his whimpers are those of a man who'll not be any further pushed, and they'd frighten the insides out of you.

He caves onto me, more out of relief than longing, but he's soon going at it full peck, and what touches me is not the sopped words he leaves on my neck but the effort it costs me to show him proper feeling in return. My heart's hard against him, and the more he gives way, the harder it grows.

"It's the proper thing," he says afterwards. "I couldn't live on like this, it goes contrary to my morals."

I tell him he's right, all along he's been right, I was only being silly and afraid, and that sends him off into his snores. Leaving me to stare into the thought that there'll never be light for me locked into this Irish lie.

XIV. The Franco-Prussian War

Jenny has grapes, real grapes, in her hair. She's drawn me over to the sideboard and is poking furious at a display of green boughs.

"I don't know what to expect," she says.

"I'm sure they'll be charming," I says.

"They are French, most of them. Escapees from the siege in Paris. It worries me."

"What does?"

"Them. I do not know how they will be. We *are* Prussians, after all."

At a loss—why are we whispering?—I look back into the room. Karl is treading the length and breadth, glancing at the clock and grumbling. He's had his beard brushed out and locks curled up special, and is making great efforts not to touch them and put them out of place. Frederick is fidgeting by the chimneypiece. Bare through the door and he's already on his second vodka. Christmas

Day in Jenny's parlor, and I don't think Joseph himself was as fretful as this, waiting for the virgin birth.

She tugs on my elbow and I turn back.

"You must think I am being silly, Lizzie."

"Nay, not a bit of it." I give her my best face.

"If they are coming here to dine with us, it must mean they have embraced Communism and are free from that blasting curse of national prejudice, which at the end of the day is nothing but wholesale selfishness."

What has them so nerved up? As far as I'm concerned, you've dealt with one frog, you've dealt with the whole pond.

Outside, the sound of wheels. Karl moves to the window and checks up and down the road.

"This must be them."

He sends Nim down to pay off the cab. I go to the mirror to make some last revisions. In the glass now I see Nim coming in, looking wan. No one appears behind her. She speaks something in German. Exclamations fly. There's a rush for the door.

"What's wrong?"

"Oh, forgive us, Lizzie," Jenny says. "We have to go straight down to the dining room. One of the men has an injury and cannot get up the stairs. How could we be so thoughtless?"

"Not thoughtless," I says, shaking my head, "not a bit of thoughtless," and a part of me feels sorry she'll not have her pageant processing down, two-by-two, the biggest animals first. She looks forward to such affairs and it will damper her mood to have it passed over.

Nine men stand in the hall. In any other house they'd be crushed, but here they've room to stand in a line crossways and to bow. I'm not the only one shocked as to their number. Nim's pallor

has gone to green, and Jenny has a croak in her voice when she says, "Gentlemen, the season's greetings to you all."

The injured man is balancing between two ashplants. In his aspect the good lords over the bad, though he isn't a man you'd ask for a direction with any faith you wouldn't be cursed at. What I suppose to be presentations are made. When my turn comes, Jenny switches to the English.

"And this is Frederick's dear spouse, Lizzie. An Irishwoman."

They dip a final bow in my direction before being led into the dining room.

Nim has to run around and reset the table before we're put sitting down. Jenny fills the time by making a theater of deciding who to put where. I make myself busy lighting the candles that have been blown out by the draft we bring in. The table is laden—dishes of tomatoes and strawberries and grapes and greengages, bowls of nuts and savories, a Russian salad—but I know that Jenny likes to keep her courses spare, and I'm curious to see if there'll be enough to sate the extra stomachs. (Spiv in the kitchen won't be happy, but at least Pumps might do as she's told and not put a foot higher than the scullery step, for she won't want so many men to see her dressed as she is, in the dreariest bonnet I could find in her wardrobe.)

I'm glad to be sat at the corner, away from the horror of making myself understood. Frederick is put on my right, Karl at the head to my left. The wine has been taken from their dandy green bottles and put into dull-looking jugs. Nim pours from these now. Once all our glasses are full—it takes an uncomfortable time for her to get all the way round—Karl bellows out a toast. At the other end, Jenny makes to stand, but remembers the wounded man's condition and sits back down. We touch glasses from where we are.

After some murmuring and shifting, Karl drops his eyeglass and clears his throat. All heads turn to this end. He speaks loud

and in the French. During his pauses, his mouth makes that sarcastic curl that Frederick says makes his enemies quake. Hair like wire pokes out from his ears, long and strong enough for a bird to land on. He's wearing his usual broadcloth. Poor Frederick, meantime, has gone all out with the silks. It can't be chance alone that his necktie matches the runner on the table.

While Karl speeches, I can't help handling the silver, which has been shined to blinding. The china has been rubbed to white by time. Invisible on the linen, it is, and brittle as the host, though it probable cost a sum nonetheless. I see my fiddling has been noticed, so I take my hand away. Folding and unfolding my napkin under the table, I wait for the soup.

With Frederick's help, by the time the second broth is cleared and the fish arrives, I've put names on some of the Frenchmen. The thin, raw-boned one is Lenoble. The one with the ragged pair of worsted gloves tucked under his plate and the busy gob tucked under his nose is Boyer. The stern one, strong-made, is Pernaudet. Ottlick isn't French at all but a Magyar. He's my first glimpse of his race, and it's a letdown, though the patch on his eye is fair and impressing. The wounded man is Bouton. He has been silent since we sat down, keeping watch. He catches my eye now and smiles like he knows what I look like out of my shimmy. I look away. Give my flush to the wall.

Frederick does most of the speeching during the meat course, which isn't long, for it contains a turkey that looks much less massive now it's cooked and put in the center of this crowd. While Nim carves, Jenny fiddles with the cuff of her blouse and, by her staring, tries to will more meat off the bone. I do my bit by refusing more than a smitch. I can fill myself up with water, I think, and reach for the third glass on the right (you only make a mistake with finger bowls once).

With pudding—fruitcake, custard, jelly, ices, nuts, and cream cheese—Nim also brings bread and butter and seed cake and macaroons and wafers in case anyone is still hungry. No one dares touch any of it, except the Frenchmen, who larrup in, but they have the excuse of being strangers.

Talk about the war starts up. Anxious that I not be ignorant of what's passing, Frederick speaks in the English about the manifestations in London in favor of British assistance to France. Jenny—in a voice far more foreign than I know it to be—tells the men that her daughter, too, is across the Channel, working with her husband, Mr. Lafargue, to end Prussian occupation, and then, of course, to bring about the final Revolution. Karl says that a German victory, and a carving up of France, would end by forcing France into the arms of Russia, followed by a new war of revenge, which would act as a midwife to revolution in the East. The men listen and have opinions of their own, which they give out in the French.

Where there is now a lull, Lenoble gives Nim a nod and she brings him two parcels he has given her to put away. The crumpled brown bag, he holds out to Jenny. She clutches her chest and cries out. Only when he insists does she take it and look inside. More yelling.

"What is it, Frederick?" I whisper.

"Dried apricots," he says. "They would have preferred to bring a bottle of something French and good, but times are bad."

To Karl they give the gift covered in newspaper.

Frederick nudges me. "They have wrapped it with one of my articles about the war, do you see?"

At first Karl is careful not to tear the paper, but the French jeer him till he rips it open. A book. He reads the title and everyone laughs.

"What is it, Frederick?"

He starts to explain, but soon stops and calls across the table.

"Mr. Lenoble, if it doesn't displease you, can you explain in English what the book is, for my wife's sake?"

Lenoble bows an elegant bow. "Madame Lizzie, the book is called *Confessions of a Breton Seminarist* and it tells of all the ways the religious men and women in France misbehave themselves."

"We used to read about the Empress," snickers Boyer, "now we read about the nuns!"

Roars of laughter. Jenny yelps and claps her hands. I sip and bide for the noise to die down before I says, "Is it true? What it says in the book?"

Lenoble wipes his mouth. "When it comes to the religious orders, Madame Lizzie, truth is worse than fiction."

I can't be sure what he means, only that it's of a familiar persuasion. I let it go.

A discussion follows about the refusal of religion by the working classes, and now about the need to abolish marriage as a next step. I open my fan and beat some air into my lung. What puzzles me is why it's oftenest married people who want marriage abolished, while the unmarried ones, like myself, want it kept safe, in case one day we might need it.

Jenny rises and opens a hand in the direction of the sofas: time to remove ourselves there. Pumps stokes the fires and lights the candles on the tree. Nim pours tea and coffee into cups on the occasional table. Frederick looks after the gin and whiskey. Karl passes round the cigars. I find myself beside Ottlick.

"In France," he says, "men and women separate after dinner."

"Oh, I think it's the same here," I says. "Only we're not the kind to go by."

More talk about the war. More speeches in the English. As far as I can tell, the only one who fails to offer something is Bouton. The longer he stays mute, the more blistering my curiosity for him grows. Perhaps he doesn't have the language to grasp what's being said, or has gone so separate in his head that he can't even hear it. Perhaps he's one of these soldiers who can no longer see the beauty in anything, on account of all the death he's witnessed, and cares least for speeches and words. Perhaps he's just biding the good moment to put in. Perhaps all he needs is a push.

"Your leg looks very sick," I says.

The room goes quiet. Jenny bulges at me over her fan.

"I hope you're having it seen to proper. We know a good doctor if you're in need."

He covers his heart and leans down into a bow.

I raise my glass to him. "To life and surviving it."

A silence now takes command, a silence made of swallowings and sighs. Out of it, Bouton's voice rises a rumble.

"Madame Lizzie, you are a tradeswoman, *n'est-ce pas*? A worker?"

"I am. Spent most of my young years in a cotton mill in Manchester, and not a bit ashamed of it."

"A cotton mill, *oui*, this is what I've been told. Is it also true that your, ah, your husband here *owned* the factory you worked in?"

"Monsieur!" Frederick is up quicker than a lady-do-naught sitting down. He disguises his haste by taking an ashtray and holding it out for Bouton to tap his cigar on. "Mr. Bouton, you speak on a complicated matter and, moreover, one that is now past. Myself and my wife now live away from Manchester." He puts the ashtray down, stabs his own cigar into it. "It is no secret that I come from a family of capitalists. Bourgeois and philistine, those were the un-

fortunate circumstances I was born into."

I can't help being impressed by Bouton's sharpness, his knowing precise where the weak point is, but I pity my Frederick more. It's not uncommon that he has to answer to this charge, not uncommon even though the world knows he worked in that mill to keep Karl and the Movement afloat. And knock me acock if I ever see *Karl* having to defend himself in this way.

"Believe me, Lieutenant," Frederick says, moving back to his chair but not sitting on it, "I never lost sight of the contradictions of my situation. I managed the mill because I had to. Destitute, I would not have been much help to our Cause. Be in no doubt, it was a hard time for me. I occupied a position I did not enjoy, and I occupied it for twenty years. What sustained me was the knowledge that my profits were also the Revolution's."

Bouton hearkens without cutting in, but he makes sure to show himself unpersuaded. Karl stares at his feet. Jenny offers the wafers round.

"I would also like to say, so that the record is clear," Frederick says now, flicking out the skirts of his coat and sitting down, "I would also like to say that in Manchester I made a point of *not* socializing with the bourgeoisie and of devoting my leisure hours to intercourse with plain working—"

"I heard you were quite the fox hunter," says Bouton, his tone as easy as a sea breeze.

I wince at the clout of it. The colors rush to Frederick's face. He throws a leg over one way and now the other. Cups his hands over his knee. Jigs up and down. The quiet is complete enough to hear the rustle of my dress as I run my palm down my thigh to dry it. I look at Bouton. I can tell by the stones of his eyes that, in spite of his flippant manner, it doesn't pleasure him to be contrary like this. He's not doing it for fun or high spirits, but rather is doing

what he thinks a soldier must when he finds himself among parlor men. He's saying the truth of real things.

"In Manchester," says Frederick, "I discovered poverty and degradation among the working people worse than in any civilized place on earth. But I also discovered a proletarian culture of significant intellectual elevation. The laborers devoured Rousseau, Voltaire, and Paine. Byron and Shelley were read almost exclusively by them. On Sunday evenings thousands filled the Hall of Science to hear lectures by their working brothers on political, religious, and social affairs. And I was there with them. I was there to hear those men whose fustian jackets scarcely held together speak on geology and astronomy with more knowledge than most bourgeois paper-shufflers possess." He tucks his hair back. Runs a finger over his lip and smiles. His esteem is recovering. "I can assure you, all of you, that even when in the service of cotton capitalism, I was never anything but devoted to the International."

"I'm certain Mr. Bouton is not suggesting otherwise," says Lenoble.

"S'il vous plait, Mr. Engels," says Pernaudet, "Mr. Bouton was simply being curious. He did not mean to cause offense."

Frederick bends forward into a bow and takes his drink back up.

"Mr. Bouton," he says, and salutes the soldier.

"Mr. Engels"—Bouton returns the gesture—"do forgive me if my questions are bold. I have been so long among fighting men whose manners were poor, I am prone to forget myself. I hope you can excuse me."

"Please, Mr. Bouton," says Frederick, "there is no need to apologize."

And, with that, it looks like it's over, the storm blown wide. Frederick sits back and slugs down. Bouton turns his attention to lifting his bandaged leg and carrying it to a new spot on the carpet.

Jenny rushes over and puts a cushion under. Ottlick turns to me with a small conversation about the weather in London and how it compares to the outside world.

"It's the only thing," he says, shaking his head, "the only thing for which this city cannot claim greatness."

I nod and smile for politeness' sake, but in truth, my interest is what I can see over his shoulder: Bouton and the winds still howling through the ruts on his face.

"There is still one thing I do not understand, Mr. Engels," he says.

Frederick pulls away from Karl's ear. "What is that, Mr. Bouton?"

"Since my arrival here in London, your role has been explained to me on a number of occasions and by a number of different people, and yet I cannot seem to comprehend it quite."

"My role?"

"Your role, Mr. Engels, your position in the International, as you call it. If you have left the situation by which you were financing it, what do you do for it now?"

This churns Karl right up. He rises—*creak!*—to stand by Frederick's chair. Slaps a hand onto his shoulder. "Mr. Bouton, please, if I may speak for my colleague. The man you are addressing, and with such ill-manner, if I may say, is our corresponding secretary for Belgium, Italy, Spain—"

Frederick murmurs something.

"And Portugal and Denmark, that's right. This, Mr. Bouton, is none other than the man in charge of coordinating the proletarian struggle *across the Continent.*"

Frederick accepts Karl's tribute with a quick nod.

"It sounds like your secretary does important work, Dr. Marx," says Bouton.

"I can assure you he does," says Karl. "Important work and apparently thankless."

With a proud flick of his head, Karl seizes Frederick's glass and brings it to the drinks tray with his own.

"Have you ever fought, Mr. Engels?" says Bouton.

His back still to the room, Karl slams down his glass. "Indeed he has!" He swings round. "Back in forty-eight he was involved in no less than four important battles against the Prussians. He himself raised the red flag over his hometown. In theory *and* in practice, Mr. Engels is an expert on war. It is not for nothing we call him our General."

Bouton smiles a conceding smile. "I did not know this history of yours, Mr. Engels, and am most glad to learn it."

Frederick receives this weak praise with an extravagant whirl of his hand. "Now that you are in London, Mr. Bouton, I hope we shall have many more opportunities to learn about each other."

Karl gives Frederick his drink and, mumbling quiet oaths to himself, returns to his own seat. He plumps down. Pulls the thighs of his breeches towards himself so that their ends come up over his boots to show a sliver of pale and spotted skin.

"And you, Dr. Marx? Have *you* ever fought?"

The grin comes so quick to my face I've to rush to cover it with my fan. I see it now. Karl has been Bouton's target all along. He's been going through Frederick to find his way to him. A coil in me loosens, and I feel I can start to enjoy myself.

Karl gulps down and wipes his mouth with his sleeve. For a grain of what has already been said, I've seen him drench bodies in bitter slang. This time, though, he manages to keep his temper. "If forty-eight has left us with a lesson, Mr. Bouton, it is the danger of inadequately prepared rebellions. It is my duty as a revolutionary leader to educate the proletariat towards its eventual destiny. Without instruction and guidance there can be no useful action.

We all cannot, nor should we all, be soldiers. To the Revolution, as to the new society, we must give according to our abilities."

"And the International? What does *it* do? Does it have an army?"

"Our Association constitutes nothing more than the bond between the most advanced workingmen in the various countries of the civilized world."

"A bond?" says Bouton. "Does the bond *do* anything?"

"Its task is to infuse workers' groups with socialist theory and a revolutionary temper."

"You mean its task is to sell your books."

Lenoble and Ottlick both fling their arms out in objection. "Monsieur Bouton, *s'il vous plait.* We are guests in Dr. Marx's home!"

Bouton ignores them. "Don't you think, Dr. Marx, that the workers would be moved more easily by appeals to direct action than by learned treatises about labor and capital?"

Uproar. Everyone on their feet, shouting and flailing about. Everyone except Bouton, of course. And me. You won't find *me* up there bawling over politics.

Karl raises up to calm the waters. "*Bitte, bitte, bitte,*" he says, and now when he has quiet and everyone is sitting again, "You know, Mr. Bouton, you are right. Ideas can accomplish absolutely nothing. Ideas never lead beyond the established situation. They only lead beyond the *ideas* of the established situation. To become real, ideas require men to apply practical force. However—and *this* is the vital point—force must be organized by the new idea. Force without the new idea is wasted."

Bouton folds his arms across and frowns. "You speak of action, Dr. Marx, but what action is your organization taking? I am sorry but I cannot believe it to be merely a coincidence that your headquarters are in the only country in Europe determined *not* to revolt."

Again, chaos. Again, everyone up and shouting. This time, though, Karl follows Bouton's lead and stays in his seat. Screened by the dancing bodies and the curtain of blue smoke, he digs his elbows into his lap and lets his head fall into his hands, reaches his fingers into his brush and scratches his scalp.

"Will the cursed peace in this country ever end?"

When things have settled, Karl leaves for the cellar to choose something to fill the empty jugs with. He plods out, followed by Frederick, and now by Lenoble, Boyer, Ottlick, and Pumps. Jenny rings for Nim and helps her bring some things downstairs. On the way, she tries to collect my eye, but I look down and sit tight. I spend enough time in my own kitchen.

I'm left with Bouton and Pernaudet. Huddled like plotters on the couch, they talk in low voices in the French. I clear my throat.

"Don't you think it gives a queer air to a place, having so many people who don't want to be in it?"

They look confused.

"London, I mean."

"Oh, London."

"Why did you choose London, gents, if it displeases you so much?"

"This was the only place. It was either here or Switzerland."

"I see. And Switzerland?"

They shake their heads as if to say, "You think here is peaceful?"

I use a stray napkin to rub the paint off the lip of my glass. "I've come to believe emigration can't be healthful for a person," I says.

The two men nod, wistful.

"You know, Madame Lizzie," Bouton says after a time, "you have the aspect of someone who has seen trouble and had to fight it."

"That I've done my share of fighting can't be gainsaid. By nobody it can't."

"You're not the same as these people"—he nods towards the door—"my advice to you is, go softly and do not lose yourself among them."

I begin to protest.

"We all have our reasons for being somewhere, do we not, Madame Lizzie? In France there is war. An order out on our heads. We cannot return, not if we want to live. This is our excuse. But you, Madame Lizzie, what is yours?"

"My excuse?"

"Go easy, Bouton," says Pernaudet, and mutters something in the French.

Bouton dismisses him. "Yes, Madame Lizzie, what is your reason for being here, away from where you belong? You must have one. We all do. If we did not, we would be back there, *n'est-ce pas?*"

"I've no place to be going back to, Mr. Bouton. This is my home. Is that what you call a reason?"

"No."

"Bouton!"

"Please leave him, Mr. Pernaudet. Though he tries, Mr. Bouton doesn't offend."

Pernaudet bows.

Bouton smiles. "Do *you* like it here, Mrs. Burns? In London. In these houses?"

"Like it or nay, it's where I find myself, and it's where I'll live myself out."

"Such a pity."

"Bouton!"

"Please, Mr. Pernaudet, I don't wish to be handled with kidskin. Mr. Bouton, I've been to Ireland only once, on a holiday with Frederick, but I still call myself Irish, and I will till the last of my breaths. Can you understand that?"

He curls his lip down. "No."

I laugh. "All right, then, can you understand this: was I to take myself off tomorrow, back to Ireland, or wheresoever, Mr. Engels's house would fall right down."

"No house for the Internationals?" he says. "My God, Madame Lizzie, where would we all be then?"

Where? Nowhere is where.

A body must be where her money is made.

Phase
the Next

1871

February

XV. The Necessary Course

The Revolution has happened. In my parlor.

Chairs overturned. Empty bottles on the chimneypiece. Half-full glasses among the plants in the pots. Fag ends in the necks of the lamps. The clod from someone's pipe stuck onto Jenny's horse painting, right where its bit ought be. And on the sofa, head to foot and snoring, their clothes screwed tight about them, morning wood standing up in their breeches: men I don't recognize.

Another fancy evening for the comrades. Another night spent with cotton in my ears and a chair against the door. And now another day spent with yesterday's smoke clogging up my bad lung?

Nay. There's something wrong in this. I must get out. I must breathe the outside air, else I'll be stuck here suffering in my heart the agonies of a caged animal till death and salvation overtake me.

I'll talk to Frederick, is what I'll do. Unload my mind on him. And by my tone he'll know I've neither leisure nor energy for

debate. I'll say the house is a problem I want no more business with. Give me a job, I'll say. A proper purpose. I can no longer be happy living in a wife's constraints. Put me to good use, send me out to do what I'm fit for. No matter how mean the task, I'll perform it, as long as it brings me a distance from this place. And there's this to be said too: outside in the world I'll keep a good spirit, and will weather the severe judgments my public actions will draw down on me, for if there's any justice, there's another world with no politics biding for me above.

XVI. A Public Woman

"You must give me something to do."

He's lying in his shirt from last night, a cloth folded over his eyes, an arm folded over the cloth. "*Ach,*" he moans, and turns his face away from me as if from a flood of unwanted light, "there is so *much* to do. So much."

"I need to get out of this house."

"Well, go. Who's stopping you?"

"The mess you left downstairs, is what."

"Leave that to the maids if you must."

"Have no fear. I won't be lifting a finger to it."

"Good." Keeping the cloth in place with an unsteady hand, he rolls over onto his side. "Now, if you don't mind, Lizzie, this head I have needs more rest."

They call him a genius. They point to his articles and tell me his mind is mighty, crushing, and I won't gainsay it, if it's down

there in black and white. Me, I can only know what I know, and that's the man, the meat and bones of him.

"You must give me something to do. Something useful. I won't lie idle like this any longer."

"Go visit Jenny."

"Oh, aye, the cure for all my ills."

He sighs, flops onto his back again, lifts the corner of the cloth, peeps out from under it. "What's the matter with you, Lizzie? You said you didn't want any more active duties. You were very clear about that when we came to London."

"I know what I said. And I'm not asking to command a battalion. I just want something to get me abroad of this god-forsaken shit-sty!"

He gives me the best thing he can find this early and in his condition. I'm to go to a convent in Hampstead, the Sisters of Providence, and plead a case for Edward Dalby, a comrade from Manchester whose wife has just died, leaving him with three young children he can't keep. The convent has refused his application because he's been unable to prove a stable income. I'm to meet with whoever will see me, Mother Theodore if possible, and convince her that Dalby's associates—and I can only suppose that means Frederick alone—will cover the cost of the girls' education. He gives me a letter, some money for the cab, and a further sum in case I need to pay anyone off.

"Now that I think of it," he says, "you're probably the best man for the case. I don't know why I didn't put you on it before."

"I must have slipped your mind," I says, taking another sovereign from the box, this one for my trouble.

•

Mother Theodore is big. Big in a fashion I didn't think nuns were allowed to be big.

"What can I do for you, Mrs. Burns?" she says.

I hear her and would like to answer, but I'm frozen in wonder at how a hole in the face so small could be responsible for what hangs around it.

"Mrs. Burns?"

I shift in my seat, pull my eyes down to my lap. "Sister, may I speak to you plain?"

"Please do."

"I'm not sure why I'm here." I look up.

She purses. Leans herself forward onto the creaking desk. "Well, Mrs. Burns, when I find myself in a moment without a purpose, I like to eliminate from my mind those things that rest beyond the reach of my powers. Would I be right in saying you haven't come here with the flickerings of a vocation?"

I can't but smile. Her eyes—alive among the stone statues and the faded pictures of the sacred subjects—catch mine, and for a moment we're two simple lasses twinkling at each other, two lasses weary of the continual calls on us to clean up other people's messes. I've come biding for a fight, but now I feel a change happen within me: a smoothing, a softening.

"You'd be right there, Sister. You won't fit me into a habit."

"Well then, Mrs. Burns, tell me, what *might* your intentions be in coming here today?"

"My husband has sent me in the belief that I can do something to further one of his causes."

"Your husband? I may live behind high walls, Mrs. Burns, but I am not deaf to the local voices."

"We're not so particular about the ceremony."

"But you live together as man and wife?"

"We do."

"I see. Go on."

"He thinks that because I'm Catholic by breeding I'd have—what'll I say?—an influence that he, being only a Calvin, would not."

"An influence? Over what?"

"Over the matter at hand."

"And what matter is that?"

"I think he's sent you a letter about it." I take his latest letter from my reticule.

She waves it away. "He has done more than that, Mrs. Burns. He has also come to see us, in person. And, as you probably already know, we have had to refuse his request."

"I do know that, Sister, and I think what Mr. Engels would like—"

"I am very aware of what Mr. Engels would like. What interests me right now is what *you* would like."

"I'd like what he wants."

"And I would like you to speak for yourself."

She joins her hands on the desk. The cross she's wearing—gold with green brilliants—gives me license to stay on the surge of her bust for longer than is proper.

"All right. I'm here to help a man, Edward Dalby. My husband will have told you all about him already. Do you want to hear it again?"

"I want to hear it from you, yes. That is why you have come, is it not?"

"If that's what you want, Sister."

"It is."

I arrange my face to a sober expression, business-like. "Mr. Dalby is a piano maker living in Manchester, and one of the soundest of bodies I know. He borrows from nobody, except in the

extremes of need, and he has such a conscience that always pays back. I'm not going to lie to you, Sister, he's a Communist and has different ideas, but he's desperate. He's lost his wife to the consumption and has been turned out of his trade for his politics. He has three little girls, Sister. Gorgeous wee things. He feels he can't bring them up at home in a proper manner, and has asked Frederick—Mr. Engels—to find places for them."

"And you think the Convent of the Sisters of Providence might be a suitable place?"

"My husband seems to think so."

"Do you think so?"

I shrug. "I don't know, Sister. I haven't thought long on it."

She clears her throat. Lays her hands flat on the desk, the pork of the fingers spreading. It looks like she's about to push herself up, but instead she sighs and joins her hands again. "I take it you do not have children of your own, Mrs. Burns."

"I don't, Sister."

"And Mr. Engels?"

"Nay, not him either."

The pause is so long and deep I can hear my lie echo about in it. Enough of the fibs and the fiction. The time for hiding is past.

"Well, Sister, the truth be known, he has one of his own. A bastard. I know it sounds peculiar."

"Peculiar? Nothing that happens in the world is peculiar, Mrs. Burns. It is simply what happens."

It's only now I've said it that I understand how hard it was to say. Burning in the face, I turn away. Through the window bars, a courtyard. And through the windows on the opposite wall, classrooms. Though my sight doesn't stretch that far, I see in my mind neat rows of identical girls, each repeating the same dree task over and over. It's mean and silly of me, but I can't help thinking of the mill.

"Mrs. Burns?"

"Aye, Sister?"

"Would you like a glass of water?" She gestures to the jug on the sideboard. I shake my head. She looks down at a page on the desk. "Tell me, Mrs. Burns, is he a Catholic, this Mr. Dalby?"

"Sister, if I may?" I nod towards the water, for I've decided on it after all.

"Please do." She doesn't move.

I get up and serve myself. "You're asking if he's a Catholic?" I says when I'm quenched and sat again. She nods. "Let me tell you something, Sister. I had a friend once. A Jew."

"Oh?"

"He used to go round saying he didn't want anything to do with his religion, and true enough, he knew how to buy a beck of pork as well as the next. But I noticed one thing about him."

"And what was that?"

"He didn't work on a Saturday. And he always washed his hands before his meals. And he never used the same knife to cut his meat as he used to spread his butter."

"I'm not sure I gather your meaning, Mrs. Burns."

"All right, then. Look at me." I lean back on the chair to show myself full glory. "I don't go to Mass. I don't deny it. But if I'm passing a chapel, I'll drop into it, to bless myself or have myself a prayer. And I'll do it even when I've money in my pocket and have naught particular to ask for."

"Mrs. Burns, are you saying I should look on Mr. Dalby as a Catholic even if, with his political actions, he works for the destruction of the Church?"

"You'd get to raise his children in the faith. That'd be your gain."

She laughs, and for a moment the bleeding heart of Christ and the mournful Mary and the Savior bearing the cross and the ado-

ration of the Shepherds and Pope Pius (may he live another hundred years) appear to laugh along with her. "You make an interesting argument, Mrs. Burns."

She gets up—wood and leather groaning—and goes to fill a glass of her own from the jug. Sends it down like a whiskey. "You do understand we're not a charity," she says, coming back to her chair. "The fee for boarding is thirteen pounds for the first year and twelve pounds for subsequent years, excluding uniform, travel, and summer holidays. Is it your, um, home-friend who would pay the sum? Thirteen times three makes thirty-nine pounds per year."

"Aye, Frederick'd pay."

"That's a lot of money, Mrs. Burns."

"Aye, a fair amount."

"It would feed five poor families for twice that length of time."

"It would, you're right."

"Give it to any of the workhouses and it would improve the lives of hundreds."

"I can't disown it, Sister, but such charity doesn't interest me. Dalby is a friend."

"And, you know, there are cheaper schools than this one."

"But this is close to our home. We could keep an eye."

"And you would not miss it? The money, I mean?"

"We wouldn't go without. Enough passes through our hands."

"And his child? Mr. Engels's child?"

"Is grown. Has a family and an income of his own."

A long silence that is relieved, final, by the knock on the door.

"Mrs. Burns, I do apologize, but this is my next appointment." She heaves herself up. I gather my things. She brings me to the threshold. Here she wavers. "It is my turn to speak plainly, Mrs. Burns."

"Of course, Sister."

"We are not a charity, as I say, but we do have expenses. Roofs that leak. Walls that need painting. You understand."

"I do."

"The fees do not always cover all the costs. There are always holes to fill."

"I know that well."

"I cannot guarantee anything, but making a contribution to the Order would certainly strengthen your case."

It would be easy to say I've naught about me. It would be easy to say I'll drop back during the week or have Frederick send something in the post. It'd be easy to keep it all for my own ends. But instead I open my purse and pass her the coins, including the one I've taken for myself. I close her fingers over the money.

"You know what, Sister? It's yours. I wish you joy of it."

XVII. The Coming

The business is well ended. A letter has come from the convent: a tuition bill. Frederick embraces me and says, "You're a wonder, Lizzie Burns, a miracle worker," and in my soul it's like a cloud has passed from a dreary scene. Once again I feel part of the affairs of the world, and though I'm breaking old promises made to myself, I find I'm better for it.

I do my morning tasks with a new energy, knowing I don't depend on them to give worth to my time, and when they're done I find I have a healthy hunger on me. I decide to have lunch with the girls in the kitchen. They give me leery looks but don't interfere with me or come at me with backtalk; they can tell I now mean to live as I please.

Just tucking in and there's the door. Jenny glides in with a stamp of pain on her. I'm not disposed to get up and make much of it. Just decided: I'm taking the rest of the day off. A Saint Monday.

Pumps finds her a stool.

"Will you have something?"

"No, no, please, don't let me disturb your lunch."

Easier said than done, with the soughs she sends out over it.

"Is there something wrong, Jenny?"

"Oh, Lizzie, I hate to trespass on your time." Her hand reaches out to seize the wrist I've left idle on the cloth.

I put down my spoon. "You girls finish up here. I'll heat mine up after."

In the morning room Jenny takes the sofa. Beckons me to sit beside her. "Forgive me, Lizzie. I'm a beast for barging in like this."

"That's all right, Jenny. Tell me what's the matter."

The matter—she proceeds by loops and zigzags, but I eventual draw her out into frankness—is that the Girls want to go to France to help Laura with the new babby.

"And you don't want them to go?"

"The war has only just ended, Lizzie. The situation there is very unsettled. It's true Laura is in Bordeaux, away from the heat of Paris. Nonetheless, I'm certain it cannot be safe, two girls traveling there alone. And especially *these* two girls. If anyone found out who they were and what their father did, well—"

"I'm sure if you explain the dangers to them, they'll understand and will decide against such a trip."

"Karl has already given his consent."

"I see."

"He's a scoundrel. A rotten scoundrel. He spoils them to death, Lizzie. And this time, it might literally be *to the death*." She covers her face and lets out a single harrowing sob.

"Oh, Jenny," I says, rubbing her back, "don't be like that. Calm down now. You're only upsetting yourself. Have some tea. You'll feel much the better for it."

I reach for the bell-cord. She stops me by laying hold of my arm. "Please, Lizzie, don't call for anything. I couldn't bear to sit here drinking tea."

"What can I get you instead? Is there anything else I can do for you?"

"No, Lizzie, I don't want to bother you any more than I already have. Really, you are too good for this world."

She separates herself from me. Rubs her face with her handkerchief. Stands. Goes to the mirror. Peers hard at herself.

Slaps her face and stretches back the skin. "Good God, look at me."

I take out the brush I keep in the drawer of the cabinet and go to her. "Here, let me."

I let down her hair and start to brush it. She closes her eyes. Though her mouth is pulled down and her cheeks sagged, though her eyes are circled round by red, the remains of her beauty haven't all fallen by. Even now, at the age when a woman's graces are bound to unfold, she's a damn sight comelier than I've *ever* been. The only thing I have over her is my hair.

Now her eyes flick open as if out of a bad dream.

"And that is not the end of it, Lizzie," she says.

"What else is there, Jenny? Let it out to me now."

And she does. She lets it out. Delivers all the particulars with no hesitatings. It's Karl's carbuncles. They're back. This time ferocious bad.

"There are days when he can only stand upright or lie on his side on the sofa. When he cannot bear the pain any longer, he takes a razor to them himself. Do you credit it, Lizzie? These little operations of his, mercy be on us, they leave these big—"

She shakes her head to rid her mind of the image.

"I cannot bear the sight of it anymore. Nim is taking care of

him for the most part. My spirits have been shattered by the incessant nursing. She seems to withstand it better."

"Is he taking the arsenic?"

"Swilling it like it is his favorite lager."

"Well, that's something."

Her head falls forward to meet her lifting hands, a gesture which tugs on the bit of mop I'm holding. I let go. "Thank you, Lizzie," she says, and, rough as a sailor with his rope, twists it round and jabs the pins back in. She leans into the mirror and inspects. "And to think, I could have had *anybody*."

It's but a slip. We make them, all of us.

"What'd you like me to do?"

"Oh, Lizzie, how it humiliates me to ask you for anything, no matter how small. You and Frederick have already done so much for us. Too much. We owe you nothing less than our lives."

"What is it, Jenny? Are you in need of money? For the doctor?"

Giving herself a last exhausted look, she moves away from her image. Takes a chair from under the writing table. Sets herself up behind it, leans down onto it. "He speaks of a salve Mary used to make for him when he would stay with Frederick in Manchester. Personally, I think he does not need a salve but to get himself to a watering place like Dr. Allen advises, but the man has his own mind, and he is unwilling to let go of the idea of this salve, which he claims will cure any class of corn or carbuncle."

"He wants it now?"

"It is too much for you?"

"Of course not."

"My darling Lizzie, I cannot thank you enough."

"I'll go and see what I can rustle up."

"At least let me help you."

"It's not a bother, Jenny, honest."

But is that all? A bit of cream, is that everything you're after?

I send her upstairs to the Mister and take myself down to the kitchen. Spiv blinks at me over the scales; a shovel of flour suspended in the air between us. I blink back, blank. I've not the murkiest idea about what went into Mary's concoction.

"Spiv, I need to make a salve."

"A what?"

"For Dr. Marx's carbuncles," says Pumps from the chimney corner.

"Oh no," says Spiv, "not likely." Puss-faced, she goes back to her weighing.

"Drop that, Spiv. We can give you a hand with it later. First, a salve. Jenny's biding."

"Is she now?"

"Get out the jars, Pumps."

"I wouldn't know the first thing about making a salve."

"Nor would I. But this, my child, is what you do for your neighbors. You help them."

We scrape something together using the soda, the butter, the linseed, the rosemary, the lavender, the basilicum, and no mean dosing of the arsenic.

"That'll put hairs on his nip," says Spiv.

We've almost beat it into a paste when Jenny pokes her head in. "I am going to run."

"What about this?" I says, nodding at the bowl that Spiv has in a vise between her gut and her forearm, arm working double at the whisk.

"I do apologize, Lizzie, but I have to be in High Holborn in half an hour. We're voting on the women's resolution."

That explains the parlor dress, the posy of flowers.

I go to see her out. She whispers to me at the door. "When you

go up with it, can you talk to him about the Girls? Knock some sense into him?"

"I'll do that, Jenny. Go on, you'll be late."

"You're a precious angel."

"Enough of that now."

"Toodle-oo!" she calls over my shoulder, and is gone.

In the hush that comes after her, we spoon the salve into a jar and put the dirty things into the basin. We listen for the kettle to boil.

"That woman'd take your liver on a plate," says Spiv after a time.

I'm looking at her holding her cheek before I realize I've slapped her.

❦

On a normal day, I'd leave the house before Moss would, my walk to work being longer than his, but on this day I feign an illness and stay till he himself has gone. Then I pack a case. The meaning of the act leaves me unmoved. It seems more important that I fold my things in a way that won't leave them creased. But then life is like that.

I walk to Mary's new place in Salford. Frederick has put her here, and it's a lovely spot, the loveliest I've ever seen. He has not moved in himself, of course, though he says that's only a matter of time. I put my case down on a shining floor of tiles.

"It's gorgeous, Mary," I says.

"Built in the villa style," she says, and now laughs like that's something funny to say.

She shows me round: the kitchen, the garden, her room, my room, the place in the sitting room where the doors have been taken away and the wall knocked down.

"Imagine," I says.

She shrugs and says, "It's a start," in an effort to make it

appear more modest than it is. "It'll do for now," she says, but I can see that she's brimming over, that a high happiness has gripped her. She has the house out of town that she wanted, and now that I've come, she won't be so lonely in it anymore. The world is well again. Things are back on their right course.

I wash and change in my room. Put my few bits into the wardrobe. My case now empty and tucked under the bed, I sit and look out the window—beyond the back wall it's possible to see the line where the chimneys give way to the woods and fields—and wonder would Moss ever be able to find this place. He would if he wanted to, if he *really* wanted to, but I try not think about what I'd do if he did, and instead think about how unfeeling it is of Mary not to ask me any questions about how I feel in myself—how any woman would feel if they were put in my situation—and I know that if I continue to sit here I'll become angry because of it and might say or do something I'll regret, so I get up and go out and try to find a job to busy myself with.

No useful task presents itself to me, however. Everything is perfect. The hearths and windows clean. The ornaments too few for grime to collect. No rugs to muster up old smells. All the little things already paid attention to. If I was to go at this place, I'd achieve nothing except knock the furniture about and make a dust. I stand in the sitting room, in the middle of the red carpet with the border of flooring all around, and I ponder the length of the coming day.

After tea, which she bare touches, she goes to her room without a word. I do the dishing up and then sit for a while in the armchair, but it's hopeless: I *must* know what those noises are. I find her rummaging through her wardrobe.

"Looking for something?" I says.

"Something to wear. Something that bespeaks the occasion."

The occasion, I've been Mary's sister long enough to know, isn't me.

"Going out?"

"Nay, they're coming here. Frederick is bringing a friend over."

At least now I know what has her so excited. It's a rare thing that Frederick brings a friend to the house, and now that's it's happening, it can only mean that he's bending to her wants, that he's beginning to turn on her finger.

"Am I to make myself scarce?" I says.

"Don't give me that, Lizzie," she says, running a hand along the line of hangers. "This is your home now, too."

She picks out a dress and holds it up against her. Looks down at herself. Kicks her leg out to flare the skirts. "Bleh," she says, and stuffs it back in.

"Who is it that's coming?" I says. "The Pope himself?"

"Who?" Her hip cocked and a finger tapping her chin, she peers in at the array, imploring the right mood to make itself known. "Didn't I say before?"

"Nay, Mary, you didn't. "

"An intimate from London."

"And does he have a name, this intimate?"

"Marx. The man Marx is down from London for the week. Staying with Frederick."

Arms crossed, I come around and, with my hip, push the wardrobe door closed.

"Watch! You'll have my fingers!"

"Mary, I thought you *hated* that man."

"Karl? Not a bit. It's his wife that's not right. He's grand, a big pet actual, when you get him out of her company. Now, if you don't mind."

She pushes me aside and opens the wardrobe again. Reaches in, as if for any old thing, and throws it onto the bed.

"I suppose it'll have to be this one. Help me, can you?"

She steps out of her flannel wrapper and into the dress. Turns to give her back to me.

"I just can't grasp it," I says, pulling hard on her ties.

She sighs. "What is it, exact, that you can't grasp?"

"Naught, except I can't understand how you can entertain this man, after all his wife has said about you. It's a mystery to me. A God-made mystery."

I poke her to tell her it's done, and she goes over to look at herself in the glass. Sucks herself in and rubs a hand down her front.

"Is it right to have him here? I'd be embarrassed. For you, I'd be."

She throws her eyes up and plonks down at her toilet table. Strains towards herself. "Is there time for the curling irons, do you think?"

I come to stand behind her. Look at her through the mirror. "Well, tell me at least, will he be expecting something? A fancy deal?"

"What he'll be expecting is less opinion from you, I'll tell you that much."

She's ready hours before they arrive, but now, when the knock comes, she runs to her bedroom and slams the door behind.

"*I'll* get it, then," I says, hoping my tone will carry through to the outside, where the men are waiting.

He's got hairy hands, I notice, when he takes mine to kiss it. And his coat is buttoned wrong. Frederick walks him in and tours him around the room like he owns it, which of course he does.

"Mary'll be out in a minute," I says. "She's fallen behind in her day."

Frederick puts Karl standing by the fire, arranges four chairs around it, and goes to get the drinks. Karl won't sit till I'm down. "*Bitte,* Miss Burns," he says, gesturing to the chair, a light moving in his dark eyes. "Please do sit down."

Frederick carries four glasses over, two in each hand. He serves us and, releasing a satisfied moan, installs himself in his chair. He drinks from one glass and holds the other on his lap for Mary.

"So where have you lads come from?" I ask, my voice nervous in front of this new stranger.

"A charity ball," says Karl, "at the—" He slurs something in the German.

"The German Club," says Frederick. He tries to cross a leg over but it slips off his knee; his boot lands heavy on the floor. "A choir concert in aid of the poor immigrants."

"By the cut of you both," I says, drawing a circle in the air around them, "that's not the only place you've been."

Frederick laughs. "You see?" he says to Karl. "What did I tell you?"

Karl lifts his glass and burps out a chuckle.

Mary appears, drawn out by the laughter and the envy it brings up inside of her. She kisses Karl on both cheeks, Frederick on the mouth, and takes her drink from him. She raises up to Karl, and goes round to touch all of our glasses, before she sits back into her place.

Frederick does most of the talking. Speaks at length and with great force about the boredom of Manchester. The dullness of office life. The commerce and its accursed tasks that are impinging on his Communism.

"I'm bored to death," he says. "I drink rum and water, and spend my time between twist and tedium."

We laugh, for though his meaning is serious, he speaks so correct, and with such humor, that to laugh is to give his speech the

true weight it's due. Karl appears the happiest body amongst us: as he listens to Frederick; as he argues with him; as he cuts in to share secret things in the German, the good temper doesn't fall from his face, and it's clear they adore each other.

Trust Mary, in the middle of such easy goings, to call attention to what we're ignoring. We, to be civil, are looking past it, over it, beyond it; *she* can't help but point her big finger right at it.

"Are you well there, Karl?" she says.

"Me?" he says, surprised.

"You look to be having trouble with your arm," she says. "I see you are in pain when you lift your glass to drink."

"Thank you for your concern, Mary, but it's nothing," he says.

And that ought be enough for a body; enough to tell her it's a question she has no business with. But Mary won't leave a thing alone, not if she thinks it's a way into a man's affections. So she keeps at him, she presses and presses, and now Frederick joins her—"She won't stop till you tell her, *mein Freund.* You might as well give it up"—till the man caves in and lets it out; till he coughs and fidgets around and, red-faced, falls to admitting that indeed there is something the matter: something carbuncular, just under his arm, which is making movement a nuisance and writing a torture.

Frederick makes light of it; it's his way of helping Karl out of his shame. "Do you believe him, ladies? This is the excuse he's been giving us for not having completed his Economics."

Karl scoffs at his friend and turns to address Mary. "It's a terrible bother, Miss Burns. The doctor has tried to drain it, but no opening or discharge could be induced. I've applied every remedy and compress known to medical science, all in vain."

Mary can't conceal her fascination. "Let's have a look," she says.

Karl waves a refusing hand.

"Pop your shirt off and let me see it. I might be able to help."

He looks at her a moment, hopeful: perhaps this Irish woman *can* help! But now he shakes his head and covers his eyes with his hands. "Christ, I've had too much to drink."

Frederick laughs. "Come, Karl, no need for reserve. You're not in London now."

Mary stands in front, so that most of his bulk is hidden behind her, and helps him out of his jacket and shirt. She lays these over him to cover his naked paunch. Now she takes his hand and levers up his arm. Glistening in the firelight, mottled red and green, it's at least the size of an egg. The sight of it turns me ill.

"Hmm," Mary says, and puts the arm back down.

"The problem," says Frederick, "is that he refuses to take the arsenic."

Karl reaches an arm across his belly, to keep the jacket and shirt from slipping off. "I have my doubts about that stuff."

Frederick clicks his tongue. "You're impossible, Karl. Drinking arsenic doesn't hinder you in your ordinary way of life in any manner. Twice a day for three or four months, and you'll be rid of this business finally."

Karl groans.

"And you need to take more exercise. It's good of Jenny that she dutifully drags you out to go for walks. I hope she doesn't allow herself to be scared off by your physical indolence disguised as your need to work."

"For goodness sake, do you want the Book written or not?"

"We do. Desperately. If all else fails, I'll make a few pounds available to get you to Karlsbad."

"Nay." From her standing position, her hips held firm in her hands, Mary demands our attending. "Keep your money, Frederick. And, Karl, you're right to stay clear of the normal prescrip-

tions. What you have isn't a carbuncle at all but an abscess. It's in a bad state of neglect, on account of you treating it as something that it's not. What it needs is a good rub with something that'll take the poison out of it. Sit tight. I have just the thing."

With that—her expert judgment given—she swishes off to the kitchen. I follow her in. The walls are too thin to permit me a speech, so instead I fix my face in the tone of "What, sister child, are you playing at?" My look doesn't escape her, and her response is to wink back at it—the scab-bag—and put the kettle on to boil.

She goes back in with Lord-knows-what stirred into her bowl. She kneels in front of Karl and soaks a bit of cotton. "This'll sting now," she says.

"What is it?" he says.

"Never you mind," she says. "Something from where we come from."

Karl clenches his teeth. He calls out German oaths. But then, after the third or fourth soaking, he grows calmer, soothed not by any special ingredient, of course, but by the attention, the rubbing in, which she makes a theater of doing, in her good dress, her knees on the floor, and her sleeves turned back.

Mary says it's only when Jenny is around that Karl acts shabby towards her, and though I've never got solid proof of this, for I don't go with them on their trips to the capital, I see now that Mary might be right. He enjoys her attention; by his gestures and words, he shows himself fond of her; this, it seems, is his real feeling.

"You have the nurse's touch," he says to her, smiling and reaching out to put his hairies on her waist.

What it is, I think, is that he's a family man; a real family man like Frederick will never be. He cares for his own blood and kin above all else, and it has never occurred to him to cross his wife or

put his friend's poor choices above her. Fundamental in his mind, more fundamental than his politics even, is the belief that his family should live high, that they should be protected from the hostile and vulgar world: if his wife sits in judgment of Mary, if she goes as far as being cruel and personal with her, then she must have a good reason, even if he himself doesn't share it.

Watching Mary now, as she helps him back on with his shirt, I begin to have thoughts I've never had before. I'm going to have your life, is what I think. I'm going to have your life, but without the mistakes. Without the need for all this carrying on. Without anything old to count against me.

I turn to Frederick, and by the arrangement of his face, I can tell he's only half-enjoying the scene; part of him is uneasy and doesn't trust it. I catch his eye, and his way of looking at me covers me with happy confusion. Pictures of a life with him, an honest life, come between me and the room, and for a moment I'm lost in them. By thinking that it might be, however, I arrive at the conviction that it never could be. My heart sinks and settles, and though I can't see into his body, I can only suppose his heart is in agreement: these are but thoughts in the air with no spirit.

With the bad winds and the lack of cabs, I've a parch on me by the time I get to the Marxes, but I'm not offered anything to lift it, and I know by the hardship in Nim's face not to ask.

"Are the Girls here?" I says.

"Gone to get new bonnets for France," she says.

"So it's definite? They're going?"

She shrugs as if to say, "Don't ask me, I only clean the pots." She takes my coat and reticule. Tries to take the jar with the salve from me. I tell her I want to present that myself, and clutch it close.

She frowns and leads me towards the kitchen, but there's fluid on my knees and a pain in my lung, after all that walking against the gales, and I have to sit on the stairs to cough it out.

She slaps my back. "Here, give me that."

"Nay, I'll bring it up to him."

"What can it be that you're so close with it? Gold dust?"

I look at the face between the graying locks. It's sincere. She knows naught about a salve. "I want to give it to him myself, that's all."

I take the teaspoon of sugar she brings and start up the stairs.

"Mrs. Burns, it has taken me all morning to get him onto his back. Please do not disturb him. I can give him the gift on your behalf later."

"I won't be a second, I promise. He's gone and ordered it special."

"What is it he has ordered?"

"A salve. Jenny says he's been crying out for it, the relief it gives him."

"A salve? Is that what she said?"

"It is and all."

She lets out the quiet air of a body that's making the best of things. "I'll be in the kitchen."

I find Karl wrapped in cataplasms and lying stiff as a stave across his divan. He's reading from a book held out to one side. He strains his neck round. "Oh, Lizzie, it's you!" He closes the book and wedges it into the space between himself and the cushions. Shifts as if to hide himself. Crosses his arms across his pot. "I cannot stand for you to see me like this. If I had known—"

"Please don't move, Karl. Stay as you are. I'll only be a moment."

Groaning, he sits up. "No, no. Be as long as you like, my dear Lizzie, it is a tonic to see a different face." It's clear his new

position pains him, and after only a moment of it, he collapses onto his side. "I would like best to hang on a tree in the air."

I make my way through the heaps and stacks on the floor, and clear a space among the papers on his desk for the jar. Now I kneel on the carpet beside him, put a hand on his forehead.

"Touching anything is nasty for me," he says. "But that feels wonderful."

"I brought some of Mary's salve. Maybe that'll help you to get comfortable."

"Ah, the old Irish salve! I'd clean forgotten about that. It used to help. Very thoughtful of you, Lizzie."

I shake my head, as if to fend off the thanks, but really I'm thinking, How many separate stories are playing out at a single time, in a single house?

"I'd rub some into you now, only I'd be hard-pressed to find a spot between your coverings."

He smiles. "You know, it is funny"—his face bright with fresh effort—"I was just thinking before you came, it would have been better if this affliction had been given to a good Catholic who could have turned his suffering to some account!"

"True," I says, "but you ought take comfort. The bourgeoisie will have good reason to remember your suffering from a true proletarian disease!"

"Ah, do not make me laugh!" He draws his legs up and splutters. "Ah, ah, it hurts, it hurts too much." He bellows and bellows, and I'm sorry for it now, for it's a pity to watch its slow and certain turning. "Oh, Lizzie, all the muck has been thrown at once."

I smooth back his hair, a pitying gesture, but I'm afraid to handle him anyplace else, for the aggravation it might cause.

"I thought I was properly back on my feet. I was working away gaily, but now this." He takes my hand from where it's resting on

his head and kisses it. Puts it between his palms and keeps it there. "I am being the best of patients. I am allowing myself to be soaked in all sorts of vinegars and limes, and smothered in remedies."

"Oh, how *well* you have to be to be ill!"

He grins, ear to ear. "Now I am back on the arsenic cure, since an end must at last be put to this state of affairs."

"I'm sure you're only delighted about that, Karl."

"Delighted indeed. Dr. Allen laughs at my reservations, and Frederick just thinks I am being difficult."

"Maybe you ought hearken to them."

"Pah! If I listened to Allen, all I would take in is that poison, and if it were up to Frederick, I would be out every morning taking uphill hikes. Fresh air, his cure for every blessed thing. I would like to see *him* walk with boils where I have them."

I laugh. He's a good man. As good as you let him be good.

"Jenny was down with us before."

"Oh?"

"She's worried about the Girls going to France."

"She worries too much."

"The war, Karl. Any mother would fret."

"Well, she need not. The war is over—she knows this—and the Prussians have prevailed. The Girls will be safe as long as they be-have like good English ladies. Besides, they are grown and need some world experience. And their sister needs them."

I touch his cheek. "You know best, Karl. I just told her I'd men-tion it."

"Thanks, Lizzie. I know you are only being a friend."

I get up to leave. He pleads an extra few minutes. "I can't, Karl. Get some rest and I'll see you soon."

He smiles, holds on to my dress. "Why don't we see more of you?"

"It's a busy time."

"When the Girls go away, my wife will be wanting for company. She does have Nim. And her contacts outside. The woman always seems to be running off somewhere. But it would be good for her, I think, to have a true friend to confide in. She'll be worried."

"It won't be easy for her. All the Girls away."

"Come and see her, please."

"When I can."

In the kitchen, Nim is standing in front of a bottle of beer. There's a glass set out on the table, but I suck from the neck. It's sour and old, but I'm glad of it. "Merciful hour, what's that noise?" I says, unable to ignore the screeching that's coming from the scullery.

"That?" She saunters over and, in a pleased manner, swings the door open.

A plague of rats; a gush.

I'm onto a stool before my knees can even whisper a complaint.

Nim folds her arms and sneers over at me. "You weren't expecting that, were you, Mrs. Burns?"

The kittens, as my cooling mind now understands them to be, scratch at the legs of the stool, jump up to catch the hem of my dress. I hiss them away and step down. As soon as I'm on the floor again, however, they rush back, the whole ragged pack, and climb up my yards as far as my waist. I serve them out full swing. Nim gets the most determined ones off with the broom and sweeps them back into the scullery. Those that escape her peep out from the shadows.

"Tommy?" I says.

She nods. "Eight in all."

"Not bad for the old grimalkin."

"We've let them grow too big. Mrs. Marx would not let me get

rid of them before. She thought she would be able to give them away as pets. But now—"

"Now?"

"Now she has finally come round. But of course she doesn't have the stomach to do it herself. She refuses to help me and I cannot do it alone. There are too many of them, I have tried."

She puts the broom away and turns to me. "It has to be done before Tussy gets home. She would not stand for it. It has to be done *now*."

Are you ever stood wanting for speech? Are you ever stood wanting for speech while inside you're yelling out for the truth of things to be spoken? *So this is it, Jenny! This is my purpose to you! Not some silly salve, but this!*

"Get a sack," I says. "I'll put the water on."

Our hands and wrists are left cut and scored, our sleeves and fringes frayed, but we make a bundle of the whole number eventual. We're agreed: all at once in the big basin. One-by-one and we'll lose our nerve and leave the job done halfways.

All of our hands are needed to hold them under. I'm startled by the struggle nature can make from even the smallest of its examples. Nim doesn't seem so impressed, being so small herself, and so strong.

Our arms cross. Our hips bump. The heat of the water stings. We exchange winces. "Your pinny is soaked," I says, to keep our minds off. She looks down and nods. I'm close enough to smell her, the German hooer.

⌇

"That German hooer!" Mary screams, and I come away from my room to see what's the matter. She has come through the door without closing it and thrown herself onto the sofa with

her hat yet pinned. "That German hooer! She's gone and ruined everything!"

It's our first summer in the Salford house. Frederick hasn't yet moved in, and I'm not holding my breath, but I'm not spiteful about it either. For I've changed about him. My pride has softened. The protection I didn't want from him before, I'm grateful for now. A roof over my head and everything provided, no question? Down on my hands and knees, morning and night, is where I ought be.

"Whisht, Mary," I says, by now long used to the overactions of her heart, "you'll have the neighbors interested."

When I look through the door she's left open, I can see the garden, and beyond that, other gardens, whole lines of them. Moss would have liked it here, on the edge of everything, where there's a quiet I've never known, a quiet that makes me wonder how I ever put up with the noise, how I ever lived in those courts without losing my wits about them. Here we have it all—the green and the air—without even the bother of the landlady, who goes to collect her rates from Frederick direct, at his own flat by the mill. This is where Mary has come from: Frederick's public chambers.

"Bitch! Bitch! Bitch!"

I close the door, walk round the sofa, and fold my arms over her. "What's wrong with you?"

She's pounding the cushion. "Bitch! Bitch!"

Sighing, I go and wet some tea. Then I sit and bide for her at the table. She comes in when she hears the rattling of the spoon against the cup.

"The Marxes have got a new maid," she says.

"So?"

"Sent over from Germany by Jenny's mother. Helen's her name but they call her Nim."

"Why Nim?"

"They like those sorts of games."

"They do? And what about her, this Nim?"

"She's had a babby."

Frederick. My inklings flock to him like moths to a lamp. I'm already counting back the nine months to October and trying to remember, was he in London or where?

She pushes back from the table to get her lungs into the wail. "She's called the bastard Freddy!" She tears at her hair, thumps at her breast. "The ugly tart has called him Freddy!"

Now, I think. Now, final, she will lose her faith in him.

I stand up. As it is when there's a death, the tasks lie clear before me. "That's it," I says. "We're leaving this place."

She stops her wailing sudden. Grapples at her throat. "Leaving?"

"We're not staying here a minute longer. Pack your things."

"Lizzie, hold a moment." She stands and reaches out for me, but I step from her.

"Do as I say, Mary."

"Hearken to me, Lizzie."

"I don't want to hear any more."

"It's to be fostered out. He's going to pay its way, but he'll not have anything to do with it. We'll not ever have to lay eyes on it. It'll be like it didn't happen."

"Did he tell you all this himself? Are these words from his own mouth?"

"Isn't it better I heard it from him?"

I feel sick. "Mary, clamp it now. I don't want to hear it."

I go into the living room and open the window: breeze in the trees and birdsong. There's such things here. It was grand while it lasted.

"Where do you want us to go?" she says, coming in on me.

"I don't know and I don't care. But it's not for us here. I don't want another penny of that man's mint."

"But, Lizzie—"

"Sorry, Mary, I'll not do it. I'll not stand here and hearken to you defend the wrong thing again."

"Lizzie, you wicked bitch." She grabs my hoop with both her hands.

Pulling free, my stitches shred. "You'll pay for that," I says.

"Jealous is all you are, Lizzie Burns. You've always been jealous of me."

"Give it over," I says, making to walk out.

"You've always wanted him."

"Don't start this, Mary," I says from the door. "You know well how I feel about him and his kind."

"The kind that puts you up and pays for your meat and gravy?"

"The kind that puts his hand on your arse in public, as if it's the most natural thing, and then asks to be a called a gent."

"Fine sentiments, Lizzie. But where are they when he hands over the rates?"

"That's to be no more. Things can't go on as they are. Mr. Engels is none of our sweat and blood, nor any way connected with us. We owe him naught. We can leave here now and still keep our heads up."

"We? I'm not going anyplace. All the matter needs is time to be forgot."

I'm gone, through the kitchen and into the yard, for I can't be doing with it.

She follows after me. "Lizzie, hearken to me, for pity's sake."

"There's no sugaring this over, Mary. There's no forgiving it."

"The child is to be given away. Nim is to keep her position.

Naught has to change, if we just keep our cool and try not to look too long at it."

Furious, I cross to the plot and go through the pantomime of checking on the cabbages. My hands have minds to tear them all up. "Here's what I tell you, Mary Burns. He'll not be for taking a wife, not ever."

She laughs. *Laughs.* "You think me a dullard? You think I don't know that?"

"I think you a fool to yourself."

"I love him."

"You ought be ashamed, still wanting the company of such a man."

"Did you hear me? I love him."

"Nay. What it is, you've already built too much onto him and you can't bear to have it fall down about you. I can see the dreams he lets you have. Hag-rode you are, by visions of the high life. You'll not go back to the old way, in town, that's what's wrong with you. You're spoilt and you'll not go back."

She takes my shoulder, twists me round. "And you, Lizzie, would you go back?"

I can't look at her but have to look over her. Over the roof to where the clear sky, the clearest blue sky, is blurring.

"Tell me, Lizzie, what's the fear in you?"

"Oh, Mary." I look at her now, and through my tears I see her calm and composed. "What if he goes and does another flit? Back to Germany or wherever else?"

She shakes her head. "What can he ever do to me that I've not already survived?"

"Every time he'll find a new way of hurting you."

"And me, I'll find a new way of keeping him." She pats her belly. "My turn will come."

Unbelieving, I watch her smile. I've never seen a lass so beaten, nor so resolved.

She kisses me and turns to go back inside.

I look down at the cabbages. "If I ever set eyes on that German hooer, I'll—"

———

Nim looks startled when I first take tight of her wrist, but now her face settles into an arrangement that says she's been waiting for this moment a long time. The animals have stopped struggling. The water is still. Our hands are still sunk in it. I'm not certain what I want to do with this thin little bone of hers, whether I want to use it to pull her to me or push her away; it feels ready to do whatever I will it.

"Helen," I says.

She blinks.

"Helen, listen to me. It's not your fault. I don't hold it against you."

She sighs and shakes her head. "Mrs. Burns, please"—there's pity, frigid pity in her voice—"do not do this."

"I'd like to help. I feel sorry for the boy. His treatment has been wrong. I feel a duty to make up for Frederick."

"No, Mrs. Burns. You must not say these things. You must stay out of business that is not yours."

"I'm sorry." Seared by her tone, I let go. I look at my hand under the water, old-looking and raw. "Forgive me."

"*Bitte*, Mrs. Burns, let's just get this done."

We lift the sack out, heavier now that they're dead and sodden, and carry it to the storeroom, lock it away from the mice.

"If I bury them, the dog will dig them up."

"The rag-and-bone man will take them in the morning. Sure, he'll be thrilled with them."

She looks at me.

"For his hogwash," I says.

Disgusted, she turns back into the kitchen.

We wipe our hands and arms dry, roll down our sleeves.

She sees me out. Opens the dining-room door on the way. Points down.

"New carpet?"

"Tell her you saw it."

March

XVIII. A Fantastic Standing Apart

News comes of a rebellion in France. The workers have seized power from the new government, and a Commune has been declared. Frederick is somber when he tells me; humorless and unsmiling.

"Doesn't it excite you?" I says. "Isn't this what we've been waiting for?"

"It is an accident of the war, nothing more. It has no chance of success."

"Nay?"

He shakes his head. "Won't last."

"Well, even so, aren't you happy that *something* is coming about?"

He looks up from his newspaper. Folds it over and drops it down. Pushes his cup to the center of the table to make room for his elbows. "Lizzie, you must understand, we have been

campaigning to *prevent* this kind of doomed outbreak. Upsetting the government, so soon after the Prussian crisis, is a desperate folly. The onus on the French workmen is to perform their duties as citizens, to calmly and resolutely improve the opportunities of republican liberty, for the purpose of class organization. Without organization and planning, without international association, the emancipation of labor is impossible."

"I just thought you'd be happy, is all."

"I'm not unhappy, Lizzie. Not unhappy at all. I just understand the reality of these things. The inevitable demise of premature actions."

I brush into my hand some crumbs from the damask, rub them off onto my plate. "So, what are you going to do?"

"Observe. See how it develops."

"That's it?"

"What more do you suggest?"

"I don't know. You could lecture the working men about what's happening. Try to get a spark going here."

"Hmm." He yawns, stretches out his limbs. "The problem is, we don't know yet *what* is happening. When we have an idea, we shall make our opinions public. We cannot jump on every bandwagon that passes." He leans back on his chair, joins his hands behind his head. "Besides, Karl is still unwell. On top of everything else, he has bronchitis now, and he complains of his liver. Under the circumstances, I do not see another course than to sit tight and wait our time."

"There is nothing I can do, then?"

"No, *mein Liebling.* Not for now. You are off the hook, as they say."

I sigh. Look out the window at the whirling of the trees and the clouds moving fast above them. The room brightens and darkens,

brightens and darkens. "Well, at least the Girls won't go to France. Not after this."

He shrugs. "I can't see why they wouldn't."

"I can see plenty of reasons, their well-being being the first."

"They will be fine."

"Karl just doesn't have the steel to stop them."

"Karl is giving his daughters the largest gift a father can give: their own free choice."

Nay, he's just soft. And you're weak. But men *are*.

April

XIX. Sacred Land

The rebellion in France has turned to civil war. The forces of government have surrounded Paris and the workers' Commune is under siege. But here, on the other side, there's only the flat routine of the weeks. The dull of waking and sleeping. The boredom of tea and shopping. The bitterness of thoughts.

I sit on my bed and look at another day drawing out in front of me and, in a shot, am back downstairs with my bonnet on.

"Pumps, I've to run a message."

"In this weather?"

"I'm not asking your permission."

"Uncle Fred says you've to watch for your lung."

"Mr. Engels."

"Mr. Engels says you've to—"

It's not my health she's worried about, the scut, but the aspersions cast on me by those who aren't free to come and go as they list.

"A bit of rain won't kill me."

"But look." She holds up the bunch of drawers. "There's still all this to do."

"Do it yourself, can't you?" I turn to leave. Change my mind and come back. "Second thoughts, go help Spiv in the kitchen."

"Do I have to?"

"Go on, and none of your cod."

"What'll I tell him?"

"Tell him I'll be home to serve the supper."

Hate to say it, the child is right. Bad in the head, you'd have to be, to go out in this. Pulling my collars up and wrapping my coat around, I turn onto Rothwell Street, go down St. George's Road as far as Fitzroy, and now up to the railway cottages on Gloucester Road. Black smoke rises up over the roofs from the engine shed behind Dumpton Place. On the corner: a pub I've often seen and know to be in Irish hands.

I skip the ladies' saloon and go straight into the main bar, empty but for a couple of daytime stragglers.

"So this is where it all happens," I says, taking a seat at the counter.

The barman stops his wiping to plant a look on me.

"You can serve me here, man. There's no law against it."

He turns out, after much goading, to be a Bert.

"So, Bert, what's the name of this place, anyhows?"

"Didn't you read the sign outside?"

"I didn't."

"The Lansdowne."

"That's all I'm asking. I'll remember it from now on."

I hold my glass out and shake it till he refills it.

"I've heard about you," he says.

"All good, I'm sure," I says.

"Wouldn't say that," he says.

He's a tough nut, there's granite in him, but after a time—after I flatter him with compliments about the cut of his bar and after I shout him a short *out* of my own pocket—he falls to speaking about his affairs: the wife upstairs and the children. He's sure to look gloomy on them, and to make as if to envy me, with my none, for he's a man raised never to speak high of himself, it only opens you up to charges, and is a waste of time, anyhows, for you can't judge a fella by the idea he has of himself.

There's a thirst on me that won't be quenched. I have another, and soon we're talking like intimates and have much in common. Like myself, he's of the species of Irish not born there—it was his grandparents who came over—and he holds no love for the newcomers.

"Grecians," he calls them. "The cut of these Grecians coming over here to take the bread from our mouths."

I like him because he appears to take my meaning from few words, and in spite of my caution, a caution that comes from the fact that I've not heard an undecent word from him, nor an oath, and I wouldn't want him to think me the type either.

"You're right about that, Bert," I says. "What we're getting now is the lowest description of Irish."

"A discredit to their origins," he says. "The Famine was a thing, but it's long over now and there's no excuse for them."

He goes to take an empty glass from a table. Puts it into his bucket and washes it around. Wipes it clean with his rag. Puts it back on the shelf.

"Can I tell you, Mrs. Burns?"

"You can."

"I'm wondering about your being here."

"You are?"

"I mean, it's a man's nature to be seen in a pub. He needs no business to be here, it's just one of his natural homes. A woman alone in a tavern, but, that's another story. There's always a reason for it. Are you looking for someone?"

"Not anyone you'd find in this part of town."

"Where'd you find him, so, if you went looking?"

"I'm told he's in St. Giles, around there."

"The Rookery? You don't want to go there, Mrs. Burns."

"I might have to, Bert."

"Full of thieves and whores and cadgers' lodgings at fourpence a night."

"I've heard."

He narrows his eyes to try and get inside of me. "Well, it's the only reason anyone from the outside would go to St. Giles. To find someone."

"Is that right?"

"And you'll never find him, whoever it is you're looking for. Any priest will tell you who's ever opened a mission there: it swallows them up. Whole families. Whole people. They mix with darkies and offcomers, and don't care a whit about it. More chance of finding a brown button in a boghole."

"You might be right, Bert. But sometimes in life we don't get a vote. We have to do what's in our hearts to do."

He's uneasy in the mind about my intentions, but he can hear from my tone that my mind is made, so he gives me the directions, and without my even having to ask for them. I put them to my memory. Across the Canal and past the Barracks. Right to the Park and down by the railings as far as the Crescent. If I have the money, there's a cab rank there, but if I'm short and have the breath to spare, I can go the rest of the way on foot: down and left onto the wide road, Oxford Street, and then, after another twenty minutes

of walking, right into the Rookery. He thinks I must be going out of religion, to convert a man or to save him from ruin.

"Your pilgrimage to the sacred land," he says.

"Not a bit of it, man," I says. "Do you see me barefoot?"

His laugh is cut short by a voice coming down from upstairs. He goes into the back room and shouts up to answer it. I use the chance to take my leave.

In St. Giles it's as if God has released His revelations and is calling closing time on the world. On the short skip from the cab to the first alley, I have to step over two bodies lying in the gutter, and get past four or five beggars, each more staggered than the next. I feel the drink rise to my head and buy an orange from a coster, lean back against a bit of empty wall to refresh myself.

"Wouldn't mind a bit of that," says the man sat on paving stones on the corner, eating an onion. "Wouldn't mind a bit of that round *this*," he says, clutching the front of his breeches.

In places like this, naught can be full enjoyed.

I give what's left of the orange to a ragged child and push on, closing my nose against the slops that are flung down and the pools that stand reeking, pulling in my skirts against the squeeze of the passing bodies: the Ireland-born and the England-bred, the dirty sons and daughters of the Hunger, come to grabble out their fortunes in the holy gutter.

I ask around for a drinking place. I'm pointed in every direction. I find my own way to a shebeen at the end of a passage. I have to dance round a dust heap that's been dumped in front of the door: the grime-glass, worm-ate, creaky-cracky door that doesn't invite opening and ought be changed along with the crowd.

The wind gushes as I open, bringing the stink inside with me. It's full. Yet hours to go before the work bells ring and it's bursting, the glut of them Irish. The man, Paudy, is glad when I ask his

name, but grumbles when I hand him back my cup, as if a little top-up will make him bankrupt. I move to the snuggery, which comes free when a pair of neckers take their display outside. The snuggery panels are bits of old doors and cupboards. Inside, the smoke is caught and the seats are rubbed raw of their cushion. I stay where I am, despite. The gap gives me a good view of the bar, and keeps my looks hidden.

A stranger man comes in on me after a time.

"It's yourself," he says, "and in your fineries too."

"Would that be me you're addressing?" I says.

"You and no one else, though I know the mistake in it."

"Your mistakes are your own, man, I didn't ask you to interfere."

Pure rotted by the lush, he moans and staggers in his clogs. Fumbles for something in his pocket. I swear you can tell a man's whole story by his comb and the number of teeth left on it. He rakes the few strands he has left across his pate.

"What is it you want off me?" I says. "Do I owe you anything?"

"Wouldn't take your mint, even if you did," he says.

"Well, off with you, then. I don't want to be spoken to."

The lush can give you a confidence that's terrible. I've always thought it, though I take a sup myself. The worst, it can blind you to the difference between what's thought and what's said.

Says he: "I only came to you to ask how you are and would you share a drop with me."

"Don't mind my health and leave me to myself where I'm happy."

"Have I seen you before?"

"You haven't."

"Are you looking for someone?"

Knowing I'll not be rid of him, I get up and push past him to the bar. On my way through I hear some things that aren't compli-

ments and some hard words, too. I sometimes think that because my shoulders are wide and my waist doesn't go in, that because my speaking holds its share of Irish, I'm taken for solid, when it's tender I really am in broad light and with sober senses.

Still, I'll not be beaten by it. I stay dogged and drink on my feet. I drop Moss's name to Paudy and some other drinkers whose faces I trust, but they can't help me.

"Never heard of him," they says.

And it's just as well, for it's all got too much in here, with the patterer bawling out the top lines from a ragged-looking *Irishman*, and now the last-dying speeches of the martyrs Larkin and O'Brien, and all the howling that goes along with it, so I come away.

Down the road, things are quieter. I sit at a table by the only window.

"What're you having?" the man calls out. "I'll bring it over to you."

"You're very good," I says, when he sets the glass down in front of me.

"Are you all right, missus?" he says.

"All right?"

"You had your head in your hands. Have you a pain there?"

I tell him I'm grand, only I don't know why I bothered with the other place, mouthfuls of dirt with your drink, the species of hole that people fall into no matter how hard they train themselves to walk around. He laughs and says he hopes I'm not saying the same about his place somewhere else, and I laugh in my turn and says I hope that crowd and all belonging to them are swept back to where they came from, and he says it's a pity strong speeches come into the mind when it's too late to say them.

He's a Noonan, and has a gentle air, dependable, so I come straight out with my business.

"Moss O'Malley?"

"Aye. Came down from Manchester. Four years or so ago."

"No. Doesn't ring a bell. He's not one of the ones that comes in here, anyway. Do you know what he does for his money?"

I shake my head.

"You might try down the Docks. That's where a lot of them end up."

I pay a boy to take me out of the Rookery to the main road.

"How much would it be to the Docks?" I says to the cabby.

"From here it'd cost you six bob, ma'am."

The spin in my head prevents me from seeing into my purse, so I have to reach in and count with my fingers. "I'm short," I says. "Take me home."

"Where's home?"

And for a moment I can't think of the address.

XX. The Horrors

Morning queer won't kill you. It's only the lush that stands inside you pickling. But if you stay lolling in it—dreaming miserable half-dreams about what you said and did—it can make your spirit bitter. The trick is "up and out": rouse yourself up and fetch it out. Clean of the old, you'll then be fit and primed for the new. Claret is the best cure. I order a glass with a rasher of bacon.

"How are you feeling?" says Spiv, bringing the gridiron over to the table and tilting it so the meat falls—*flop!*—onto my plate.

"Fine, Spiv, thank you. Has Mr. Engels had his breakfast?"

"Ages ago."

"What did he have?"

"The usual."

Toast with butter and jam, porridge with salt. Eggs once a week. Kidneys if the energies are down. Cold ham or tongue if there's guests. And the papers for company; always them.

"Get the cheese from the stores," I says, for eating has given me an appetite. "And the jam. And if there's no fresh bread to spread it on, bring me the plum duff instead. I'm dying for something sweet."

Tussy and Janey call while I'm still halfway hungry. They come right into the kitchen and take stools to join me at the table.

"We've come to say goodbye," says Tussy.

"So you're going after all?"

"Of course! There was never any question of canceling. We just had to find the right moment."

"And you decided on this one?"

"We can't delay any longer. The baby is ill and Laura is alone with it. Paul has gone to Paris."

"Won't it be dangerous?"

"Well, if the barricades tempt him to go in for fighting—"

"Nay, I mean dangerous for *you*. Traveling over there at such a time. What if someone finds out who you are? They'll think you're working for the Commune and you'll be shot."

"Oh, Aunt Lizzie, we appreciate your concern, but there's no need to worry. We intend to travel under assumed names. And by all accounts, Bordeaux is a tedious place. Laura says she's bored. She wishes to be back in Paris. I think she would have gone with Paul if she had found someone to whom she could have trusted the child."

I offer them food, they refuse, and I'm glad, for the truth is, I'm tired to death and not at all well, and as much as I love them and want to be good to them, right now I'm craving my own company. Oblivious, they stay on and tell me their travel plans, how the railway line has been cut off so they have to catch the steamer, and other such details that on an average day I'd enjoy but today I can't

even keep track of. My chin slips from my hand and my head falls
to my chest.

"Aunt Lizzie?"

"I'm sorry, Girls."

"You are tired. We should leave you."

"Excuse my manners. It's just I'm not feeling the best."

I stand to see them out, but they wave me down.

"Stay where you are, Aunt Lizzie. We know the way to the
door."

I don't argue.

Tussy touches my shoulder on her way out. "Look after yourself, please, Aunt Lizzie. Why don't you call on Dr. Allen?"

I go back to bed and have a cry. I'm sad to see the Girls go, and
am worried for them, but what upsets me more is my behavior just
now, the mistakes I made in front of them. And last night, too, going about in the world, letting loose Moss's name in the society
of strangers. And Frederick. He must take some of the blame. For
leaving me idle when there's a revolution going on and plenty that
could be done. And for not taking me with him anywhere, never
showing me anyplace. And Mary, well, isn't she the first source of
it all—

Sleep doesn't come. I weary of thinking, and yet thinking keeps
me up. Old troubles come back. I'm crushed with shame. I can't
bear to be inside my skin. The horrors have hit me full-strong.

⁓

Frederick announces himself with a rap of his stick, and I put the
flame under his supper to warm it. I'll not move from here, nor
will Mary from her dressing table upstairs, till we hear him come
through and the door locked behind him.

"I'm home."

I look out. "Sit down. This'll be ready now."

"Too kind, Lizzie," he says, though he stays stood and keeps his coat on till Mary comes down, for he knows she likes to help it off.

"You look tired," she says.

"It will be the death of me, that place."

"It won't be forever, Frederick. You weren't meant for there forever."

We sit at the table and watch him with his food. We can't last till this hour to have our own, which to the foreign mind must be a failing, though it doesn't seem to trouble him. He knows we're ruled by a different tide, and he seems to enjoy being under our scrutiny.

"Here, have another spoon."

"I cannot refuse, Lizzie, it is so delicious."

Between mouthfuls he talks about the mill, the little bits of business he thinks we might understand, but there is only so much of this talk that Mary will stand, the mill being somewhere else now, somewhere she no longer is, and if she cannot be there herself, in the midst of it, knowing everything, then she'd rather not know anything at all.

"Something happened to me today," she interrupts him to say.

"A thing good or a thing bad?" he says.

"Good, I think."

We look at her. She appears surprised to have got our attention so easy.

"Or bad, maybe. I can't be certain." She looks into her cup. "It was in the park."

"You were in the park today?" I says, knowing she has not left the house.

"Nay, not today. Yesterday, it was. Yesterday."

I give her a stern look. I'd have reason to remember if she'd

gone to the park yesterday, such an event would it have been. Fact is, she's only speaking to speak, to be heard to be saying something. For in the silence Freddy lurks.

"Come on, then," Frederick says. "What happened?"

"God, now that I mention it, I doubt myself. It could've been a dream. Aye, what it was was a dream. One of these nights, I had a dream."

He's grown huge, the bastard boy, in the dark. Her promise not to name him, not to conjure him up in any aspect, has done naught but store him in her every thought. She tells us some made-up dream about finding a babby in a basket in the park and searching the paths for its mother and being unable to find her and having to nurse the thing herself, and it's impossible not to see Freddy everywhere in it.

"Does it have any sense, do you think?" she says.

"Not a bit," says Frederick with a click of his tongue. "You are bored, that's what's going on. These fantasies are the outcome of separation only, and the lack of things to do. You need some recreation. We should go to the theater this Saturday. I will check what is playing."

"The theater?" She covers her eyes against it. "I couldn't bear it. All those false feelings."

Frederick sighs and folds his arms across.

"Don't decide now, Mary," I says, taking her hand away from her face. "See how you feel on the day." She gives me a smile, weak but there. I squeeze her hand. "It might help you to think on other things."

I take Frederick's empty plate to the kitchen, and put some time into preparing his pudding. He'll be off soon, back to his own place, so it's right that they have a moment alone. I can hear them whispering. If I stopped humming and strained an ear, I'd get the

tone of what's going between them. But, in all sincerity, I don't care to know. I've found pleasure in things as they are, and see I can be happy.

It's Mary, as it happens, who has gone blind to what's good.

"Which is it?" she says when he's left. "Is he living with us, or isn't he?"

And in truth it's hard to tell. Every day he leaves money on the table, and in the evening comes back to eat what the money has bought. Then, when we retire, he goes out again and leaves more money on the table for the next day. Sometimes he visits Mary's room. Sometimes he stays away for days. Sometimes he wants that we're talking and laughing. Sometimes he wants that we're quiet and out of the way. Always he expects that we do only what it pleases us to do. Never does he invite us to join him on his social rounds. For a time, so, he is provider and we are family, and for a time, for me at least, that's everything and fine.

"What matter where he lives, Mary, aren't we getting on grand?"

I don't miss the mill. Like a fish to the bowl, I've taken to the kept life. Its close bounds. The safety and the ease of it. The empty hours and the eating for something to do. Each morning I'm woken by the first bells, the faraway sound of them, and am set tossing by the picture of Lydia and the other girls rushing through the gates and to their places. But once they've died down—the bells and the pictures—I roll over and sleep till they strike again at noontime.

Twice I've been woken by Moss come to call my name outside the house. Only twice. The second time I almost get up and go to the window, but then I think, Next time. Let him sweat it a bit. Of course, so painful is it to him to sweat long at anything, there's no next time.

No matter what time I rise, Mary is rare up before me. She bides till she hears me put the kettle on downstairs and then she calls me to her room, where it's fetch me this and do me that, for I'm the scab, the hanger-on, and she believes I must moil like a slave on account of it. I know to oblige. To refuse would be to prove what she already credits about the world—that one of its halves is against her and the other taking advantage—and who'd suffer the brunt of that rage, only myself? Though she's my flesh and kin, I can't claim to know her limits. There's naught to say she wouldn't pin the guilt on me for a trifle and throw me to the street as a justice. This much, I'm long enough to be wise to.

With just the three of us to think about, the house is easy to keep without her help, and the message rounds don't tire me more than they keep my spirits up and my lungs clear of carpet dust. At first the local shopkeepers are wary of me, and some are regular rude, having heard uncommon rumors about my position, but I don't take on to notice. Instead, I hold their eye at the counters and don't flinch with my orders and make sure to get into some easy talk about the stresses of doing business with the cost of the rents and the up-and-downs of the prices, and with some light-hearted grumbles, too, about the peculiar duties a woman has to face when her sister goes bedridden, and like this I soon have them on my side and eating out of my palm. It helps that Frederick is generous with his allowances, for it lets me go for the better cuts, the choicer brands. At the same time, though, I'm careful to keep a shilling over for my own private ends: a cold glass at the alehouse, a shampooing at the haircutter's, a bottle of Rimmel's toilet vinegar, a penny for the savings jar.

For the whole of the p.m., meantime, she lies on her linen and doesn't move except to drink my preparations and follow me with her eyes gone dull. To the same measure as I've surrendered to

gratefulness, she's surrendered to dejection. It'd be easy to blame *him,* but she can't pretend to have been ignorant of his history when they first upped shack. The truer truth has to be that she's doing it to herself, that it's a malady of her own making, and that most of it is for my benefit: a touch of the plague she'll riddle us both with if she doesn't grow with child, and quick.

"Mary," I says to her one day, "you might well be lying here in front of me, but I'll be effed if I know where you are."

It's like she doesn't hear me, she's gone so far in on herself. She rolls her eyes over me and moans like her voice is coming from another room, and it's plain the company she's now keeping closest are the thoughts put in her head by the devil, thoughts that give her to believe that having a babby will bring vengeance on the Marx maid and snare Frederick once and forever: a single stone to kill the two crows preying on her happiness.

I don't tell her what I think, for what I think is, It'll never happen. In all the weeks I've been here, I've not seen any red on the sheets, not even a fleck from the normal courses, so it can't be like before when her belly wouldn't hold the babbies in, but must be that she's gone the same way as myself: dry as a bone from too much gained and lost.

"Keep up your heart, Mary. Ward off the woe-filling thoughts. Bear patient what He sends and for what He doesn't."

But she doesn't listen. She stays in bed listening only to herself. Hoping and praying for the impossible. Wallowing in the bitterness and the spite that sinks her ever further backwards and in, in, in, in till seven o'clock draws near and she sits up and calls for hot water, and I sponge her and dress her and put cucumber on her eyes and pour her out a nip, and she goes to wait in the armchair for his return. He comes in spent after his day of dealings, but he usual finds the forces to sit with her and give her his

attention while I heat the dinner. Alone with him, she comes over happy. I can hear her spouting it from the kitchen. But then at the table, if she earns less than his every regard, her jealousies and her disappointments seep up, and she starts to cark: she is tired, she is bored, she is lonely.

"I'm taken in a wrong sense by everybody," she says. "That's why I'm stuck here with nobody calling."

She doesn't set out to be a whine. I'm sure she comes down on herself for it afterwards and vows to change and be different. But it's a power stronger than her. For there's a part of her that hasn't matured, a part yet too wet to understand that, as helpmeet to a man, a woman must be ready to cease to be the first. She must be thankful for his fondness, but never count on it as her sole right and title.

The average man wouldn't stand for her, but our Frederick endures her by digging out the truth and by making her share in it. "If you are lonely, Mary, couldn't you call on the girls from the mill? Your old friends?" He also has an appetite for indulgence that I've scarce seen in others, though if you ask me, he indulges her *too* with his pets and his coddles, for in the end it's her who exhausts first and has to be put to bed. If it's one of their nights, he does the honors, but ten times of the long dozen it's left to me. Once I've given her the Godfrey's and sent her off, I go back down and finish with the house, and if he's staying a bit, I bring him a drink.

"You are too kind," he says to me. "How did we ever manage without you?"

"I'm sure you managed grand." I take the rug from the couch and put it over his legs. He hams a kiss of gratitude on my hand, and I can't keep from a smile.

"Mary could learn from you," he says.

"Oh?" I says, turning away to tend the fire.

"She would only have to watch you for a day to learn how the true proletarian copes. She who has not lost the spirit which is her class."

I hang the poker and the blower, pull the elbow-chair over to sit next to him. "Mary watches me plenty, Frederick. I can swear you that. But she'll only ever learn for herself and in her own time. She'll not have anything pushed on her."

He looks into the new flames reaching high. "There is a truth," he says.

I sip my drink and he does the same, and you'd have to be stone not to notice the charge that goes between us.

"Was it difficult for you, Lizzie, with this Irishman?"

"Arrah, it was and it wasn't. The way I look at it, you can't change the bodies that walk the world, but only help them. And if they end up not wanting your help, well then at least you know. And knowing, you can decide things for yourself."

He laughs a good sort of laugh. "You are a strong woman, Lizzie."

"No stronger than anybody would be in my place."

I tip us another short and throw on the last bit of log. He keeps me up long after both are gone, trying to convince me of some argument or other.

"You know, Lizzie," he says when final he rises to leave, "I look forward to our little chats."

"I do so myself," I says.

I guide him over to the door, for he's gone and drunk himself into a stagger.

"Easy now," I says, keeping hold of his arm while he gets his coat on.

There's a moment, then, when it's like he's pulling me towards

him. But I don't know. In the late hours things can look different to what they are.

Soon after, there's a visit from Lydia. She knocks on the door but won't come in.

"Can't you step in a minute, for Jesus sake?"

She shakes her head and plants her feet.

"Arrah, Lydia. Frederick's gone and Mary's in bed. No one's going to bite you."

"I'll bide here for you."

I sigh out a holy curse. "Right then," I says. "Hold on."

I wrap myself up and, before leaving, poke the fire up so it'll be warm when I get back.

We head to the nearest pub. She lets me pay. Doesn't put a hand near her pocket.

"We miss you in the place," she says.

"I miss you too."

"You do in your hat, you've landed the life."

"I'll have to find a situation of my own soon. I can't live off him forever."

"A situation of your own? Lizzie, my love, Manchester has already talked all it can talk about you. Its mind is set and won't be changed. You might as well ride the hog as long as it lasts. You've naught to lose now."

I look at the heads lined along the counter, pretending not to listen. "Mind your own effin' businesses," I call out to them, and take our drinks to a table where we'll not be wigged.

"How's Jamie?" I says.

"Well, he's the reason I've called on you. We're going to be wed."

My heart sinks to my stomach. "Ah, Lydia, that's great news. When'll it be?"

"In the summer. St. Mary's and then back to the house."

"Ah lovely."

"Will you come, Lizzie?"

"I'd not miss it."

"You're certain now?"

"Of course."

"I'm only saying because Moss will be there. Him and Jamie go back."

"Don't worry about that. I've no grievings with O'Malley."

"That's good, Lizzie. I'm glad."

We hug and clink glasses, and when we're over with that, I get another round.

"Will I tell Mary as well?" I says when I'm back.

"Nay," she says. "Don't."

"She'll find out, Lydia. It'll hurt her not be asked."

"I can't, Lizzie. I'm sorry."

On the walk back, before parting ways, she says, "How is she, anyhows?"

"Mary?"

"Aye."

"The same, only worse. She has ideas of a babby."

"Heaven save us, that's all she needs."

"Don't worry, it won't happen. I don't think she can, if you catch my meaning."

"Well, thank God for His cruel mercies."

It takes me weeks to warm up the courage to tell Mary about Lydia and Jamie. Then when I do, it happens easy as morning waters.

"Mary, I've something to tell you."

She's scouring the coppers and humming a sunny-sounding air, and she's been like this for a number of days now, up at the

crack and cleaning and cooking and shopping and caring after Frederick, and I don't know if it means she's turned the corner on the bad or if she's gone all the distance into it.

"Mary, can you hear me?"

She stops her humming and beams over at me. "I can hear you grand, Lizzie, what is it?"

"It's Lydia."

"What about her?"

"She and Jamie—"

"Are going to be married?"

The rag falls from my hands and into the bucket.

"Is that what you've been wanting to tell me all this time? Tiptoeing round me and looking for your moment?"

I feel ashamed and hide my face.

She lets me squirm on my stool for a long minute before bursting into wild laughter. "My darling Lizzie! What on earth were you afraid of? This news calls for a celebration!"

She throws her work down and hares out of the scullery. I follow her and, in the parlor, find her uncorking a bottle of Frederick's good stuff and pouring from it into two tall glasses.

"To love," she says, raising up.

"To love," I says, gulping down in one.

When the bottle is polished, she runs up to her room and spends the rest of the day sifting through her clothes, and sewing and stitching.

"We're going out," she says when she appears some hours later, dressed to the neck.

"Out?"

"To celebrate."

"Mary, are you all right?"

"Grand, only I'm sick of the sight of these four walls. It's time we got off our bunches and saw a bit of the world."

"We?"

She throws one of her old gowns at me. "Here, wear this."

"I will not. Your size doesn't even fit me."

"I've taken out the waist. The length ought be fine."

So stunned am I, so caught, that I don't resist when she pushes me into my room and starts pulling at my laces.

"Slow down, Mary."

"We'll be late."

"Where is it you think we're going?"

"To Trafford Park."

"You're joking, aren't you?"

"I happen to know they're showing some famous pictures there tonight."

"And what would *you* be wanting with famous pictures?" No sooner is the question out than I've answered it myself. "Did he tell you that's where he's going?"

"He said he wouldn't be home for dinner, so I've put two and two together."

"Nay, Mary, what he *actual* said was he'd be dining at the Club."

"Club, my arse. It's to Trafford Park he's going. Anyone who's anyone, that's where they'll be."

The roads to Trafford are so choked, the cab has to let us out on a distant bend. We hold up our hems and walk it.

Says Mary: "What did I tell you?"

The hall is new and has glass walls that don't topple only by a high miracle. There's a queue at the door to get in. Mary walks up to the top and declares herself the wife of Mr. Frederick Engels, mill owner.

"Mr. who?" says the livery man, but Mary scorches him such a look that he lets us in anyhows.

Inside is baking with the crowds and the lamps lit high. Some of the women have come without their crinolines and are walking with their dresses straight and dragging.

"Is that for fashion or to save space?" I whisper to Mary, but she pretends not to hear. She's on her tippies and peering out over the heads for Frederick.

A spot of sand on an effin' beach.

Determined still, she takes my hand and leads me round. What pictures I can see through the gaps are natural and blessed as to their kind; the frames huge and gold.

"We're going in circles," I says when we pass for the fourth time the archangel with his mickey swinging.

"All right, cease your moaning," she says, and asks a man for the direction to the refreshment room.

"Just over there," he says, pointing to the throng to the left of the fountain.

"Nay, not that one," says Mary. "The first-class place."

He frowns. "Ah well, that's outside in the tent, madam, but—"

We push out.

"What has the rich bodies so fascinated about tents?" I says.

Mary shuffles forward and puts on not to be with me.

It turns out recommendations are needed to get in. The man at the entrance is making *no exceptions*. After some wheedling, however, he allows Mary five minutes to find her husband.

"But heed me, madam," he says, "if you do not come out after that time I will go and look for you myself."

I'm glad to stay outside. The air is a blast of goodness after the heat and the rot. I find a dark place and watch the bodies going in and out. When the tent flaps are pulled back, I get glimpses of the

larry. Frederick's there. She's right about that at least. I light on him dancing with a body that isn't Mary's.

Now: dancing with Mary.

Now: pulling her aside by the elbow.

Now: I can't see either of them anymore.

Mary comes out well after the time granted her. "Right," she says, grinning huge and happy, "ready for home?"

Back at the house she demands a cold bath and insists on sitting in it for longer than can be healthful. I'm still there trying to coax her out of it with a warm towel when Frederick comes in. He opens the door to the room and stands leaning on the frame. He's dead silent except for the smell of spirit and cigars roaring across at us.

Mary takes the sides of the bath and pulls herself to a stand. I rush to cover her, but she swipes the towel away, and now, like a drunk waking from a stupor, I see for the first time what the whole of Manchester can't have missed: a hump where her belly has swelled. I clasp my mouth and step back, for though she's received the beginnings of many, it's a shock to see her gone large.

Oh, Mary Burns, what species of mother will you be?

I don't think I've ever seen Frederick with a look on his face so dirty and black. I watch him for as long as he stays there, unable to speak except to wipe his mouth and glower. I watch him and what I see is a man who understands, as I do, that it's all very well to be sincere and to hate falseness, but we also have to get on in the busy world.

Says Mary when he's had his angry moment and is gone: "It'll all be fine once the babby is born. He'll come round to sense then."

Her new happiness, I live it like a purgatory. When at night I sit with my drink in the kitchen gone cold and listen to her snoring above me, it feels like we're souls waiting to be damned. For no

matter which way this goes—a babby lost or a babby born—one thing is for certain, we're bound for a bad place.

Suffer, Lizzie, and be still.

June

XXI. Church

The Commune in Paris has fallen. Tens of thousands have been killed. And we—we!—have become famous on the back of it. Notorious, overnight. Now when people pass the house, they peer in and try to see through the blinds. I can't go two yards without someone making a comment on me. Or get onto a bus without a mole fluttering at me over his paper. The milkmaid won't call. The butcher cuts my orders from the bad end. And the baker, he near throws my bread across the counter. Men watch us: two of them, at the bottom of the Hill, with notebooks, taking down the comings and goings. Unsigned letters arrive, threatening our lives. Yesterday a brick come through the parlor window. "Foreigners, go home!" said the bit of paper wrapped around it. We're famous, aye, and it's a terrible aggravation for the nerves, and it's all Karl's fault; who else? During the whole life of the Commune he stayed silent, *observing*. And now, as soon as the thing collapses, he comes

out with his article, his mighty effin' address about the Commune being a foretoken of the coming World Revolution, and it goes public, spreads like a wood fire, and everyone gets to thinking *he* is the mind behind the doings. The puppet master pulling the strings. The leader of an international Communist conspiracy.

"Conspiracy?" I says.

"That is what they believe," says Frederick.

"And what, may I ask, are you doing to change their minds?"

"We have made it very clear, Lizzie, that our Association is a public one, that we have no interest in secret plots and conspiracies. The fullest reports of our proceedings are published for all who care to read them. Anyone may buy our rules for a penny."

"Don't give me that, Frederick. You're enjoying it. The attention. The rumors. And I don't like it. It's dishonest. What did we have to do with the Commune? You said yourself, there was naught we could do from here to help the cause in Paris. As for Karl, the state he was in, he was unable to mastermind the evacuation of his own bowels. We didn't do anything to bring the Commune about, and he can't go around claiming we did. It's not right."

"That is not what Karl is doing, Lizzie. His address does not claim anything for us. You speak from a place of ignorance. And, for your information, although contact with Paris was difficult, we took advantage of every opportunity to help the Commune leaders in tactical and strategic matters. And if anybody should ask, this is what you must tell them. You must keep your false ideas and your prejudices to yourself."

"Christ, Frederick, I can't talk to you when you're like this."

Today Karl is to read his address at the Club. We're all going to give our support.

"The French won't like it when they get wind that Karl is taking the credit."

"Stop worrying your head, Lizzie. Many members of the Commune were also members of the International. And for those who were not, a shilling laid out in pamphlets will teach them all they need to know about us. They themselves will come to see that the Commune was child of the International, *intellectually*."

The Club is packed with bodies and all languages spoken. The usual faces are here: the London comrades, the women, Jenny in the first row. But there's also a whole lot from the outside. Newspapermen. Police agents. Local shopkeepers. Reactionaries. Wags. I stand at the back near the door.

Frederick takes the stage first. He introduces Karl with stories of the big man's early life and education in Germany, his activities here and abroad, his role in the International. There's a polite applause before Karl himself gets up. We're expecting a bit of a joke, to clear the atmosphere, but he does no such thing. Clears his throat and reads straight from the page. Dry and serious. There's some murmuring. A bit of giggling. And now when Karl gets to his piece about the Commune being the glorious harbinger of a new society, someone burps to try to get a laugh up and disturb the solemn mood, but that's the extent of it. There's an ordinary applause when he's finished. Some cat-calling, but less than you'd think, considering.

Karl lumbers off and Frederick gets back up to take questions. They come in the guise of insults, most of them. But Frederick is quick with the right responses, just enough honor and sincerity to take the sting out of the attacks. He doesn't get riled, nor does he resort to insults himself, and this—when he has the public to himself—is when he's at his most seducing. He can handle his words like no one else, and even if you don't catch their meaning

first time, you hold on to them, somewhere, they've been said with so much believing.

When the questions run dry, he takes a turn at a speech of his own. He holds no paper. It all comes from his mind. He walks up and down, away from the lectern, and uses his limbs to make signs in the air. He opens his jacket, and now it comes off, and there's a power about him, and to hear him you'd think he's a religious man. I can't say he knows better than the priests, but his words come out as good as Bible words: familiar and true. As he talks on, my mind wanders over them, dips in and out of them, and I fall to thinking about Mary; how when Frederick came along she made a show of flinging her Church off like a worn-out shimmy. She stopped going to Mass as soon as she worked out his bent, and was quick to tilt her scorn over those who keep at it, no different than a drinker sworn off the lush who judges harsh those who still have their noses in it. But she clung—for dear life, she did—to the superstitions. The ghosts and the whispers. The spells and the fairies. She didn't ever lose that.

I'd catch her picking a bit of bread off the ground and making the sign of the cross over it, then kissing it and saying a Hail Mary.

"What in Jesus' name are you doing?" I'd say.

"Just in case," she'd say.

And when I'd find her burning candles to the Sacred Heart or dousing cabs and train carriages with holy water: "You never know. It's best on the safe side."

And I believe it'll be the same with Frederick. Sooner or later he'll have need for the faith he's turned from, and will come back to it. The prayer I hear in his speech is proof, if I needed more, that his religion hasn't had its day. Already, I know, there have been moments in his life when the strong arm of God has pushed him onto his knees. I only hope that, when the next moment comes,

the Lord will give him the wisdom to know it's wasted breath to pray for the soul of a dishonest woman, and that he ought do the right thing by me well before time.

I leave before the speeches are over. Jenny looks to be next in line, and I just can't be looking at her, spouting off in a room full of men. I go outside and look up and down the road. I know St. Giles to be close, and I need to find my way there. I've decided to have another look, this time with a clear head. I was mistaken the last time. I tripped up. The pubs were the wrong idea.

I get directions from a girl in a fancy drapers. On my way I don't pass a single English subject but only foreigners going about without proper covers. There's bad bodies among them, and they think me one of their own. From a shop door, an idling scamp whistles at me. A dark mop with a tray of wax birds comes into my path and won't let me pass till I give her out some words. Hooers cackle from the upstairs windows. From under some awning a man—a foul streak of oil—steps out and opens his coat to show a line of spectacles hung. When I give him a penny, he tells me where the Catholic church is found.

On the pew farthest to the back, a row of bodies is biding for confession. I've not come for that, so I go farther up. To save my knees from kneeling, I perch on the edge of the pew and lean forward over the armrest. In front: the high altar dressed in white and gold, the tortured body of Christ. Behind: the slide of the priest's grille, footsteps, whispered penances.

Of the sacred life of the Calvins I know little, but I'm up on this much: they don't like bodies to shrive themselves to priests, and in this they're the same as the England Protestants. Me, I think if you can stomach it, there's probable value to be got from it. How can you tell yourself straight to God and know He's hearkening? What

good can you draw off a Jesus that lives only in your head? What advice?

I put my chin to rest on my knuckles. It's hard to set about this right.

Soon tired of sitting, I go and put a shilling into the box under the Blessed Lady, light a candle. "Mary is our heavenly Mother and the Maker of all things. She knows every person and every thing, every thought and every secret we commit. She's the here and after, the present and future. She's the every place. She who believes in her can't be unhappy, for she can't be alone."

"I haven't seen you here before."

He wears no whiskers. He's bare out of his time.

"No, Father, you wouldn't have seen me. I'm new to this place."

"Father Killigad." He touches his chest. "I'm the priest here."

"Hello, Father."

He looks up at the Mary, crosses himself. "Will you put me in your prayers?"

"I will, Father, if that's what you want, but it might do you more harm than good."

He doesn't laugh, but doesn't get nettled either. He's used to us, being Irish himself. "Putting someone else in your prayers is a great gift."

"Even if they've asked you to do it?"

"Even then. *Especially* then."

He joins his hands—palms pressed flat like a pup in preparations for his Holy First—and bows his head. The strain in his face, he must be pushing one out for me.

When he's done, he touches my arm and leads me over to the top pew. "Will we be seeing you for Mass?"

"Sunday is a hard day for me, Father. At home like. And it's a bit of a way. I can't always get free."

"Are you being prevented?"

"Prevented? Only by the housekeeping, Father."

"Forgive me. I ask only because there are some who feel obliged to hide. I know maids who fear losing their positions."

"If you knew my name, Father, you'd know my position."

"Oh? And what is your name?"

"Engels. Wife of Frederick Engels."

He shakes his head. "I'm sorry, Mrs. Engels. The name means nothing to me."

We sit in silence a time, equal in the eyes of the Lord.

"Would you like to do penance, Mrs. Engels?"

"I'm not big on the officials, Father."

"How long is it since your last?"

"A long time."

"What sin is it that you're afraid to confess?"

"There's naught in me that God doesn't already know."

"But have you asked His forgiveness?"

"In so many words?"

"There's nothing the Lord won't absolve, Mrs. Engels, but you must ask Him. He'll not intervene without a plea. You must own up to your sins, admit you've done wrong. You must show Him you know you're a sinner."

"Well, if He doesn't know that for Himself, Father, He's deaf as well as blind."

He sighs, folds his arms across as if to say, "What is it about our lot in England?" He stands and goes around the pew to loom over me. Clasps his hands in front. "Sunday Mass is on the hour, eight to midday. I hope to see you there soon, Mrs. Engels."

"Father, just a minute. I'm being contrary. I'm sorry."

"You're being nothing I haven't seen a hundred times before, Mrs. Engels."

"Listen, Father, you're right. What you're saying, I'm agreed with it. Would you take my confession now?"

He is triumphant. "Follow me."

When we're good and settled in the box, he slides back the grille.

"If I was God, Mrs. Engels, what would you tell me?"

"I'd tell you to try my life for size, see if you'd fare any different."

"Do you think your life has been harder than anyone else's?"

The knees are at me already. Nowhere to put your arse. "Nay. I've been lucky. Luckier than most."

"If God was to live your life, how would He live it differently?"

"I suppose He wouldn't be on His own so much."

"Jesus spent long periods alone, Mrs. Engels. He suffered as we suffer."

I look down at the shadow of my hands, cut across by light from the gap where the curtains don't full meet. "I fear London doesn't agree with me, Father."

"How so? You are lonely here?"

"It's worrying my mind."

"London is?"

"I thought it would be a fresh start. But it's the same, isn't it, no matter where you go? I thought I'd be a stranger, a face in the crush. But it's all pursuing after me."

"You feel London is pursuing you?"

"Nay, Manchester is pursuing me. London is watching me."

"Mrs. Engels, I—"

"Jesus, would you listen to me? I'm bare making sense."

"Who is following you, Mrs. Engels?"

"Nobody, Father. Only the past."

The wood creaks when he shifts to bring his face close to the grille. There's not a nook in the church the sound doesn't reach.

"Are you here with a message, is that it, Mrs. Engels?"

"I'm looking for someone, Father."

"Yes?"

"Moss O'Malley. He came up from Manchester some years back. A man of strong faith."

"O'Malley? I don't know him myself, but I can send the word out. We have many friends in the Church. Voices carry quickly. Are you wanting a meeting? What's your message?"

"I don't know. I've naught prepared."

"Should he find you?"

"He could, I suppose, if he wanted."

I give him the address.

He repeats it back and now pulls the panel half across, whispers something so low I can't make it out.

"What's that, Father?"

Slam.

Black.

Am I off, or are such manners political in a priest?

My bonnet is off before I'm through the door. Seeing Frederick's hat not yet on the hook, I allow myself a bellow.

"Up off your arses, he'll be back any minute!"

I make for the kitchen, loosening ties and tugging on buttons as I go.

"Pumps, if I find you in that bath again, you'll know all about it!"

I'm stopped on the second step by voices coming through the parlor wall. The door opens and Pumps appears in the hall with an arrangement on her face—eyes wide as an owl's, brows touching the fringe of her cap—that can only mean Jenny and Karl.

I hurry my ties back into their knots, my buttons back through

their holes. Pumps reaches an arm out as if to present me, but I push past her in the tone of "I can usher myself in."

In the parlor the middle doors have been folded back and the good table has been set. They're all sat round, eating.

"Lizzie, you're soaked through," says Jenny. "Where on earth did you get to?"

I don't feel called on to make excuses in my own house. "I thought you were dining in town. In that *restaurant*," I says.

"We changed our minds, *mein Liebling*," says Frederick. "You were right. It was full and uncomfortable. It makes a better celebration to eat at home, just the four of us. We thought we'd find you already here."

"I had some things to do," I says.

"Well, you're here now," says Karl, to prevent a scene, "that's the main thing."

"Go get changed," says Jenny, "and then come and join us, please. I've been overseeing things. The girl was going to do broccoli and gravy with the fowl, but I had a look at what there was and I thought some savory rice and a curried sauce would be more amusing, or?"

Side-splitting.

"As long as Camilla wasn't put out."

"Oh, she was delighted. She says she loves a change."

In the hall, I put my wet back against the wallpaper, close my eyes, and breathe.

"Better?" says Jenny when I return in my good dress.

"Much better," I says.

The dinner is curious, but I'm supposing usual to its kind. I'm left to eat alone. The men have already cleaned their plates. Jenny's is still full, but she's only pushing its contents from one side to the other; none of it goes near her mouth.

"Lizzie, we've been talking about the success of Karl's address," she says, "and what a nightmare it has been for us personally. Nothing short of ruinous to our private life. We have no peace day or night. The *Telegraph* was around again yesterday. And now there is a journalist in New York who wants to come over and do a feature. All that way, can you imagine?"

Aye, and for what?

"It certainly is making a devil of a noise," says Karl. "I have the honor to be at this moment the most abused and threatened man in London. But I have to say, it really does me good after the tedious twenty-year idyll in the backwoods."

"Well, you've never looked healthier," I says.

They laugh.

I miss the Girls.

"How have things been here, Lizzie, for you?"

"Fine. No complaints."

Pumps, puss-faced, appears in the doorway. She looks at me. Usual, Frederick allows her to take her supper with us, but with the Marxes here she's not sure which foot she's standing on.

"You can take these away, Pumps," I says. "And bring in the pudding."

"Didn't you like it, ma'am?" she says to Jenny when she takes up her plate, still packed with food.

"It was delicious, Pumps, thank you."

There's quiet till Pumps is gone.

"So, what now?" I says, to break it.

"Good question," says Frederick.

"The refugees are the priority," says Karl.

"Refugees?" I says.

"The Communards," says Jenny. "Hundreds of them. Come to London to escape the forces of repression."

"Oh. More of the French."

Jenny blinks at me. "Didn't you see them, Lizzie? Thronging the streets around the Club? Thin as sticks and with no clothes on their backs. Their only belonging that bewildered air which encircles them."

"I saw them," I says. "I just didn't know what they were."

"Proper accommodation will need to be found for them," says Frederick.

"And then we must get them educated," says Karl.

"Yes. They must be taught the significance of what they have achieved," says Frederick.

"And they must be made aware of their mistakes," says Jenny.

"Won't they know these things already, for themselves?" I says, tired now after the food.

"Some of them might," says Frederick. "But we mustn't presume a high level of self-consciousness or theory in these men."

Karl nods. "Our main aim now must be to make the Commune's historic experience available, firstly, to those who were directly involved and, subsequently, more widely. We must analyze theoretically the lessons of the rebellion and thereby turn spontaneous sympathy into the conscious desire and ability of the proletarian masses to carry its cause forward to victory."

"Oughtn't we be hearkening to what they themselves have to say?" I says. "They being the revolutionaries?"

"Of course, Lizzie," says Frederick. "No one is suggesting otherwise. But many of these men are infused with a mood of failure and disappointment. We must press upon them that the Commune was merely the first attempt at working-class government, and therefore destined to failure. And that this failure is part of the necessary course. For you see, Lizzie, the death of the Paris rebellion is more historical than its life. Its dying is only the beginning."

The beginning? How many of those must they have before they start to see they're the end?

XXII. The Art of Being Well

Dr. Allen comes and orders me onto my back.

"You've been called in error," I says. "I'm not ill."

"Mr. Engels tells me you've been coughing."

"I'm not one to fly to the medical man every time my throat tingles."

"He doesn't like to hear it. He says it won't leave you."

"I've had a cough since I was a child, Doctor. It's what you get for growing up in Manchester."

"Is that so."

"Aye. Since back-when I've had it, and till my death I'll have it. My wind gets wheezy and it hurts, and then it doesn't. That's always been the way of it."

"He says you insist on going out in bad weather. Getting wet in the rain."

"Mother of Moses, I've never known such a talker."

"Exertion is the instigation of your illness, Mrs. Burns. You must be careful against agitation of all kinds and against excessive application."

"English, Doctor?"

"Stop your running about. Too much exercise can imbalance a woman."

I throw him a look.

"Well, at least wait for a clear day, Mrs. Burns."

He feels around me. "How are your knees?"

My knees? Growing more and more watery. Bare a bend left in them. Not long till I'll be obliged to walk with a stick. "Grand."

"And down here?" He presses down into me. "Do you have urgency?"

"Urgency, Doctor?"

"Passing water."

"I've never been able to hold it long, if that's what you mean."

"Is there a sting?"

"Nay." Sometimes.

"Hmm. I feel something here. A small swelling. Nothing to worry about in the immediate term. But we'll have to keep an eye on it."

"We're getting on, Doctor. We can't expect to be well, most of us."

He recommends that I stay inside and revive. Makes up a prescription for something he knows I won't get. For the fact of it is: we're oftener killed by treatment than disease.

July

XXIII. The Other Half

In search of a missing slipper, I come through the middle doors of the parlor, and there on the chair in the corner, on the wolsey bought special for the move, is a strange man, lounging.

"I'm afraid Mr. Engels is from home, sir."

He sweeps his wet hair back. "I was told to wait here."

"You'll have to come back."

"I am sorry, but that was not what I was told at the door."

"Sunday is what you ought've been told. We receive on a Sunday."

"That's no good. No good at all."

"If you have a card, I can make sure Mr. Engels gets it."

"A card, a card, that's very well, a card is something, better than nothing, but now that I'm here and have been made sit for so long, and with the water coming down outside, and being without a proper coat and liable for a soaking, maybe all these factors

considering I should be allowed to see the lady of the house? A short minute from her schedule is all I ask, *s'il vous plait.*"

A pause; a tiny gap into which the whole world could fit.

"Bah, of course! You must be Mrs. Burns!" He stands and bows. "Delighted and honored. The name is Delamer"—he opens his coat and settles back into my afternoon—"Roland Delamer. Just in from Paris."

"Welcome to London, Mr. Delamer."

"*Merci, merci.*"

"And if you are still here Sunday, I'm sure Mr. Engels will be happy to receive you."

"Still here Sunday? Mrs. Burns, with the situation at home as it is, I shan't be leaving London until long after Sunday. Ah, the things I've seen." He closes his eyes and, like an actor of the stage, shakes his head. "The weight I carry."

The fashion of his collar, up at middle-cheek, makes it seem like he's peering out over a wall and not liking much what he sees: now the pictures, now the carpet, now the ornaments, now the lamps. He smoothes his hair over the other way and looks back at me.

"You'll have met some others, Mrs. Burns? Communards who have fled the repression?"

"A few."

Torn carpets, I have, from the volume of them coming through, and I've noticed it's the ones with the look of butchers, stern and strong-made, who are ashamed about bringing their filth higher than the kitchen, while it's the ones grown delicate from bookwork who waltz about and stamp their prints deep. And even by the standards of the dainty fellas, this one here is spare and thin, a ballroom the fitter place for his shoes, time enough on the barricades to macassar his brow and whisker.

"It's as I thought. For everywhere I look in London, I see French faces, my brothers, my comrades, and they all have the same aspect, the same eyes filled with the same horror. It's an abominable situation. The things I have seen. The things I have seen!"

I don't conceal my sigh. "I'll order some tea, Mr. Delamer, and you'll have a cup. But then I must ask you to—"

"Not Dull-a-mare, Mrs. Burns. D-E-L-A-M-E-R. De-la-mer. Of the sea."

I pull the bell-cord, and now harder, and am glad when no one stirs to answer it and I have to go myself. "Do excuse me a moment, Mr. Delacey."

Burns. Of the fire. *Enchanté.*

I find Spiv in the kitchen, picking the chicken.

"Spiv?"

"Name's Camilla, ma'am."

"What day is it?"

"It's bird day, ma'am."

"And what day is bird day?"

"Bird day's the day I'm stuck in here as always, not a sinner to help me."

"It's Wednesday, Spiv. Today is Wednesday."

"Aye, ma'am, bird day."

"And what day do we receive?"

"Sunday, ma'am."

"Too hard to remember?"

"No, ma'am."

"The only house in the country that dares, God forgive us."

"Aye, ma'am."

"Aye, ma'am, aye, ma'am, three bags burst ma'am, but what's there a gent doing in my parlor on this, a Wednesday?"

"Couldn't say, ma'am."

"Couldn't say."

"Bird day, ma'am. Been stuck in here, not a sinner to help me. Ain't seen no man."

Even the blunt ones would cut you with argument.

I nose out Pumps in her room, melting candles and putting her knuckles into them.

"Put that out."

She laps her tips, pinches the wick.

"Didn't you hear the bell?"

"The what?"

"Is that wax going into your ears?"

Unmade bed. Scab on the arm. Pinny a doubtful white. A day in the mill and she'd know what from what.

"What have I told you about callers?"

"None past the door when Uncle Angel's not here."

"Mr. Engels."

"That's what I said." She scratches herself. "Oh, and as well, I'm to take their card and tell them to come back on Sunday. And if they don't have a card, I'm to write down their name and their current residence."

"The rule isn't for saying but for obeying."

"All right, don't overcook, Aunt Liz."

"You have to be firm at the door or they'll put on us, these frogs."

"I don't know what you're on about, I didn't let anyone in."

"Now look at where you've got us. Frederick not back till supper, our stores empty, and another one on our hands till Jesus knows when. The shape will be pulled out of my day entire. I just pray he doesn't want a bed for the night."

"No need for a song and dance, Aunt Liz. Do you want me to go and talk to him?"

You do what you can, and that's all you can do. You tell them whose house they're in, and why a stray caller isn't a light thing, not here. You tell them to keep a special watch on the French, for the French are ignorant of what's done and what's not, most of them being *refugees,* which means on the run and penniless and with nowhere to put down their heads. You tell them it's forgivable they decide to call on this house, and it's forgivable that once inside they forget their manners and overstay their time telling their grievings, darkening the rooms with wild words and dead faces, and giving eye to the sofa, hoping to put themselves on it. But the truth is, we can't help everybody who comes. We have to draw a line. It won't do the Revolution any good if a lodging is made of our parlor and Frederick is kept from his work. You tell them all this, you go blue in the face, and still it doesn't sink. Still they let pass any creature that can hobble. And it's hard to pin on them any wrongdoing. So sometimes the only thing for it is a swift clip round the ear.

Back down in a fresh dress.

"We'll have tea direct, Mr. Delacey. You'll have to pardon the running about."

"Oh no, Mrs. Burns, I understand. I have a wife myself."

It takes Pumps three trips to bring all the tea things, so concerned is she with her bobs and her ribbons.

"Thank you, Miss Burns, that'll be enough."

"A sweet girl. Is she your daughter?"

"Niece." Half-niece. Plenty-removed.

"Well, I knew there was some connection. There's the same heat in your eyes."

The same heat that burns.

"Weak or strong?"

"*Comme ça.*"

"Milk?"

"Some lemon, if you have it."

"Of course." I call Pumps back in, much to her thrilling. "Bring the gent some lemon."

"Ma'am?"

"Slices, Miss Burns, slices."

"I hope it's no trouble."

"Not a bit of it, Mr. Delacey, after all you've been through."

He takes his cup from the tray and holds it out for pouring, but in a mean way, close to his chest, which obliges me to stand and reach over. And, now, just when I'm at my most uncertain, up on pointed toe and with no free hand to lean down on—she's gone and brought me the pot that needs a finger to keep the lid on—he parts his whiskers to show his teeth (good and strong) and the front of his jacket to show the lining (silk, no less) and the lip of the inside pocket (abulge with money notes, a terrible lot of capital to have clear all at once). Tea pours over the lip of the cup onto the saucer and fountains down onto his fingers. He lets everything drop. Most of the tea ends up on his shirt and breeches. The wolsey—praise be—is saved.

While he prances and yells, I find myself calm. How queer his speech is, I think as I watch him dance across the carpet and pull the scalded clothes away from himself. How it has changed from before. As a man in his cholers, I wouldn't have guessed him French. German or English perhaps. One of the efficient races. But not French.

Pumps comes in with the lemon. "Sir, are you all right?" she says.

"What does it bloody look like," he says, as far from French as I am.

"Why don't we get those off you, sir, and we'll give you—"

"Pumps! Go get a cloth and fettle up this mess."

Two curtsies, the scut manages, in the middle of the chaos.

"I'm awful sorry, Mr. Delacey," I says, handing him some napkins, "my mind went elsewhere and I didn't know where I was."

"Mrs. Burns! It would do you well to train your mind on matters, particularly the handling of hot things. You would be surprised how many people are injured or even killed by accidents in the home."

Fine advice. From a rebel.

We fall into an uneasy quiet. I could ask him about Paris and what he did and saw there, test him that way. But you never know with that. It can bring you to places you'd rather not be.

"Sandwich?" I says instead, and seeing now that they're the ones left over from Sunday, I give them a sly sniff as I pass. Tolerable. He takes one and puts it in whole. Chews. Rearranges his crotch. Swallows.

I sip and shift round and am about to call time when he fixes me a stare. He pats his pocket, the one with the money, as if I've forgotten about it, a swelling as big as one of Karl's carbuncles.

Says he: "So a chat, then, Mrs. Burns?"

I put my cup down, fold my arms across.

"Is there something you want, Mr. Delacey?"

"A quiet one, are you, Mrs. Burns?"

I ignore his wink. "What is it you want? I run a busy house."

He takes up a second sandwich and begins to play with it. Turns it like a coin till the bread turns gray. Puts it back on the plate. "So what has Mr. Engels been up to this past while?"

I look past him, out the window.

"And Dr. Marx? How is his health?"

"I don't know what it's like in France but here, Mr. Delacey, you oughtn't credit what you read in the papers."

He leans towards me, arse lifting right off. "So you see a lot of him?"

"A lot of who?"

"Marx. Dr. Marx. The Red Terror Doctor."

"What is it you're after, Mr. Delacey?"

"Bah, nothing in particular, Mrs. Burns, anything you want to give me, any small thing."

I rise to a stand. "I suggest you come back on Sunday."

He stands too, and talks fast, his speech slipped right out of foreign. "Is it Marx who started the Paris Commune, Mrs. Burns?"

"It was the proletariat as did *that.*"

"But guided by Marx and the International, am I right?"

"You ought know more about it than me. You *are* a Communard, aren't you?"

"Tell me, Mrs. Burns, now that Dr. Marx has waged war on one government, does he have plans to wage war on every government in the world?"

"If you're looking for information on Dr. Marx's activities, you ought read the Association reports, they'll have what you're looking for."

I start to gather the tea things.

"Leave that, Mrs. Burns, I'll be out of your hair in a jiffy, I just want to have a little chat with you, a head-to-head between friends."

I pick up the teaboard. He tries to take it from me. I grip it tight. He pulls. I pull back.

"Boo!" he says, giving me such a fright that I go foot-totting backwards. He clatters it down on the good table.

"You ought leave now, Mr.— "

"What do you make of the rumors?"

"I try not to listen to blather. You listen to blather and you get to believing all species of things."

"Wise words, Mrs. Burns, wise words. But isn't it interesting, fascinating, I'd say, what they're saying?"

"I don't know what they're saying about any cursed thing. Now it's time for you—"

I make for the door, but he lunges forward and takes tight of my wrist. He puts a hand over my mouth, skin too soft for a soldier, the smell of scented water. I'm not afraid. I look into his eyes and see his own fear, and that way I'm not afraid. Slow, he takes his hand away and steps back. Before I start screaming there's a moment, an empty moment, when there's naught but stillness between us. He breaks it with a wink.

"Get out!" I'm so loud I can hear myself against the walls. "It's not a bit of a Frenchman you are and I want you out!"

"Oh now, Mrs. Burns, what's all this? Let's calm down now, shall we?"

"I'll howl the road down, don't think I'll not."

"Now now, darling, just a couple of minutes, that's all I'm after. We're looking for the inside track. The story behind the story. Inside the home of the Revolution. The other half gets her say."

"Out, I said. Out!"

He shows his hands in the manner of "I surrender." "All right, all right, you win," he says. "But just in case you change your mind." He reaches into his jacket, slides a card and a money note, a whole five-jack, between a cup and the pot. "And there's more where that came from," he says, and is gone.

The door slams.

Rain.

Pumps comes in looking pale.

"Nay, child," I says, "I'll clear this. Go put the chain on the street door. And don't tell Frederick about any of it."

I take the teaboard down to the kitchen. A stitch in my chest but steady hands. I throw the card in the stove, bide till it burns away. The money note, I've already slid into my sleeve.

XXIV. Eruption of the End

It's all quiet at the Marx house. Nim opens the door only wide enough to peep.

"I was passing," I says.

She makes room for me and I step in, but no farther than the matting.

"I'm not staying. I just wanted to give you this."

I hand her the money note in an envelope I've asked Pumps to prepare: "Helen" written in big letters.

"What's this?"

"I don't know," I lie. "Something from Frederick."

She looks at it, suspicious, but now puts it away.

"She's in her room," she says.

"Oh, she's here? I thought, with the quiet, she was out."

She shakes her head, mournful, and points me up.

There's no sound in Jenny's room apart from the clock ticking.

I almost don't notice her sat in a chair by the window, a blanket too heavy for the season spread over her. She turns to me without a greeting. I go and stand in front of her. She takes my skirts and pushes her face into them.

Soul of my body, what is it now?

"Laura has lost the baby."

I go cold. I'm a monster.

"Oh, Jenny, that's terrible. When?"

"Two weeks ago, but with the state of the French post, we only got the news yesterday."

She covers her face. Tears escape. She falls forward and gives herself onto me. And now she weeps out. All down my front. At first I'm kept stiff and ungiving by the mean crook of my spirit that continues to look black on her, but my palsy gives way to shame and sadness when, by some higher interference, I come to understand there's no harm in what she's doing; it'd do the sorry world good if we all sat down and cried out for ourselves. I take strong of her and bring her into me, holding her head so she'll not raise it and see the water that now comes from my own eyes, for my own sins, and the babbies I could never have as a consequence of them.

Like this we are, for a long time. Long enough for the light in the room to change, for the heat of the day to dry the swelter off my back and to put it back there again.

Jenny draws away. I give her the tissue from my sleeve to wipe herself with. She thanks me without looking. She's found in the shades of the empty fireplace a place to put away what she's let out.

"I'm sorry," she says.

I touch her shoulder and keep there. "What is Laura going to do?"

She shakes her head. "It is no longer safe for Paul, and he has crossed into Spain. She has stayed behind with the boy, who

is himself ill with dysentery." She puts a hand to her mouth and shuts her eyes. "God, if anything happened to *him* now, that would just be the end."

"Naught of the sort will happen. Aren't Janey and Tussy there with her? They'll make sure she and the boy are well looked after."

Jenny sucks her lips in and nods. "Karl has written and told them to follow Paul across the border, where at least they will not be arrested. But I think they should just come home. Find a ferry that will take them and go."

"They'll come home soon enough, don't you worry."

"Oh, Lizzie, thank you for saying it, but I find it hard to believe."

"Oh, Jenny, whisht now."

I bring her over to the bed so we can sit side-by-side.

"Karl has taken this news very hard. He is beside himself."

"It'd be hard for any grandfather."

"It is the drop that has made the vase overflow. With all the extra work the exiles have made, he was already suffering from overstrain. But now? Now he is on the edge of falling down. And I cannot help but be affected also."

"Jenny, it is only normal to feel it."

"You are lucky, Lizzie. It is different for you. And you have Frederick. A man of action rather than emotional reflection. An uncomplicated man, a man on the move. And with such an appetite for life, life as it is. I can't imagine him suffering in the same way."

"I'm not sure about that, Jenny. He's had his share of losses. We all have. Now come, no more talking. Let's get you lying down."

I guide her head to the pillow.

"I don't want to sleep," she says, but she stays put.

I sit beside her till she goes off.

"It's going to be all right," says Mary, and at first I think that, because we're in Smithfield Market buying our vittles, she means we're all right for brass and have enough to cover us for the week.

"Aye," I says, "we ought be all right," and wave at the fishmonger to put more shrimps onto the scales. "We'll get these as a treat, and if we run low, we can have turnips and taters till we're flush again. No point scrimping or we'd never have anything nice to put on the table."

Hearing me go on, she laughs and tells the monger to throw in a few mussels to make a proper measure. "My piggy little sister Lizzie," she says, "your mind has but a single track. I'm not talking about money!"

"You're not?"

"I'm not."

"What *are* you talking about, then?"

"I'm talking, Lizzie, about *this.*"

She opens her shawl to show her tummy. She pats it open and public.

"Well, pray forgive me, Mary, but aren't the two subjects one and the same? Isn't a babby by Frederick like a hen that shits gold?"

She gives me a face. I jab her an elbow. The monger clears his throat. I take the fish from him and put it in the basket.

"What I mean is," she says, "I can tell this one's going to be all right."

"I don't doubt it," I says, for I've learnt that going against her is only another way of convincing her of her rightness.

"It's going to be a healthful little boy."

"A boy will be lovely, Mary."

She takes my arm and leads me away: *she* leads *me,* the sick guiding the sound. We go through the rest of the Market

without seeing anything worth halting for. I don't understand why we still come here at all. The eatables are low in grade and the place is infested with Irish. I can't see any reasonable sense to traipsing all this way up when we can well afford the shops over where we are. And what's else, I don't understand why she insists on coming with me. I'm well capable of doing the shopping without her escort. I just hope it's not because she still wants the busy world to see her illness and to make tavern talk out of it. I hope she's learnt her lesson after that holy rup-and-rumble at Trafford Park. Or is that hoping against itself?

We come out on High Street. My idea is to catch a bus outside one of the factories on Great Ancoats. I try to steer us onto the nearest course there. I ought know better, however, than to have my own ideas when it's in Mary's company I am. On Thomas Street she tugs at my sleeves and drags me in the direction of Deansgate.

"Come," she says, "I want to show you something."

"Not a chance. I want to get home and cook this fish before it rots the whole way."

"Arrah, don't be such an old woman and come on."

A shortcut through the warehouses, a turn by the dressmaker's, a skip and a march, and she has me stood at the window of a shop, upper-quality if the people coming in and out are to swear by.

"What am I supposed to be looking at?" I says, playing blind to the babby's crib in the display.

"Don't give me that," she says. "You can see it well and good."

And in fairness it'd be hard to miss, it's such a roaring festoon of a thing: flowers carved into the wood and silk bows tied onto the frame and butterflies pinned to wires and hovering over.

"What do you think?" she says.

"I think it's a bit early to be thinking about cradles."

"Nonsense. No new mother wants to be caught with everything

to do at the last minute. Better to get these things early. He'll be out and born before we know it."

Letting out a satisfied titter, she draws me closer to the window, then closer again, till my skirts are wiping the glass.

"Isn't it just the nattiest?" she says.

"Gorgeous," I says. "Now, is that it? Is that everything you wanted me to see?"

She scowls at me. Takes my bonnet strings and yanks them down. "Damn your arse, Lizzie, would you ever grow a bit of patience?"

Before I've the chance to fix myself or even understand I've been unfixed, she has me parading again, this time down the street past the toy shops and round the pub on the corner.

"Where in hell's name are we going now?" I says.

"Shh," she says, hastening her stride. "For once, can't you just flow along?"

Ring-a-ding-ding! We're in through the door of somewhere. A shop. A shop with only one small square window in the front that gives so little opportunity for light it requires gas even during the day. The bit of sun that does stray in is caught and turned brilliant by the shelves of porcelain and silver that run round the walls to cover every inch; every inch except the bit of the back wall where a tiny door has been cut, and where now a man—lanky as a pole and yellow as a crow's foot—is bending through. He stops before he comes all the way out. Stays with his head and feet on this side and his arse on the other. Speaks with surprising force for a body folded into such an arrangement.

"Mrs. Engels!" he says. "How delightful to see you again!"

"Mr. Lambert," Mary says. "Always a pleasure."

"Give me one moment, my dear. I've to finish something in here and I'll be right out."

"Take your time."

Once alone, I take her wrist and rasp into her ear. "Explain to me, please, what we're doing here."

"Ow," she says, "get off."

"Well?"

"Come on to feck, Lizzie. What do you *think* we're doing here?"

"Oh, this is dandy, this is just effin' dandy."

And I don't bother to give out more than that, for I know there'll be no gain got from crossing her. My only comfort is that this appears to be a higher class of slop-shop than I'm used to. It seems, at least, to be the species where your things are taken for hard coinage instead of the usual fags and gin.

While we wait, I can't help tapping out my irritation on the counter. Meantime, Mary ogles the loot.

"Oh, look at those," she says, pointing to a set of silver tea things. "They must be worth a pretty penny. The poor sods can't have been happy losing *them.*"

I look away, but find there's no place to look *to.* Left and along the racks: boots and braces and the lives of bodies hung. Right and up to the ceiling: plates and forks and spoons, Manchester's hunger brimming over. Down and beneath the glass of the counter: a thousand private pockets turned out, snuff boxes and fob watches and card holders—

I close my eyes to it all, but then there's still Mary tee-heeing beside me—what side of this place can she possible find funny?— and the smell of emery powder and benzene to keep my stomach keeling. After what feels like a generation, Lambert stoops through the door and, with a crack of his brittles, opens himself to his tallest stature.

"So what can I do for you?" he says. "Are we buying or selling today?"

"We're selling, Mr. Lambert," Mary says.

"Good, good," he says, rubbing his hands like I suppose he's expected to. "And what do you have for me?"

"Something special," she says.

"I like special," he says.

"In that case"—she takes her shawl off her shoulders and puts a finger on her brooch, the one with the green stones set in the shape of a clover—"you're going to like *this*."

Lambert cranes over the counter to twinkle at the treasure revealed.

"How much can you give me for it?"

"Give it here and I'll tell you."

She unfastens it from her dress and holds it under him. His nose twitches as if to sniff the air round it. The hairs in his nostrils shiver and appear to reach down to stroke it.

"Well, how much?"

"I can't say straight off." He screws his face up. "I'll need a good look at it under the light."

"Well, be quick about it, Mr. Lambert. There's other places we could go to."

He holds out for it. "I'll be as quick as a flash."

She dangles it over. "Good man yourself. And remember, I'm no panhandler looking for her next meal. I'd sooner walk back out of here with none of your cash than with too little of it, do you grasp me?"

He nods. She drops it in. He's gone. She grins at me as if to say, "Isn't this a lark?"

We're left waiting another span. I try to be still and offer my feelings up, but there's only so long a body can keep mum without bursting out.

"Mary, he gave you that brooch for your birthday."

"Don't start. He wouldn't even remember. And I certain won't miss it. My priorities are changed."

"Priorities? If you want the wretched crib so desperate, couldn't you ask him to buy it when the yoke is born?"

"I could, I suppose. But there'll be so much to do, and so much will be asked of him then. I want to get as much as I can out of the way by my own account and without disturbing him before time."

It's the rational sense she makes that worries me most.

"Stop your worrying, Lizzie. It's all going to be grand."

She puts a hushing hand on my arm and then goes off for a little tour of the shop, humming and purring on her way. The shelf of clocks, which Lambert must keep wound as a torture for his wife, count out a ragged time, *tick-tick-tock-tick-tock-tock-tock*—

The door opens and Lambert ducks back in carrying a little purse. Mary takes it from him. Doesn't stop to count what's in it before gathering her yards and hurrying out: *rrrrring-a-ding-ding-ding-ding!*

"Terrible sorry," I says on my way out after her, "do pardon us, please," though I imagine he's delighted to get away easy as he does, not the whiff of a haggle left in our wake.

Round the corner again and I light on her tearing, crinoline aflare, towards the cradle shop.

"Mary!" I call out to her. "Slow down, for godsake. Remember you're not well." And I've a share of complaints myself.

By the time I make it into the shop after her, the purse has already been handed over, and a man the shape of a skittle, bald of pate and bulging at the waist, is putting the coins into little piles on the counter. Over his shoulder peers a woman dressed as a nurse; dressed as one, but not an actual one. I can tell, for I saw many nurses in the lock hospital and got to know them well, and none of them bore semblance to this one, none wore a hat of this

shape or an apron of this cut, none wore faces of this knit. The only reason this one is here is to make the customers feel easier about parting with their mint. The only reason this one is here is to sell more crib.

"Good afternoon," I says, beating my chest to get the lung going.

"Oh, and *that,*" says Mary, gesturing over her shoulder without turning round from the counter, "is my sister." Her shoulders are rising and falling with her heavy breaths, and her voice, I notice, has gone weak and whispery. "That's only my sister, Miss Burns."

"How do you do, Miss Burns?" the nurse-body says.

"Alive," I says.

The nurse-body doesn't break from her fearsome stare. The skittle glances up from what, at this stage, must be his third tour through the coins.

"Don't mind her," Mary murmurs to them. "Don't mind her, and tell me, please, what's left to pay off."

The nurse-body produces a book from a drawer. She opens it—*creak*—and puts it on the counter in front of the skittle. He runs his finger down the page.

"Ah, here we are," he says. "Mrs. Engels, no?"

"Aye, that's it," says Mary.

He takes his pen up and dips it. Scribbles something down. "Six shillings and sixpence from three pounds and ten makes three pounds, three shillings, and six."

I watch Mary nod, then watch as the nod turns into an ill-looking loll. She leans forward onto the counter and looks in danger of slumping onto it. I don't move to prop her, for it's only a rig she's playing, a dodge to get something off the price. Or just to make a pageant of her condition.

The skittle looks over his spectacles. "Mrs. Engels?"

She doesn't answer. She's too busy wiping her face of a wet that isn't there.

"Mrs. Engels?"

"Aye?"

"Did you hear what I said? There's three pounds, three shillings, and sixpence owing on the cradle."

"Aye, that's quite right." She rubs her handkerchief over the palms of her hands and sweeps back what's come loose from her hair. "Three pounds, three shillings, and six, that's where we are."

"At the rate you're going, you should have it bought outright in no time."

"In no time, thank you. Thank you."

She turns and, with a feeble toss of her shawl, shows me she's ready to leave. I smile a vague thanks to the two behind the counter and reach for the door. On my way out, though, I hear a noise behind me, a creaking and a whimper, and glance back to see Mary stumbling in her boots. I look to the nurse-body. She narrows back at me, mistrusting the scene. Mary reaches out for the closest object that will take her weight. She finds the iron railing of a cot. The nurse-body coughs a rigid cough.

"Please read the sign, Mrs. Engels."

Mary moans.

"We ask customers to kindly not touch the items on display. If you need to rest, you are welcome to sit there." She raises an arm— rod-stiff, no elbow in it at all—and points to the pair of chairs by the door.

"Don't worry yourself," Mary says, and steps away from the cradle. "I'm grand. It's all grand."

Step. Shuffle. Dodder. Totter.

I'm beginning to feel anxious. I move back inside, but am wary of going to aid her. I'm lost as to what part I'm supposed to be

playing in this game, or what she hopes to gain by it. Final she makes it to the seat and sits heavy onto it.

"Do you think—" She presses the backs of her hands against her brow, then her cheeks.

"What is it, Mrs. Engels?" the skittle says. "Are you unwell?"

"Do you think I could bother you"—swallowing and licking her lips—"Can I ask you for a glass of something to drink. I don't know, all of a sudden, I feel—"

A gurgle and a heave then, and she's letting vomit. Frozen, we watch it outpour. Follow it drain down over her and collect into a puddle on the floor.

Then the hysterics. From the nurse, a cater-and-wailing I can't make end nor side of. From the skittle, an unmanful shrill.

"My boards! My good boards!"

I rush over to Mary, kneel beside her, and push her head down between her knees. More comes, gushes, splashes onto my sleeves and seeps into my trail. The oysters we ate in Smithfield are there, black globs of flesh in the stew, though I doubt they're to blame, for I had the largest share and I feel in perfect hale.

"Get her out!" the skittle shrieks. "Get her onto the street!"

But there's no shifting her now. It's pouring too fast and too heavy. All we can do is bide for it to waste.

Minutes, it takes, and minutes more for her breathing to return.

"Lizzie," she says then, and I have to pull close to hear her under the howling of the other two.

"Aye, Mary?"

"I think I vomited."

She turns to look at me. I glimpse death dark in her cheeks and in the pits round her eyes. "Christ, Mary, what's happening?"

"Naught. Lizzie. Naught at all. Only we'll need to get a cab back. Have we any ready left on us?"

"We do, I think. Can you stand?"

"Well, no one's going to carry me, are they?"

I pull her onto her feet. Her hair is matted and she smells like a drain broke. The skittle and the nurse-body pinch their noses and jig at the edges of the creeping pool.

"You'll have to pay for the cleaning! We'll have to add it to your account!"

I put a hand round Mary's waist and steer her towards the door.

"For the love of Christ," I says, "be a bit useful and hail us a cab."

We wait outside in the air. It doesn't take long for the skittle to find us something, so desperate is he to get rid of us from the thereabouts of his shop.

"Stop!" he yells at whatever is passing. "Stop please!"

He throws himself in front of a cab before it can get full round him. I'm left to help Mary up alone while the driver busies himself with his horse. The skittle and the nurse-body hover by the shop door and keep their safe distance. Mary is burning a fever and is weak as water. I need to get both hands onto her bustle and heave to get her in, and it's only then, doing this, that I see it on the back of her skirts: the stain.

It's a sight to make you think of Jesus at the post. It's a sight I see and understand, and yet I disbelieve it and tell myself it can't be true. Despite the number of babbies that have come and gone before, despite of all of those that have swelled her up and then let her down, still I can't own that this blood is real. I imagine telling Lydia and it coming out sounding like a lie.

"A miscarriage in a cradle shop, Lizzie? Are you pulling my leg or what?"

Back at the house, the day-maid Aggie is putting her coat on

to leave. I give her an extra shilling to run and fetch Dr. Gumbert and Frederick.

"I don't need the doctor," says Mary. "Just get me Frederick. I want Frederick."

By my fierce eyes, Aggie knows to ignore her.

I sponge Mary in the bath and put her in the bed with a pan by her side and a dish of beef tea on her lap. Soon Dr. Gumbert comes and gives her something to sleep.

"Tell me this is the last time, Doctor," I says to him when she's snoring. "One of these times will have to be last."

"This may well be the last, Lizzie," he says. "This may well be. Get some rest, both of you, and I'll be back in the morning."

When it's getting dark and gone time for excuses—the rogue better not even try to come at me with any—Aggie knocks and says she's looked every place, the Mill, the Club, the Hall of Science, the Exchange, the Warehouse, but he's invisible to be found, and nobody could tell her where he is. Which can only mean he's taken one of his personal days, the ones he thinks we don't know about, to go and hunt the foxes. I thank Aggie and give her the next day off for her troubles. She thanks me in return and asks is there anything she can do.

"Keep tight about this," I says. "That's all I want of you."

He doesn't come that night, or the next. Five days we have to bide for him to grace us.

"I'm told you've been looking for me," he says when final he makes it through the door, fresh of face and looking younger by years. "I was away in the country."

"With the foxes again?"

"Is that a crime, Lizzie? Your tone certainly suggests so."

I sigh and nod in the direction of her chambers. "She's waiting for you in there."

He looks at the door, and now it's his turn to sigh. He lets it out, long and loud. "I *told* her I'd be away and wouldn't be around. Is everything all right?"

"Frederick?" Her voice comes though the wall with surprising force. "Frederick, is that you, my sweet love?"

He freezes like a thief caught by the light of a peeler's lantern.

"Coming, my dear," he says, and strides forward.

I catch his cuff. "For the love of Christ, leave off her for a bit."

He takes my look and gives me one back that says, "I'm sure I don't know what you mean."

But he's no dullard. He understands what has happened and is only acting oblivious to smooth his path past me.

"Oh, Frederick," I hear her say when he goes in to her. "My darling Frederick, thank God it's you," she says, as if he was the savior of her situation and not its first cause.

"My Irish lass," he says, "what has you like this? What have you done to yourself now?"

And once again we're but where we are: torn between what is and what ought be; blest and curst in even portions.

XXV. Hereafter a Blank

There's rules for sending letters to the house. Frederick's five commandments. One: close your envelopes careful. Two: seal them over the glue so the wax touches all four flaps. Three: send secret things in a pack. Four: when addressing your letter, don't use his name but put "Miss Burns" instead. Five: put no other envelope of address inside. Anything breaking these rules ought be handled with care and treated with suspicion.

"Know anything about this?" he shouts through the wall.

I leave the landing skirting boards and go in to him. He's waving a bit of paper in the air. On account of the sudden weather—the heat now pounding at us along with the rain—he has stripped his top down to his innerwear, and is damp all over and pongs of mead.

"What is it?" I says.

"You tell *me*."

"I don't know, I've never seen it before."

"It came with first post. I threw it out because I judged it another of these sham begging letters we have been getting. I did not think on it again until I heard you outside. It's addressed to "Mrs. Engels," which I can only presume to mean you. I wanted to show it to you to be certain it is not anything to worry about or report."

"I'm not expecting anything, Frederick." I'm firm in voice. "It's naught only the usual litter."

I rub my rag around the base of a lamp.

"What does it say, anyhows?"

"Here." He holds it out. "Have Pumps read it to you. I really have to get back."

I call Pumps to the parlor and give it to her.

"Drop that face and give me the gist."

"It's just an address."

She reads it out.

"Again."

She reads it again, and I have it this time.

"What's the signature?"

"There is none."

The address is in St. Giles, but on the Covent Garden side. I can tell by the women with baskets on their heads: flowers for the Market. I knock on the door. He's dressed in his coat when he answers.

"We'll go down the road. I know a quiet place."

We walk through the heat of the lanes and passages.

"Aren't you too hot in that?" I says.

He looks at me out the side of his eye. "You haven't changed."

"You have. You're gone soft. And you've lost the best of your hair."

He orders me a gin. He has a lemonade. He pays for them himself. Counts out from a pile of coppers in his hand.

"You've been asking after me, Lizzie."

"I have."

"What for?"

"Don't let your head swell. I only wanted to see if you're all right."

"I'm grand. Alive."

"I can see that."

"What wind blows you to London? Are you down here now with your man?"

"I am. We're up on Primrose Hill."

"Well for some."

I take from my drink. It bites my throat. "So Killigad told you, then."

"Killigad?"

"The priest in the church here."

"Oh, him. It was another voice told me, but it could well have come first from him. I don't know him personal, I go to another place, St. Patrick's, but I know he's a friend."

"I thought the Church looked dark on you and your kind."

"Arrah, that's only the bishops, putting on a face. They preach against rebellion, but they know, as well as anyone, that fighting against Protestantism is fighting against England and fighting for Catholicity is fighting for Ireland."

The quick heat of the drink has given me a cramp in the stomach. "Have you eaten, Moss? We should get you something to eat. We should go to a restaurant."

"A what?" He shakes his head. "I have enough to eat. If you have any loose money on you, you can give me that."

"I'm not giving you any money, Moss. I don't know where it'd go."

"It won't go to the drink, Lizzie. Can't you see I'm off it?"

"How do I know you're not just putting that on for my benefit?"

"Christ, you really haven't changed."

"Does anyone?"

He sighs and shakes his head. "What are we doing, Lizzie? What has us here together?"

"I don't know."

"What do I mean to you?"

"An old friend. It's a big place, this London."

He doesn't say anything to that. Stares into the lemonade he hasn't touched.

"How much do you need?"

"Anything you can spare."

"What's planned? What are you all scheming?"

"It's all work for the good."

"Ireland."

"What other good is there? Have you gone entirely English in your feelings, Lizzie?"

"Nay, Moss, of course not. Only I made a promise to myself not to get involved. I don't want to know anything about it."

"I'm not asking you to be involved. It won't be like last time. We only need a bit of funding, is all. To get things rolling."

I imbibe in a single gulp, and it goes down easier. "I'll see what I can do."

I get up to leave. He takes my hand. I let him have it. "I'm off, Moss. I've a dinner to serve at home."

"Well, now we know where to find each other."

"I'll be in touch."

At the door, I risk a glance back. Once such a gradely man, he's become large and hard-breathing. And yet I feel I've never been without loving him. Which puts me in a place where I don't know

how anything will be. All I know is that my life will hereafter be blank, and any color of thing could arise to fill it.

⁓

"How are things going to be now?" I says when I open up to the dark morning and see Frederick there, blue-nosed and white-cheeked from the cold and the shock.

He doesn't answer me, just stands there looking like the heart's been torn alive out of his body.

I step back and hold open. The glow of the candles reaches out to take him in. He stoops under the doorpost—the house isn't built for the foreign body—and I see then he's brought Dr. Gumbert with him.

I bob a curtsy. "She's in the bedroom."

We all go in. While Gumbert looks her over, Frederick paces the flags, window to chimneypiece, as if impatient for her to rise out of her death to greet him. I stand and watch the fire in the grate perish.

"Didn't you see anything ailing about her?" Gumbert asks.

"Nay," I says. "It's like she wasted overnight."

Behind me I hear Frederick's tread make a sudden halt. "She had a cough," he says. "But we presumed it the effect of a cold. And she had pain from time to time but—"

I finish to save him from further excuses. "But the Lord Himself knows Mary liked to indulge in a headache."

"Hmm," Gumbert says, and goes back to his examining.

I poke at the fire though I know it's in vain. In truth, I'm scattering the coals and choking the flames. Frederick doesn't take up his pacing again. The room is still to the silence of his halting. I turn and am met by his eyes snuffed like yesterday's lamps. I test

a smile on him, but it makes no impression: a howl hitting a wall and no echo coming back.

"Are you all right, Frederick?" I says. "Can I get you something?"

"*Nein*. Thank you, Lizzie." He goes to look out the window, and there he stays, looking, even though there's naught to see, for I've darkened the panes.

Feeling more alone than I've ever felt, I turn from his back to the bed. Gumbert has his hand inside her night rail and is feeling round her belly. I don't know which is worse: to follow the lump of his hand under the flannel or to move up to her face where the grimace waits.

I knew this was going to happen.

You're not meant to know, but when you look back you sometimes remember a feeling that's like a prior knowing. The face she made from the bed last night—her eyes rolling up before the lids had come down—was the same she used to make from the bloodied child sheets, and I had a sense that this was the last time I'd see it, that this was her farewell to me.

This is it, I thought. This is her now, gone.

I'd pictured her dead before. In those moments of selfishness and envy when thinking can't be controlled or kept from the evil corners, I imagined what I'd gain if she were to die and pass over. I imagined a world that didn't contain her, that didn't brim over with her, and I felt freer in it, and better off. But flickerings of this kind can't be compared to the knowing of real death. Such knowing occurs like an awakening, a sudden switch from night to noontide. "All these years," it says, "all these years you've ignored the pallor of death worn over her. If only you'd opened your eyes you'd have seen she's been dying since the first time she swole with a babby for him. Now the hour has come to grant it. She had no

living child to make her suffer in the rearing, but instead had enough dead to knock her down and leave her eternal wrecked."

And what an awakening it is! What a rousing! What a wrenching from what is comfortable and safe! For though I can still say in my mind that it was *him* who made her sick, the rage in my heart keeps being against *me*; against *me* for letting her be done by him; against *me* for watching by as he killed her by inches.

Says Gumbert: "Hmm, it's probable her heart gave way."

Says I to myself: "God forgive me, but I can well believe it."

Frederick sees him out. I follow their whisperings as far as the sitting room. They slink outside to speak private among men. I go to the window and twitch the blind. They're stood in the middle of the road, in the full force of the wind. Frederick's head is bent so far forward it's near resting on Gumbert's shoulder. Gumbert's mouth is brought to licking distance of Frederick's ear. Looking at them, it makes me wonder do they think I've lost my senses altogether. Can't I see them? Don't I know what they're talking about? "A bad death," they're saying. "A consequence of the lush and the search for pleasure."

Frederick comes back in and leans against the wall. Scratches at his forehead. In his arrangement there's hardness and there's wildness. He hunts the room for something to accuse. By now I've learnt to know him and to trust him, but I'm not free of fear. Saints of men have been known to make dreadful acts under the influence of grief.

"What day is it?" he says.

"Tuesday," I says.

He's yet to cry; we've both of us yet to do it. I think to be held might help bring it on and get it past. I move into the room where it'd be easy for him to come and give onto me, if such was his desire and intending. And indeed he does come to me. But instead

of an embrace he takes my hand and lifts it—lifts it as if to lead me to a dance or to kiss it—and then lets go of it sudden. Drops it so that it falls limp into my skirts. And a relief, it is, for he'd begun to squeeze it hard.

What he does now I wish Mary could be alive to see: he charges past me to her room, flings open the door, throws down by the side of the bed, and prays.

"Mary, Mary," he says between his German orations, "Mary, Mary, forgive me, Mary."

It's a bad and awkward scene to watch. A voice speaks inside of me: "Get up out of that and let her rest in peace. I'll not have you easing your conscience telling her things that matter little now." And there's pleasure in it at first, hearing what's innermost, but I soon judge it cruel. To silence it, I set myself to making the place ready.

I think the end of every task will bring an end to Frederick's supplications, but I'm wrong. He stays down: elbows dug, hands melded, throat scratched by the volume of godly words fetched up. When I've done all I can do on my own, I go to him and put a hand on him. Mary's bottom lip has slipped from the top, and her jaw has fallen down. She's glaring at us. And who'd blame her?

Frederick lifts and turns his face to me.

"What now?" I says again, for I need to know. Mary was the only true kin I had on earth. Nobody could split us. We were got in the same tin or we weren't got at all. When I looked in the glass, two faces looked back. Is there a place possible with myself alone in it? "Tell me, Frederick, what's to happen?"

Letting a quiet moan, he says, "We'll talk about it after the funeral," and then, as if a bell has rung, he starts his crying. The sorrow in me is a deep feeling too, but I don't allow it, not yet. It'll get naught done but pour itself more.

I send the neighbor's boy out for Lydia and Father Logan. They're here in no time and with all the bits needed to wash and compose her.

"Is *he* all right?" Lydia whispers, gesturing at Frederick collapsed over himself on the elbow chair. "Will he want to help?"

I shake my head. "He's grand where he is for now."

Lydia asks can she have the night dress we cut off Mary. She wants it to make new patterns with, and I give it to her glad. As Beloff used to say, "Every good bit of cloth ought be made into something else."

After we've bathed her, they go out to Frederick and leave me alone to do the cotton. I can hear them murmuring on the other side of the wall, which takes some of the closeness out of the task, makes it seem a shared and dirty thing.

"You're only getting in the way, Mr. Engels," I hear Lydia say. "Go home and have a wash, get your letters writ and the notice published. Come back this evening when everything's arranged."

There's some shuffling, and rattling, and the glug and slam of a glass.

"Do whatever you have to do," he says. "Don't hesitate to get the best. I'll look after it."

Then the door bangs. With the sound of him gone I'm calmer, and after a minute I settle down to it and do the best I can according to Logan's instructions.

When I'm finished I call them back and Logan unfolds the habit he's brought.

"Is that the best there is, Father?" I says.

"A simple funeral is wiser, Lizzie. You don't want to grate on the feelings of any."

"Didn't you hear the man before, Father? There's money to be spent. And isn't it occasions like this that give money its value?"

Lydia comes between us. "How about we use this habit, Lizzie, and we'll get her a good set of beads, the best we can find."

Begrudging, I agree, and she goes for them.

When she comes back, they're so good-looking and dear, I have to turn away while she weaves them into her hands.

Night is already down when the men come and put her into the box. We've to do the beads again, and her hair and the habit too, but once she's out for show in the sitting room, I can say we've done her justice. We light more candles and put rows of chairs about. Flowers arrive, and sandwiches and raw spirit; gifts from round the town. Bodies known and bodies unknown to me pass through. On their way they boil water and make tea, pour glasses of whiskey and set out plates of beef and ham. Some linger only a minute, others stay longer to kneel and join the responses, or take a chair and share in the talk. At first, they're afraid to speak above the breath, for fear of being the first to laugh, but soon the room is filled with the excitement that comes up at such gatherings, and they get louder and bolder, turning their talk away from Mary and towards their own living cares.

Some time after eight, the house thronged, Moss arrives. I haven't seen him since Lydia's wedding. Waist thickened, trousers unbraced and coat unpatched, shoulders lowered and skin mottled and eyes sunk: is this the same man I near wed? He's come in the company of Jamie and Kit and Joseph and Dan and some other Fenian boys, a gang of seven or eight. They offer their condolences to me with manners that can't be doubted, but once they've come away from me and taken up their drinks, they feign a menacing cast, stood together in a bunch and glowering about like it's the peelers they are. It's plain they've come in force to make a point, about rich factory men ill-using Irish women to death, or some such guff. I only hope they'll tire and sooner go. I want no trouble.

Not long after, Frederick returns. Jamie sees him appear at the door and nudges Moss. Moss does the same to his neighbor, and soon they're all shifting about in their boots and sniffing and rubbing their noses along their sleeves as if preparing for fisticuffs. Frederick doesn't even see them. He has come with a man, a lank with a plume in his hat and a bag of tools in his hand; it's this Mr. Plume who takes up the whole of Frederick's attention. He tows him over the side of the box, and together they look over Mary. They huddle close like plotters. Size her up like a rural does a sow.

The room has gone quiet to watch them. Whispers go round, but don't reach me. There's such an air that if someone doesn't tell me what's going on, I might smother in it. The Fenian gang shuffle away from the wall and make a ring round the three: Mary, Frederick, and Mr. Plume. Moss comes to me with his cap in his hand.

"Lizzie, I feel obliged to tell you, for I think you ought know. They want to make casts of her face and hands."

"Merciful Jesus."

"Now, if you like, we can—"

"Leave this to me." I push through. "Lads, step back. I'll deal with this."

I take Frederick into the bedroom, get rid of the bodies gathered there, and close the door behind us.

"Are you trying to mortify me?"

"It would be something to keep, Lizzie. Something we would have."

"Something we'd—?"

"A memory. A souvenir. Is it such a bad thing to want?"

"This is a great shock for us all, Frederick. And we must each of us find our ways to bear it. But this isn't the way." My speech rises high out from me. "This is *not* the way!"

I run from the room and into Lydia's biding arms. "Poor petal," she says. "My poor poor petal."

When Frederick comes out again, he looks tense and difficult, like he no longer feels his place among us. Under our hard gaze, he shows Plume out and, after a whiskey and some words with Father Logan, goes himself. He doesn't appear again—thanks be to Christ—till the Thursday morning at the graveside.

There, he doesn't join in the prayers. I'm sure he's happy to have them—the marks they make in the wind that would otherwise roll across the field unchecked—but he has a look on his face, a superior look that says, "This is a habit I've long since grown out of." Of course, if he'd been there at the closing of the box; if he'd seen how her hollowness and ash turned to a radiance that the oils and the candles couldn't full explain, he'd now understand that religion isn't something light to be taken up and put down, like a book.

Back at the house again, the party goes on till the place is drunk dry. It's past midnight by the time we're left alone; past midnight and well gone the hour to talk about our affairs. I don't want it put off another day. But Frederick has other matters on his mind.

"I received this."

I stop the dishing up and turn to him. He's sat on a stool by the fire, holding up a letter.

"It's from Karl."

"Read it to me."

"You won't like it."

"Frederick, tell it out."

He unfolds it slow and reads. When he's done, he bends forward, pinches the bone between his eyes.

"Is that what he has to say?" I storm the bucket. The crocks have rare known such fury. "Thinking about money at such a time. The man's a savage."

"How do I reply? How do I even—?" He starts to whimper.

"It doesn't merit replying, Frederick. Let him souse in a bit of silence from you."

"The poor girl loved me with all her heart. He doesn't see it. He doesn't care."

"Put it away now. And wrap that blanket round yourself proper or you'll freeze."

When I'm finished with the dishes, I go to wring my hands over the heat. He swigs a sup from the bottle and hands me the end.

"You know what, Lizzie? I didn't just bury her today. I buried the last vestige of my youth."

"Does that mean you'll be looking to get it back, your youth, or are you going to give it up and live like a grown man at last?"

A silence comes down on us like a heavy curtain falling. I give way first, for a man can keep holding the weight forever. "Listen, Frederick"—I crouch at his feet—"what's to happen? I want to know how to think about us."

He puts a loose strand of my hair behind my ear. "You can think about us however you want. You are free."

I sit back onto the floor. "Freedom? I don't know what it is. And I don't want it."

"Come on, Lizzie, get up from there." He comes off his stool. "Don't dirty yourself on the ground." He takes my wrists and drags me to my feet with a force I'm sure he doesn't intend. He looks as surprised as I am when we finish locked into a standing embrace.

My stomach is turned over and my head in a rush even before he lifts me up into his arms and takes me to the bed. I let him pull me free of my bodice and my crinoline, and I let him fetch me, gasping and fraught. Afterwards I cry and he holds me. Then he cries a bit, and tears at his hair as well, and I have to bite his hand

to pull him out of his frenzy. Then we are quiet. We watch the candles lean and dart sideways with the draft.

"I'll not live hid away like she did."

"Are you talking about marriage, Lizzie?"

"I am."

He shakes his head.

"I'm talking about a good life, an honest life. I want to live proper."

"What does it mean, this *proper*?"

"I know you have your own ideas, Frederick. And I know they're different and brilliant, and there's naught wrong with that. But I have a mind too, and, let me tell you, it's full of worries."

"Come, Lizzie, what worries you so?"

"I've not a family left. Only my half-brother Thomas and his rotten children. I've long given up chance of having my own. We're not getting any younger. Isn't it time to settle up?"

"For the love of God, Lizzie, these terms you use."

"For those who survive it's hard, Frederick. But we're lucky. We've the bond that unites those who have been loved by someone now dead."

"What has the marriage institution got to do with such a bond?"

"Naught. Naught at all. But it'd be a seal. It'd make it actual and known. And it'd be a great gift to me. You'd be giving me peace and comfort."

"My gift is love and protection. You can depend on me without registering your dependence."

"It wouldn't mean the end to your freedom, Frederick, I swear it. You won't have children by me. I'd put naught on your path to obstruct you."

"Why are you insisting, Lizzie? What is this new mania?"

"It's not new. It's as old as I am."

"Do not tell me you have always dreamed of being a wife, Lizzie, because I shan't believe it."

"Nay. Not a wife. What I've always wanted is to be able to hand myself over when I'm tired. To put down tools and know I'll not starve for it."

"Can't you do that anyway, with my support?"

"I'm not sure, Frederick. As it is, I'm not sure if I can ever rest full."

He lies back and looks at the ceiling. Picks at his whiskers and makes as if to contemplate. I pull the sheets up.

"I do not want you to be in hopes, Lizzie. I have to live according to my convictions."

"What about the feelings of your heart?"

"Lizzie, listen to me," but he doesn't say anything more.

Sudden, over the bed, the spirit of Beloff looms: "Christ, girl, don't kick over your own trough."

"I understand your position, Frederick, I do."

"But do you truly, Lizzie? Do you understand that I cannot offer you more than a spoken vow. Can that be enough for you?"

I turn to the wall. "I know what it is. Your heart is in her keeping forever."

"Lizzie, that's not it."

"I can't compete with a dead woman."

"Lizzie, no."

I turn back and take hold of him, look steady into his eyes. "Just promise you'll be honest with me."

"I'm the most honest man in England."

"Don't lie to me about your women and the rest of it."

"I shall never hide anything important from you." He pulls me in. "And you? Do you accept what I can give you?"

In the end, I'm moved by the fear of saying no. But that can grow to be love too, same as any other beginning.

Phase
the Last

1871 - 1872

August

XXVI. Private Property

I am as you see me. A pauper woman on an expensive couch. I don't pretend to be something more.

Our mother—may her soul find cushion in heaven—didn't last on this earth long enough to pass much down, but I do remember one lesson she gave us. "Give thanks for what you get," she said. "Be thankful for whatsoever life bestows on you." And all my life I've kept her teaching close and tried to be true to it. But this time spent in London has brought about a change in me. I've learnt to be more like you, Mary. You who, if the Queen put the hair of her head under your feet, still you wouldn't be satisfied.

Before, I might have found myself saying, "Thanks be" when Frederick was gone out and the maids were busy with jobs and I had rule of the morning room; "Thanks be to Jesus" when the doors to the parlor were folded shut and the bottles of spirit in the cabinet in reach; "Thanks be to Jesus God Almighty" might have

slipped out natural and easy, for I used to think that to do other-wise—to be silent in the face of a gift—was like sinning.

But these days, at moments like this, I'm mindful that, though I was born low and have been raised in station, I don't need to fall on my knees to enjoy what's rightful and mine. I think, This is my lush and I will drink it. I think, This is my foot and I will undress it. I think, This is my stocking and I will throw it. I think, This is my carpet and I will rub it, if that's what pleases me.

You'd be proud of me, sister, if you could only see me.

XXVII. The Wheel of History

I listen to the house: the cupboards and the cabinets and the hangings and the ornaments gathered up in an unnatural silence.

Upstairs, I find Frederick from his desk and lying belly down on the couch, his arm fallen limp over the side, a page of bond on the rug by his hand. I fear he's been like this since first post and might be like this for some time yet. Hours—days—it can take him to get over a letter from his mother.

He groans. "I can't let out a fart without that woman finding out and expressing some Lamb-of-God opinion on it."

"Come, Frederick. Try not to let her come on top of you. Would you like to take a walk? A bit of fresh air would do you the world of good."

"She's got her hands on Karl's address, and now she too thinks he's to blame for the whole French debacle."

Thirty years gone from home and—Christ have pity on him—
he still needs her say-so. I look at the unopened packets of paper
on his desk, the books piled and biding. "Why don't you get back to
work, Frederick?"

He pushes his face into a cushion.

"Come on, now. Don't be like that."

He comes up for air. Twists his neck round and rests his ear
down. "She takes as gospel every police invention and piece of slan-
der invented by the Paris gossipmongers. She raises a hue and cry
about a few hostages and some houses burned down. But the forty
thousand slaughtered by the forces of repression, does she have a
single word to say about *them*?"

I'm unmoved: she's never had a word to say about *me* either,
and I don't see it vexing him so.

"Frederick, she's your Mammy. Everybody's Mammy drives
them up the wall. That's what Mammies do. And, anyhows, how
can she know any different? You say yourself that if you had to rely
on the German rags, you'd know only lies."

He moans. Sits up. Combs back his hair. "You're right, Lizzie. I
am sorry for my mood."

"That's all right, Frederick. Now back to work, there's a good
man."

He gets up. Goes the opposite way to the desk. His shirt hangs
loose from his breeches. He leans on the windowsill. Outside, a day
with a winter countenance and a summer constitution.

"I'm dining at the Club tonight."

"Again?"

"I'm sorry to miss another one, Lizzie. But these Frenchmen
are like children. They need my supervision or they start fighting
with each other. With Karl recovering in Brighton, I'm the only
one who can give them proper counsel." He comes away from the

window. Tucks his shirt in. "Which reminds me. Could you do something for me?" He goes to the desk and writes something on a bit of paper. Gives it to me with two sovereigns from the box. "I'd do it myself, only this mood I've fallen into leaves me little inclined to the task."

"What is it?"

"One of our Communards has been evicted from his lodgings. A young trooper by the name of Troplong. The landlady needs to be paid off."

"Isn't there a fund? Doesn't Mr. Jung look after that side of things?"

"Come now, Lizzie, we all have to loosen our purse strings."

"We all of us, meaning us and us alone."

He makes not to have heard. Goes back behind his desk and sits down. "He'll also need something to go on for a few days. Until we find him a situation. The address is written there. It's in Soho, not far from the Club. Give the money to the landlady in my name and obtain a receipt."

I'm about to refuse. On a point of principle, I'm about to tell him I'm over being his runner—at some point the money spout will have to be plugged—but I decide, in this moment, to use the trip into town as an opportunity.

"That oughtn't be a problem, Frederick. But are you sure that's enough? I'd hate to go all the way and find myself short."

"Maybe you're right. Better to be safe."

He lays out another coin. I put my cheek out for a kiss. He gives me a whole line of them: brow, nose, lip, chin. I come away before he loses charge of himself.

"Oh, and, Lizzie"—he peeps round the door and calls down the landing—"give her a bit of a scare, can you? The landlady, I mean.

Just enough to make her think twice before turning our working heroes onto the street again."

I give the paper to the cabby. "I'm going here."

"Dean Street, ma'am?"

"That's right."

"Quick as a flash."

He takes a queer route, down narrow lanes bare fit for a carriage, up roads I've never lighted on before, and we're there in no time. A grubby-looking tavern. A green door. A scrawn of a boy lollying outside. That must be him. "Mr. Troplong?" He looks up from the ground. There's a familiar flavor to his eyes. "Have we met before? Have you been to the house?"

"No, madame."

"In that case, my name is Mrs. Burns."

"I was expecting—"

"Well, you got me."

His sack of things sits by his feet. He looks only just out of the bed, with his hair plastered down and his combinations coming out the ends of his coat. "She put me out."

"Could be worse. She could've done it last month, when the rain was coming down like ten thousand."

I knock and a girl answers.

"She's busy, ma'am."

"Who's busy, child?"

"The lady of the house, ma'am."

"So she's in, is she?"

"She's in, but she's taken up."

"No worries. I'll be here in the hall till she has a moment."

"Sorry, ma'am, I can't allow that."

"Arrah, be reasoned, girl. Won't it save you answering the door

to me every minute from now till midnight, and aren't I halfway in as it is?"

Mary used to say my feet were like boats, that in the last detail God mixed me up with Moss, whose dainty little yokes keep him upright only with the help of the angels. I follow the girl's gander down to them—my boat-feet—and we stand together a minute, marveling at their reach: several long inches over the threshold, and solid as blocks, hobnails like rods, no hope of closing a door against them.

Defeated, she lets me in, and I beckon Troplong to follow.

"Wait here," she says, and bolts up the staircase.

The hall is a dark passage with bare boards and peeling wallpaper. There's a smell of piss and rotting meat coming up through the kitchen doors. "Not so bad," I whisper back to Troplong. He moons at me, half-mazed.

We're not long biding before the lady herself comes tearing down the stairs, screeching and flaming like a hooer of the apocalypse. The girl follows her down; puts herself to cringe behind her skirts.

"Whisht, woman!"—I hold a hand up, a sovereign between two fingers—"There's this if you want it. You can take it and be happy, or we can go and give it to someone with a bit of sense."

"Four shilling a week plus board," she says. "That's what I ask and it's as fair a price as you'll find. He's a month owing. That there sovereign'll bare cover the vittles he's ate. Gut of a cow, he has. I ain't running no parish."

"I'm sorry, Mrs.—?"

"Gambon. *Miss* Gambon."

"Miss Gambon, my good woman, I'm not here to bargain with you. This amount will clear what's behindhand and get him through to October, do you understand?"

"I don't know who you think you is, and I don't bloody care neither. He knew the price before he went and took the room, didn't he? I want him out. Ain't having no more with the foreigners."

Our eyes lock a long minute. I make sure to see a tremor come to her lashes before yielding.

"All right, Miss Gambon." I take a crown from my reticule. "Fair is fair. Each of us has to make a living, and you deserve to be compensated for your labors." I make a sudden step forward. She doesn't flinch, but behind her the girl shrinks further and gasps. "But mark me, Miss Gambon, these here coins will secure our soldier till October, bed and board, and we'll not hear a peep from you till then."

She purses. The gingers on her top lip bristle. She holds out her claw.

"And another thing. If we catch on you're treating this hero shabby, we'll make sure you'll be spending this, and more of your own, on fixing the windows."

I dangle the coins a minute before dropping them in. A second and they're jangling down into the pouch of her gown.

"Now, if you wouldn't mind writing me up a receipt."

"A what?"

"A receipt. For what we've just paid for."

"This ain't no shop. This here is a home, and a respectable one."

"Can you write?"

"Excuse *me,* of course I can write."

"Then write this down. *Two pounds received to cover Mr. Troplong's bed and board till the first of October eighteen seventy-one.*"

"It were a sovereign and a crown you gave me. One pound, five shilling."

"Well, put that down, then, woman. And hurry. I've other places to be."

She shakes her head and her wild locks flare. Sends the girl off to fetch the paper. "Don't know who you think you is. The a-ffrontery I've to face in this place."

When the receipt is done, I make as if to read it. "This look all right to you, Mr. Troplong?"

He looks at me. Now at the paper. Back at me.

"Is it signed, Mr. Troplong? Can you read her name?"

"*Oui.* Yes."

"Grand so. You can give Mr. Troplong back his key now, Miss Gambon."

She frees it from the hoop on her hip and tosses it at him with a sneer.

I fold the paper into my pocket. "We'll hold this in our care. We like to keep track of the legals. Now, if you wouldn't mind pointing me in the way of St. Giles, I've another appointment waiting for me there."

Moss doesn't look surprised to see me.

"I was in the area," I says.

"I'll get my coat," he says, as if women callers at peculiar hours are part of his regular day.

"Don't bother. I'll come up."

He squints at me, queasy.

"Aren't we intimate enough, Donal Óg O'Malley?"

There's four mattresses in the room. Two men. Moss nods at the door. They leave without a word.

"My privates," he says when they're gone.

"You're a sergeant now? How many under you?"

"These two and seven others."

My face, I'm sure, doesn't hide my disbelief. "You're doing well for yourself."

"A man can't fail among his own people."

He makes little circles on the floor, unsure where he ought be going.

"I've no drink in the place, but I can wet some tea."

"I'm fine for tea, Moss."

I sit on the only chair. He takes the mattress facing.

"So what can I do for you?" he says.

"You can let fall the performance, for a start. There's naught you can do for me, and you know it. You've asked me for help and I've come to talk on it further."

"What's there to talk on? You know what we need."

"I do. And I'm here to tell you money is tight right now. There isn't the flow there once was. There's been an intake of Frenchmen, and they have to be looked after."

"The French have sympathy for us."

"The French have their own problems."

He sighs a long sigh. "And the man you live with. His lot. Don't they have guns? Can you get us some?"

I shake my head. "They're book men, Moss. Organizers of things. They're not involved in the fighting side."

He shrugs. "I suppose people must fill their time with something."

I turn a deaf ear to his tone. "Aren't you getting what you need from America?"

He doesn't answer. Scratches instead at an itch on the back of his leg. By the look of the place, I wouldn't wonder if he's ravaged by fleas.

"A donation would mean we wouldn't have to turn to crime."

"I'm not here to stop your crime. If I give you money, it's because you ask for it and I care for you."

"So you'll give it?"

"I didn't say that. I have to think on it."

"How long more do you need for your thinking?"

"I can't just make it appear. I've to get it into my purse, and that can be work. It doesn't just lie around."

"Can't you tell him? Ask him out straight? We could make, you know, an alliance."

"Nay, Moss. Forget that idea. He's a friend of Ireland, he supports your struggle, but he thinks your tactics foolish. I've often heard him say it. He's against secret societies, and he looks down on conspiracies, they all do. So you ought get that right in your head now. If I give you anything, it'll come from me, Lizzie Burns, and me alone."

There's a knock. One of the men pokes his head in. "Sorry to disturb, Sergeant, only the other men are here." Moss waves him out. The man nods, first to Moss and now to me, a holy show of respect, like he's in audience with the bishop. I can't help smiling at it, for it's proof for what they say: the man that's down has stones thrown at him; the man that's up has his chair lifted.

"So, will you give us the money or not?"

It's offhand, too short, and I'm tempted to remind him that, if anyone owes anyone, it's *he* who owes *me*: *he* took away my chances of having children, *he* robbed me of my birthright to a normal life, and it would do him good to think on it before speaking.

"Moss, listen to me now. If I gave you something, you could use it on yourself. Get yourself somewhere proper to live. Set yourself up with a job somewhere."

He shakes his head. Runs his nose along the length of his arm. "I've no want for such things now. There's bigger matters to fix."

I find this hard to swallow. Isn't a clean home and a stable situation what we're all of us after, whether we're high or low, English or Irish?

Feeling sad for him—naught but death will wean him off his wild ideas of a free Ireland—I turn to look through the dirt on the window: a view of bricks and, between the two facing buildings, a thin slice of sky.

"Do you get out at all, Moss? Or is it *all* about the old country now, with no room left for a bit of distraction?"

"Distraction?"

"You ought make time for enjoying yourself. I don't like to think of you stuck in here all day, scheming and plotting and making yourself mad. We could go out one night together. To a show. Or a tuppenny hop. I'd say there's grand places for dancing around here."

He strikes down on his thigh. Now holds the striking hand out in a pleading manner. "Lizzie, are you only here to torment me? Do you have any intention of helping us?"

Like after a cold gust on the face, I'm woken to my senses. I gather my ends and stand to leave, more to hide my embarrassment than out of a desire to be gone. "I'll see what I can do."

On my way out, he gives me the bit about an Irishman's duty to take action. "We must fight," he says, "or our names will go down in history as naught more than braggarts." And it's an affecting speech, it touches the roots of me, though really I know it's only the same Manchester story repeating itself. I'd be a fool to believe it'll be any different on the second telling.

∽

It's Lydia who tells me. I see more of her now that Mary's gone, now that there's less shame to having me as company. Salford being too far to come, she sends messages through Frederick at

the mill, and we meet in town. I always get her a bit of cake and put a nip of something in her tea. She appreciates my good offices, though it'd gall her pride to say it.

"Moss wants to meet with you."

"What for? I haven't seen him since Mary's thing. What have we to say to each other?"

"He's a changed man."

"I don't give a fourpenny feck what he is."

"He's writing poems now, I'm told."

"Poems."

"And I hear he's taken the oath."

"Against the drink?"

"Aye, that. And against the Queen."

"Mercy on us, the double whop."

I don't go to him, despite the pressure of my feelings. Instead, like a man gone feral, he comes to me. Walks right across to Salford to knock at the house. I don't let him in. We talk through the gap in the door.

"No flowers?"

He seizes his hips with his empty hands. "Can we go somewhere?"

"Anything you say to me, you can say to the neighbors."

"I've come to ask for your help. Won't you hear me out?"

"I'm listening."

He sighs. Looks up and down the road. Brings his face close and lowers his voice to a whisper. "Can I trust you?"

"Desperate men must take risks."

His face reddens, but he keeps it down. "Have you heard about Colonel Kelly and Captain Deasy?"

"Arrested for plotting. I heard. It's in the news."

"Well"—he swallows—"I've come to tell you our plan."

I slam the door. Put my back against it. Stay like this a minute. When my heart settles, I go to the window. He's still outside, muttering to himself and using the edge of my step to scrape the muck from his boots.

"All right, you moocher, come in. But don't take anything off. You'll only be staying long enough for me to kick you out on your back."

He refuses my offer of a short but takes a hot coffee with milk. I pull him over a chair.

"I'd sooner stand," he says.

Between slurps, he gives me out the particulars. There's a new man, come from America. A man called Condon. A man of action. Under his command, they're going to get Kelly and Deasy out from under the law.

"Where are the men being kept?"

"Bellevue."

I let out with a mocking laugh. "You're going to break them out of Bellevue?"

"Not a bit of it," he says with a seriousness that'd take you by the throat. What they're going to do, in fact, is rescue the men when they're being taken from the jail to the courthouse. The police van will be ambushed when it passes under the railway arches on Hyde Road, the keys will be nabbed, and the prisoners will be delivered to freedom.

"I see. And where would my money go in all of this?"

"We've no firearms. We've to send someone up to Birmingham."

I fold my arms across. I'm frowning, I can tell. "Better to be alone, Moss, than in bad company."

"Look who's talking."

I almost laugh. "It's from *my* bad company you're looking for help, and don't you forget it!"

He winces.

I don't relent. "And another thing. It's a swindle, if you ask me, this Fenian business. Organized by smart Americans who are playing off your dreams to make money for their own excesses. It can only be that someone's making money out of this, Moss, and I can see it isn't you."

He listens to me. Bides till I've had my rant right out. "Can you help us or not?"

I look away, at the floor, at the walls, but I can't think my feelings away. "When is it planned for?"

"The eighteenth."

"I can't give you money."

"We're not asking for much."

"Did you hear me? I said I can't give you money. Hyde Road, but, is only a short walk from here. I'll keep the doors open on the eighteenth and you can come if you need somewhere. That's the most I can do."

He seems happy with this; he sees the size of it once he's thought on it a moment. He holds out a cool hand. I overlook it and bring him to the door.

"Would I be right in saying you're off the booze?"

"Thirst produces thirst, Lizzie, and naught more useful than that."

September

XXVIII. Means to Satisfy

The Girls are home looking adult and abraded. Janey appears to have dwindled to her bones. Tussy is pale in the face and has dark lines under her eyes. They come to the parlor door to greet us, kiss us on the cheek, and fill us with their new scents, but once this duty is done, they fall back to where they were, collapsed on the couch among the crowd of bickering Frenchmen.

It's a new lot. Communards just come over. Frederick gives me all the names. He manages it without interrupting the rumpus, and I'm thankful for it.

"What are they arguing over?" I says.

"The Commune," he says. "Why it failed."

We'll be here a while.

Frederick goes to join in. I take a seat outside the circle, by the second fireplace, and try to catch Tussy's attention. I want to ask her about France. I want to sit with her and have her tell me everything

from beginning to end. What did they see? How is Laura coping after the loss? Is it true they were all arrested? But she can't be reached. My looks land unheeded on her cheek, her ear, her neck, so taken is she by the man Lissagaray, with his untamed handkerchief and disheveled hair, who is now reaching so far forward on his seat to pay her court that he might as well be lying across her knee. Janey can't be got either. She, too, is fascinated by the foreign attention. Beside her, the man Longuet has put his hand on the brocade a dangerous distance from hers, and she's busy finding reasons to bring it ever closer. It's a touching spectacle, a real bowel mover, and it hasn't gone unnoticed by Jenny, who, after a last attempt to put herself between the straining bodies, comes away and demands my company, downstairs, immediate.

"In the kitchen, Lizzie. Please."

I let her off and leave her fume a minute before making my way down. I find her playing tragedy queen on the square of floor between the stove and cupboard. Nim has put herself out of the way, in the far corner; her eyes, like gems in the gloom, meet mine; something passes between us, something I don't recognize nor have a name for.

"It's disgusting," Jenny says.

"What is?" I says, turning from Nim to give the once-over to the leftovers from the lunch we weren't invited to.

"Lissagaray. He's twice Tussy's age. He must be stopped."

I find a drumstick intact and smell it. "I'm sure it's only innocent."

She halts, mid-pace, to take full possession of me. "Oh, Lizzie, you can be so naive. Has anyone ever told you how naive you are?"

Seeing a row threaten, Nim gives Jenny a plate of fruit and sends her out with it. "Go on now, Mrs. Marx. You have guests."

I sigh and drop the drumstick onto the plate, make to follow Jenny up.

"No, you stay, Mrs. Burns," says Nim. "I need you for something."

She looks up the stairs for anybody who might be coming before closing the kitchen door. She takes me into the scullery, closes that door too.

"What is it, Helen?" I says, close enough to her now to see her fretful and quickened. "What's the matter with you?"

"You must take this back." She reaches into her clothes and comes out with the money note, the same five-jack I gave her before. "I cannot account for it, Mrs. Burns. If it is found in my keeping, they will have questions I cannot answer. It is burning a hole in my pocket. Please, you must take it back, with my thanks."

"If you can't use it, Helen, give it to *someone* who can."

My meaning is plain to her, but he's a subject she'd rather not talk on. Given the choice, she'd die with her tongue under her belt and the identity of things hidden. She looks lost and exposed, like a little animal living outside its defenses for the first time. But there's no help for it now.

"I understand, Mrs. Burns. But how do you suppose I get it to him? Everything leaving this house is tampered with. It would be lost."

"Can't you go yourself? Aren't you free to travel on your day off?"

"I have promised to stay away."

"Promised? Who have you promised? Him or *them*?"

She pushes the five-jack against my breast. "Please, Mrs. Burns, no more of this. Take it now."

I close a hand over hers in an effort to get it away from me, for I can't have this money either. If I have it, I won't be able to hold on to it for long: I'll end up giving it to Moss. And I mustn't do that. I mustn't have a reason to see him again. I mustn't start once more on the old round.

A call comes from upstairs and Nim runs out to answer it, leaving the note to drop to the ground at my feet. I bend down and crunch it into a ball and curse money for ever having come near me.

The comic singer has just come off and we're biding for the flash dancers. In the third or fourth row, we are, right up the front, a tuppence more than the places farther back, and for what? To be howled at, is what. Howled and hurled at by the children of St. Giles who come down from the heavens and nab the good seats not paid for.

"I've a surprise for you," I says.

"What is it?" Moss says.

"If I told you," I says, fanning away the heat from the gaslight, "it wouldn't be a surprise anymore, would it?"

Beside me, a girl with feathers in her tatty-looking bonnet calls out a filthy saying, and her intimates, the gang of roughs thick-spread about her, burst out.

"I swear they're getting worse than the boys," I says, and he laughs and takes my hand into his, lays it on his thigh.

The lights dim, a drum is beaten, and the spectacle begins again. In the dark, I lean in and kiss him on the rough of his cheek. I feel my hand squeezed as a response.

Afterwards, we eat something quick from a stand, and now he takes me to a tavern, a quiet place with only ourselves and the Holy Ghost in it.

"I thought we were going to go dancing?" I says.

"I'm gone too old for that," he says. "All the jostling and the noise. Aren't we as well off here?"

"You don't even drink! I'd be imbibing alone, and there's something improper in that."

He shrugs as if to say my drinking and my habits for doing it are my own business.

"Arrah, you're useless. I won't go home without a dance. I've been looking forward to a dance all day."

"Stand up there and give us a jig, can't you?"

"Stand up yourself, Moss O'Malley. Seeing as you're too embarrassed to go with me to a real place, you can dance with me here."

"I will *not*."

"Get up out of that, there's nobody about. What's stopping you?"

"There's no music."

"We can make our own."

I drag him up and start him off. "Stay with me," I says, and hum a melody to keep his step in time and his feet from stomping on mine.

"Does this song ever end?" he says.

"Don't be lazy. We all have to work for our ready."

But I see he's not finding the fun in it, he can't summon the proper pleasure, and I feel sorry for him, having to do what doesn't come natural because he feels obliged. "We can stop if you're tired."

"Aye, let's sit down. Please."

He gets something soft and I get something hard, and we drink. "To our love," I says to myself when we touch glasses, "to our love and the day without end." As soon as I think it, however, my mood sinks. I'm not used to happiness, and to feel it now makes me afraid. What if I can't make him feel it too, at any cost?

"I'm afraid," I says.

"Never be afraid," he says. "And if you are, tell no one."

He gulps from his drink. Wipes with his sleeve the wet ring his glass leaves on the counter. He's got to be a quiet man, I can see

that now. Learned his lesson, he has, about giving out too much, about revealing himself before he's aware, so now he does the other thing, which is to lock away feeling and impart little. And, if I'm honest, I like it this way; I prefer them quiet. I've had enough of talking men who use superior phrases to tell you naught. Moss, he'll tell you anything you wish to know, but in few words, because words are no use; there's no way to ever really say things.

"Give us a poem," I says.

"Not a chance."

"My God, has the soul been drained out of you along with the drink?"

He scoffs. "What would a poem be worth to you?"

"I won't know *that* till I hear it."

He ponders this a second. "All right, but you must swear not to jeer."

I throw my eyes up: "I swear."

He taps a finger on his glass: a show of thinking.

"Well, do you have one or not?"

"Hold on, it has to come to me."

Another moment, now, and he clears his throat and, keeping his eyes down, moans out a few passages.

"What was that?"

"A lament for departed lovers."

"Is it your own?"

He doesn't say anything. "It might be my own," his silence says, "or it might be someone else's, and it's your own ignorance that prevents you from knowing the difference." Once upon a time, such a silence might have smothered me, or it might have made me want to smother *him,* but right now I feel him nearer to me than anyone else in the world; right now, in this quiet, my heart warms with attachment to him.

"Moss?"

"Aye?"

"Do you think you can forgive my spurnings in former days?"

He shakes his head. "I try not to think about times gone. They're gone for a reason. To be forgot."

"So you don't ever think about it? About us, before?"

"I do, of course, but I don't encourage it in myself."

And I know what he means. I can understand that. To think on what's past will only bring regret into your life and make you sad. But does he miss me at all? Would he ever want me that way again? For him to say he has found distance from our earlier mistakes is not enough. I need to know, does he yearn? Does he have wants?

"I reckon it's time for your surprise," I says, for I suppose the sight of money, if naught else, will excite some feeling in him.

"Oh?" he says, and indeed, he does appear roused. And why should I judge him harsh for it? A love with no interest does not exist. We always expect something for what we give.

"Hand me my bag," I says.

"Your bag?" he says.

"Didn't I give it to you? To mind?"

"I didn't see you with a bag all night. Are you certain you had one?"

"Of course I am. A reticule, it was. With beading on it. You know the one. Where did I put it?"

He checks around the stools and now around the floor where we danced. I delve into my pockets: maybe he's right, maybe I didn't bring it, maybe I put the money in here instead? But, nay. There's no mistake. I had my bag. The vision of it comes to me now: sitting on the floor between my feet in the theater.

"Christ. I left it in the penny gaff."

"What was in it?"

"Money. For you. A whole five pounds."

At first he's stiff and dumb, so surprised is he to discover he possesses the powers to change my mind. Only now does it dawn on him that his labors might have been in vain, the reward for his work lost. He jumps to a stand. "We ought go back and find it. Someone might have handed it in."

"Oh, Moss, where on earth do you think you are? It'll be gone, and you know it."

Desperate, he looks at the air all around him, as if God, the Great Doer of Justice, might drop a note down to replace the one lost. His desperation, however, turns quick to distrust. His eyes narrow at me. His arms fold across. How soon the aspect of things can change.

"Do you think I was born yesterday?"

"For godsake, Moss, this is no rig. I'm telling you, I had some money that I was going to give you, and I lost it. That's the fact of what happened."

A hand goes up to cover his eyes from the horror of it. A curse flies out from between his clenched teeth.

"I'm sorry, Moss. Really I am. I'll try to get you some more."

He whips his cap off the counter and uses it to swipe his empty glass onto the floor, where it breaks into sharp pieces. "I wish I knew what you wanted from me, Lizzie Burns," he says on his way to the door. "I just wish I knew."

XXIX. New Needs

The fury of my love comes late and slow. Over the course of days, it seeps up from the bottom till it rings in my temples and pumps at my neck. The effect of it, however, is to strengthen me. To make me more calm and correct. All of my thoughts, now, are fixed on a single purpose: to make another five pounds to match those I lost.

The butcher advances me a pound, but says if it's not cleared with the rest of the account by Friday, he'll put a penny interest a day on top of it. The baker refuses to give me anything. He points at a sign by the till.

"Oh, for godsake, what does *that* say?"

"*No credit given.*"

"Can't you make an exception? Mr. Engels is the most honest and reliable gent in the parish. He'll have you paid off in no time."

He shakes his head and says that may be so, but these little sums the housewives borrow from him add up to fortunes, and it's

getting him into trouble with the bank, not to mention the menfolk who come and give him earfuls about handing over cash to their women without their authority. He has stopped with it altogether, it's not worth the trouble.

"If it's extra money you need," he says, "go and pawn a candlestick like a normal woman."

Candlesticks, aye. And plates, too. And jugs and tobacco jars and inkwells. I get good prices for them all. By his manner, I can tell the broker believes I'm handling goods that came to me by crooked means, and it hurts my pride to be rated so, but I suffer the wound and go on, for I'm on good terms with my Almighty and am justified: if I don't do it—if I don't make back the full sum—it'd be as good as telling Moss my word has no value and my affection is not to be trusted, and that would be the death of me.

"Girls, I need you to turn out your money boxes."

Pumps snorts. "For what?"

"The books are running short. We've all of us to pitch in to make up what's lacking."

Snap. Snap. Spiv is breaking beans into a bowl. "I don't have a penny spare. *Snap.* You know my earnings. *Snap.* How could I hope to save anything from them? *Snap.*"

Truth only comes through a hard process of searching: I've been to their room and have found, hidden in a box beneath the bed, a porcelain pig filled with coins.

"Don't make me go up there and get it myself," I says.

Spiv stops her work. Grips the lip of the bowl. Heaves a sough out into the air. Wipes her hands on her pinny and leaves the kitchen. We listen to her go up. And now, our hearts athrob, we listen to her come back down.

"He wants you upstairs," she says.

"You'll pay for this," I says.

"Lizzie, I have just had a disturbing meeting with Camilla. She informs me you have asked her to part with her savings. Is this true?"

I'm feeling too much to answer.

"Lizzie, answer me, did you plan to appropriate the maid's savings?"

If a feeling is there, it'll come out somehow. And now, without warning, it gushes. All the cruel words a coarse woman could say, I say to him. I call him a beast and a hound, and tell him he doesn't know who I am or how I live, what I have to put up with under his roof, and I'd be beholden if he'd get on his horse and walk the rest of the road on his own. I'm off to pack my bags, I says, and go a new route; any route that won't involve him.

And the queer thing is, he listens. He doesn't answer back or dash to defend. Instead, by his mettle, and the length of his silence, he gives open passage to my vent. Each barb I throw at him, each prickle and each spine, he takes into his grip and holds it firm, just as the rural grasps the nettle so as not to be stung by it. If his point is to exhaust me, he succeeds, for after a few rounds, the spite starts to drain out of me and I get calmer by degrees. Bit by bit, my mind clears, and once again I'm able to see the lines on his face and the faint stoop in his back, the mark on his cheek of an abscess still not full healed, and am reminded that he, too, has hardships: he, too, has been knocked up by the difficulty of life.

"Don't forget," Mary used to say whenever I came down sharp on him, "don't forget how early he rises and how late he retires to keep us all fed and dressed."

I'm loath to give over to pity or be swerved by his virtues, so I try to ward them off with fresh thoughts of his poor conduct—his meanness as a father and his reckless generosity as a comrade—and, from these, I find fresh umbrage to take, and my wounds

break out as new and my tongue itches once more. But the truth is, I'm already tired of the effort it costs me to stay cross, and am beginning to feel the pangs of remorse, for I know I can sometimes get things out of proportion and damn people for venial things I've made mortal in my thoughts.

"What is this all about, Lizzie? Tell me out straight. What has got into you?"

"I need some money, is all."

"What do you need it for? Don't I give you enough? Are you left short in any aspect?"

"It's not for me."

"Well, whom do you owe, then?"

I hesitate. It's rare he knows what's in my mind. Things trouble me and I don't tell him; that has always been the way. Ought I give this to him?

"Nobody," I says. "I don't owe anyone anything."

"I'm glad to hear it."

He rests his knuckles on the desk and leans down on them.

"I have noticed you've been going out a lot of late. Would you like to tell me where you have been spending your time?"

"Nowhere in particular. I need the air."

"Are you gambling?"

"Frederick, please."

He doesn't soften to my tone, but keeps his wary eyes locked on me. "Pumps tells me you have grown fond of the local drinking houses."

"I stop to rest on my rounds. Has that been made a crime?"

He shakes his head and sighs. Sits back into his chair.

"I have decided, Lizzie"—he crosses a leg and smoothes the wrinkles of his trouser—"I have decided you must go to Ramsgate."

"Ramsgate?"

"You leave on Friday."

"Not a chance."

"You are not being given a choice. This is an imperative."

"No way, I won't go."

"There is to be a conference here in London. A private meeting of the Association. Things have got out of hand with the French. We need to settle these blasted disputes. Tighten discipline. Establish some organization."

"And while all this is going on, I'm to be shipped off to the seaside, is that it?"

"Karl has insisted that Jenny leave London for the duration of the conference. If she stays and becomes involved with the organizing and entertaining, there is every chance it will attack her nerves and she will become ill again. She has chosen to leave for Ramsgate, and you will accompany her."

"This is your excuse? This is the story you've invented for sending me away?"

Transporting me. Sailing me up the water.

"It is not a story. You need a break. I fear London is overexciting you."

"Christ, Frederick, would you listen to yourself? Ramsgate? What'll I do there? Can you tell me that?"

"You will take the cure. You will bathe. You will practice your Irish melodies."

"I will die."

"You will come back your old self, Lizzie. Or you won't come back at all."

XXX. And Forty Nights

So it's to Ramsgate we're dispatched. Ramsgate, because it's more salubrious than Margate. Ramsgate, because Brighton is only London by the shore and Scarborough costs too dear on the railway. Ramsgate, because, though the lodging rates are higher, the patients are more interesting. Ramsgate, because here the motto is safety for the shipwrecked and health for the sick.

"I thought we'd take our first dip this morning," says Jenny, looking up from her novel.

"This morning?" I says, looking out at the sea, where the buoys are touching the bottom, and the coal ship by the pier is lolling on its side, and it's taking an age for the horsemen to drag the bathing machines out all the way. "Oughtn't we wait for the tide to come in?"

"The farther out the better," she says. "Fewer spying eyes. Besides, I have already put our names down for a machine. Eleven o'clock."

She goes back to reading her book, and to twirling her parasol, and I wonder how she doesn't get exhausted doing the two things at once, when it's draining all my energies just to get comfortable in this damn penny chair. I lean out of it for a bit of relief and, while so bent, decide to take off my boot and pour out what's got in. Before putting it back on, I sink my foot down and lift up the sand with my toes. If it was up to me, I'd set the morning aside for this only and wouldn't care a whit about the old rogues who'd turn their eyeglasses on my legs.

When the hour comes, we go to the area with the bathing machines. A man wearing a check suit and cap ticks us off the list and directs us to the horseman, who conducts us to a green-colored machine.

"Can't we have that one there?" says Jenny, pointing to one painted bright as a Gypsy van.

"As you like," he says.

We watch him hinge his horse to the box.

"Business seems to be going on prosperous," I says to him.

"With respect, missus," he says, "you ought've seen it in July. Couldn't get near the water, you couldn't, for all the machines and all the ladies wanting a dunk."

Mortified, Jenny climbs inside and bides there. I stroke the horse's nose till the man is finished hinging and mounts.

"Ready when you are, missus," he says.

When I get inside, I see Jenny has already changed into her bathing frock. I find it no trouble to change into mine while we're being pulled out, the sand under the wheels being so flat and hard. Smooth as it is, though, the journey to the water isn't an easy one, given the smell of feet and rotten fish that fills the little room.

Eventual the machine comes to a stop. I'm eager to open up and let some air in, but we have to be patient while the man frees

his horse. We sit and listen to the sea lapping against the under-side of the box. Jenny twists the strings of her frock and hums.

"Right you are, ladies," the man calls out after a time, and thumps the side. "Fanny will look after you from here."

Jenny bides till she's sure the man is good and gone before opening the front hatch. I look out over her shoulder. Wading waist-deep towards us from a neighboring machine is the woman Fanny, a burly pip in a flannel jacket and a straw bonnet.

"Fine day for it," she says, and lowers the hood of our machine till it makes a tent over the water.

"September," says Jenny, "is England's July."

Fanny beckons Jenny in. "In your own time, ma'am," she says. But she fast loses patience with Jenny's toe-dipping and gasping—"The longer you wait, ma'am, the harder it gets"—and now takes grip of her waist and well nigh lifts her over the steps and into the freeze. It'd make the perfect look for my locket, the shock on Jenny's face.

"Will you be going under, ma'am?" Fanny says now, putting her fat hand to rest on the top of Jenny's head. The most Jenny can do is blink back, for the cold has struck a palsy into her as prevents the liberation of anything other than a tooth-chattered sough. Fanny takes this for a blessing, and plunges her under: bonnet, baroness, and all.

"Now you," she says, looking up at me.

"I think I'll pass," I says, stepping back into the box.

"Come on now, you've come all this way. You'll regret it if you don't."

I sit back onto the bench inside. Wrap my coat round. "Let that be on my own head, woman."

"You'd leave your friend to bathe on her own?"

I look over at Jenny and her blue lips, and at her eyes shot red

and her hair hanging lank to the shoulder. "I'd leave each body to do as she pleases," I says.

At lunch, Jenny doesn't leave it alone.

"I cannot believe you didn't get in," she says, as if I've done something to her personal. "You Irish are all talk," she says, "all talk," and she goes on and on, till I'm sick to the dentils of hearing it and jaded with exhaustion, and I give her to understand as much, with some unkind words about her own Germankind and their tight fists.

There's silence between us now, and it looks likely to continue for the rest of the p.m. Which suits me grand. For it leaves me to sit and to think untroubled by her patter and nonsense. I sink back into myself, and when I tire of wondering about what ought be done about everything, I find no small amount of pleasure in the sights and the sounds of the sands. When a huckster advances, Jenny doesn't break her vow of silence to send him away, so I'm able to take a good look at his corset laces; I even buy a couple. From the coster's basket, I take bloaters and shrimps, and pies and cakes, and eat them right here, for all the crowds to see, without her blather about keeping from food that thickens the waist. And pleasure atop all pleasures, I listen unbothered to the music, and tap my foot to it, and put a penny in the tin if I think it earned.

Most of the Ramsgate minstrels are fake darkies, but there's one who comes by most days before the tea bell is rung, at three o'clock or thereabouts, and he's a real one: a black; a real black man. He dresses in a suit of red stripes and, apart from the bad expressions he makes when singing, and the touch of a crook in his leg, he has lovely looks such as common bodies won't admire. Though I don't put it out for Jenny to see, I find myself getting nervous when it comes his time for coming; I feel like a sick babby

when I see his figure limping up the beach towards us. He sings alone, with no instruments behind him, and I know he's noticed me, for at our stretch of the sands he'll do two songs instead of the usual one—an opera bit and now a new air from the Americas—and God's grace be on him, a smoother tenor I haven't heard since eternity. If I thought I wouldn't be put away for it, I'd go to him and give him every coin I possess—all I've saved for Moss and everything I can find on top of that—for a pinch of his lips and a stroke of his hair.

What must it feel like to the hand?

"I used to like darky music, but it is stale now," is Jenny's usual, but today, joy of joys, she has it buttoned, and what's else, he's giving his best performance yet. What he's done is, he's rolled up his trousers and paddled himself into the low water, and by stamping and kicking his foot, he's using the sea as a drum, which catches the attention of every chair for two hundred yards. There's not a shake, not a tremble in his voice, which washes up over the rows to drown us. Before him, we're stiff and scurvy-looking, white like melted butter in a pan.

In the pause between songs, he takes a large square of card from his basket and holds it up. After showing it round, he puts it leaning against a rock so everybody passing can see it. I muster the courage to tap the shoulder of the lady sitting on my right side, not the species Jenny would talk to, but I take people as they come.

"I've gone and forgotten my eyeglasses," I says to her. "Can you tell me what the darky's sign says?"

"Why, my dear, you ought get a chain." Glad to be distracted from her string of beads and her snoring husband, she sits up and peers over the bodies in front. "Let's see. It looks like an advertisement for his evening show."

"A show? Does it have a direction? Can you see?"

"Yes, there's something. But it's out of town, in Pegwell Bay. You'd have to get a cab."

"Oh, that wouldn't be a bother. My husband has such a fondness for the darky songs, he'd drive a hundred mile to catch a night of them."

She looks at me, unfooled. "I don't have ink to write it down."

"That's all right. If you tell it out for me, I'll remember."

The darky's second song is a slow keen about the hardness of life and the wanting to be rid of it, an unfortunate subject for Ramsgate, where even the healthiest are made more healthy, but the notes carry such power that we forget who and where we are, and there's more than one lady who has to reach for her handkerchief. The applause is generous enough—my own clapping near sends me to a stand—but this being England, and England being the rottenest, stingiest place on earth, few bodies come forth with the loot when he circles with the silver shell he uses as his tin. I make sure to flash my coins so he knows not to take off before he gets to our row, and while I'm dropping them in—a whole florin this time—I also make sure to give him sympathy with all of my eyes. He smiles down at me and tips his hat, and with a gentleness and a frankness that our race has lost through too much society, he says, "Thanking you kindly, ma'am. All of us at the Three Crowns tavern in Pegwell do hope to be seeing you this night."

He leaves me burning red and struggling to swallow. The neighboring lady leans over in her chair and, under her shawl, passes me her hip flask. "Looks like you need this."

I don't refuse it, and when I give it back, she takes a snort herself.

"If you could," she says now, "would you prevent the marriage of a white with a colored?"

"Well—" I falter. My throat's yet burning from the spirit, and my heart thumping from having one of them so close up. "Well, I'd never try to separate those who loved."

She settles back and takes up her fancywork. "I quite agree. Love *is* a gift given down from God that no human being should steal. But I don't think a union of black and white very likely either, for I credit the darkies are no more disposed to marry us than we to marry them."

I look out at the gray sea. "I suppose that's one way of putting it," I says.

Jenny makes it the whole way through dinner without opening, but back at the lodgings, the sight of me pinning up my hair and changing into my good gown fetches her voice up.

"All sorts on the beach today," she says.

"Same as ever," I says.

"I think I'll get dressed as well. Have a look in the paper at what is on."

As soon as she's in her bedroom, I'm out the door and, in no time, up the crescent. Instead of going all the way to the rank on the pier, I manage to convince the gent on the corner to give me—an ailing matron—the cab he's just flagged and to hang on himself for the next. But for all that, I'm yet too slow.

"Yoo-hoo! Lizzie! Where are you going? What is your rush?"

I turn to see Jenny appearing round the corner, the streetlamps putting a yellow shine on her frippery. In my mind, I picture myself lunging into the cab and rushing off into the night, leaving her here to wave and bawl after me, but in ordinary truth, I stay stuck where I am, one foot on the cab step.

"I feel so good after that swim today," she says, nodding a greeting to the gent who holds out his hand to help her up. "And since it was cold, it did me twice as good. I believe I'm building up

a good stock of health. What damage could a naughty late night possibly do?"

The cab moves off, and I feel I can't look at her, for she speaks as if every night till now she's been in bed with the gas out before nine; as if she doesn't wake up from her p.m. nap going "I'm bored" and flying off to the offerings of any old place: concerts, lectures, balls, novelties, amusements, mediums; you announce it, she does it. Nay, I can't look at her, so I turn to stare out into the darkness.

"Where were you thinking of going?" she says.

"No place in particular," I says.

"Well, no place is not very fun, is it?" She laughs, the sharp edge of frantic. "How about the Marine Library? Suit you? Thursdays they have the raffling tables out. We could stake a shilling, Lizzie. That would be amusing, or?"

The conference is only to last a week, and yet I've been put here for a month and more: here, where one day is so much like its neighbor that it's no easy matter to say which is which and, filling each night, the same desert sands.

October

XXXI. Love Pursues Profit

I come home old and extinguished. My belongings still in the cases, I lie on the bed and wonder whether I'll ever get up again.

Frederick knocks. "May I?"

I let him take off his boots and lie on the bed beside me, because I know it's a gesture he's making.

"How was the conference?" I says.

"Interesting," he says, and is afraid to say more.

By touching his cheek, I give him license. "Go on. Tell me."

He props himself up on his elbow. Speaks with energy and emphasis. A group of Frenchmen, he says, led by the man Bakunin, have raised a commotion about a resolution that was passed calling for the creation of proletarian parties in each country. They are against parties. They are against rules. They believe in anarchy, total human freedom. The International, they say, is becoming authoritarian.

"What they can't seem to understand is that revolution is the most authoritarian thing there is. It was the lack of centralization and authority that cost the life of the Paris Commune. "

"So what is going to happen?"

"The most difficult thing will be to get the different sides together and ensure that the differences of opinion do not disturb the solidity and stability of the Association. I fear there will be a split."

"Let's hope it doesn't come to that."

He hears the weakness in my voice and offers a sympathetic smile. "But that is not important now, Lizzie. How was your holiday? Did you manage to enjoy it at all?"

I turn my head on the pillow to look at him, the curves of his youth still visible beneath his clothes, and I'm reminded of what Mary said to me soon before she died.

"Don't go with him, Lizzie," she said. "If something ever happens to me, and you're left with him, let him off to other fields. Don't try to take what I had for yourself. I could manage it, but it'd kill you. Moss is more your kind. I was hard on the man, I know, but I see now he would've suited you well. I don't think that door is full closed. If you gave him another chance, I think it'd work out for you both."

There was truth in this, as much truth as can be held by late-night phrases, but it's also true that her words came from a resenting place, for she knew that, since her illnesses and perhaps even before, Frederick had turned his eyes in my direction; she knew she'd already lost him—her life—to me.

I brush back a fallen bit of Frederick's hair. "I'm tired to death, Frederick, and not at all well."

"I thought it would have done you some good."

"And maybe it did. I just need to rest now."

He carries his shoes to the door. "I'll have something sent up."

I lie here, looking up at the plaster patterns on the ceiling, till I don't even know I'm on my feet again.

Away from him, raging lusts devoured me, but now that I see him in the flesh, I'm slow to feel anything. It's cold to be near him, he's so stiff and so white. Is there anything in his looks or his behavior that merits the dreams and fancies I had in his name? I can't see it; I can't see anything that lights a flame in me; he's not at all as I remembered him: not as handsome, not as eager, not as free with the poems and the flattering remarks. In truth, there's not a thing about him—not a single thing!—that would keep me from criticizing him in my mind, and calling him rotten names, and hardening my heart to him, and shutting a corridor of a hundred doors against him. And I wonder now, have I acted too fast—have I made myself ridiculous?—by paying for this room in this slum of an inn.

"Where have you been?" he says.

He doesn't hold out a hand, nor say an affectionate word; he has no indulgence for me, no fondness. Instead, he closes the door and uses the key to lock it, and checks under the bed, and opens the wardrobe to see if the previous guests have left anything behind. It must be that he doesn't see anything attractive in me; it must be that I look worse now than before the seaside, and I find myself wishing for a philter that would make me young again and fetching: a smooth mouth and a firm bust are what's needed to bring his furies up.

"I've been out of London, Moss. I had to go away."

"Well for some."

"Is it?"

"Where were you?"

"What does it matter where I was?"

"Answer me."

"In Ramsgate."

"Ramsgate? Fucking *Ramsgate.*"

"My sentiments precise."

He goes to the window and looks out. Draws the curtain on what he sees.

"Is this to be my welcome back, Moss? A foul mood? A drubbing?"

He turns to me. "Forgive me. It's just I don't know what to think. You make a promise to me and then you disappear."

"I'm here, can't you see? Better now than never. And my promise is still good. I've never gone back on a promise, and I'm not about to start."

I take off my bonnet and gloves. Put them on the table by the bed.

"Well, Moss O'Malley? Will you be hanging round long enough to take off your jacket?"

He undoes his buttons slow, which gives me the chance to forgive him—to forgive his unshaven face and his patched-up clothes for not belonging to the man they once did—and I'm sudden conscious of the beauty of the patriotic life he leads, the baldness and the simplicity of it, a single goal that turns the vain concerns of the average man into meaningless trifles, and my feelings for him reignite: a blaze of love.

"Come here," I says.

"Where?" he says.

"*Here,*" I says, gesturing to the bit of floor in front of me.

He comes and gives me a kiss not meant to go beyond itself.

"What is it, Moss? Don't you want it? Don't you think of me in that way anymore?" *Poor as you are, and as desperate for my money, are you still too proud to lap up another man's leavings?*

"Nay, Lizzie. It's not that. It's just, I wouldn't know what to *call* it."

"Call what?"

"This. What we're doing."

"Misery," I want to say. "Call it misery, which is what loving is for all women." But I don't say any such thing. Instead, I wet my mouth and offer it to him, for when something is there for the grasping, you either choose it or you don't, and you can't blame anyone else if you go away with naught.

I take his hand, put it inside my skirts, and let it be there a moment.

"Nay," he says, but what I hear him say is "Aye," and his eyes repeat it, and the four walls echo it.

I give him the love that comes from a need, a sore distress; he gives me the love that comes with a reason, a motive, which can only be a diluted kind of passion: thin milk with no real nourishment. I read the signs of his ardor and am certain they mean I'm of little account with him, except as a purse to root in. There's no use blinking the matter: to collar my mint is what he wants, and he's waited so long for it now, his thirst has become entitlement. The world has treated Lizzie Burns well, and he's come to believe that he—the man who once set her free so she could live the better life—is deserving of the same. It's a state of affairs I'm not happy with; it's a situation I mustn't allow. I'll give him money, as much as he wants, but there must be feelings, also, in the bargain.

"Remember," he says when he's done and is panting on the bed beside me, "remember your promise."

I use his shirt to wipe the sop that he insisted on spilling outside of me. "Have you ever known me to break a promise? Haven't I always kept my word to you, even when it brought danger to my door?"

~

The eighteenth arrives, the day the rebels Kelly and Deasy are to be liberated. I keep the doors of the Salford house open for Moss, as promised. Then I go out for the day. I walk to Market Street and look at the shops. I go along the Medlock, running purple with an evil-smelling dye. I tend Mary's grave; take away the weeds and put a new plant down; say a few prayers. I eat a baked potato from a stand. And, when the time comes, I bide for Frederick at the mill gates and walk him back to his private lodgings.

He no longer minds to be seen with me outside. In his heart, he has given up on the mill and, as a consequence, has lost interest in knowing what behavior a man in his position ought be showing. He doesn't hear the voices that speak of him, nor does he feel their eyes, for, in spirit, he isn't here anymore but in London with the man Marx, working to make the world right.

At his lodgings, I make him something to eat from what's there, and then we have a drink and play a game of cards. When I rise to leave, he rises too, he wants to walk me back, but I tell him to stay where he is. I'm tired and all I want to do is sleep. And, being a gentleman, he doesn't require further reasons than this.

It's dark when I get back at the house. When I light a lamp, I see there are six of them: Moss and five unknown to me.

"That's too many," I says. I point to Moss and two others. "You, you, and you can stay. The rest, you'll all of you have to find somewhere else."

The men I choose to send out don't object. They tip their caps and disappear, one by one, a minute between them. I put the remaining men down on a rug by the back door. "If the peelers come in the night, you're to run. And if they catch you, you're to say you broke in and hid yourselves while the people slept. Is that clear to you?"

I put myself straight to bed. Sleep refuses me, however. I can feel the men through the wall—the threat of them—and it keeps me from giving way.

Sometime in the early hours, Moss comes, as I knew he would. I pretend to be gone, but I'm not fooling him. He sits on the bed where my legs have made a crook. Puts his hand on my thigh.

"Did you manage it?" I says.

"Aye," he says. "Kelly and Deasy are both free men. We can be proud of that, at least."

I sit up in the bed. His figure is a mass of black in the blue. "What happened?"

"You don't want to know."

"You came in here to tell me, didn't you? So get it out, and let's be done with it."

"A man got shot. An Englishman. A peeler."

"A peeler? Christ. How?"

"I'm not sure. There was so much commotion. Shots were fired. You couldn't tell from where. The man who shot him probably didn't even know."

"Were you seen fleeing?"

"There were people looking on, aye."

I draw away from him. Bring my legs up so I can lean on my knees. "The law won't stand for a peeler shot, Moss. They'll hunt you all out. All the Irish in Manchester will be rounded up. Anyone even suspected of being on the Hyde Road today will be put hanging."

"They've already caught a number of us. We were lucky to get away."

"Go back to Ireland, Moss. Go back to where you never ought've left."

"Nay, I can't. I've burnt my bridges there."

"What'll you do, then? You can't stay in Manchester. You must get out."

"I'll go to the capital. I'll go to London."

"Do you know anyone?"

"We're strong up there."

From beneath my night rail, I take out the pouch I keep tied around my neck. I find his hand in the dark and push a couple of coins into it. "Here, have this. You'll need it to get you through the first couple of days."

He thanks me, and when I settle back into the bed, he lies with me.

When first light comes, he gets up and washes himself at my basin. The scars on his back make fearsome arrangements in the gloom. When I see him about to turn back to me, I close my eyes. When I open them again, he's gone.

XXXII. Its Soul Comes Forward

"*Mohme* tells us you had a wonderful time."

They sent a note asking to see me. It's been so long, there's so much for us to catch up on, I hoped to be received alone. And I believed my hopes realized when Janey told me at the door that Jenny and Karl were from home. But then, coming into the parlor, I was given a lesson in the futility of wishing for anything: Longuet tossing about the place like the bad weather, heaving and sighing and bored with everything; Lissagaray too light on his toes to be trusted, though it's clear Tussy has taken to adoring him, so coming-on is she in her manner towards him.

"But *Mohme* also said you didn't get into the water. Isn't that what she said, Mr. Lissagaray?"

"Indeed, that is what she said."

"I'm surprised at you, Aunt Lizzie. We'd have thought you made of hardier stuff."

Nim lays out some cold mutton and some pickled salmon. She looks pale and withered, she appears to have shrunk several inches closer to the floor, and there's a shiver in her hand as she prepares the plates. Now, when she gives the food round, she sends imploring eyes over at me. "There is trouble," they say. "There is trouble and you must help me fix it."

I drink my tea and pick at some meat, and when I feel I've put in good time, I rise and announce that I need some fresh air.

"A good idea," says Tussy. "I'll go with you." She takes my arm and leads me out, but not before giving Lissagaray a starry look and telling him to sit there, she'll be back, right back.

She brings me through the kitchen—Nim puts on not to notice us—and into the garden.

"You look happy," I says when we are outside.

"Do I? For once, therefore, the exterior aspect is matching the interior feeling!"

"You mother spoke to me about this man."

"Of course she did. She's *obsessed*."

"She's concerned."

"She has formed a bad opinion of him out of nothing. She has no grounds to take against him."

"There's his age, Tussy. He's no chicken. Some would say he's gone past his time."

"Ah! These bourgeois anxieties about propriety and time. Do you really go in for them, Aunt Lizzie? I believed you to be someone with a more independent attitude."

I shake my head. At her age, I too thought it'd be a great glory to have thoughts opposed to all people, to dispute against the whole world. She's no worse than I was.

"I'm not speaking for myself, Tussy. I'm telling you only what your mother said to me in Ramsgate. It's painful to her to see you

with this man. She's suffering for it. She doesn't want to see your youth wasted. Heaven forbid you wake up alone in five years' time, too late for you to find a proper mate."

"Good God, the woman is such a terrible bore. And she has turned you into the same. Let us talk of other things."

Before an atmosphere is let form between us, I brighten my tone and ask her about the conference: who was there, what was said, where it will all lead. Her answers—as high as they are careful—get us the whole way round the garden.

"Well, Tussy, you certain explain it better than *they* do."

Back in the kitchen, I pretend to be alarmed by the amount of work our day has created for the maid.

"Go on up, child. I'll help Nim with these few things and I'll be right there."

Shrugging and sighing, she obeys.

Once we are alone, Nim doesn't delay in coming at me.

"Calm down, Nim, and tell me what's the matter?"

With a stricken look, she takes a letter from her pinny and gives it to me. "It's from Freddy," she says. "It arrived while you and Mrs. Marx were away."

Not thinking, I bring the paper to my nose to smell it. "Is he all right? Do you want me to take him something?"

"No. A gift would not be well received."

"Well, what is it, then? What does he want?"

"He is not clear. The note was obviously written in excitement and anger. There are unkind words said against all of us. He speaks of wanting to be left in peace. I fear he, too, is living the consequences of Dr. Marx's speech on France. It is possible he is being harassed. By the newsmen. Or someone from the government."

"I'll go to him," I says. "I'll find out."

"Would you? You would do that?"

"Tell me where he lives."

"I hate to put you out."

"Give me the direction, Helen, and I'll go."

"It's way over. In Hackney. Two buses."

"I'm not afraid of a bit of travel. Tell me out, where is he to be found?"

"I have it written somewhere."

"Nay, Helen. My memory is in my ears. It's what I hear that sticks. Say it twice, and I'll have it then."

The cab stops opposite a covered market.

"Ain't going no farther than this, ma'am. From this end of town myself, I am. Ain't got nothing against it. But I've fares to get, don't I?"

"You're not cheap either," I says when I pay him off.

"Worth it, ain't it, ma'am, on a day like this?"

I ask a stander-by for directions. She sends me a long stretch past building sites and across fields. A man now explains the route through the terraces. By the time I get to the place, I'm wet through, even with the brolly. I'm tempted to save myself a final soaking by going straight to the front door, but there's no point coming all this way to cause upset, so I go round the lane and up the backs like Nim explained.

He answers the door himself. Built broader than his father. Rougher cut.

"Who are *you*?"

"Freddy? My name is Lizzie Burns. I'm a friend of your father's."

He doesn't appear surprised. He's a man that's finished being surprised by the world. "I'm having my tea."

"You told us you've been having trouble, and we want to get to the bottom of it. We want to help."

He gives the end of the door a light kick. "All right. We can talk here."

I lower the brolly and glance out to the weather. "I'll not be a tick. In and out before you see me."

He pushes his hands deep into his pockets and sighs. Nods me inside.

A woman, not near his match in looks, is at the table. On her lap a babby, bare dressed.

"What a love of a child," I says. "What's he called?"

"Who in blazes are you?"

On the table, two places set. Bacon and potatoes. A smell of turnips too, though I can't see them put out.

"Freddy? Who in God's name is this?"

"Lizzie Burns. That *friend* of my father."

"The famous Mrs. Burns, is it? That's all we need now."

"I'll not stay a minute. Go ahead and finish your tea."

Freddy sits and chins to the empty chair. The woman rocks the babby and fumes over at Freddy. The babby grabs at her breast and pushes his face against it. She takes it under the arms and sits it down hard.

"Will you have something?" Freddy says.

"I'll not, thanks. I'm on my way to my own. Go on now, don't let me get in your way."

He gets back to his food. Big healthy gulps.

"Where have you come from?"

"Primrose Hill."

"Where on earth?" says the woman.

Freddy uses his thumb to point to her. "This is my wife, Sarah. And that's my son, Harry."

"Nice knowing you. He's a dote."

"Shame on you coming here."

"Sarah, I'll deal with this."

One, two, three, four tubs put out to catch the droppings from the ceiling cracks. They beat out a time uneven enough to set you wailing. Freddy finishes and brings the teapot over. Puts a mug in front of me.

"Drink that," he says. Hands like plates. Nails eaten away.

"You're very good."

Harry starts to cry.

"Must give him his feed," Sarah says, and brings the child away, draws the curtain across. Gone, she's a bigger presence than when she was here; a shadow on the wall.

"Were you at work today, Freddy?"

"I was."

"And is it going well for you?"

"Well enough. It keeps us going. In charge of my own lathe now. The prospects are good for moving up."

"Good for you."

He offers to roll me a fag.

"Thanks, dear, but my lung wouldn't take it."

He lights up and moves his chair to the stove so he can flick his ash into the fire.

"So, Mrs. Burns, I take it my mother showed you my letter."

"Tell me, Freddy, what's the matter?"

"The matter?" shouts Sarah through the curtain. "You know what's the matter, Mrs. Burns!"

"Leave this to me," Freddy shouts back.

"Did something happen? What has you so upset?"

He pulls on his fag. Breathes out a heavy cloud. "Don't mind my upset, Mrs. Burns, and tell me what you want. What is it you's after from us."

"I'm after naught, Freddy. Naught at all. I've come to help."

"Drop the bull. You has us caught up in something. Something we don't want to be caught up in."

"For the life of me, I don't know what you're speaking to."

"I'm a union man, Mrs. Burns. I do my bit. But I know what Marx and your man Engels do, I know what they want for the world, and I ain't saying I don't have no regards for it. I do. It's just I've a family, and I don't want no strife for them."

"Believe me, Freddy, your father doesn't want any strife for you either. Why don't you tell me what happened."

"Don't let her off easy," says Sarah.

"I told *you* to shut up," he says.

Now, slow and fierce, he uncurls a finger, turns it towards the floor. Through his vest I can see his tissues taut. "There were a man here. There were a man here, asking questions."

"When?"

"A couple of weeks back."

"What kind of man?"

"A man who said he knew you. Your lot."

"Did you let him in?"

A clattering from behind the curtain and Sarah comes haring through it. Comes to stand by Freddy. From over in his cot, Harry bawls. "Napoleon were how he called himself," she says. "Louis Napoleon. Mean anything to you, Mrs. Burns?"

I think on the name a minute. *Napoleon? Louis Napoleon?* I look out the window, as if a memory of the man might be found there. A cat sits on the back wall. A wind blows through the ivy and the weeds. It has stopped raining, but it looks about to start again. "I don't know a Louis Napoleon," I says. "Did you tell him who you are, Freddy? Did you tell him where you come from?"

"We didn't tell him anything. Despite what you might think of us, Mrs. Burns, we ain't thick."

Relieved, I shift forward on the chair and reach out to put a reassuring hand on Freddy's knee, but he draws back from me. "It was probable only a newsman, Freddy, sniffing about for a story. Don't worry yourselves about him. He was a chancer is all he was. You don't have to worry, your family isn't in danger. In future, just be careful about who you let in."

"We don't know nothing about this Communism business, and we don't want to know. We're just trying to get by."

"In that, we're all on the same keel, Freddy. Doing our best."

Wrapping my shawl around, I make to leave.

"What I'll do is, I'll come back in a couple of weeks' time and check up on you, just to be sure."

"We don't want you back here," says Sarah.

"I'll come back just to be certain things are settled."

"Don't, Mrs. Burns," says Freddy. "Keep your distance from us."

I nod as if assenting to their wishes, though I've no intention of honoring them.

They follow me to the door. I swing it open myself and step out.

"I'm sorry we've brought this worry on you," I says.

I rummage about myself for the bits of coin I have hidden about me, and, slow, no flash moves of the hand, I drop them into the pocket of his jacket.

"Your father asked me to give you this."

He looks at his pocket, as if revolted. "He don't need to do this."

"He wants to help."

"He must be doing well for himself if he can spare so much."

"Don't worry for him, Freddy."

"We have enough, Mrs. Burns. We don't need it."

"It's a fool won't take money that's offered him."

He shakes his head. Takes the money out and holds it up in his open palm—four shiny coins lying flat on his scored and blackened skin—for me to reclaim.

"If you won't use it, Freddy, then give it away. Or put it into the union. It's yours and that's the end of it."

He flinches when I touch his arm.

"You know where to find us if you need something," I says.

"We've never asked for anything."

"I know, Freddy. But you can now, if you need it."

He doesn't say anything. Looks at the ground.

"I'll be back," I says. "When I can, I'll be back."

I go down the path and pull open the back gate. The coins fall on the stone behind me, the chimes of a beggar's tantrum: flung away now but sure to be rooted after when the times come hard to require them.

It occurs to me on the journey home, and as the days and weeks pass, it lives within me as a new certainty: it's a thing to be changed and put right. The boy isn't in the gutter yet, I've seen bodies in brutaler situations than his, but he *is* unsteady. For the son of a wealthy man, he's too much taken up with the effort of surviving. If word was to get out, Frederick would be judged a shoddy father, and it's a name that can't but paint me as well. And God's truth, I can't shoulder another load of shame in this life. To have this knowledge, and to fail to do something handsome to correct it, would be to take the good out of having anything at all.

I have no choice. Only one road lies before me. From this day on, every farthing I spend will be a farthing less for a creature on this earth more deserving, so every farthing I spend must be matched by a farthing put aside for him. Compared to what goes to Karl and the Cause, what I take will be like spit in the sea. It's to

rebalance the accounts that I'll do it. At the end of the day, it's the poor that must do things for the poor.

Aye, it's a thing to be changed and put right. But it must be careful done. Charity is best pulled off so that, if someone asks, nobody knows.

November

XXXIII. Love Brings Death to Itself

The letter carrier brings a note from Moss. I step out and ask him to read it.

"Commemoration of Manchester Martyrs. Tomorrow. Eight o'clock p.m. Sixteen Maynard Street. Come. Or have you decided against me again?"

I thank the boy and send him away with a penny. Come back inside and put the note in the fire.

Decided against him? Until this moment, I didn't know this is what I've done; now I see that it is.

I sit by the window and look out at the winter coming on, the trees at the bottom of Primrose Hill trembling, and I think that the only pity—God's greatest rig—is that the people we want to help are so seldom those who want it; the desperate, we decide against.

And is it any different with love? Isn't love the reverse side of the same medal? To love is to have, but rare does it happen that

what we have is what we love. Love buys cheap and seeks to sell at a higher price; our greed is for gain that lies outside our reach. We desire those who don't desire us in return.

The wind comes to rattle the panes. I pull a rug over my knees, and realize, now, that Moss must be told. I must go to his commemoration and make it clear to him: I'm cleaned out, my money is needed elsewhere, by a cause more noble than the delivery of any nation. That we loved once, long ago, is not in question. But it does not give him a claim on my means. He is to leave me alone and stop looking at me to fund his ideas. If he insists on staying in London, he is to make as if I've emigrated or passed over.

He will play with me, of course. He will say that he has heard this before, that between us it'll never be for the last time; there'll always be another chapter, a new phase. We are bound by invisible string; tied to our wrists is a length of Diamond Thread; we cannot make the final break. And when his playacting doesn't work, he'll become angry, as is his nature. But his nature will only strengthen mine. I will stand in defiant endurance of it.

"Your love?" I'll say. "I wouldn't want it again at any price."

The Manchester peelers put out a reward of three hundred pounds for the recapture of Kelly and Deasy, two hundred for the seizure of anyone known to have attacked the police van. Mobs maraud the streets in search of stray Irishmen to drag away. The peelers roar like fire through the District and Little Ireland and Ancoats and Hulme and Salford, and hundreds, thousands are rounded up. They knock on my door, but seeing only a matron living alone, they don't overturn the furniture like they do in other places; a quick sniff around and they're gone again. I pray to God Moss has made it to London and won't be found. Frederick reads

me the newspapers, and every day it comes as sweet relief when his name isn't spoken with the others.

"Are you looking out for someone in particular?" says Frederick. "A relative or a friend?"

He has noticed my nerves, which I'm too nervous to hide, so I tell him out. I was involved, I says. I hid some of the Fenian men in the house. It was an act of loyalty. An obligation I had to my people. He's nettled at first. He judges me foolish for risking arrest in political actions that, on account of their lack of proper forethought, are destined to end in disappointment and failure. Once his piece is said, however, he softens, and his admiration comes out, free-spoken.

"You are no ordinary woman, Lizzie Burns," he says, and kisses me. "A fighter, just like your sister."

Three men are convicted of killing the peeler during the rescue. They're to be executed outside the New Bailey. Frederick wants to go and watch, it being just a walk away. He thinks it an event of importance that we oughtn't miss. He says that if there's no reprieve given and the executions are carried out, they will be the start of a new phase in the struggle between England and Ireland; a true Irish rebellion might follow. And, after that, perhaps even a revolution in Britain.

Says he: "Ireland lost, the British Empire is gone, and the class war in England, till now somnolent and chronic, will assume acute forms."

Important or not, I'm not fain to go and see it. I think it gruesome to make a spectacle of a man's end. But when the news reaches me that the priests have banned us from attending, I turn proud and decide to join Frederick, after all. There ought be witnesses. A free road oughtn't be given to the ruffs and bandits who are sure to make a Protestant mockery of something that's sacred.

By the time we arrive on the morning of the event, huge crowds have already formed. Men, and women too, and babbies. They've been here since last night, it seems, roughing it out for good vantage. The beerhouses are doing a capital trade. Singing, laughing, shouting, brawling: it's like a national holiday. Pushing through, I don't hear any Irish voices till, by some miracle, a man gets through the line of peelers at front of the scaffold, climbs the barricades, and begins to speak out on the plight of Ireland and the bad things the hangings will bring about. He's dragged down, and while the peelers beat him, he's taunted by the mob, wild and terrible.

We take places where we can find them, outside Sidebottom's tobacconists. At the strike of eight on the jail clock, the men are brought onto the scaffold. A yellow fog has come down, but when the air moves and a clearing happens, it's possible to see the leather straps that have been passed around the men's waists, their elbows held by loops, and their hands fettered to the front of their bodies. The man Allen comes first, his face white as a sheet. O'Brien, next, is holding a crucifix and praying out. His words are passed back through the crowd.

"Christ, hear us," he's saying. "Christ, graciously hear us."

Larkin, the third man, has lost control of his legs and is being held upright by a warder on either side. He stumbles up the flight of steps and has to be half-carried to his place.

The three men, stood now beneath their ropes, turn to each other and give blessings. Before the cap is put over his head, O'Brien takes hold of Allen's hand and kisses it. It's a sad scene; I keep being about to cry.

The ropes are put over their heads. Larkin faints to his right. Now, held up by a warder, he slumps to his left. I can't bear to look, and yet I do. The hangman pulls the lever and the three men drop.

The rope holding Allen sways for only a short time, and now hangs still. The other two jerk and swing for many minutes. The crowd break their silence to share their revulsion, to delight in it. The hangman goes down the steps that lead underneath. The ropes bounce as he tugs down on the men's legs to end their suffering.

We make our way out of the crowds and walk home without saying a word. Only once we're well inside and our drinks are poured can we bring ourselves to talk a little.

"Well, all you lacked were martyrs," Frederick says. "And now you've got them."

I look into my glass and try to put a shape on my feelings. "It was well organized, that's for certain."

"Good planning. That's what that is."

I look out the window. Naught to see only the fog. "That's me done now," I says. "I've had enough of the politics. I want a quiet life."

He nods, understanding. "You've had a long and hard run of it, Lizzie. And it won't be long now till you get your rest. I'll be rid of the mill before you know it. Then we'll be in London, and you'll have a proper house, run by people. And Tussy, and Jenny, and plenty of friends to go about with. I was even thinking that, before the move, we could take a trip to Ireland?"

I drink down and sigh out. "That'd be nice."

I'm not prepared for this moment. In spite of the stink of death that lingers all around, the happiness rises up from a deep place, a great and earnest feeling.

What can you do, only press ahead?

～♪

Maynard Street is as I expect: a back room in a falling-down house. Inside the door is a table with piles of caps stacked. I'm the only woman, I see. I keep my bonnet on.

Word is sent to Moss that I've arrived, and he comes to bring me in. He throws a boy off a stool to let me sit down. "Thanks for coming," he says.

The crowd is the common sort, and the speeches are the same; common things are hard to die. The lives of Colonel Kelly and Captain Deasy are recounted. The particulars of their rescue are gone over. Prayers are offered that their new lives abroad will be happy and long-lasting.

After a pause to allow a more somber mood to settle, the three martyrs Allen, Larkin, and O'Brien are invoked. These men, we're told, were put to death by the British for an act they didn't commit. The peeler was not murdered, as the authorities say, but was caught by a stray bullet during the normal course of his duties. None of the executed men could have fired the shot. Their fingers didn't touch their triggers. Witnesses put them in positions where a clear mark would have been impossible. Their arrest and hanging was a spiteful act of revenge: an act of war. And it's a war, now, that's being fought, and it'll go on till the independence for which our fathers yearned, struggled, and suffered is won.

A minute's silence is observed. A song is sung. Moss reads a poem. The meeting is moved to a tavern down the road.

"Will you come for one?" says Moss.

"Nay, I've to get back," I says.

"Well, you're good for coming out."

"It's the last time now."

He looks down at his feet. "If that's what you want."

"And I can't give you anything. I've other things to look after. And, anyhows, I've no guarantee you wouldn't be hurting people off the back of it."

I hear myself, and I wince, for I'm only being righteous, a hypocrite. I know what a rebellion is, what it looks like on a man's body.

"If it isn't in your heart to give it, Lizzie, then we'd rather not have it."

There's no hint of the anger about him. If he's feeling something, it's compassion: pity for human shortcomings. Men like Moss are easy once you know it's in your power to leave them.

"I don't want to know what it is you're up to, Moss. What actions you have planned. If you get caught, I won't be visiting you in jail. I'll not be a visiting woman."

He gives a gentle nod, as if to say, "I understand."

"You're to forget about me, do you hear? I'm going to vanish out of your life. Don't bother about me anymore."

"No one's stopping you from going your own way."

"That's right. So this is the last last-time I'll be seeing you. This is the end with no fresh beginnings."

He reaches out a hand to show me the right road away. "Go on, then. Off with you. But do this, Lizzie Burns. When you get back to your big house, and you fall to believing whatever it is you like to believe, remember it was *you* came looking for *me.* I didn't ask to be found. Not this time, not the last time, not ever."

March

XXXIV. A Secret Society

Janey's engagement dinner, and Longuet himself does the cooking. Sole in a cream and cider sauce. I'm wary, but it turns out to be better, much better, than that beef he made for us at New Year's. This, at least, has been heated through. We're served by the men Wroblewski and Brunel. Two lieutenants like them oughtn't be let up; they ought be confined to their chairs and have their every need attended on, but they seem to want to do it. They're making a game out of it. Fussing with napkins. Sniffing the wine before they pour it. Ooh-la-la-ing when they lift the lid off a salver. Pointing at our plates and explaining what's on them, what went into the preparation, on the chance that we'd want to fix it for ourselves and not make a German muck of it.

It's the first time I've seen Nim sitting at the table for a whole supper. They've put her in a privileged position, at the center beside Jenny, and she seems comfortable enough there, in her gay

dress and with her educated graces, her laughter always well timed; a good humor that's hard to account for, knowing the state of the kitchen that awaits her. Toasts are made. Wedding dates are debated. Our faces turn red from the lush and the heat of the fires. Karl cries. Frederick makes jokes about Karl's lack of any except unbidden emotions. The only spot dulling the high shine of the evening is Tussy. She raises her glass when it's called for, and she answers with politeness the questions directed to her, but it's clear her effort is forced, that her true feelings are out of temper with the celebrations. I'd wager she's angry because Lissagaray hasn't been invited; I'd bet my life that's what's wrong with her. She has fought with her parents about it. What we're witnessing are the final vapors of a tantrum. No Lissagaray, no ball.

The pudding is baked apples, which everyone agrees are delicious. Not even Jenny leaves something on her plate for manners. A round of sweet wine, and now brandy, and the party moves to the second fireplace to play games. Nim stays at the table to clear up.

"Can't you leave it till tomorrow?" I says.

"I'd prefer to make a start on it now," she says.

"Well, let me help you, then."

She doesn't object. I load plates onto a salver and carry it to the kitchen. On the way back up, at the top of the kitchen stairs, Tussy catches hold of me.

"I need to talk to you, Aunt Lizzie."

"I'm helping Nim."

"This is important. Please."

It goes against my mood. Whatever she has to tell me would be better kept till we're not so overtook with drink; I'd rather it waited till I'm clearer of mind and have more patience for it. But I oblige. Out of obligation, I oblige.

She takes me upstairs to her room. The fire has wasted out, leaving the place gloomy and cold. She lights a lamp and puts it on the bedside. Sits on the bed and wraps herself in a rug. Makes space for me to sit beside her. I stay where I am by the door. The lush pounds behind my eyes and in the tips of my fingers.

"What's the matter with you, Tussy? Aren't you happy for your sister?"

"That's not it, Aunt Lizzie. I rejoice for Janey."

"What is it, then?"

Her eyes glimmer big and wet in the light. "I, too, am engaged to be married."

Sudden, the appetite for the drink I've already drunk leaves me, and I turn dizzy and sick. "Oh, Tussy." I go to the chimneypiece and lean on it. "You haven't told them."

"You know they disapprove of him."

I look into the grate, at the burnt bits and the ashes. Why can't people learn to keep themselves dark? Why must they insist on telling themselves out? For now I must do what it isn't my job to do: I must try to turn her away from it.

"Aunt Lizzie? You are happy for me, I hope."

I turn to look at her. Her face is open, awaiting my indulgences. "Perhaps if they knew how you really feel."

"Oh, they know. They *know.*"

"They think it an infatuation."

"They hate him. He is a free thinker, that's why."

I come away from the chimneypiece. Take my support from the bedstead. "Tussy, I don't understand it. Why would you want to marry a man your parents disapprove of?"

She throws the rug off her shoulders. Clasps one hand to her breast. Points at me with the other, accusing. "Oh no. Not you as well!"

I flap a hand in the air to dismiss her pointing finger. "Have some reason, girl. They see what you cannot because you're under the sway of feelings. They have your best interests at heart. You must find a match that suits the family, that fits with the position that your parents desire for you."

She jumps to a stand. Paces forward. And now back. "Oh, God. Everyone is against me. Everyone! Even you!"

"What were you expecting, child? You think me so different?"

"Not anymore. Not after *this*!"

"Tussy, I've heard enough. I'm going back downstairs."

"What? You're just going to leave me. Leave me here alone?"

I try to make the door before my temper rises. But I'm too slow. My hand hasn't yet reached the knob when the drink in my gut spits its poison up.

"Why can't you keep your business to yourselves, you people? What do you want us to do with these secrets you insist on making public? Carry the load around so you don't have to? Do you ask us, before you empty your dirt upon us? Nay, you just decide for yourselves that this is the best course, as if you had special rights to our understanding. Well, here's a thing, Tussy Marx. We don't want to know what's inside you. We couldn't care less for what you carry about in your private wraps. We struggle enough with our own cares as it is."

I leave her gasping and sobbing into the quilt.

Back in the kitchen, I beg Nim for some water and quaff it down. "I think it's time I go home."

She steadies me with a strong hand. "It's early yet, Mrs. Burns. Sit there and get your head straight. They'll be done soon."

I sit in the chimney corner and watch her work. When she's close to finishing, she boils up some tea. Stirs me a mug. Now she sits with me. We talk about the rising price of things, to be saying

something. The dogs are barking in the yard. Laughter and clapping waft down from upstairs. I don't hear Tussy coming down. She must be feeling the indignity that comes when you let go of what's hidden; let her steep in it.

"Thanks for the tea, Helen. My strength is up, I think. I must get myself home."

She gives me some leftovers in a dish. "Take this with you."

I accept it with a smile.

"I was thinking, Nim. I might go back to see Freddy soon. The scandal seems to have passed, but we ought make absolute and sure there's no danger facing him."

"Mrs. Burns, please don't."

"It'd be a chance to bring him something, if you have anything you think he'd like to have."

She shakes her head in a sad way. "No, Mrs. Burns."

"This time, however, it might be an idea to tell Frederick. He has a right to know I'm going."

"Don't. Don't tell Mr. Engels anything. And don't go there, to Freddy. It's none of your concern. I was mistaken to ask you to go before. It was a misjudgment on my part."

"Far from it, Helen. I was glad to go. And Freddy, I'm sure, appreciated the—"

A new seriousness takes hold of her. She takes the dish back from me and puts it on the table. "Sit down again, Mrs. Burns."

"I'm grand standing."

"Sit, please. I can see if I don't tell you, you will cause further harm."

"Tell me what?"

She leads me back to the chimney corner, but I don't sit in it.

"Mrs. Burns, you should know. Freddy is not Mr. Engels's son."

The words knock me out of myself, leave me struggling for sense.

"What, what are you saying?" I says, feeling sudden sober.

"Mr. Engels gave the boy his name in order to save the father from ruin."

The father? The question comes, but I stop it in my throat, for I've neither the right nor the need to ask it. I understand—sudden—that it's Karl she's speaking about.

"It was a fine and admirable thing Mr. Engels did," she says. "I don't see why you must suffer in ignorance for it."

I hear the words—these words intended to exonerate—and I feel naught, naught except the unease that comes from being told that something is fine and not being able to feel that it's so, like being blind when people talk of the earth and the sky.

"Is what you say true? The simple truth?"

She nods, solemn. "I'm sorry. I don't understand why you were never told." She turns her face to the floor, so it's impossible to know what she's feeling in herself.

I no longer feel the drink, but only the numbness that comes after a shock.

"Thanks for your frankness. It can't have been easy."

She gives a weak smile; a thanks of her own. I make to leave.

"The leftovers?"

"Nay. You've plenty of mouths to feed here."

On the way back up, I pause in the hall a moment, to fathom it. What is worse, I wonder: to be Mary and to believe for all your life a false thing against Frederick; or to be Jenny and to know the truth of what Karl did, and to live with it. It's confusing to know.

And what about Frederick himself? How ought he be judged? By putting the man Marx before everything—by being more loyal to *him* than to his own woman, his own name, his own *life*—he has made of Karl something like a wife. Those of us who really love

Frederick have had to fight over what remains after Karl has had his way, and in truth, there's rare much there to wake up to.

Curse these infernal times! How is a body meant to think about them? The most I can say is that it's no better here than in Manchester; no easier to get a grasp on the working of things. The wide views and the fresh air I once hoped to find have been replaced by the same dark courts and winding passages that lead nowhere.

Back in the parlor, Janey is playing the piano and Jenny is singing, her voice restored after the attacks of pleurisy; stronger and clearer than ever before. I sit in my place, beholding, and unexpected chords stir within me: sympathy and pity and esteem. A woman must expect trials, a politics woman more than most, but to watch your maid grow big with your husband's bastard is a calamity requiring inhuman forbearance to live down. What agonies she must have suffered. What lonely hours passed. What grit to keep from falling down. What cleverness to have Frederick deliver her from the shame. I've been led into a mistake about her: she's a good wit and a survivor; in my eyes, twice the person she was.

And Karl? Karl, there, with his god's beard and his foot beating out the time? How often we admire the wrong thing.

XXXV. The Administration of Things

Frederick is distracting himself with preparations for the first anniversary of the Paris Commune. Running up and down the stairs, barking orders and firing off letters, behaving like he's too caught up to see me sitting here with my bowl of broth, biding my moment to come at him. I've left the door of the morning room open, to watch his comings and goings, and to glower at him. How he can act like it's just another day, it passes me to understand. Is it a virtue, this capacity he has to saddle the evil that others have made? To go about with his good name in tatters in order to make right another man's error? Am I wrong to be ill-judging him? Ought I be looking up to him instead? Ought he be returned his halo, rather than stripped of it?

When I see Spiv bringing up his lunch, I call her in and tell her to leave the tray here. "Today he'll have his midday meal at the table, like a good husband."

She goes up to tell him the news. He comes down some moments later, looking cross.

"I don't have time for nonsense, Lizzie."

"You'll have time for this, when I tell you. Sit down."

He sighs. "Camilla, take the food upstairs and close the door on your way out." He puts half an arse on the chair. "What's this about?"

"I know, Frederick."

"You know what?"

"I know Karl's the father."

He throws his eyes up and rolls his head round as if seized by a mortal attack of boredom. "Are you claiming this knowledge came to you only recently?"

"Yesterday. Nim told me."

"Rubbish. You've known for years."

"I was never told."

"I didn't see the need. The situation was perfectly clear."

"It was? So you told Mary, then?"

"Yes."

"You did?"

"She was sick with it, so I told her. The envy took her over and I thought she was going to do herself harm, so I gave her the truth, yes."

"And?"

"She didn't believe me. She went on believing the lie."

"Ha! And why wouldn't she, that woman who loved you to death? You made her demented with your stories and your traveling and your affairs, you made her so she didn't know where to put her faith. May you rot in hell for it!"

"I refuse to believe she didn't know, despite what she said and how she acted. And you, I think you knew too."

I shake my head, exasperated. "You have always had a too high opinion of our minds, Frederick Engels. We're far more ignorant than you give us credit for. Far far more."

"Pah!" he says, and we shake our heads in unison.

"What a mess," I says now. "And for what? For Karl?"

"For the Cause, Lizzie."

"The Cause. The Cause."

"Yes, the Cause."

"Whose idea was it?"

"Mine."

"Liar. It could only have been Jenny's."

"What difference does it make? Together we did what was right."

"Does Freddy know?"

"*Lizzie.*"

"Does he?"

"No. He has been protected from it."

"He has a right to know."

"Go softly, Lizzie Burns. You're wading in high waters. Don't get out of your depth."

His hard arrangement gives me to understand that this is all I'll pull from him today. I get up before he has a chance to. I want to be the one who calls an end to proceedings; I want to be the one who walks free. I put my coat and bonnet on, and leave by the street door.

"Thought you had a hangover!" he shouts after me.

The thing must be done, and no one else around here will ever do it.

Sarah answers with a big and grubbed-up Harry on her hip. She looks up the road.

"Don't worry," I says. "I've been careful."

"Come in. You've come all this way, you might as well stay for some tea."

The room looks knocked about and neglected.

"Freddy?"

"There's a man sick. He's working a Sunday to cover."

"Will he get something extra for that?"

She shrugs. Puts Harry on the dirty floor while she boils the water. She gives me the tea in a glass. "Sorry. The cups is all broke. Harry kicked them off the table. Lucky there were nothing poured or he'd of been scalded."

I close my eyes and try to fight off the image. I wish people would keep from telling me *anything*.

She sits across from me. Takes Harry back up. "He won't be home now. He'll go out for a few, after the day. Won't be back till we're well took to bed."

I nod. Stir my tea. It puts you off, seeing through to the milk churning round.

"Is that all right for you?"

"Grand."

I reach over and put a stray butter knife out of Harry's reach. A proper scrub is what he needs. And a scissors put to his hair. You'd mistake him for a girl, under the grease.

"Have you come for anything particular, Mrs. Burns? Can I help you with something?"

She's expecting more money. She's being careful with me, handling me soft, for she thinks she can get it out of me and not tell Freddy about it.

"There's been something on my mind, Sarah."

She narrows, mistrusting.

"I was just wondering, has Mrs. Demuth ever come? Freddy's mother?"

"No."

"Wouldn't you like to meet her? I could set it up."

"That's Freddy's business."

"Wouldn't he like to see her from time to time?"

She shrugs. "He might visit her on his days off, for all I know. I barely see him."

"And the fosters? Are they in touch?"

"It's for the better they're not."

Harry starts to hit and kick. She stands and, holding him under his arms, offers him to me. "Here, can you take him? He's driving me mad."

He stops howling the moment I get touch of him. "Lord have mercy, the weight of him." He pinches and smears and puts fistfuls of my dress into his gob.

"Is that your good clothes?"

"Don't worry about that."

She has me feed him some pap, and afterwards I give him a ballad. He stares at me, tranced, through all the verses, and, when I'm finished, sinks his fingers into my cheeks and pulls them down. There's a stroke of sadness, now, giving him back, for it's one of those things that's hard to leave off once you've taken to it.

"You never wanted any of your own?"

"Sure, aren't wanting and getting worlds apart?"

"You can say that again. I never wanted anything, and look what I got."

I come away. "Tell him I called, anyhows."

"Is there anything you want to leave for him?"

I think a moment. I could tell her now and be done with it: *Freddy's father isn't who you think it is.* But in my mind I see that I won't tell them anything, not ever. And I'll never be back here again

either. It's not my place. These people don't belong to me, and I don't belong to them. "Just give him my love," I says.

She walks me to the door. Her disappointment is plain.

I rub Harry's cheek and brush his hair out of his eyes. "Look after him, won't you?"

I get a bus as far as the Park and, in spite of the drizzle and the line of waiting cabs, walk the rest of the way. I approach the house on the opposite side of the road, glance in as I pass. The windows are bright. The fires are up and the lamps lit. Naught looks lacking. I'll be home for supper.

There's a fight on in one of the warehouses, so the Lansdowne is deserted.

"How goes it with the radicals?" says Bert.

"Don't be at me today."

"The usual?"

"Nay, give me a beer. I've to go easy. Heavy night last night."

"Anything special?"

"An engagement."

"Your own?"

"Get away with you."

I watch him pull it. "Mind you put a good head on."

I stay at the counter and he tells me the local news.

"Do you know either of the men?" he says.

"What men?" I says.

"Fighting."

"I don't. What are their names?"

"Don't know. I was wondering if you knew them."

"I'm not the newspaper, Bert."

"I can see that."

"I come here to take a sup and to get away."

"I'm sorry for asking, Mrs. Burns. Forget I said anything."

He takes up his cloth and goes away to clean something.

"Sorry, Bert. Come back. Don't take it on. The world isn't fit for me today."

He comes back wearing a generous smile. "I've got just the thing for you."

He's got his hands on a bottle of the homemade stuff. He'll put a nip in my flask if I don't tell anybody where I got it. I refuse him at first. It'd only keep me here and put me in the way of another hangover. But as we talk, and as our subjects become nearer, the need gets the better of me.

"Sure, give me a taste of it now and let's be done with it."

"There's a good woman."

It's hard going down, and runs fast to the head; a heavy kind of pleasure. He joins me for a second drain, and our mouths now loosened by it, we fall to talking about the thoughts that have been busying us. I tell him where I've just come from.

"So you went back?" he says.

"I did," I says.

I stop short of telling him the reason for my visit. But I give him everything else.

"The world isn't fair, Bert. There's some that die for want of a child, and there's others that have no real care for their own. It's true what they say, children are wasted on their begetters."

"Come now, Mrs. Burns. It's only parents themselves that can know the true pressures of it."

His words sting, but I allow them in exchange for another quick go. He grants it to me, and one to himself, too, which opens him to speak of his own trials, bedaughtered as he is.

"But we can't get down about it, can we, Mrs. Burns? We have to take our bits and ends of happiness where we can find them."

"Aye, Bert," I says. "We've to let things alone, else we'll never be easy."

He nods away to that, and I nod along in my stead, and the next I know myself, I'm opening my eyes and being looked at.

"Child, is it yourself?"

She's trying to get my arm into the sleeve of my coat.

"Come on, Aunt Liz, let's get you home."

"I've lost track. Is the supper ready?"

"Put this on you."

"Did you come on your own?"

"Come on, take my arm."

"Is he fed? Did Spiv manage without me?"

"Stop your flustering and get a hold of me. Night, Bert."

"Night, Pumps."

The air sets me aching for a spend. We go up a lane and she stands in front.

"Stop moving," I says, for I've to hold her skirts for balance.

"Hurry up," she says. "We ought to get you home and out of those damp things."

"Nay," I says, helping myself up. "I'll lie down as I am so I can sleep the extra minutes in the morning."

XXXVI. A Higher Authority

To mark the anniversary, there was going to be a rally for five thousand. But now, at the last moment, the owner of the hall where it was to be held has refused us admission. French Communists, he said, weren't allowed to meet in any hall in London. If he'd known who we were beforehand, he'd never have agreed.

Frederick is livid. "Since the philistine is sure to be unwilling to lose the ten guineas rent, and since we shall sue for damages and shall get them too, it is obvious he's being compensated by the government. I think we should chance it anyway. We shall gather a smaller group and go along quietly. If we find the door locked, which is probable but not certain, we shall put the man in the witness box and see what can be made of the affair."

The door, we find, is indeed locked. Not a sinner in sight. Once we've shook at the bolts and caused a bit of a scene, we make

our way to a room on Frances Street and have the ceremony there. Speeches are given. Resolutions are adopted. Frederick decides to invite everyone in earshot to our house for a drink and a song. Cheers go up. My day falls to rubble.

I track down Jenny and ask her would she like to share a cab back.

"Why Lizzie," she says, unable to hide her surprise, "I'd be delighted."

We sit side-by-side. She lets me take her hand. Moves in close. Fixes her skirts so that they fall over mine. She compliments Frederick on his speech. I can't bring myself to say anything about Karl's. I tell her the Girls are looking ever handsomer, Janey most of all, since the engagement. She thanks me in a tired way, and, to my own surprise, says no more about them. I myself have to poke at the subject to get it up.

"Do you still worry about Lissagaray?"

"No. I've grown weary of worrying. I have forbidden the relation, and I expect that to be the end of it."

"You're going to lose her to someone, Jenny. I daresay she might be happy in a marriage where her husband is a sort of father and could teach her."

She shakes her head. "More education is not what Tussy requires. A strong man, a solid man, that is what. A provider. I couldn't save the others from their fate, but I still have a chance with Tussy. She, at least, must be kept clear of the dangers that our political life has put in her path."

Her regret shows as a passing shadow on her face, and I find myself drawn into sympathy. The fate she's afraid of is her own: a wifehood devoted to making up for her husband's poverty and putting away his sad mistakes. She's right to want Tussy—at least *her*—saved from it.

•

The doors open to the hordes, by midday the house is full to the beams. With all the craving stomachs, every bit of vittle that goes up comes down as crumbs on the plate. The order from the pastry cooks is soon exhausted, leaving us to rely on our own preparations, and Spiv is set teaving to keep up. Pumps is doing her utmost, but she can't be counted on for a prompt return, not with all the flitting and tossing she tries to squeeze into her runs. Frederick has already been sent down the cellar stairs more often than is right for a body of his age and standing. And it's not for the cheapest bottles he's dispatched either, but for the dustier, dearer ones that are then sloshed about the place as if the merest ale. The better the lush, the easier it goes down, and it's wise to be heedful and watch your measure, but it seems the French can bear a great deal of pleasure, for they don't ever refuse what's offered them, nor even wait to be offered in the first, and what's left now is not a soul sober among them.

The whole thing has put me into a coat of sweat, and into a humor too that would raise the hair on the devil himself.

Says one of them from the crowd, "Are we to be denied some tobacco after coming so far?" And Frederick, like a dullard, dashes off for the box.

Jenny gets up a German song. She leads into the strain, and the Girls join in, and now Karl. When they're finished, Tussy calls on Frederick to give us a bout of "The Vicar of Bray."

"All right," he says, after much coaxing, "but I cannot guarantee I shan't mess it." He takes a gulp from his tumbler and, holding on to the chimneypiece, makes the mime of a tipsy drunk clinging to the edge of a bar counter, and everybody laughs. When there's

some hush again, he begins, trembling at first but soon steadfast. He's left alone for the verses; the Marxes chime in for the refrains.

"And this is law, I will maintain, unto my dying day, sir, that whatsoever king may reign, I'll be Vicar of Bray, sir."

The clapping goes on well after Frederick has bowed and sat down, and threatens to go on an embarrassing length, till Karl strikes the punch bowl with the rim of his eyeglass and a hush spreads over once more. The big man stands, teeters, and is put right by Tussy. He waves her away and plants himself well into the carpet. Takes hold of the openings of his coat, gives his throat a rough throat-clearing. He gives a speech in the French. When everybody bows their heads, I understand he's asking for a minute to remember the Paris dead, and I bend down in my turn. Out the side of my eye, I see Jenny crying behind her fan. Lissagaray and another man tussle to be the one to pass Tussy a handkerchief. Janey has fallen sideways into Longuet's arms. I wonder why I'm not feeling the proper feeling. I try to bring it on by thinking of Mary, but it doesn't come. These things can't just be called up, like a servant from below.

The minute over, Karl takes up with his speeching once more. The crowd raises their glasses and turns to face me. It takes me a moment to realize they're proposing me.

"To our hostess, Lizzie Burns," says Karl.

"To Lizzie Burns," says Frederick. "Proletarian, Irish rebel, and model Communist!"

"Lizzie! Lizzie!"

I'm lost for what to be saying or where to be saying it. "Thank you, gents. Our home is your home. Now, would you ever sit down and make it so? You'll have me mortified standing there in your gaiters."

Laughter, clapping, some more cheers.

I go down to the kitchen to come over it with a bit of dignity.

Spiv is sat at the table, having her bit.

"What's wrong with you?"

I turn to the stove and don't feel called on to explain.

She fetches me a fresh glass from the cupboard and fills it from her bottle. "She who goes to bed sober falls with the leaves in October."

I take it, and it helps me on.

Back up in the parlor, the serious business has begun.

"Too many false prophets have polluted the field," Karl is saying. "Now is not the time for sects and factions and discord. Now is the time for unity and for discipline. Now is the time for optimism. Now is the International's time."

Frederick sweeps a fierce look round the faces, and musters an applause by it.

"The anarchists, that plague of bourgeois rats, consider any revolutionary uprising to be justified as a step towards the total destruction of society, and so run about giving their support to spasmodic uprisings, wherever they take place. We, on the other hand, do not expect a quick revolution, nor a partial one. The failure of the Paris Commune has shown us that Communism will only be possible as the act of the proletariat all at once and simultaneously!"

"Hear, hear!"

"Well said!"

"Murderer of freedom!" It's the ill-dressed old gent in the upright chair who speaks: a stranger to me and to this house. "You have said it, Dr. Terror! With your own words, you have proved yourself an authoritarian, a murderer of freedom!"

"Who is this man?" says Karl, almost laughing. "Who brought their grandfather with them?"

"Who are you?" says Frederick. "Speak your name."

"Equality without freedom is a fiction!" he says. "Equality without freedom is a myth created by swindlers to mislead fools!"

Frederick springs to his feet. "Get this anarchist worm out of here!"

Five, ten men answer his command. Numbed by the lush, they stumble over chairs and knock down bottles and glasses to get to him. The man doesn't struggle when they put their hold on him, nor when they pull his coat up over his head and lift him onto their shoulders like a coffin.

"Equality without freedom means state despotism!" comes his muffled call as they carry him out to the hall.

I put myself among the herd that follows the procession out, but instead of turning left towards the street door like the others, I steal right, down the kitchen steps. Spiv is washing plates in the scullery.

"Didn't it say in that character of yours that you play the piano?"

She gives me the daggers.

"Go on up, you're needed to lighten the atmosphere. It's gone dark."

She wrings out her rag and slaps it onto the side of the bucket.

"Well, isn't it better than wiping at these?"

"I'd quicker wipe a thousand of these, and a thousand arses after them."

"Don't give me that, and go on. Get it past and done. I'll finish this for you." I take the bottle of champagne out of the sink where it's been steeping in cold water. "And bring this up with you as an extra excitement."

She takes the bottle from me and stomps up. "This is some life."

I bide till I hear the first notes struck, delicate as a bull at a gate, before going out the area way.

I find Moss turned towards his door, fumbling with keys. I come up behind him and float a hand against his shoulder. I see he's made a toilet of bear's grease and has brushed his breeches of their stains.

"On your way out?"

He jumps, alarmed. Sighs and shakes his head when he lights on me. "I thought we'd seen the last of you."

"I'm out for a walk and this is my way."

"You've never been one to keep your word."

He yanks the door towards him and, with a holy curse, forces the lock to turn. "I can't stay. I'm on my way to a meeting."

"Suit yourself. I only came to give you this." Untroubled by the bright daylight and the beggars creeping around, I hold out my purse: the house surplus for four months, not an enormous sum, but tidy enough to deliver a man from anxiety.

He flashes up and down the road. "Christ, Lizzie, put it away."

I laugh at his nerviness, and drop the purse back into my skirts. All business now, he takes my arm and walks me off.

"What changed your mind?"

"What does it matter? Do you want the mint or not?"

"Come with me to the meeting. You can make your donation there. It'll be most welcome."

"I'm going nowhere near another meeting."

"I won't take the money unless you come. You're not giving it to me. You're giving it to the Cause."

"You're mistaken, Moss. I'm giving it to you. You're the Cause."

If this touches any feelings in him, he doesn't make a display of them, except to tighten his grip and pull me closer.

I'm taken along by his slow walk. My mind calls out against

going with him, but my body doesn't hearken. Down the alleys and lanes, through the courts, I let myself be led. When we get to the church, I says, "Where on earth are you taking me?" but it's too late to sound anything except false.

We go inside and walk up the main aisle to the top. He knocks on the sacristy door. A head peeps out and looks us over before letting us in. The sacristy is as you'd expect. A small window. A table spread with white linen. A wardrobe for the gowns. A shelf for the holy things. Candles and chalices. Jugs of wine and water. Bells and books and vases.

"Mrs. Engels!" says Killigad. "Welcome!"

Stood around the priest, leant back against the walls and the furniture, squatted down close to the floor: an amount of men, no less than two dozen. Many of the faces I recognize from Manchester. Albert and Joseph and Kit and Dan. Here, too, are the three I hid in the house after the rescue of Kelly and Deasy. And many others that I don't have names for.

"This here is Lizzie Burns," says Moss, presenting me. "She's come to make a donation. Give her the welcome she deserves."

I put the purse on the table, by the pile of holy books. "I just don't want to know how you're going to spend it."

An applause erupts, and a round of cheers, and now the men get into a line to greet me. Many of them are yet young for whiskers, and most have holes in their knees and their elbows, but by the strength and soberness of their grip, they do honor to themselves, and to Manchester, and to the other country. I feel overcome. I'm not someone who sheds abundant tears, but abundant is how they now come. There's no sadness compared to the loss of home.

Moss comes and puts a hand on me. "You were right to come, Lizzie."

Feeling weak, I fall into him, and he takes me.

"Oh, Moss, it's not about what's right or wrong. When you don't have a choice, it's not about that. My feet brought me here, and I couldn't stop them."

Laughing—wanting to shake off my sorrows—he swings me round. "Well, Lizzie Burns, why don't you show me what those feet can do!"

My view blurred by tears, I mimic him as he jumps up and down. It feels like my knees might burst, with the uncommon strain, but I don't stop. He takes my hand and we turn round like children in a jig. Another man joins to make a circle. And another and another, till our stomping can be heard all through St. Giles.

XXXVII. Nothing Is Final

Dr. Allen, the physician of all misery, tells me again that I must learn to rest and mend myself, else my complaints will worsen and, if I'm not careful, carry me off at any moment.

"What did the doctor say?" says Frederick.

"The usual," I says.

He smiles. "The man knows nothing. What you need is the fresh air that comes from a good walk." He stands and pulls me up after him. "Come on."

We leave as we are, half-bare: he without his jacket and I without anything to cover my head. There's a breeze, but not cold; it runs through my hair like a soothing hand. We cross the road and stand at the bottom of the Hill, looking up. The sheep have been shorn and there's lambs. The strollers are few, it being a weekday.

"What do you think?"

"I've never been to the top. Imagine, Frederick. Near two years, and I've never thought to climb it."

"Well, no time like the present, *mein Liebling.*"

We go up the path. The spring flowers are out, dancing.

"The weather's picking up," Frederick says. "The new season is coming on."

"Aye," I says, "it's fine now," though I still insist on the fires and the hot brick in my bed.

After only a few steps, my chest was already hurting; now that we reach the top, I've no breath to spare. We sit on the bench, and little by little my faculties return.

Up at such a height you can see all of London, the big pile of it. It's a sight to make you think of God and the things carried out on His responsibility and the places built on His behalf. Frederick takes in a deep breath and moves his gaze across the entire length of it. "The British don't know how to build a city."

"Or tear one down."

He laughs. "The Romans, like the Greeks before them, believed that membership of an actual physical city was a condition of true civilization. English public life, by contrast, needs no town. Its elements already exist in every man's household."

Happy here, we sit another while.

I ask him about work.

"It's good, I suppose." He thinks Karl ought resign from the Council and return to his theoretical work. The second volume of the Book must be finished soon, or it'll never be.

"And what about your history of Ireland?" I says. "Are you going to get back to that?"

He sighs. "I will. As soon as order has been established in the Association."

Which can only mean never. A woman knows order is only a thought with no reality to support it.

My bladder begins to strain; we make our way back down before it fails me. While waiting to cross, we both fall to looking at the house.

"Do you ever miss Manchester?" I says.

"Sometimes," he says. "Not really."

"And Mary? Do you miss her?"

He looks off for a moment. And now back, his eyes bright with a smile that can only mean, "You can't miss what never left you."

Back inside, I go straight upstairs to my bedpan. A minute and there's a knock on my door.

His boots are already off and he has the ties of his shirt loosened.

"Turn around," he says.

He undresses me all the way.

"Now lie down."

I do as he commands, not under the sheets, but on top of them. I open my legs so he can get the full regard. It's the hope that I—*me, this body here*—might be his happiness that makes me fearless.

He feeds his bit out the front hole of his trousers and climbs onto me. I make no attempt to control my feelings, which come out of me now through my mouth. He, on the other side, stays silent, as ever. Silent except for his eyes.

"Say something," I says. "Anything at all. Please, just say it out."

"Shh," he says.

I can feel her in the air around him, pushing him on, and in this moment I don't care for myself; I will disappear into her, if it'll make him mine.

"Say her name."

"Lizzie, be quiet."

What is it? What's stopping him? Doesn't he know that I'm willing to nothing myself, to think of my body as if it was another's, if it means he'll look no further than me?

"It's all right, Frederick, I know what you're thinking."

Releasing a loud groan, he clasps a hand over my mouth. "Shh! Don't say another word!"

At first I feel crushed, and cry inward to myself, for I know he once delighted in hearing her speak: from their first meeting to their last, it was "Let us hear, Mary," and "Don't stop, Mary," and "Whatever you say, Mary." But the hurt soon vanishes, because I understand now, as he rushes towards his discharge, that my words—whatever they are and whenever they are spoken—are unsafe to him, for they have the power to reopen sad subjects.

He shivers free of his wants, and falls onto me, panting. I bring my hands to rest on the wet back of his shirt. As he heaves, his gut presses down into mine, making it hard for me to catch my own breath, but I let him be and don't move to topple him, for I notice, too, that I have all the air I need, that I am full in the awareness that no body was ever nearer to him than I am now.

Moaning to show his fulfilment, he lifts his weight up and puts it onto his elbows, though still I feel our hearts bound tight in a mutual feeling. He kisses my nose and my mouth. Smoothes back my hair. Smiles.

"How is it," he says, "that I always feel as if you are trying to find me out, when in truth I have nothing to conceal?"

I shake my head, embarrassed, for sudden *I* am the one who has been caught with her thoughts bare.

"Nay, Frederick, you mustn't feel that."

He caresses my burning cheek and searches me through, and he must see—he can't fail to behold it—that, at bottom, I love him no

less in knowing he has cared for others and might any moment cease to find interest in me; indeed, I love him all the more as a result.

He winks and I wink back, and we grin at each other for a long time. Now—his desires restored perhaps—he brings his mouth to my ear and nibbles on the soft part where another woman might keep a jewel. And he says it. He does.

"Oh, Lizzie," he says. "Lizzie, *mein Liebling.* My love."

In Paradisum

1878

Praise the end of it. The expert has come and pronounced me incurable, so at last—long last—I can rest without hope. For it's the hope, at the end, that causes you to suffer. It's with hope that you lie with no spirit in you, racked by a mind's fever that sets you to beat your breast and pull your hair and speak wild and dangerous prayers; and it's the hope that, in the next moment, kills the quick of your life and sinks you into a waste from which you don't rise unless they lift you out to do your dirty business. But with hope destroyed, you see life for what it is, and you welcome death, for you know now that it's equal, and there's always joy in anticipation, joy and gladness that you're not one of them; not Spiv, who must care for my evacuations; not Pumps, who must soak my feet and feed me broth with a spoon; not Frederick, who must make the beds at night and light the kitchen stove in the morning. It's them you pity. With things still to work for.

Dr. Allen comes and goes, and the boy who brings the medicines. They fill me with such an amount of morphia that the slow return of the pain is all that tells me I'm still alive. The famous swelling in my bladder: I know once it no longer gives off its heat, I'm gone.

And I'm not afraid. What comes afterwards can't be worse than Eastbourne. Or New Brighton. Or Bridlington Quay or Great Yarmouth or Worthing or the Isle of Wight or Baden or any of the other potholes I've been dragged to for the cure. Every soaking, every wrapping, every gulp just another stride towards God taken, if only it could be admitted and spoken on.

One day, in Karlsbad, a man with a head like death skinned over says to me, he says, "What are you here for?"

What am I here for? I need to take a moment to think. And then: "What else but for the emptiness of life they provide?"

By the way he looks at me, I can tell he thinks there's something wrong in my head. *That,* he thinks, is why I'm here.

Pumps comes to raise my legs. And put the cushion under me. And turn me to the other side. She's returned from the finishing school in Heidelberg more wild than she went, and I can tell from the roughness of her handling that she's resentful of the work. Worse, her time away has given her airs. She refuses to sleep in the same room as Spiv, who's now forced to roll out her mat on the kitchen floor, and in the evening she eats with Frederick in the dining room, the two of them alone. I sometimes hear their useless patter coming up through the ceiling, the scrape of their knives on the good plate.

I watch her now, the whiteness and plumpness of her arms and neck; the rotten health of her. It'll be her turn one day to have

this agony, to be wiped and sponged into a mortified shiver. Till then, there's no point expecting her to know.

"Pumps," I says.

"What is it? Are you in need of something?"

"Moss will have to be told."

She rolls her eyes. "Don't worry about that now. Go to sleep."

"Newgate jail. You'll have to go."

"Head down now, Aunt Liz, and get some rest."

"He'll wonder if I don't come. He'll wonder."

I start up in the night. Except it's not the night but the day with the curtains drawn. Tussy is here.

"Sweet child," I says.

She rubs the cold out of my hands, and tells me the time, and the place, and who is here with her.

"I'm alone," she says.

And she always is. Never brings the man Lissagaray with her, though I know she's always at his side; the shadow that comes between her and the family; the black shade on the freshest years of her life. Happy is the child that's never taught concealment.

"Your mother? Your father?"

"In heaven."

"Heaven?"

"I said Malvern, Aunt Lizzie. The spa at Malvern."

Malvern. The place we go when we pass over, alone and friendless, with only secrets to fill our purses.

Everything is memory. I close my eyes, and the moth I've just seen beating itself against the lamp appears in my mind as a picture, and I can't see what separates it from the others that present themselves to me: the scenes from my early life, the comings and goings of long ago, the things that haven't happened. Old and

young and never to be, they are all the same, no difference between them, just pictures that come between us.

The release is forgetting.

I tell Pumps to send for Nim. More and more, when I'm alone, the picture of Freddy pays me hidden visits. He comes and takes up the empty spaces in my mind, the caught moments, and I must have his news. How is he keeping? Is he coping since Sarah ran away with everything?

But when she comes, she's too small, speaks too soft, and I've fallen too far in a waste to listen.

I hear my name, and I see you, Mary. Offering me something. Or is your hand out, asking? Do I owe you? Have you something old to count against me?

There's a pause in my breath, and for a long moment I think it mightn't come back. But now it does. A frothing. A babby's gurgle. A sound dreadful enough to bring Pumps down from her room.

She turns me on my side and slaps it out. "Better?"

Better.

The world doesn't happen how you think it will. The secret is to soften to it, and to take its blows. But a person doesn't understand this till all chance of acting is past. How can we know when we're young and busy hardening ourselves against the winds, and dreaming of a time when things won't require us to be hard at all; how can we know that, in fact, we're living our only life?

I open my eyes to see Lydia, crying. I close again and let her have it out.

Awake, and she's still here, on a chair that's been moved near me. It's late. The lamps are lit. The fire crackles and spits.

"You came up all this way?"

"Of course we did, Lizzie."

Jamie is sat beside her, his cap wrung out in his hands.

"You're very good to come."

"Don't, Lizzie. Save your forces."

I sit in my wet and watch them. They turn their gaze to their laps.

A minute and Frederick comes in, breathless. Spiv and Pumps come after him. And a man, a church man. Lydia and Jamie shuffle over to make room. Frederick kneels at the bedside and takes my hand. The church man comes to stand behind him.

Is it that time already?

"Mrs. Burns, I'm Reverend Galloway from St. Mark's Church in Regent's Park."

I moan at him in the tone of "And I'm Lizzie Burns, a Catholic."

"Lizzie, the Reverend Galloway is here to marry us. We're to be wed!"

The girls whimper. Lydia lets out a sob. I can't part my lips, they're so parched. Pumps has to spoon me a bit of water before I can speak.

"Would it count?"

"Of course. We have a special license."

"An English blessing?"

"Does it matter?"

"Only if it's a dishonest thing."

He comes off his knees to hover over me, his face so close it's only a blur. "No, Lizzie. Don't think that. It is my desire too."

I nod my assent, knowing that his actions come not from his own desires but from a wish to give me something; a gift that will please my God and ensure me a good death. The man opens his book, speaks out his Protestant words; short and not unfamiliar;

666666

6666

6666

beautiful. When called upon to kiss me, Frederick goes for my forehead, his whiskers like a scour on my skin. Spiv comes forward with a bit of paper, a pen, and an inkwell. Frederick flattens the paper onto the mattress. Now he dips the pen and presses it in my hand. Closes his own hands around my own to keep me steady. Brings the tip to touch the page. Everyone waits. There's a quiet that'd burst your ears. A mark on this page and I, this poor woman here, will be his ever, Mrs. Engels.

"Frederick?"

"Yes, my precious love."

"What will it be like?"

"What will what be like?"

"Communism."

Water rises to his eyes and falls over onto his cheeks. "Now is not the time for that, Lizzie. Can you make your name? Can you do that? Do you need me to help you?"

You think if you ask enough questions you'll get to know what they're like, but you won't. You think there's something there, something to find. The truth is, there's naught but what you have in your mind about them. In front of us aren't our husbands but the stories we make of them, one story good till a better one comes to replace it, and it's only afterwards that this is understood; only after you've loved and hated them for what they never were; only after it has ceased to matter.

Acknowledgments

Mrs. Engels is a work of fiction. It has been enriched by the work of many scholars, historians, philosophers, and observers from the nineteenth century, the twentieth century, and today. It owes its greatest debts to Tristram Hunt, Roy Whitfield, David McLellan, Isaiah Berlin, Yvonne Kapp, F. H. Peters, Alistair Horne, Liza Picard, Judith Flanders, Asa Briggs, A. N. Wilson, Jerry White, Alan Kidd, John Newsinger, Jack Doughty, Henry Mayhew, and, of course, Karl Marx and Friedrich Engels.

I owe a great debt of gratitude to Iñaki Moraza, Trezza Azzopardi, and Rebecca Stott for their help with things both on and off the page; and to my agent Rebecca Carter and my editors, Philip Gwyn Jones and Pat Strachan, for their unswerving faith and resolve. I owe further thanks to the School of Literature, Drama and Creative Writing at the University of East Anglia for its generous financial backing.

About the Author

Gavin McCrea was born in Dublin, Ireland, in 1978 and holds a B.A. and an M.A. from University College Dublin, and an M.A. and a Ph.D. from the University of East Anglia. He currently lives in London, England, and northern Spain. *Mrs. Engels* is his first novel.

Mrs.
ENGELS